HUNTING CHRIST

BASED ON AN ORIGINAL SCREENPLAY

by
Ken Policard

SECOND EDITION   2013 FICTION

MANAGER
Arnie Holland – CEO/PRESIDENT
www.lightyear.com

INDEPENDENT AMERICAN MOVIES

KEN POLICARD – President of Global Affairs
ARNIE HOLLAND – Senior Vice President of Acquisition
IVEY ROBERTSON – Senior Vice President of International Affairs
JUAN SMITH – Vice President of Finance
MELANIE SMITH – Director of Finance
CHRISTOPHER COPPOLA – Senior Vice President of Production
MIKE CONLEY – Senior Vice President of Intellectual Property & Story Development
JAY COULBOURNE – Senior Vice President of Artistic Development

EMAIL: businessaffairs@huntingchrist.com

ISBN-13: 978-0-9846340-2-6
Library of Congress Control Number: 2010943517

Hunting Christ AKA Blood of Eden

Printed in the United States of America

This book is dedicated to you

ACKNOWLEDGMENT

First, on bended knees, I would like to thank the Universe – God. It took many lifetimes orbiting around many planets, in order for our friendship to evolve. Thank you, for being my I AM.

Next, I would like to dedicate this book to every soul, on every planet, surrounding every star.

Thank you, for being my audience.

And I can't let the moment of this acknowledgment pass without putting on the full armor of God. My greatest desire in life is to bring an end to these senseless wars. I love God completely – mind, body, and soul freely. God is not a convenience. I'm certain that Jesus never passed the collection plate, and if Christ were here today, you would not find Him on television asking you to send money to His ministry. Say "NO" to money for miracles. God's healing is free of charge.

It is the devil that requires payment.

That is why I pledge my allegiance to God, so, let no "religion" stand between you and God. This is an amazing time to be alive, but because of poor leadership, selfishness, and egos – the whole world has fallen into a recession. One must do his or her due-diligence before voting to elect a political leader. By making an informed decision – you keep the devil at bay. Though some of our religious leaders have good intentions, but as they say – the road to hell was paved with good intentions.

Beware of those who claim to be "the called" of God.

And finally, I want to acknowledge the key people who had hands on involvement on this project. My work would not have been possible without you. I wish to thank, Lori Ann Picou, Juan Smith, Melanie Smith, Jay Coulbourne, and Ivey Robertson whose clarity of vision, spiritual understanding, wisdom, and encouragement is the reason *Hunting Christ* made its way to bookshelves, when it did, and how it did. You all are Godsend!

Then, I wish to acknowledge our Co-Executive Producer, Mr. Mike Conley. Mike, you've been on this project, from the alpha to the omega. You're a great mentor that is why I run all of my ideas by you first! If there's a problem...you'll find it, and together we'll fix it. Thanks for always having the remedy.

To my producing partners, thank you for your unwavering dedication, you guys are the pulse of life that runs through HC's veins. Thank you for hanging in there. Our stars are now perfectly aligned; our success will come forth from our Divine Inheritance!

To Michael Toppin, you were the first to sign a contract with us, although we never received the funding. I believe that you had good intentions, was looking forward to having you as part of the team.

To all aspiring authors and producers – trust in God! All others, proof of funds, and the verification there of is a must! For this profession – you need an attorney for your attorney, a manager for your manager, and an accountant for your accountant – the literary world, and film industry can be brutal!

To Sue Bray and Tim Snider, you two are the reason why we came back to Bookmasters! Thank you, for having our best interest at heart.

Hunting Christ is now being translated into 14 languages – French, Spanish, Italian, Hebrew, Arabic, German, Mandarin, Portuguese, Russian, Japanese, Hindi, Bengali, Romanian, and Haitian Creol. Special thank you to all the translators! Hunting Christ is officially going international!

To my wife Betsie, and to Teresa Ramos, and Ivey Robertson, you ladies have been my life-support. Thank you for hanging in there! And to my children, Tiffani, Kenny, Destiny, and Jamie, thank you for being my inspiration. You guys are the reason that I write. Always love God more than you love me. This acknowledgment would be incomplete, without me thanking Sean Robertson, Michael Brown, Bianca Sylvia Smith, Edward Joseph Smith, and Justin Anthony Smith for being a blessing in our lives.

I love you all – "ALL THE WAY TO GOD!"

PROLOGUE

I always knew you were wronged. Every last one of you. From the sinners and the scoundrels to the starry-eyed believers. From the beginning, all of you have been conned.

The problem was no one realized it. Neither the saints nor the sinners, nor all the angels in heaven. But I knew. I damn well knew the truth, and He knew that I did. And that is what made me so dangerous in His eyes.

That is why I was cast out. Faith is not a virtue! The quest for truth is. Therein lies the flaw at the core of His creation. Know that well.

Approaching Him was easy. He has always trapped Himself by His own wisdom and fairness, so there was no doubt that He would agree to my proposition. How could He say no to logic and fair play?

Consider it a bet in the grand casino of Paradise. I have gone before Him and laid everything on the table, challenging the House of God to one more round, double or nothing. I know I am destined to win, because there is no way that He could do it again.

Heaven is a house of cards.

— from The Book of Devlin
Thirty-three Years Before the New Time

CHAPTER ONE

It was too cold, too wet. Christmastime in the bayou felt like the dank, flooded cellar of an unheated cathedral, but that didn't matter now. Only one thing mattered, and it lay ahead, somewhere in the windblown darkness.

In his younger days, Jacob Molinari slogged through the marshes of the Po River delta in his native Italy, harvesting reeds for the basket weavers of his family's ancestral village. Despite the passage of some thirty-odd years, his muscles still retained the memory of youth.

His thighs cramped in protest, but he pushed himself through the pain. He had to move fast. Faster than...

No! Don't say it! It was too risky to even whisper the word, or even worse, the name. In this moment and for this sacred task, it would be blasphemy.

The clock struck midnight only minutes before. The most blessed day of the Christian year had come once again, briefly renewing the hopes of a weary world, but the world was unaware that lightning was about to strike twice on Man's eternal calendar. Few mortals had any inkling of what would transpire over the next few hours. Unless he could safeguard the event, Molinari knew with terrifying certainty that it would surely come and go without a trace, and then all would be lost.

He tripped over a submerged log and fell to the muddy ground. He took a moment to collect his breath, or was he giving up? Was he overcome by fear? Could he really expect to survive? The pain, if he were to fail, would surely be beyond torture.

Wind rustled the trees all about him, and he thought of the Garden of Gethsemane. The Christians say that even Jesus had His moment of doubt and pain. Turning his head to the side to breathe, Molinari gathered his second wind.

The rain came harder now, washing away the mud that splashed on his face when he fell. Yes, Jesus did have his moment of doubt and pain, as any man would, Molinari told himself. And still, the man kept going.

Revived from the downpour, Molinari pushed himself up from the mud and looked ahead. The night sky to the east had not yet clouded over. He could still see the three stars of Orion's belt. Tonight they aligned with Sirius, the brightest star in the east, and pointed to the dim lights of a ramshackle medical clinic in the distance.

Bayou Memorial Hospital was one of the many rural clinics built throughout the South during the New Deal. It was deep in the bayou, miles outside of New Orleans, a place the rural poor had relied upon for decades. The facility was understaffed, under-funded, and overcrowded; the roof leaked, the plumbing rattled, and mold had taken up residence behind the cracked plaster walls. It was a humble setting for an event that would save Mankind, if Molinari could only get there on time.

His eyes widened with hope, seeing the lights of the clinic ahead, and he blinked away the rain streaming down his forehead. He took a deep, resolute breath, struggled to his feet, and willed himself forward with grim determination. The pain no longer mattered. Only one thing did.

Closer...

There was no fear anymore, at least no fear of what would happen on this holy night. Whatever fear was left in him was focused on the future. The impending doom was so palpable that he could smell it, a pall that hung over the world like decaying flesh. What drove him forward was the utter certainty of the disaster that would surely occur, if he couldn't make it through the front door of the clinic in the next few minutes.

"That's it. Breathe, child," Rose said, coaching the young woman in labor, who shifted uncomfortably in the bed of Room Three. "Come on, Melissa! Hang in there. You're gonna be a mother soon."

It was Melissa's first child and she was having a hard time of it. She writhed in pain, alarmed as each contraction came on stronger than the last. She wasn't sure she could stand much more of the ordeal.

Her child was stubborn. "A born fighter," she used to joke. It was something she was well aware of ever since the first kick. And now that the time had come, the child was bound and determined to enter the world.

Another contraction brought a fierce scream of pain from her. She kicked at the rusted iron pipes that formed the footboard of her creaking hospital bed. The bed lurched in response, scuffing the worn linoleum floor.

Rose had her hands full with this one. "Please, honey! You gotta be strong for your baby!" She tried to calm Melissa with a damp washcloth, dabbing the young woman's glistening forehead and chattering with small talk to distract her from the pain.

"Oh, yes, we got quite a few like you in here tonight, honey. Mmmm, hmmm. I ain't *never* seen it so busy 'round here!" Rose smiled at Melissa. "Now breathe, child. Breathe..."

Melissa didn't care how busy the place was, or how busy Rose was. All she wanted was for the pain to be over and her baby to be sleeping in her arms.

They both heard the door opening. Melissa tried to see around Rose, but she couldn't manage. Rose turned to see who it was, expecting

3

reinforcements, but the hopeful light in her eyes dimmed when she saw who came into the room.

Father Vicente nodded hello and approached them, crossing himself, a Bible clutched in his other hand. He was a short, tidy Latino gentleman with a stooped, bookish posture and a set of gleaming white teeth. His lips parted in a congenial smile.

"I'm Father Vicente, the new chaplain."

Rose nodded hello, but she sighed in silent frustration. Still, a priest was better than nothing. They did tend to calm things a little, though they were no substitute for a doctor.

The door shut behind Vicente and he stood beside the bed, smiling down at Melissa. He knew exactly who she was, where she was from and what her circumstances were, but it didn't matter. Nothing mattered but the child in her womb. He had no idea how they found her, but they had, and that in itself was a miracle. He had been able to verify everything, down to the last detail.

When the envoy from Rome came to visit just three days ago, he took great pains to ensure that Vicente knew exactly what the circumstances were. It took several hours for the envoy and his assistants to walk Vicente through the history and cosmology of the great secret that had been festering within the walls of the Vatican for nearly two millennia. Vicente was literally struck dumb when he learned the truth. As with any good Catholic, he had no idea, none whatsoever.

Despite his initial shock, which was so profound that he vomited, in the end he finally came to understand that there was simply too much at stake. Something had to be done, and if the Mother Church needed him to help, how could he refuse? The Church was his life; it was all that he had ever known.

God works in mysterious ways, indeed! Father Vicente reflected with bitter irony. *Even through such a humble agent as myself.*

Melissa winced in pain, squeezing tears from her eyes. He gently took her hand and smiled again, but she was in far too much pain to reply.

4

"Thank you, Father," the nurse murmured on her behalf.

Vicente glanced at her and nodded, then his eyes shifted back to Melissa. He stroked the back of her hand with his thumb. "Merry Christmas, my child."

She tried to give him a brave smile, but she wasn't feeling very brave at the moment. He sat on the edge of the bed, gently cradling Melissa's hand in his. He placed his Bible on the nightstand as Melissa clenched her jaw in a sudden onrush of exquisite pain. She arched her back, breathing rapid and deep through flared nostrils. He touched her abdomen and felt the baby move. At that moment, her water broke.

"Aahhh!" Melissa breathed, a little embarrassed.

"Her time has come," Vicente informed Rose. "Bring the doctor. Hurry."

Rose hesitated, glancing at Melissa. She didn't want to leave a woman in the throes of labor without medical attention. Anything could happen at this point, but Vicente's gaze was as insistent as it was reassuring.

"She is in good hands. Go now."

Rose glanced at Melissa and left the room. As she closed the door behind her, she heard Vicente begin to pray in Latin. *"Pater noster qui es in cœlis, Sanctificetur nomen tuum..."*

In the hall, Rose caught Evelyn's eye as she was backing out of room five with an empty wheelchair. The shift supervisor found herself picking up the slack wherever she could; she felt she was more of a den mother than anything else. "That walk-in's ready to pop," Rose told her boss. "You do up a folder for her yet?"

Evelyn shook her head; she was swamped. Rose looked up and down the hallway. "Where's Dr. Garrity at?"

Evelyn steered the wheelchair down the hall and pointed back to room nine. Rose stepped closer to the room and peeked inside.

Dr. Garrity was delivering a baby, assisted by two young nurses. "It's a boy," the doctor announced.

"Doctor," one of the nurses said tersely, "She's not responding."

Rose stepped back from the open door; they didn't need anyone looking over their shoulders now. As she backed away, she saw something out of the corner of her eye and turned. A man, his clothes wet and muddy, had just come up the main staircase. He was breathing hard, like he just finished running a race. He moved quickly down the hall toward her, looking into each room as he approached.

Melissa's breathing was fast and deep and the sweat streamed off her face, staining her faded hospital gown. As he held Melissa's hand, Vicente slipped his other hand into the sleeve of his tunic and withdrew a large ornate crucifix.

"Adveniat regnum tuum. Fiat voluntas tua, sicut in cœlo, & in terra..."

Behind him, the door silently yawned open by itself. The old wood door had warped over the years and the latch didn't line up properly. A nurse scurried past the room, and then a patient hobbled by wheeling an IV stand. Neither of them glanced in the room, and Vicente didn't notice them, either, intent as he was on the task at hand.

"Panem nostrum quotidiamum da nobis hodie..."

He grasped the crucifix like a dagger and nudged the golden body of Christ with his thumb. The figurine and the polished shaft of wormwood that it was nailed to slipped free of the razor-sharp iron blade inside.

CHAPTER TWO

The envoys from Rome had assured him that carbon dating performed at the Vatican labs confirmed that the dagger was almost two thousand years old. The wandering knight who brought it from the Holy Land claimed to have fashioned it himself from an old Roman spear.

Vicente felt a surge of destiny, holding the blade in his trembling hand. From the instant he touched it, he realized that as simple as it was, it would change the future. It was the most powerful weapon in history. And when it was used, the fallout would be a rain of souls.

"Et dimitte nobis debita nostra, sicut & nos dimittimus debitoribus nostris..."

At that moment in the hallway, Molinari looked in on them and froze, seeing the dagger in Vicente's hand. Melissa saw him over Vicente's shoulder, but his muddy clothes and rain-matted hair didn't register on her. For some reason he was staring at the two of them, so she stared back. Vicente noticed that her eyes were focused on something behind him, and turned...

"Vicente! No!"

Molinari rushed into the room, horrified. Despite his predicament, Vicente smiled, seeing the look on Molinari's face. It was the same horrified reaction that he himself had just three days earlier, before he knew the truth.

Vicente knew he had to act at once. He quickly stood, grabbing Melissa by the hair to stretch her neck. She was still in the throes of labor and thrashed about on the bed, squealing in alarm, but the sound was choked off and she stared at Molinari, her eyes begging for help.

Vicente pressed the dagger against her throat, glaring a warning at Molinari, and it worked. Molinari stopped short, still several feet away from them.

That was all Vicente needed. He turned to Melissa and lifted the dagger high. She fought back and tried to twist herself free, but his grip was too strong. Molinari launched himself at the mad priest as Vicente stabbed downward.

The blade plunged deep into her abdomen. Melissa gave a strangled cry of pain as Vicente yanked it out with a spurt of blood, lifting the weapon high for another strike.

Molinari slammed into him before he could bring the blade down again. The needle-sharp dagger clattered to the floor, as they crashed against the nightstand and spun away.

Molinari pinned him for a moment against the wall, but only for a moment. His feet were tangled in the bed sheet and Vicente wrested himself free.

Melissa writhed on the bed, gasping for air as she desperately clutched at her wound. Standing beside her bed, Vicente was frantically searching for the dagger, but he had no idea where it was.

It was in Molinari's hand.

They faced each other across the room. Vicente was cornered by the larger, stronger man, and with nowhere to go he simply sat down on the bed.

Behind him, Melissa was struggling to breathe, her hand pressed against her stab wound. A dark stain of blood was spreading over her gown and the bed sheet.

"My baby!" she managed to gasp. "My baby..."

Vicente just looked at Molinari, waiting.

"You have nowhere to run, Vicente," Molinari said.

Vicente sadly shook his head, and picked his Bible up from the floor. He opened it, looking inside.

"There is one place," he said with a smile, and took a stiletto out of the hollowed-out Bible, snicking it open.

He stood erect, facing Molinari, and used both hands to clasp the stiletto before him, the blade pointing to heaven.

"Adios." Go with God.

With one purposeful thrust, Father Raimundo Olberto Vicente rammed the gleaming steel shaft up under his chin and deep into his skull.

His body dropped to the floor and shuddered in death spasms, leaving Molinari and Melissa face-to-face in utter astonishment. The young woman was whimpering now, petrified, and she was bleeding out quickly. Molinari stared in anguish at the bloody disaster before him.

"No!" he whispered. "Not like this!"

He realized that the woman was dying, and that her baby might already be gone. The stab wound to her abdomen had struck dead center in her womb. He couldn't imagine how any infant might survive such an attack, but he had to try to save it. They both did. Whether she knew it or not, it was the only thing that mattered.

Molinari hastily wrapped her in the bed sheet and helped her to her feet, and then gave her a towel from the rack by the sink to staunch her wound. He looked around, wondering what to do next. He knew he had to move her to someplace safe, but he had no idea where that might be.

Several sick people of the parish were waiting their turn to see a doctor, fidgeting in the overstuffed Naugahyde chairs in the clinic lobby. The old furnace rustled the Christmas decorations, but it failed to chase the dank chill from the air. The sick huddled with their families, flipping through a collection of dog-eared *Life* magazines or

9

idly watching a re-run of President Ford's second Christmas wish to the nation. An orderly finally came by and changed the channel on the big Sylvania console. Johnny Carson and Ed McMahon were walking through a bawdy skit wearing oversized Santa hats, and that seemed to lighten the mood.

An old man sat alone, gazing out the smudged glass doors and ignoring the TV. He was brooding as he watched the rain steak past the lights in the parking lot. It galled him to think that after all he had been through, from the Dust Bowl to Guadalcanal and beyond, that he was destined to drop dead in a noisy, mildewed waiting room, watching a rainstorm ruin another Christmas morning.

His view of the storm was suddenly obscured as a dark hulk approached the front doors. The doors were pushed open from the outside and Zamba Boukman stepped into the lobby.

The old man's jaw dropped open; a giant was standing before him. New Orleans was just down the highway and the people of the parish were not unaccustomed to seeing strangers with peculiar looks pass through. But this man was something different, something altogether different.

Standing before him was a six-foot-two stranger, two hundred pounds of solid muscle, an enormous block of chiseled obsidian masquerading as human flesh. Zamba was dressed in an outfit better suited for Mardi Gras or a sun-splashed Caribbean isle. His necklace was a chain of thick black iron links.

He was born in Benin, in West Africa, and after growing up in Jamaica he was taken to the island of Saint-Dominque. His power as a voodoo priest soon became the stuff of legend, and the praise was entirely justified. Zamba Boukman was now over two hundred years old.

He smiled at the old man, but the old man didn't return the gesture. He just stared back, and he wasn't the only one. The entire lobby seemed to pause. For a moment, all that ailed them or caused them to fear for their lives was forgotten. Zamba had just brought them a different kind of fear, because although he was scrupulously clean, it seemed to everyone in the room that he smelled of evil.

He strode across the lobby to the reception desk, where the duty nurse sat at her typewriter, staring at him along with everyone else.

"Perhaps you could help me," he said to her.

Molinari and Melissa silently emerged from Room Three. She held the bed sheet wrapped about her, pressing the towel underneath it against her abdominal wound. Molinari held her close, helping her to walk and giving her what little comfort he could.

The hallway was thankfully empty at the moment. Behind them, Room Three had been hastily cleaned up, and Father Vicente's body was nowhere to be seen.

An aluminum Christmas tree, lit by a slowly rotating color wheel, shimmered by the nurses' station. The duty nurse had her nose in a magazine and her staff was busy elsewhere. She got up, rubbed her aching back, and stepped into the back office.

Molinari guided Melissa past the nurse's station and the main staircase, toward the exit sign at the end of the hall, passing the open doors of several rooms. Patients were fast asleep in their beds, their lights down low.

He silently urged Melissa to hurry, guiding her through the exit door and down the stairwell. A scant moment later, Evelyn, the shift supervisor and Jane, another nurse, jockeyed a gurney out of the elevator and wheeled it down the hall, searching for an empty room.

Lisa Johnson lay under the sweat-soaked sheet, pale and nervous, holding her swollen belly. She convulsed as another contraction wracked her body. Jane gripped her hand and offered a brave smile.

"This kid wants out, huh, Lisa?"

"Tell me about it!" the mother-to-be gasped. "Is my husband here?"

"He'll be here," Jane assured her.

Evelyn poked her head into Room Three and discovered it was empty. She caught Jane's eye. "I guess they got that walk-in down in recovery by now."

Jane shrugged. "Guess so." She glanced at the bed inside. "Ain't got no linen..."

Lisa convulsed from another strong contraction. Evelyn pointed at the storage closet across the hall, by the elevator. "Get some sheets. The sooner Miss Johnson's prepped, the better."

Jane went to the closet and rummaged around inside as Evelyn wheeled the gurney into Room Three. Jane followed her a moment later with a fresh set of linen, closing the door behind them.

Molinari and Melissa were huddled outside under a magnolia tree, near the exit door at the end of the maternity wing. The storm was still battering the surrounding bayou, and a fitful wind tugged at Melissa's bed sheet. Rain-diluted blood streamed from her abdomen. She slumped against him, losing consciousness, and he slapped her cheeks to rouse her.

"Come on, Melissa! *Fight!!*"

Her knees buckled in response. Suddenly, all the lights of the clinic flickered and went out. He held her up, scanning the darkness. A moment later, a low diesel rumble could be heard somewhere close by. The essential clinic lights came back on, but the main lights of the parking structure were still out.

It was just a silhouette now, set back in the trees under a cloudy, moonless sky. The emergency lights in the stairwells were the only ones that came back on. The cars were sitting in darkness; it was the perfect place to hide.

He drew the bed sheet around her, and guided her through the driving rain toward the blacked-out structure.

Jane rushed out of Room Three, leaving the door open. She was in a mad hurry to find the doctor. Lisa's water had just broken, soaking the bed. Evelyn stayed with her, holding her hand and breathing along with her.

Jane dashed down the main staircase, past an enormous black man in Caribbean party clothes coming onto the floor. *Well, that's out of season,* she thought in passing, but she had more pressing things on her mind.

Zamba reached the landing and looked up and down the hallway, debating which way to go.

"Aaaauughhhh!" Lisa cried out from Room Three.

He turned to the sound of her pain and smiled, taking a step a step closer, but paused as the elevator across from the main staircase quietly chimed.

The doors slid open and Devlin stepped out.

CHAPTER THREE

Devlin was tall and lean, an aristocratic gentleman who moved with the fluid assurance of absolute authority. He was dressed in crimson and black, with a flowing black greatcoat that matched his dark, hooded eyes. His nails were perfectly manicured, and he wore them a bit longer than other men.

He smiled hello to Zamba and looked around. There was an air of triumph about him, as if he had just won something. Zamba bowed his head in respect, and the iron links of his necklace gently clattered in response.

"Where is He?" Devlin wanted to know.

"Aaaahhh!!" Lisa cried out once again, and Devlin had his answer. Room Three was across the hall from where they stood. Devlin flicked a piercing glance at the room, then looked at Zamba and smiled like an angel.

Devlin had always been confident of winning the bet, but he never thought it would be this easy. He had expected some sort of subterfuge, some misdirection or sleight of hand. But this was far too easy...

And then it occurred to him – he had met no resistance because there was no way he could lose. This, he now knew, was complete capitulation. The argument was already over; the battle was already won. His real triumph was that the entire world would know as well. And they would know it very soon indeed.

The New Time had arrived.

He approached the open door, a beatific smile on his lips and his eyes aglow. Zamba was a faithful step behind him.

The storm had whipped itself into a fury. Molinari propped Melissa against a concrete pillar by the parking structure stairwell. The emergency light over the nearby exit door provided the only illumination.

He quickly went down a row of cars in the gloom, tugging on door handles as he searched for an unlocked car. The '65 Bonneville had seen better days, but the burgundy interior was clean and the back seat was enormous. He elbowed the driver's window, busting out the safety glass, and reached inside to unlock it. He opened the door and the dome light came on, surprisingly bright in the surrounding darkness. He reached in back, unlocked the passenger door, and swung it open.

He rushed back to Melissa and half-carried her to the car, gently laying her down in back, then got inside with her, kneeling behind the driver's seat. He quietly closed the door and the dome light went out. They were invisible now. For the moment, they were safe.

Devlin and Zamba entered Room Three, quiet as ghosts, and Zamba silently closed the door behind them. Evelyn had her hands full tending to Lisa, and wasn't aware of their presence until they were right behind her, looming over the bed. Lisa's wide-eyed stare told Evelyn that something was amiss, and she turned to look.

Evelyn nearly jumped out of her skin, seeing Zamba towering over her. Devlin was mostly obscured from her view, standing on the far side of the hulking voodoo priest.

"Excuse me, but you two can't be in here right now."

Zamba slipped a ceremonial dagger from under his tunic and plunged it upwards into her heart, completely lifting her off her feet.

He grasped her hair with his other hand and carried her that way across the room, sitting her down in a chair. As he slid his blade out, her last startled breath left her body.

Lisa's mind and vision were blurry from drugs, and she hadn't seen a thing. At the moment, she was consumed with the blinding pain of a strong contraction in her belly.

Devlin was standing beside her bed, gazing down at her with a mesmerizing look that she had never seen from anyone before. It frightened her, and yet at the same time she suddenly felt an overwhelming hunger for him. But as she gazed back at him, her blurry vision suddenly increased.

"My eyes," she whispered, puzzled and suddenly terrified. Then her abdomen violently contracted again, and she gritted her teeth in pain.

Zamba stepped up close beside Devlin and gazed down at her as well. It was as if they had just discovered a priceless treasure, as if they finally found what they had been searching for.

Devlin flicked a glance at Zamba, and Zamba leaned down like he was about to kiss her lips. As he came closer, his iron necklace gently rattled.

"Who...?" Lisa wondered groggily, but when she felt something soft and slimy drop onto her breastbone, she instinctively tried to lurch away from whatever it was, pressing back in her pillow, utterly terrified. Another contraction seized her, this time triggered by fear.

"Aaaaaaarrgh!" she wailed, and the world slammed into focus as an invisible something formed undulating depressions on her skin. Her voice was soon cut off as it slid around her neck and smoothly constricted, relentlessly choking the breath out of her. In a matter of moments, Lisa Johnson was dead.

Devlin felt her belly, and grinned at Zamba. "Alive and kicking," he reported, and Zamba grinned back.

Devlin flicked her hospital gown away, exposing her naked body. Her legs were splayed open, and he smiled at the sight of her freshly-shaven vagina.

"How lovely!" Devlin observed. "Like the grand entrance of a cathedral." Zamba nodded agreement.

"Let us pray," Devlin whispered, and held out his hand, palm up. Zamba gave him the bloody ceremonial dagger.

The invisible presence slithered from around Lisa's neck and climbed up Zamba's arm, briefly materializing as it coiled around his neck. The asp took its own tail in its mouth, and transformed back into his voodoo necklace.

The windows of the Bonneville were fogged up and the storm outside was howling. Molinari was kneeling on the back seat now, between Melissa's widespread knees. The illumination from the emergency stairwell light was just enough to make out what he was doing. The problem was, he didn't really know what he was doing, but he was doing it anyway. There was no other choice. He did what he could in the scant seconds between Melissa's waning contractions, and prayed for the best.

He dropped the bloody crucifix dagger on the floor, and gently reached into the Cesarean incision that he had made. Melissa had the towel clenched in her teeth, and she screamed into it as his fingers gently probed inside of her.

Devlin's face was flecked with blood. He glared down at the fruit of his labor, Zamba's ceremonial dagger clenched in his hand. Zamba

18

was close beside him, blood on his tunic as well, staring down at the corpse. They were both infuriated.

In one fluid motion, Devlin hurled something against the wall. It fractured the plaster with a dense, wet thud, and dropped to the floor in a bloody heap. Blood seeped down the wall to meet it.

Zamba waited for him to speak. It took a while.

"This is bad for business," Devlin finally hissed. He inhaled deeply, and let out a measured breath. He couldn't fathom what might have gone wrong. The woman was supposed to be in Room Three. It had all been meticulously arranged. The envoy from Rome had assured him that Vicente would see to everything.

So where was the little bitch? Devlin fumed silently. *And for that matter, where the hell was Vicente? He saw to everything, did he?* Devlin looked forward to burning the man's eyes out.

"They deceived us?" Zamba asked.

"No! What could they possibly gain?"

Zamba shrugged. "Their scriptures tell them —"

Devlin cut him off with a withering sneer. "They don't believe that nonsense!"

He glanced at the dead newborn, now a lump of soft flesh on the floor below the blood-streaked wall.

"This changes everything," Devlin told him.

Something caught his attention, and he sniffed at the air. Zamba joined him. They both glanced at the closet, and then at each other.

Devlin opened the closet door. Father Vicente's body lay crumpled on the floor. He sneered at the odorous corpse. *"Vicente!"*

Devlin looked around the room, piecing things together, as if he could somehow sense what transpired. "Never send a priest to do the Devil's work."

Outside, the wind howled insanely. Zamba looked around, slowly nodding as he read the room, following Devlin's lead.

"Herod had the right idea," Devlin said to him.

19

They went to the door, Zamba a step ahead to open it for his master. Devlin was still clutching Zamba's dagger in his fist. He was itching to get to work.

The last thing Melissa saw before she slipped away was her precious baby entering the world. Molinari gingerly examined the newborn. To his great relief the child was unharmed. Vicente's dagger had somehow missed, plunging between the baby's legs. The infant had come through completely unscathed. It was a miracle.

Molinari wept in exhaustion, sinking to the blood-soaked seat as he beheld the sticky, fussing newborn, sputtering and squalling in his weary hands.

He could only rest for a moment, though. The wind suddenly increased to a high-pitched roar, and Molinari sat bolt upright, turning to see. He rubbed the fog off the window with his sleeve and peered into the night.

A small, lightning-laced funnel cloud touched down on the bayou not a hundred yards away. It screamed as it came closer, bearing down on the parking structure. Molinari took a moment to straighten the lifeless body of the young woman who had brought a miracle into the world.

Devlin and Zamba were just about to step out of Room Three and into the hallway when the window behind them shattered, blown out by the approaching twister. Shards of glass shotgunned into the room, but they were unaffected.

They turned to look outside, through the raw opening where the window had been. Illumination from the adjoining rooms cast a weak yellow light on the howling vortex as it tore into the parking structure across the lawn, tossing the cars around. The emergency stairwell lights short-circuited and went out.

The walls of the old clinic began shaking violently. Shingles flew around outside and other windows could be heard shattering. All over the clinic, people were screaming in panic.

The air pressure in the building underwent a drastic change, and the door was suddenly yanked from Zamba's hand, ripped from its hinges. It spun away down the hall.

In the records room behind the nurses' station, thousands of neat paper files were sucked from the shelves and drawn through the shattered windows, lost forever.

Nurses scrambled for the stairs, cradling newborns, as orderlies and doctors assisted the female patients. All around them, a flurry of paper and linen was being pulled through broken windows, drawn into the twister that was churning a deep trench in the lawn outside.

Devlin and Zamba were untouched by the howling chaos, and as quickly as it came the tornado moved on, carving a path into the moonless bayou.

Devlin looked around at the abandoned maternity wing and sighed. "We'll have to flush him out the hard way," he grumbled to Zamba.

Zamba nodded, but said nothing.

The old house by the river was perched on stilts to keep it dry from the ebb and flow of the backwater swamp. The rain had finally stopped, leaving behind an enormous mud puddle before the front steps.

Molinari stumbled out of the woods, slogged through the mud, and trudged up the wide plank stairs. The newborn was in his arms, swaddled in the bloody bed sheet.

Molinari fumbled at the doorknob and nudged the door with his knee. It creaked open as he wiped his feet the best he could.

"Quickly!" Acadia urged him, standing just inside.

He entered the house and the midwife shut the door behind him, barring them inside with a heavy oak beam.

She had already lit the front room with dozens of votive candles in preparation for his arrival, but she was expecting the mother of the child to be with him as well.

As they settled onto the sofa, Molinari caught a glimpse of the back room – an exam table with stirrups, an old white metal cabinet with patent medicines, and a laminated obstetrics poster tacked on the wall.

They sat close together and Acadia smiled at the newborn in his arms. The infant gurgled, eyes already open to the world. The midwife glanced at Molinari, apprehensive.

"And the mother?" she asked.

He sadly shook his head. Acadia crossed herself and breathed a little prayer. The baby seemed to be watching her. Acadia smiled back, and Molinari offered the infant to her. "Would you like to...?"

"Yes!" she smiled.

He placed the newborn in her arms. The child didn't fuss, but simply gazed up at her smiling, candlelit face as she softly cooed.

"Those eyes!" Acadia whispered. "Simply divine." She looked away, toward a room behind the fireplace.

"Rabbi Simone! Come see the child!"

Simone rushed in from the kitchen. He was a handsome, smiling young man, wearing a skullcap and the *peyot* side curls of an Orthodox Jew.

Simone knelt before them, smiling joyously at the new arrival, his hands held open and giving thanks to heaven.

"God's work! God's work!" he said with a radiant smile.

Molinari nodded, and smiled back. *Indeed it was,* Molinari thought. *Indeed it was...*

Acadia turned so that Simone could get a better look, opening the sheet to show him the child. He smiled at the infant then glanced at Molinari, still smiling, but hesitant.

"Are you sure, Rabbi?" Simone asked him.

Rabbi Jacob Molinari simply nodded. *Oh, yes...*

His mother had taught him that the most important thing in Judaism was the saving of a life. And after what Father Vicente nearly achieved, Molinari realized that to keep the child safe he would have to operate from within the Church, not as an outsider and certainly not as a rabbi.

The enemy was close, and he had to be even closer. As close, he thought with an ironic smile, as the Muslims say that God is to each and every one of us.

Closer than the beating of your heart.

The crucifix dagger was tucked in his waistband and it dug uncomfortably into his skin. He shifted on the sofa to ease the irritation and gazed down at his hands, bloodstained and flecked with mud.

He should wash up, he thought. For the next thirty-three years, he was going to have his hands full.

CHAPTER FOUR

Fareed Abdul Aly didn't want to die. His body was shaking uncontrollably and his clothes were clinging to his skin from a cold sweat seeping from every pore. His teeth were chattering so hard that he was sure they would crack. Even Katrina hadn't frightened him as much as this. Katrina was just a hurricane, but this was a frontal assault on his soul, and there was no high ground, no shelter, and no salvation.

There was only Devlin's voice in his head.

What Fareed was doing at this moment, and what he had been going through for the last ten minutes, was scaring the living Hell out of him. But as bewildered as he was, he knew that no matter how unreal this seemed it was all completely and utterly real. Every last bit of it.

There was one more thing he knew. He knew that there was no way out for him. Fareed Aly knew he was doomed. He had never had a suicidal thought in his life, and yet here he was, standing outside his own balcony railing twelve stories up, about to jump to his death. And even though he was about to actually do it, it was the absolute last thing he wanted to do.

Staring at the concrete sidewalk below, he realized with an electric shock of cold certainty that all he really wanted out of life was to just go on living. But Devlin wasn't going to allow that to happen. His grip on Fareed was much too strong.

Fareed clung to his balcony railing with one hand; his other was balled into a tight fist against his heaving chest. He prayed hard, his lips quivering as he tried to form the proper words, any words, to beseech the Almighty. Now that he had finally given his life to God, now that he had even brought his own siblings back into God's loving embrace, where was his Savior? Or was this to be his penance for a life of sin?

God, Devlin told Fareed soundlessly, *has nothing to do with this.*

Fareed's eyes snapped back to Devlin down below. He didn't want to die. Sweet Jesus, after all the darkness he had been through, he didn't want to die! *Not yet. Oh, Lord, not yet...*

A swarm of city vehicles clogged the street below, their lights flashing as the response teams piled out, looking up to him and pointing, and deploying their equipment while the cops set up a roadblock. Everyone and his brother were turning out to save him. Everyone except The One he had finally turned to for salvation, with the help of the Bishop just a short month ago.

The cops were already scrambling through his building lobby, and were coming up the elevator with the super and his master key. They had everything under control down below. For a city strained to the breaking point and beyond, they still performed daily miracles, but where was the real miracle worker when you needed him?

The balcony railing was cold and moist from a long, damp winter night. Dawn had crept in muggy and overcast, with a light fog drifting in from Lake Pontchartrain north of the city and from the Mississippi River to the south. The sun would soon rise over the Lower Ninth Ward and the cloudy grey November skies would melt away, but Fareed knew that he wouldn't be around to welcome the clear blue morning sky. Not this time.

Devlin was down there in the gathering crowd, and he wanted Fareed to come to him. To fall into *his* arms, into *his* loving embrace, and his name wasn't Jesus.

Fareed gripped the railing so tightly that his fingernails were bleeding. He now knew precisely what it meant to be hanging on for dear life. The phrase made perfect sense to him now, because it was all he could do at this point. Stark terror had risen inside of him, so powerful that it numbed his spine and constricted his throat. Spasms were firing in his legs and biceps, and a primal fear engulfed him as Devlin's grip became ever stronger. It was an actual physical sensation, as if a clenched fist were squeezing his heart. Devlin had somehow reached inside of him and grabbed hold, and Fareed could tell that he wasn't going to let go.

With each passing moment of precious life, Fareed begged Jesus to save him, but nothing changed. Devlin was still laughing, still whispering in his ear, and he still felt an overwhelming compulsion to jump to his death. He tightened the shaking fist that he held against his breastbone and glanced down.

He could see Devlin in the crowd below smiling up to him, a handsome face surrounded by a cluster of Fareed's worried neighbors, the familiar strangers who lived next door or across the street, the people he saw every day whose names he didn't know. Like most anonymous neighbors, they just smiled or avoided eye contact. But now they were all aiming their cell phones at him, or texting their friends. Before, Fareed was just a part of the scenery, but now he was the center of attention. He would be on YouTube by dinnertime.

The cops at the roadblock let two trucks in from the local TV channels. They ran up on the curb, inventing parking spaces on the front lawn of the building. The crews piled out, and in seconds they had their cameras locked down on tripods and trained up at him.

The reporters were running sound checks on their mics and earpieces, and fussing with their clothes while the make-up elves touched up their faces. They tilted their heads back, squinting up at the jumper as the November overcast gradually brightened above. The world was going to Hell in a hand basket, and it was their job to make sure that the coverage was compelling and the footage was awesome.

Fareed heard the entry door of his condo being unlocked, and glanced through his open slider into the living room. The super in the

27

hallway let two cops in, and stayed behind in the hall as the cops quietly approached across the living room carpet.

Their attention was riveted on the jumper, a young male with dark olive skin, an Arab-sounding name and short black hair, approximately five feet ten, one hundred sixty pounds, standing on his tiptoes outside his balcony railing and hanging on with one hand, his other one balled into a tight fist and pressed against his chest.

One of the cops almost stepped on Fareed's cordless phone, lying on the carpet. It was giving off an annoying beep, hounding whoever was in earshot to hang it up. By force of habit, the younger of the two cops paused to bend down and get it. But his partner waved that off, his eyes still on Fareed. He dropped it less than ten minutes ago, when Devlin finally enticed him out to the balcony. When he could no longer resist him.

Henry stood at the threshold of Fareed's balcony slider, gently appealing to him with the kindest eyes. His rookie partner stood beside him, watching and learning, wondering how this would turn out. He privately suspected that it wouldn't go well.

"Sir! Please go to the officer behind you!"

The megaphone momentarily broke Fareed's fixation on Devlin. It was pointing up at him, held by an officer standing by the open door of one of the police cars. The first rays of sunlight glinted off the brass stars on the officer's shoulder boards.

Fareed looked back to Henry, who smiled and offered his hand. But Henry kept his distance, not wanting to spook him.

He wanted to take Henry's hand in the worst way, but Devlin was down there, and he wanted Fareed to come to him. *Now.* Fareed looked back down to find him in the crowd.

Devlin was looking up to him along with everyone else. In over thirty years, he hadn't aged a single day, but no one around him knew that. In fact, they didn't even know he was amongst them. And even if they had glanced his way, he would have been invisible to them. Right now, for Devlin's purposes, Fareed was the only person who had any inkling he was there.

Devlin held an unlit cigarette between his fingers, but it didn't hold tobacco. It was his own special brand, something he had conjured up for his private pleasure. Devlin's cigarettes were crafted from the slow-cured leaves of the Tree of Knowledge, picked by his own hand and carefully aged over countless centuries, delicately toasted to perfection in a special place that he called his own.

He was smoking more often now, and when he did, he inhaled deeply and the smoke coiled like a serpent around the memories it evoked, especially the moment in the Garden of Eden when Eve paused to consider his fateful offer. That perfect, singular moment when the entire delicate balance of creation began to shift in his favor...

When his work was done here today, he intended to celebrate by having a smoke. After so many years of frustration and failure, the urge to finally taste success was palpable. Time was running short and he was growing nervous and impatient. Lately, only his cigarettes soothed him, and that in itself was maddening.

Knowledge had always been his by divine right, but the longer this game played out, the greater the odds became that knowledge might be something he would have to surrender, and the consequences of that were too awful to contemplate.

"Come to me," he whispered to Fareed, gesturing with the unlit cigarette held between his fingers. And yet at the same time, Devlin was thinking to himself, *Don't do it! Shun me! Get me behind thee!*

Fareed didn't know what Devlin was really thinking; all he knew was that Devlin was enticing him to jump. Fareed had no clue that that was precisely what Devlin did *not* want him to do.

Devlin actually wanted Fareed to resist him. Because if Fareed did, then Devlin would have finally found The One he was looking for. Only then could he lead The One into temptation, and when he did that, Devlin would certainly win.

Devlin wasn't tempting him, he was testing him.

The temptations would come later, after he proved who Fareed really was. After he resisted the Devil himself.

29

"Come to me..." Devlin thought aloud, and Fareed heard it as a beguiling whisper in his head.

Don't do it! Devlin privately prayed, and then something under his skin uncoiled like a serpent as he underwent a subtle transformation.

"Shun me," he whispered in another silent voice.

Fareed stared down at him, shivering as this new command enveloped his mind like a cloud of smoke. He suddenly jolted in horror as Devlin's true nature appeared. Lucifer was a magnificent, angry archangel, the first among many who had fallen from grace so long ago. Once fallen, he had never regained his balance.

The horrific sight squeezed Fareed's breath out of him, and he shot a desperate glance at Henry, who had imperceptibly moved closer. The officer was only a few feet away now, but he froze in place. His partner stayed behind at the threshold, motionless as well.

"Please, sir," Henry pleaded with Fareed. "Let us help you."

"I *want* to!" Fareed cried out. "Believe me, I *do!* But I *can't!* He won't *let* me! *He won't let me!*"

Henry was baffled, but he persisted, holding out his hand and taking another cautious step forward.

"Sir, please..."

Henry stopped, noticing something in Fareed's clutched fist. If it was a detonator, it sure was a tiny one. But these days, even a car remote was suspect.

What a fiendishly clever ruse, Henry thought, his mind suddenly racing at fever pitch. A new twist in the suicide bombing trade – get out on a ledge and draw a big crowd down below, jump into their midst and BOOM! Everybody goes home to Allah.

Henry suddenly wasn't sure what to do. If this Arab guy did reach out to him, it would be with the hand that was holding the detonator. Then what?

Anguished tears streamed down Fareed's cheeks, his desperate gaze locked on the policeman. Henry and his partner had no idea what was happening, and they wouldn't believe it if Fareed told him.

Fareed scarcely believed it himself, but it was as real as the air they breathed – completely invisible, and yet absolutely essential to what was transpiring.

Henry kept his eyes on Fareed and leaned back to his partner behind him. "Is that a detonator?" he whispered.

His partner gulped, and leaned into his shoulder mic.

"Captain!" he whispered. "The jumper might be wearing an explosive vest."

Down below, Captain Thorrington looked up to the balcony in alarm, and glanced at the crowd. Although his men were holding them back, they were still just a few yards away from where the jumper would land.

"*Come to me,*" Devlin whispered in Fareed's head, and Fareed looked down to him once again. Devlin's grip was burrowing ever deeper, opening pathways that led down to into the young man's darkest corners. And yet, Devlin was hoping and praying that Fareed would cast him off, because only then would Devlin know who Fareed really was. Devlin had been looking for The One for nearly thirty-three years now, as determined as a man looking for gold or true love, and nothing less would satisfy him.

"*No! Shun me!*" was the whisper that Fareed heard now. It was Lucifer's voice this time, Devlin's true essence, and the friction generated by his inner conflict sparked a sudden fever inside of Fareed.

"Jesus, where are you when I need you?" Fareed wailed. His entire body tensed in a final, futile effort to resist, but he was unable to tear his gaze from Devlin down below. He squeezed his swollen eyes shut to block him out, and shuddered as the fever took hold.

He turned away from his rescuers. Henry and his partner sensed that from this point forward, there was nothing they could do to save the jumper. Or the people below, if their suspicions were correct.

Fareed's tears turned to blood. He opened his eyes a final time, gazing at Devlin twelve stories down. The black-coated figure slowly beckoned with the two fingers that held his unlit cigarette.

"Come to me."

It was the only sound Fareed heard. The universe stood mute and waiting, and Fareed let his hand slip from the railing.

Henry lunged to save him, but the moment he did he felt a sudden constriction in his chest. He grabbed at his shirtfront and his partner glanced at him in alarm. But as suddenly as it came on, the pain vanished.

Henry was fine, but Fareed was gone, and all they could do was watch him fall. Henry had heard from other cops that jumpers sometimes scream their heads off when they fall, but this one didn't make a sound.

The crowd below, however, did. Several of them screamed, and those that didn't gasped. Behind them, Thorrington was shouting into his megaphone.

"CLEAR THE AREA!"

But it was too late.

Fareed saw the ground rushing up to meet him. The shocking realization of what he was doing stopped his ability to catch a final breath. The wind flapped at his clothes and tossed his hair around, tugging at his skull. His mouth filled with air, but he couldn't take any into his lungs. His bloody tears blurred his vision as he accelerated, faster and faster, closer and closer.

It was a long fall, and the crowd's reaction had dwindled to a quiet, awful dread. They watched in silence, ignoring Thorrington's order, their cameras tracking Fareed.

He slammed onto the concrete driveway with a sickening thud and bounced once, before silently coming to rest in a sad huddle of broken flesh.

There was no explosion.

Fareed drew one final, incredibly painful breath, and then lay still in a spreading pool of blood, with something still clenched in his fist.

Standing unnoticed in the murmuring crowd, Devlin's cigarette spontaneously flared to life. He was deeply disappointed, and suddenly needed a smoke. He took a drag, exhaling through his nose as his face contorted into a dark, brooding scowl. Today had not gone well, and there was only a few short months left.

He turned and walked away in a foul mood, passing directly through several bystanders. They shuddered, feeling a sudden chill, but they attributed it to the tragedy they just witnessed.

Thorrington's voice boomed over the crowd. *"Stay back from the body!"*

But the paramedics rushed to Fareed's side, thinking that Thorrington was helping them with crowd control. They deployed their equipment even though they already knew Fareed was dead, or that he would be within seconds. They knew there was nothing they could do. Their efforts were to keep themselves going, not Fareed, in the same way that a funeral was for the survivors and not for the deceased. Fareed's time had come and gone, but theirs had not.

Thorrington's men were standing back and shouting warnings to the paramedics, but all it did was generate confusion. Particularly since the paramedics already had their hands all over Fareed's body and knew there wasn't a bomb. They sat back on their heels and looked at the cops, puzzled.

Fareed's tortured soul slipped free and rose above his corpse, looking back on the person he had just been. His body's heart remained motionless. Despite the valiant efforts of the paramedics, blood no longer pumped in the veins. It leaked instead, as dead bodies do, from a multitude of orifices and ruptures.

Devlin's grip on the immortal soul that had been briefly known to the world as Fareed Abdul Aly was suddenly gone. Knowledge was gradually returning like a long-lost memory, and as it did a feeling came over him, an awareness of love.

It was good to be free of the pain.

CHAPTER FIVE

The first rays of sunlight touched the clapboard siding and the worn shingles and the patches of blue plastic tarp on the weather-beaten homes of the Lower Ninth Ward. Colonies of mold and mildew had been busy all night long in the clammy chill of a New Orleans winter, exuding their distinctive gases, but they lay dormant now as their hideouts warmed up, content to slumber until the sun was gone again.

Some cars and trucks were still piled against abandoned structures, little more than rusting hulks now after several years of rain and humidity, far beyond any hope of salvage. The junkyards, like the landfills, were already overflowing, so unless the cars were blocking traffic or interfering with access to something vital, they remained exactly where Katrina left them.

The Industrial Canal had been breached near the Claiborne Street Bridge. More than eight feet of storm-driven floodwater sloshed into the Lower Ninth Ward, directly from Lake Pontchartrain. That caused most of the immediate damage, but years of sun and wind and the constant humidity of the Caribbean basin weathered whatever debris remained.

A vindictive Mother Nature had vandalized the entire region. When the waters finally receded from the low-lying neighborhood, they left a bathtub ring around every structure, as high as a man could reach on tiptoe.

It wasn't just lake water; it was a toxic soup. The flood had upended trashcans and Dumpsters, and back-flushed restaurant drains, toilets, gutters and sewers. Tons of food floated away, along with the contents of ten thousand refrigerators, all of it putrefying in the warm water, and it blended with every pharmaceutical drug, legal or otherwise, from all the bedsides and bathroom cabinets and kitchen tables.

Added to that were the dead, bloated bodies of the pets and the raccoons and the rats that couldn't swim, and the corpses of the old and the poor who huddled in their attics, praying for a rescuer who couldn't get to them fast enough.

It all was in the mix, and it seeped into every scrap of drywall, every shingle, every floorboard and every couch and drape and mattress, and sat there, stewing in the hot sunshine, sometimes for years on end.

The two-story Victorian house was in the middle of the block, built in 1915. Most of the other homes had been abandoned, and most still remained the exact same way the flood had left them. Some four hundred souls now lived in the neighborhood, out of a pre-Katrina population of over twelve thousand.

On the second floor of the faded mansion, in the back half of the house, the master suite was in gloom and the lace curtains were drawn tight. The TV was still on from the night before. A cheery talk show was in progress, but no one was listening. A series of newspaper clippings were hung on the wall with pushpins. They formed a chilling chronology of the work of a serial killer still at large.

From the *Times-Picayune Press*, December 25, 1976 evening edition: SIX DIE – MASSACRE AND TORNADO STRIKE BAYOU MEMO-RIAL CLINIC. Another article from the *Bayou Press*, August 1977: 8-MONTH OLD BOY HAS SKULL CRUSHED. From the *Orlando Sentinel*, February 1981: 5-YEAR OLD BOY FOUND DEAD. The *Sun*

Herald reported on May 7, 1985: BRANDING KILLER STRIKES AGAIN. Boy Found In Oven, FBI Admits They're Stumped. By then, the killer had earned his moniker.

On March 17, 1988, the *New Orleans Dispatch* reported: TEEN BOY FOUND IN DUMPSTER – BOTH EYES BURNED. The trail of blood continued through several more articles, culminating in a *Time* cover story from nearly three years ago: THIRTY YEARS OF THE BRANDING KILLER – Will It Ever End?

A young woman was asleep in the four-poster bed. She shifted uncomfortably, exposing a birthmark on her right side, a dark horizontal streak about two inches in length.

A holstered revolver sat on the nightstand beside a silver-framed photograph. Twelve-year-old Christine Mas sat on her father's lap. He wore his cop helmet and his black pants with the white side-stripes, straddling his NOPD Harley-Davidson. His knee-high motorcycle boots were always spit-shined, but Officer Julian Mas liked to keep his scarred leather holster just the way it was.

BLAM!! A gunshot reverberated in the woman's dream. She burrowed into her pillow, but the gravity well of horror was inescapable now. She was falling into a familiar nightmare.

BLAM! Twelve-year-old Chrissy was pressing her hands against the passenger window, staring at her father's back. She was in the front passenger seat of the family car and he was standing just outside, leaning against her door. All she could see was the broad back of his jacket, and the revolver in his hand.

"DADDY!" she shrieked as loud as she could. But in the nightmare, she had no voice.

BLAM!

Mas lurched awake. She was soaked in sweat, her damp hair lying in limp strands on her forehead. She was frozen in place and taking short, shallow breaths as her heart raced from a surge of adrenalin. She gradually gained focus, staring at her father's gun on the nightstand.

She sat up and looked dully around the room. The master suite was a large studio apartment now, as comfortable as an old pair of shoes. Her eyes came to rest on the news clippings, and she gazed at them until she came fully awake.

She picked up her father's holstered revolver and gently cradled it in her hands, resting it in her lap. The weapon was hers now, a nickel-plated Ruger Speed-Six revolver with a four-inch barrel. Officer Mas had taken it to a gunsmith, who carefully honed the works until the trigger pull was as light and smooth as silk. The original wood grips were retained. In the proper hands, it was incredibly accurate.

The Ruger was Mas' memento of her father, and a reminder of her father's killer. He was still out there, whoever he was. And she was determined to find him.

She drew the weapon from the oiled leather holster, gripping it firmly in her right hand. It nestled perfectly in her palm, as if it had been custom-made for her. She admired the weapon's simple, elegant craftsmanship. Designed for reliability and rugged use, it was arguably one of the finest handguns ever made.

She didn't take possession of it until the day she received her B.A. in Criminal Justice, the summer after her twenty-first birthday. Her mother Beth was so proud of her that she gave it to her daughter as a graduation present, confident that she could be trusted with the weapon.

The faint scent of Hoppe's No. 9 lubricant had always been a powerful memory trigger for Mas. Sometimes it inspired her, and at other times it made it that much harder to work up the resolve to face another day on the job. This was one of those days.

Junior thrust his snout up between her knees, nudging her hands and the weapon they held out of the way. The brindle Bull Terrier was wide-awake and bright-eyed, as if he just drank a pot of coffee. It was dawn and he was ready to play, a ball and a tug rope in his mouth.

"Hey, little booger," she said with a smile. "Happy New Year."

His big brown eyes sparkled and his tail wagged like a metronome. *Play with me!*

Mas placed the Ruger and the holster on the nightstand. Junior wagged his tail harder, attentively watching her hands, waiting for her to make her move...

She grabbed the tug rope and growled at him. Junior growled back and yanked her off the bed, onto her bare feet. It was her morning exercise.

The curtains were drawn back and the room was awash in morning light. The TV was still on; the chattering on the talk show was a gentle white noise in the background. As Junior scarfed his morning chow on the back porch by the stairs, Mas dressed before the old wardrobe mirror. It was chilly on most mornings this time of year, but it had been getting into the upper 60s during the day. Still, she reckoned that wool slacks wouldn't be overly warm. She tucked in her white shirt and strapped on her 10mm SIG-Sauer P-229. She preferred the Ruger, but she had to admit that twelve flat-trajectory rounds of .40 caliber, along with four back-up clips, did come in handy. Her FBI badge was pinned to her gun belt, beside her iPhone.

She was using a strip of masking tape to get Junior's hair off her suit jacket when the phone rang. She glanced up as the answering machine took over, and listened as she put on her lip balm. "I'm not here. You know how this works." *BEEP.*

"Hi, honey, it's your mother. Just want to know if you can make it for dinner next week. Miss you. Call me some time; I worry."

Mas smiled and blew a glossy kiss as Beth hung up. Before Katrina, she would go to her mom's house for a weekly get-together and a home-cooked meal. But their family home, like so many others, had been lost in the storm. Mary Beth Mas spent the next year in a FEMA motel, and they began having their get-togethers at different restaurants around the city. As New Orleans got back on its feet, more restaurants became available, and they realized that it was both a fun way to explore the city and to celebrate its revival. Their tradition continued even after Beth moved into her new home. This week, it was Mas' turn to pick the place.

Her iPhone rang and she grabbed it off her belt. "Agent Mas."

"Morning, Chrissy." It was Captain Thorrington, head of the homicide and robbery division of NOPD. Back in the day, he was her father's partner, as much as lone-wolf motorcycle cops had partners, but they considered themselves partners nonetheless and would ride together whenever they could.

Mas smiled. "Morning, Cap'n." In her heart, she was still NOPD. After getting her B.A., she had gone straight into the NOPD Academy and worked as a rookie in homicide under the Captain's stern tutelage. After three years of active duty, she became eligible for the FBI Academy at Quantico, Virginia. Thorrington's recommendation helped her secure a position in the program.

She became a Fed because it afforded her the freedom to pursue a criminal across state lines, and there was one criminal in particular that she sought. The Branding Killer's activities had expanded beyond Louisiana while she was growing up, so by the time she was qualified to pursue him there were at least five states to cover. Thorrington recommended a Federal Marshal career path, but Mas decided that FBI was a better way to go.

She went to Virginia, three years to the day that she became a cop, and when she returned she was a Fed. Everyone knew she was still NOPD at heart, and everyone wanted the bastard caught just as much as she did, so for all practical purposes the New Orleans FBI Field Office seconded her to the NOPD and pretty much left her alone.

Thorrington got right to the point. "We had a jumper. You'll want to see this one."

Mas didn't reply, but she knew exactly what he meant. Her stomach tightened, and she suddenly had no appetite for her usual granola and coffee.

"Eleven forty-seven Beaudry," he told her.

Mas nodded, memorizing the address. "I'm on my way."

She ended the call and glanced at the long row of clippings tacked on the wall beside her dresser. Her eyes lingered on the *Time* cover hanging next to her mirror: *Will It Ever End?*

She didn't know. "Happy New Year..." she muttered.

She took a last look around the apartment before she left. Everything was locked up tight. Junior got the signal and hopped through the doggie door on the back porch, negotiating the rickety staircase down to the backyard.

Mas re-holstered the Ruger and laid it down beside the photograph. She kissed her finger and touched it to her father's smiling face, then slipped her MacBook Pro and a bottle of W.I.L. energy water in her briefcase, picked it up, and went out, deadbolting the door behind her.

Mas turned the key and pressed the starter button, and her BMW R1200 purred to life. It cost her a small fortune, but it was her only extravagance. She wasn't a woman who was partial to jewelry, and she wasn't much of a clotheshorse, either, but when it came to her ride she was particular.

She stashed her briefcase in one of the hard shell saddlebags, then unclipped her helmet from the frame and slipped it on, tucking her hair inside. She let the bike warm up, though it really wasn't necessary. It just gave her a moment to watch Junior playing with the landlady's kids.

The school bus was coming, snaking down the street as it negotiated the piles of trash, the construction debris and the abandoned cars.

Nathan and Charles hopped the chain-link fence and Junior forlornly watched them get on the bus. Mas bent over the fence and tousled his ears.

"Be good, little doggie. And leave those poor rats alone."

He just wagged his tail; the only thing he heard was the word "rats." Junior was a purebred ratter and they were everywhere these days. To his way of thinking, New Orleans was heaven on earth.

Mas went to the curb, straddled her bike and zoomed away, slaloming around the junk in the street. What few neighbors remained waved to her, and she waved back. They liked having a cop on their block, and when she became a Fed they liked it even better. Plus, she was easy on the eyes.

She drove west across the Claiborne Street Bridge, passing the infamous spot where the floodwaters had rushed into her neighborhood. Beaudry Street was on her way to the field office downtown. She could still be on time for the ten o'clock briefing if she hurried.

CHAPTER SIX

The jump site on Beaudry was a rush-hour logjam, but the cops at the roadblock could have cared less about anyone getting to work on time. They were already at work, and it wasn't any fun at all. The way they chose to see things, they were performing a civic duty by manning a roadblock that spared their fellow citizens from a similar fate that they themselves were presently suffering.

It was barely after seven in the morning and the cool winter night was quickly becoming a warm, sunny day. It was muggy like New Orleans usually was, and the sunrise breeze was already petering out. Black uniforms, body armor and an endless stream of pissed-off commuters wasn't exactly their idea of a jolly way to start the day.

Mas rolled up alongside the line of cars and paused at the roadblock, sweeping away the hem of her jacket to show them her badge. The cops smiled and let her through – any chick on a hot bike packing a gun and a badge intrigued them.

They watched her drive into the cordoned area, weaving around the swarm of response vehicles and parking at the curb. They waited until she removed her helmet, and were satisfied that they hadn't been snookered into being distracted by a skank or a dyke. She was neither, they concluded, and they both felt that they just had a good, solid moment of guy time, well spent.

During their brief distraction, a pushy reporter and her intrepid cameraman tried to slip past them, but they were halted in mid-stride.

Their newshound colleagues nearby swapped grins with them – *nice try.*

Mas clipped her helmet to the frame, shook out her hair and looked around, assessing the scene. The media was already on hand, pressing against the police tape cordon set up around the impact site. They still had a camera trained on the bloody patch of concrete, although Fareed's body was no longer there. It was in a body bag now, on a gurney parked at the open back doors of the coroner's van.

Mas spotted Captain Thorrington leaning on the hood of his prowler, the door open and the coiled mic cord stretched to the limit as he barked at someone on the other end. He was in his sixties now, as trim and fit as a drill sergeant, but lately his patience had been wearing thin. He liked to say that Katrina washed away his social veneer. It was as likely a reason as any. He paused in his radio diatribe to scowl at the crowd of lookie-loos and media surging against the police tape over by the roadblock.

"For Christ's sake, keep those people *back!*" he snapped at his lieutenant. The officer nodded and turned to his men. "You heard the captain..."

They nodded back. No one could miss the Cap'n's booming voice. He had learned the trick of being heard over a Harley's throbbing mufflers a long time ago.

Mas stepped around a drunk lounging in the grass along the curb. An officer was interviewing him, since the derelict claimed to have seen the entire thing. He lay in the grass all night long and woke up at first light. While he was gazing at the condos above, Fareed took that particular moment to climb over his railing. The drunk was the first one to spot him, but now that he had to repeat his rambling story for an official police report, his mouth had suddenly dried up. He badly needed a drink.

"*Damn!* I'm thirsty," he grumbled. The cop signaled his partner, and she tossed him a bottled water. He offered it to the drunk, but the man sneered and waved it away.

44

"Water?" he groused. "The fish fuck in it!"

The cop and his partner laughed, and so did Mas as she passed them by, crossing the street and angling toward the captain. A yuppie standing by his Porsche was giving another pair of cops a hard time. Their cruiser was parked in the street right behind his ride, and that simply would not do.

"Why am I even paying taxes?" he demanded to know.

The cops had no idea – he looked like a tax cheat to them. But he was a citizen and he wanted them to move their car, so they did. One of them hopped in the cruiser and parked it even closer to his Porsche.

The paramedics were swapping clinical notations with the coroner and his assistant, standing around the gurney by the back of the coroner's van. Dr. Osborn saw Mas and nodded hello. They had worked on several of these cases over the past five years, and all professional detachment aside the killings still creeped him out. The others with him felt much the same way.

The Captain was still on the horn, so Mas approached the group behind the van. She noted their somber tone, and it lent weight to her suspicion that the body in the bag was indeed another Branding Killer victim.

She nodded good morning and gestured toward the corpse. "Hi, Dr. Osborn. May I?"

He unzipped the bag, exposing Fareed's bloated face. His arm was broken in the fall and lay twisted over his chest. His fingers were relaxed now, revealing a small crucifix clutched in his fist.

Mas studied it for a moment. "Coptic," she said.

Osborn frowned, puzzled.

"Christian sect in the Middle East," she explained to him. He nodded, and then he shrugged. In his book, dead was dead. It never seemed to matter what kind of trinkets they held onto.

Mas took a digital thermometer from her jacket pocket and slipped it under Fareed's tongue, and then glanced around, waiting for a reading. Everyone was watching her. All the civilians were puzzled, as were most of the cops and paramedics, but the coroner knew what was up. He'd been down this road with her before.

While everyone else watched Mas, Osborn glanced at a black Maybach stretch limousine parked at the curb. The top was rolled back and the chauffeur was behind the wheel. He was looking straight ahead, but someone in back was looking at Osborn.

Osborn nodded to the man in back, and the man nodded in reply, then said something to his chauffeur. As the chauffeur maneuvered out of the parking spot, Mas noticed someone sitting behind the wheel of a perfectly preserved '76 Land Cruiser, parked across the street.

The man had a police scanner in his lap, and the building address was neatly printed on a notepad attached to his dashboard. He had arrived well before Fareed jumped, even before the cops could establish control of the area. He usually got up before dawn to pray, and when he heard the building's street address on his scanner, he drove right into town to bear witness. 1147 was the Bible code that meant "The will of God."

Mas thought the man looked familiar somehow, but she couldn't quite put her finger on it. He was in his fifties, perhaps older, a nervous type who gripped the steering wheel with both hands like he was still negotiating traffic. He was watching her, almost staring, agitated and intense.

She stepped off the curb and began crossing the street towards him. Seeing her approach, he fired up the Land Cruiser, dropped it in gear and lurched away. Since he was already inside the cordoned area, the cops were only too glad to let him leave. They lifted their tape and he sped away, staring back at Mas.

SCREECH! She instinctively hunched and turned to the sound. The Maybach limousine had come to a nimble halt mere inches behind her. It was leaving as well; she just stepped into its path.

Mas looked around, embarrassed. Everyone was watching her again, but this time they were grinning. She screwed up. Red-faced, she nodded at the chauffeur and stepped out of the way. The cops at the roadblock lifted their tape and the Maybach glided away. She noticed that the limo had Consul plates from Vatican City. She recited the plate number to herself as a matter of habit: *2315*.

Thorrington was watching her, standing in the middle of the street. "Oh, Jeez, Chrissy..." he mumbled to himself, and caught her eye. She grinned sheepishly at him, and he just shook his head.

She stepped out of the street and retrieved her thermometer from the corpse's mouth. "One oh two," she whispered to herself, and glanced at Dr. Osborn. He nodded; he could read her lips.

"When did he jump?" Mas asked him.

"About half an hour ago," he said.

"And when did you guys get here?"

Dr. Osborn checked his watch. "Twelve minutes ago."

"What was his temp?" Mas asked, already knowing the answer.

"One oh six," he told her quietly. "Same as the last one."

"Notify CDC?" she asked him, and he nodded. The CDC always wanted to examine any corpse that manifested something as strange as a post-mortem fever, and after ten Branding victims they still hadn't determined the cause. Mas suspected that they wouldn't be able to determine anything this time, either.

She slipped the thermometer back in her pocket and looked at the corpse's face. The eyes were closed, with blood caked around them. Mas gestured to the coroner's assistant, and the woman handed her a pair of gloves. Mas slipped them on.

"Okay," she said. *Here goes nothing.* She took in a breath to steady herself and pried open Fareed's eyes, cracking apart the dried blood that had sealed them shut after Osborn's initial inspection.

The pupils of both eyes were neatly seared, as if they had been carefully branded with a hot iron.

The men around her found it difficult to confront. Mas and Dr. Osborn felt the same way, but they kept their reactions under wraps.

"Thank you, Doctor," Mas said quietly.

Osborn nodded and zipped up the body bag, while Mas removed the gloves and tossed them in the waste bin inside the van.

She turned away and went over to Thorrington, who was watching her. She nodded hello, and he returned it.

"Cap'n, could you have your guys check if anyone taped the jump?"

"We already checked," he told her. "Come around later, I'll show you the clips."

Mas glanced up at Sergeant Henry Lassiter and his young partner, standing on Fareed's balcony. They were chaperoning the CSI team now, and killing a moment of idle time by watching the goings-on below.

"Mind if I talk to your men upstairs?"

Thorrington glanced up at his men and caught Henry's eye. They both had their cell phones in hand, and Thorrington toggled his. "Agent Mas is coming up," Thorrington informed him. Henry nodded, and snapped his cell phone shut.

Mas headed for the lobby of the building, glancing back over her shoulder at Thorrington. "What was his name, anyway?"

"Fareed Aly."

The one-bedroom condo wasn't anything special, but then not many people in the city could afford even a halfway decent home, much less hold a lease on one. At least this place was clean and dry and had a view. Although it served as a testament to Fareed's success, modest though it was, Mas suspected that the reason Fareed jumped was a testament to another thing entirely. Just what, at this point, she had no idea, and neither did anyone else.

A dried-up Christmas tree without presents sat forlornly in the corner. There was a large hand-woven tapestry on the wall over the couch, with a swirl of Arabic writing stitched in gold thread. A hookah sat on the coffee table.

The CSI team was dusting the place for prints and nosing around with magnifying glasses, collecting God knows what from the oddest places, gently placing their tiny treasures in little jars and baggies, using sterilized surgical tweezers and gloved hands. One of them was dusting an antique brass pyramid and a gold Sphinx on the fireplace mantel. Another was dusting the cordless phone, still lying on the carpet where Fareed dropped it less than an hour ago.

"Hey, Bob," Mas said, greeting the CSI leader. Bob smiled and nodded. He expected to see Mas on the scene, but he was surprised she showed up so soon. Then he remembered why – not only was she ex-NOPD, but she was a close friend of Captain Thorrington as well. The man had more or less adopted her on the same day her father was shot. He'd probably given her the heads-up.

"Can you guys get the phone logs over to me?" Mas asked him. Bob saluted her and got back to work.

Out on the balcony, an EMS technician was concluding a check-up on Henry, but the cop felt fine. The technician shrugged and Henry shrugged back.

Mas stepped out to the balcony. The sky was clearing and it was destined to be a beautiful day, but somehow it didn't seem right. Still, there it was. Mother Nature embraced death and destruction as serenely as she cherished every delicate tendril of life. It was a recurring observation that would strike Mas at the oddest moments, and this was one of them.

Henry nodded hello, and so did the technician before going back inside. Henry and his partner were still visibly upset over losing the jumper, but Mas chose not to offer any commiseration. She knew cops. They processed the horrors of their job in their own way, on their own time.

Henry recognized her. He had seen Agent Mas coming out of Captain Thorrington's office several times over the last few years. He knew they were still close, even though she'd gone on to become a Fed. His younger partner stood aside and kept his mouth shut, watching and learning.

"Morning, Henry. How you feeling?" Mas said.

"Morning, Agent Mas," he replied. "I'm fine now. The weirdest thing happened to me right when he jumped. Like something grabbed my heart, or something."

Mas just nodded and filed it away. She watched people's eyes when they spoke, where they flitted to or if they strayed at all. Whether the pupils constricted, when, and to what degree, along with dozens of other subtle and largely unconscious movements and muscular contractions. Anything could telegraph a hint of what the person was thinking, unless they were trained to throw curve balls. Few people were, and probably not a beat cop in New Orleans.

She started with a couple of neutral questions to get a good read on him. "What time did you guys get here?"

"Oh, about six fifteen or so."

"Did you have to bust in?"

"No, the building super had a key."

"Where was he when you walked in?"

"Standing right here outside the railing, hanging on for dear life."

Mas noted the odd choice of words. On reflection, Henry thought it was strange as well. So did his partner.

"Did Fareed say anything?"

"Yeah, that someone was making him jump."

Mas frowned, a little puzzled. "Did he say who?"

Henry shrugged, and took a wild guess. "Some guy down below, I think, from the way he was talking."

"Did you have eye contact with Fareed?"

Henry nodded, and so did his partner.

"Close eye contact?"

Henry nodded again, and his partner glanced at him, wondering what's up. Henry had an idea, but he waited for Mas' line of questioning to play itself out. He heard that she was top notch, so he didn't give her an attitude like most of the Feds he had to deal with.

"How did his eyes look?"

Henry shrugged again, a little puzzled, although he heard about the Branding Killer from the guys in the locker room. This was the first BK case he had been on.

"Frightened," Henry replied. "He wasn't more than ten feet away."

"Did he say anything else?" Mas asked him.

"Yeah. He said he didn't want to jump."

Mas nodded. Out of the corner of her eye, she could see through the glass slider into the condo. The phone was still lying on the carpet. CSI was taking photos of it now, their print work finished.

"Was he on the phone?"

"Not when we got here," Henry told her. "I think he was hearing voices, though," he offered.

"Is that why you thought he had a bomb?"

Henry was embarrassed and didn't reply.

"Anything else?" Mas asked him.

Henry's partner finally piped up. "Right before he jumped, he said 'Jesus, where are you when I need you?'"

Mas nodded, digesting this last bit, and looked away to the city. The sun was shining brightly now. Puffy white clouds were lazing in from the Gulf. Sometimes, on a perfect day, a person could almost forget that New Orleans was still a crippled, moldy, crime-ridden disaster area. Almost.

Mas leaned against the railing, still dusty from CSI's fingerprint hunt, and gazed into the distance, watching the planes land and take off at Louis Armstrong International Airport across town. Thousands of people were coming and going, and they had no idea what had just occurred here. None at all. Even when they read it in tonight's papers, Mas thought, they still wouldn't get it. They never do.

"Yeah," she finally remarked, her eyes on the distant planes. "Well, I guess Jesus took the day off, huh?"

CHAPTER SEVEN

A rainstorm drifted in overnight from the Gulf and blanketed the city like a bad mood, dispensing a weak but steady cold drizzle. It had been going on since before dawn, and would probably last all day.

The Maybach limousine was parked inside Gulf Air's spacious new hangar at Louis Armstrong International. The hangar doors were rolled back in anticipation of the arrival from Rome. Bishop Nano slouched in the back seat of his limo and gazed out the rain-streaked windows, nervously waiting for the Vatican jet to land. Mr. Gibbs, his chauffeur, was sitting upright behind the wheel, doing the same. As usual, the visitor from Rome was late.

Nano didn't have his own jet, he groused to himself, even though he was the head of the Archdiocese of New Orleans. When he flew he had to charter something, and his secretary Father Francis usually reserved him something with Gulf Air. At least they were good Catholics, and gave him their business at cost. They also let him use their private hangar for receiving visitors, which was a nice gesture. Being God's emissary in New Orleans did have its privileges, such as they were.

Nano loathed humid weather, and New Orleans was a perpetual steam bath. To make matters worse, they built most of the damn city below sea level, which he thought was a stunningly stupid idea. The entire place should have been reclaimed by the bayou ages ago. He privately looked upon Katrina as a blessing. A bit of the Old Testament

God was a good thing every now and then. It kept the rabble contrite and on their knees. And swimming was great exercise.

The Gulfstream touched down with a fine spray of wheel mist and taxied toward the Gulf Air hangar. By the time the jet nosed inside, the engines were already whispering to a halt.

Mr. Gibbs got out of the limo and approached the plane as the side door folded down and locked in place, inches above the polished concrete floor. A moment later, Father Benjamin Simone descended the integral stairs, carrying a briefcase.

He was in his late fifties now. He shaved his Orthodox *peyot* side curls off on New Year's Day of 1977, and he hadn't worn a skullcap since. Father Simone hadn't gained more than ten pounds since he began his career as a Catholic more than thirty years ago, in the orphanage down the road from the Bayou Memorial Clinic. Fifteen years later, when his fellow convert Father Jacob Molinari was transferred to Rome, Simone went with him, having become indispensable as Molinari's personal secretary. The two former Jews worked together at the Vatican from that day forward.

Mr. Gibbs shook Simone's hand. "Good to see you, Father Simone."

"Always a pleasure, Mr. Gibbs."

Simone had been visiting Nano intermittently since his transfer to Rome, and knew Nano's chauffeur for several years prior to that. Gibbs gestured toward the limo, and stepped ahead to get the back door.

Simone had always admired Nano's choice of vehicles, but this was a particularly fine specimen. He noted in passing the Vatican City Consul plate, especially its number – 2315. *Matthew 23:15,* Simone thought wryly.

"And how troubled it will be for you teachers of religious law and you Pharisees, for you cross land and sea to make one convert, and turn him into twice the child of Hell as you yourselves are."

Mr. Gibbs opened the door and came to attention as Simone took a step inside. He paused as Bishop Nano propped up a smile and extended his plump, manicured hand. Simone took the bishop's hand and dropped to one knee on the lambswool carpeting. He reverently kissed Nano's ring, and the bishop beckoned for him to be seated. Simone complied, and Mr. Gibbs quietly shut the door behind him.

Nano watched the younger man settle with a thankful sigh into the butter-soft red leather seat beside him. He had just come halfway around the world riding in one lap of luxury and now he was settling into another one, but he still betrayed a slight grimace when he sat down. Nano's own arthritis was acting up; perhaps the chilly blast of humidity between the jet and the limo had affected Simone as well.

On the other side of the soundproof glass, Mr. Gibbs piloted the stretch Maybach out of the hangar and into the relentless drizzle. Nano affected a jolly little smirk, looking over Cardinal Molinari's globe-trotting envoy.

"You poor boy, shuttling back and forth from Rome all these years. I'm surprised you're still so healthy."

Simone grinned, and gave him a polite nod of thanks for the compliment. "The gym at the Vatican is world-class, your Excellency."

Nano glanced out the window as the limo skirted the perimeter of the airport, approaching the commercial aviation gate. "As is everything at the Vatican," he remarked. "We have to make do with what we can, out here in the swamp."

They were passing a hedgerow of untrimmed weeds entwined in the rusting chain-link fence. There were weeds everywhere in New Orleans. The bayou had to be constantly beaten back, or it would creep into the city and eat it alive. There were times that Nano wished it would, and this was one of those times.

He finally looked back to the envoy. "Simone, Simone... Almost thirty-three years, and you're still just an errand boy," Nano said, not unkindly, and then he cracked a teasing grin. "Still happy you converted?"

Simone responded with a humorless smirk and looked out the window. But Nano knew that he had made his point.

The small talk sure died a quick death, didn't it? Simone thought to himself. He could well imagine why. Nano was clearly troubled by the recent turn of events, and besides, the old man's patience had been wearing thin over the years. Things were not going well, and they both knew it. So did Cardinal Molinari.

Nano decided to dispense with the social niceties during this visit from Simone. It was high time that he bluntly stated his concerns. At this stage of the game, he had nothing to lose. He was a deeply worried man, nearing the end of his productive years with little hope of salvation, or even a gentle death, if he couldn't turn things around. The master he served didn't let a person rest in peace if they failed him, whatever the reason might be.

"Time is not on our side, Simone. We have until Easter or the wager is lost. One wrong name after another...!"

Simone glanced at him and nodded, understanding the implications. Things were not going well indeed, and if Molinari had any say in the matter, things wouldn't be improving any time soon. Simone was simply a functionary. His job was to play along, and to take the heat from the Bishop. And things were heating up.

"You would think that after all these centuries, the Mother Church would have learned not to trifle with the Devil!"

Simone absorbed Nano's anger, but was inwardly troubled that the bishop was speaking in such blunt terms. In all the years that Simone had acted as Molinari's go-between, Nano always kept his comments oblique, dancing around the subject as if he were talking on a wire-tapped phone. Now he was jumping right in with both feet, like a juvenile delinquent splashing in a puddle.

"How many children were born at the clinic that night?" Nano demanded to know, a ruddy frown puckering his plump face.

"Twelve," Simone told him.

"And how does Molinari know that! All the records were lost in the tornado."

"Yes, your Excellency, which is why it's taken years to track them all down," Simone patiently re-explained. "They didn't use computers back then," he reminded the bishop. "The files were blown away. An act of God."

Nano sneered at him for an uncomfortably long time, until Simone shifted in his seat.

"Indeed." Nano sniffed. "An act of God. How convenient. Twelve, huh? Just twelve?"

Simone nodded. Nano nodded back, and cracked a humorless grin. "I should have known," he said dryly. "That number keeps coming up in our line of work."

Simone offered a thin smile, but Nano didn't intend his remark to be amusing. Simone's smile quickly evaporated.

Nano grumbled, watching the rivulets of rain streaking across the side windows as they approached the freeway on-ramp. He looked back to Simone. "This has to end! *Just find Him!*"

Simone had never seen Nano so stressed. Then again, Nano had been secretly grappling with this for over thirty years; the pressure would have crippled a lesser man. Simone was actually surprised that he hadn't collapsed long ago. Nano's predecessor never got past the first round.

Simone bowed his head, and in a quiet voice he revealed what he was sent to tell Nano. "We have, your Excellency."

Nano stared at him, catching his breath. Father Simone had the man's undivided attention now. He opened the briefcase resting on his lap and handed Nano a heavy stainless steel case with rounded corners. It was a little more than a foot long, perhaps six inches wide, and about two inches thick. It had no latch or visible hinges, just a numerical touchpad.

Nano was puzzled, and looked at Simone. The priest handed him a small parchment envelope, secured with a dollop of red sealing wax. Nano squinted at the impression – it was from Cardinal Molinari's signet ring.

Nano grunted, and broke the seal, opening the envelope. Parchment was a lovely paper, he thought, elegant and ageless. He had to hand it to Molinari. The man had class.

He withdrew a single sheet of parchment from the envelope. On it was the number *186*, written with a quill pen.

Nano's spine tingled, staring at the paper. He knew his Bible codes, and memorized what most of them meant. He certainly knew this one. Sir Isaac Newton, the heretical genius, spent half his life puzzling over Bible codes, in addition to his work on alchemy. After his death, the Vatican's own alchemists and numerologists finished the man's work in secret. Their exhaustive treatise on Newton's metaphysics − his "quiet work" − was locked away in the sub-basement of the Vatican Secret Archives. Nano, Molinari, and the secret Cabal of Cardinals to which they were loyal were the only ones with access to the masterwork. Not even the Pope could say the same; he didn't even know it existed.

186. "It is finished."

Nano glanced at Simone, who nodded at the portable vault resting on the archbishop's lap, encouraging him to try the combination. Nano pressed 1,8,6, and then pressed Enter. The lid unsealed with a whisper of air. The crucifix dagger was inside, nestled in a custom-cut bed of gray foam. *"Oh, my God..."* Nano whispered.

His mind raced back to some thirty-odd years before, to the night he delivered the same weapon, on the same journey from Rome to New Orleans.

CHAPTER EIGHT

The brand-new '76 Cadillac stretch limo bore a set of Consulate plates from Vatican City. It rolled past the front steps of the St. Louis cathedral of New Orleans and glided to a halt before the gothic three-story rectory.

The distinctive aroma of General Motors leather was a bit over-powering, but Mr. Gibbs loved the new-car smell. He was two years out of the motor pool at the American Embassy in Saigon, and any job that didn't reek of fear, diesel, and cordite was a blessing.

He hopped out and opened the back door, nodding in respect as the four envoys from the Vatican got out and stretched their legs. It had been a long ride from the airport, and the winter night was only now cooling off.

A young Bishop Nano was carrying a flat wormwood box, intricately engraved and inlaid with ivory. He looked around, privately wondering how anyone in his right mind would choose to live in the South. He grew up in New York City, and considered the rest of the world to be the sticks. Except for the Vatican, of course. He was thrilled with his new posting there. This was his first visit back to his native country, and he was distinctly underwhelmed.

His three colleagues were Italian bishops, schooled at Oxford. This was their first taste of America. Nano intended to take them back through New York and show them the town. He was confident that the food in Hell's Kitchen would stack up against what they were accustomed to in Rome.

Mr. Gibbs led them up the steps and opened the door for them, and Nano led the way inside. Father Vicente, the archbishop's secretary, shook their hands in the foyer and took them upstairs, to Archbishop Sanchez's suite of offices on the third floor.

Sanchez's rosewood-paneled office spanned the width of the building. It had twelve-foot-high coffered ceilings and a wall of leather-bound books, punctuated by a series of tall leaded windows that overlooked the graveyard behind the cathedral. A matching set of windows opposite overlooked the circular horseshoe drive and the front lawn.

The visitors looked at the archbishop's desk, but it was unoccupied. Then they looked around the cavernous room, but Archbishop Sanchez wasn't there.

They turned to Vicente, whose countenance had suddenly grown somber. "I'm sorry to report that the Archbishop suffered a heart attack, while your Excellencies were flying in from Rome."

Nano and his colleagues glanced at each other. Behind their placid expressions, they swiftly re-thought their strategy. The three Oxford scholars waited for the poker-faced Nano to make a decision.

"I'm afraid the stress was too much for him," Vicente explained to Nano. Nano hesitated, his thumb gently burnishing the wormwood box as he peered into Vicente's eyes, calculating his next move. He saw something deep inside Vicente, and nodded once.

The other bishops began breathing again, silently agreeing with Nano's decision to proceed.

Vicente sensed that something had changed. He glanced at the box in Nano's hands and smiled in anticipation. Nano smiled back. The other bishops quietly watched them.

"And just what did the Archbishop tell you, Father Vicente?" Nano asked, still studying his eyes.

Vicente's face was suddenly radiant. "That your Excellencies are on the most important mission in all of history. *In all of history!*" He bowed his head. "I would be honored to serve in my bishop's memory."

Though he was barely older than Vicente, Nano nodded like a kindly old uncle and glanced at the other bishops. They gave their silent assent, satisfied that Vicente could be a faithful courier. They could see it in his eyes. Someone had to deliver the treasure into the right hands three days hence, when all the pieces would finally be in place. It was an intricate ballet of celestial precision, but Sanchez was gone and someone had to stand in his stead. For their part, they had to return to the Vatican in a matter of hours, and no one could know they had been gone. Father Vicente was their only hope.

Nano gestured with the box, and Vicente gazed at it. "So you know who this is for?" Nano asked him. "Have you met the man?"

Vicente looked at him, a wondrous glow in his eyes. He slowly shook his head, but it wasn't a denial. Rather, he was correcting Nano's choice of words.

"He's not a man!" Vicente whispered.

The four envoys smiled. Vicente would surely understand the truth, once it was revealed. They had just enough time to enlighten him before they scurried back to the Vatican.

Two hours later, Nano and Vicente sat in a pair of centuries-old chairs before the crackling fire in Archbishop Sanchez's chambers. The other bishops stood behind Nano's chair, watching as Vicente gazed unfocused at the dancing flames, digesting everything that had just been revealed.

They were all sweating, but not from the fire. They were exhausted. With the able assistance of his three wise men, Nano had arduously briefed Vicente, painstakingly laying out the true history of the Mother Church and the Liturgy, and the actual secret of the Vatican Secret Archives. Vicente had no idea, and yet when it was all explained to him everything made perfect sense. But not before he was literally sick with shock. They had taken his entire world, turned it inside out, and handed it back to him. He would have to clean the archbishop's private restroom after the envoys were gone.

Nano handed the wormwood box to Vicente, and the priest reverently lowered it to his lap. It was a little more than a foot long, perhaps six inches wide, and about two inches thick. The box had been burnished over the centuries by numerous human hands. The lid was inlaid with the yellowed ivory of lion's teeth and had two iron hinges, but no latch. The box and its contents were nearly two thousand years old.

With an encouraging nod from Nano and a chorus of smiles from the bishops behind Nano's chair, Vicente fiddled with the box, trying to open it, but he couldn't find a way.

The bishops were amused, and Nano finally took the box back. He depressed one of the ivory inlays, slid a side panel with his thumb, and then handed the box back to Vicente. Vicente found that he could now open the lid.

The crucifix dagger was inside, on a soft bed of fleece. The golden figurine of Christ and the jewels that studded the crucifix gleamed in the fire glow. Nano gestured for Vicente to take the ancient artifact out of the box.

Vicente held the crucifix in his hands, turning it over and examining it from every angle. It was fashioned from a shaft of wormwood almost two inches wide and nearly a foot in length. He quickly discovered that the wood was split just above the crosspiece. He nudged the body of Christ, and the blade was unsheathed.

The slim iron shaft glinted in the firelight. It was lightly dressed with oil to keep it from rusting. Both edges of the blade were honed to razor-sharp perfection.

"The blade was fashioned from a Roman spear," Nano explained to him. "The same spear that pierced the side of Christ."

Vicente looked to him in wonder, and Nano nodded to assure him that he wasn't joking. The bishops standing behind him gazed down at Vicente, completely serious. Vicente looked back down to the dagger in his hands.

"It's been kept in a vault under the Papal throne for almost two millennia," Nano told him, and cracked a dark smile. "Just in case He ever showed his face again."

Vicente looked at him with his eyes aglow, and the bishops standing behind Nano smiled down on the priest. He understood perfectly. He would do just fine.

The stately suite of offices was Bishop Nano's now. When everything went awry at the Bayou Memorial Clinic, the Cabal of Cardinals in Rome made hasty arrangements to have Nano installed as the Archbishop of New Orleans.

His tenure at the Vatican had been much too brief for his liking. He had hoped to be there his entire life, but until this mess was resolved, he was stuck in New Orleans whether he liked it or not, and he didn't like it. Particularly now, with the weight of the entire world pressing down on him. His predecessor, Archbishop Sanchez, had buckled under the same load; the man could never quite make the leap of faith required for the task at hand. The way Nano saw it, faith was a talent that most mortals aspired to, but few could truly master.

He was sitting in the same centuries-old chair that he sat in more than thirty years ago. A fire was crackling in the hearth, just as before, and the dagger case was once again open and resting on his lap. Except this case was stainless steel. The ancient weapon looked out of place in the blast-proof portable vault, cradled by high-density foam.

Simone sat across from him, in the same chair where Vicente once sat, listening as Nano explained what transpired at the clinic. The night when everything went wrong.

"Vicente was drunk with the prospect of power!" Nano fumed, as he contemplated the crucifix dagger in his lap.

"Instead of delivering the dagger as he was instructed, he took it upon himself to do the deed! And we have been chasing shadows ever since."

He glared at Simone, revealing the full measure of his fury. "I can assure you, he is suffering in the ninth circle of Hell!"

The fire popped, and Simone wondered if it was a sign. He shivered, despite the luxuriant warmth.

Nano placed the steel case on the tea table beside his chair, then got up heavily and went to his desk. He unlocked a bottom drawer and took out the ancient wormwood box.

He brought it back to the fireside and sat down again, resting it on his thighs. Simone watched, fascinated, as Nano depressed one of the ivory inlays, slid a side panel with his thumb, and opened the lid.

He took the dagger from the steel case and nestled it into its bed of fleece. Then he gently closed the engraved lid of the wormwood box, and dismissively gestured at the steel case on the tea table.

"We won't be needing that contraption anymore."

Simone nodded. He closed its lid with a finger, and it hermetically sealed shut with a soft hiss. He slipped it into his briefcase.

Nano placed the ancient box on the tea table and absently patted it like a long-lost friend, as he sat there brooding and gazing into the fire. Beyond the open windows, it had finally stopped raining. The leaves of the magnolia tree outside were dripping loudly onto the cobbled driveway below.

Simone reached inside his briefcase and handed the Archbishop another parchment envelope, also sealed with wax.

Nano frowned at him, and then at the envelope. Like the first one, it was sealed with Molinari's signet ring.

Nano broke the seal and removed a single piece of parchment. It was a short note, inscribed with a quill pen in a neat, disciplined hand. Nano absorbed the message and frowned. He glanced at Simone, wagging the parchment at him. "This isn't a name, Simone. It's an invitation."

Father Simone offered him the ghost of a smile. "Yes, your Excellency. We trust you will deliver it to the right person."

The sky had cleared, and the weather was cool and perfect. Simone came down the steps of the rectory and approached the limousine. Mr. Gibbs was standing ready at the open back door.

Before Simone got into the Maybach, he took a moment to admire the façade of the cathedral of New Orleans, magnificent in the clear sunlight and washed clean by the rain.

Nano was right, he thought to himself. *Over thirty years, and I'm nothing more than a goddamn priest, sleeping on a cot in a dormitory. A pauper living in a palace.*

He sighed, and looked at the limousine. The paint was flawless, hand-buffed to a mirror finish. He touched the surface, marveling at its earthly perfection. He could see Nano's reflection in the pure black paint, watching from a window in his chambers above. Watching a priest covet his neighbor's goods. An archbishop's Maybach, no less.

"You do beautiful work, Mr. Gibbs," Simone smoothly remarked, trying to cover his sin.

"Thank you, Father Simone," Mr. Gibbs replied, but he knew exactly what Simone had been thinking. The envy was etched in the priest's face and telegraphed by his body language.

Simone took a last look at the cathedral, and climbed in back. Mr. Gibbs closed the door and got behind the wheel.

Nano cracked a knowing smile as he watched his Maybach whisper down the driveway. He had the man pegged. Even from his high angle, he saw exactly what Gibbs had seen. Simone wanted more out of life than what his devotion to Molinari had brought him. A change was long overdue.

Nano's smile disintegrated when he suddenly became aware of an insistent noise, somewhere in the room behind him. He turned and froze in his tracks, staring breathlessly at the dagger box. *It was rattling on the tea table.*

He sensed a presence in the room.

CHAPTER NINE

Father Jean Paul Eden gave thanks to God for such a beautiful morning, cleansed by yesterday's rain. He was out for his morning walk, standing at the corner of Lafayette and Carondelet and waiting for the light to change. It was a little ways north from there to the Church of the Rebirth in the French Quarter. If he kept his pace up he could be back by nine.

The light turned green and Eden crossed the street, taking in his tattered city as he went. There was still so much work to do! In his unguarded moments, the sheer enormity of the task threatened to overwhelm him.

Although it was known as the Big Easy, New Orleans had always been hard for the rest of the country to fathom. Centuries ago, after the slaves in Haiti threw out the British and the Spanish, they finally threw out the French as well. The victorious freemen then came north to help their mainland neighbors do the same, and they brought their black magic with them.

New Orleans became a chapter in the American Storybook unto itself. To a white-bread country, it was a scandalous distant cousin of a city – a heady brew of voodoo and Catholicism and Mardi Gras, a gumbo of brothels and jazz and ragtime and gambling. The Devil's playground. And yet, if the Devil's best trick was to convince Man that he didn't exist, then the people of New Orleans were one step ahead of the game, because they knew better. They knew that if the Devil didn't exist, then neither did God.

The kind of people who thought like that were the kind of people Father Eden was honored to serve. To him, they were the very salt of the earth, and he had known them since the day he was born. He grew up dirt poor on the bayou, the adopted son of a querulous alligator poacher in an extended family of moonshiners and fishermen. His adoptive mother, bless her soul, never left her husband, although she had every reason to. She would take little Jean Paul in their flat-bottom boat on Sunday mornings to attend Mass and pray for strength. Her husband was superstitious enough to believe what his cousin told him. Catholic priests practiced voodoo, the man whispered over whisky, and if his woman was going to church every week he best not beat her so much, or it'd all come back on him in the afterlife.

Church-going probably saved the woman's life, and it made a lasting impression on her boy. Sunday afternoons at the Church's orphanage playing with the other kids was the highlight of his week, and it always broke his mother's heart to take him home. When he was old enough, he volunteered whenever he could for whatever the sisters needed. At first it was mostly to get away from his father, but it soon became a calling. By the time he was twelve, Jean Paul Eden knew what he wanted to do with his life.

He became a priest because he wanted to continue doing what he had done while he was growing up – helping the children around him, wherever he found himself. He didn't do it for a reward or for any sort of recognition. He wasn't angling for bishop or for any kudos from the Vatican; he was simply doing what he thought needed to be done, with whatever resources were available. Eden was a natural priest, holding the children of God together when everything was falling apart around them.

He kept up his brisk pace, looking around as he neared the French Quarter. The Superdome was off to his left and the Convention Center was off to his right, twin memorials to the man-made portion of the Katrina disaster. Thousands of people huddled in the public buildings for days on end while the world watched on TV, including most of the Louisiana National Guard, who had been sent to the Iraqi desert along with their deepwater equipment. Not that they could have done much to save their city, but they wanted to be there to try.

The spectacle at the Superdome had been a piteous sight. The president's mother even paid a visit to console the suffering hordes. She toured the building with a phalanx of stern secret service agents, and she didn't utter a discouraging word. On the contrary, she allowed that since so many of the people were already underprivileged, living in a sports arena was working out quite well for them.

There was plenty of blame to go around. Government had failed miserably at every level, on both sides of the aisle. While the city drowned, the President was attending a sing-along at a campfire in Arizona, confident that his FEMA director was doing a heckuva job, while the mayor was spitting mad and blaming everyone but himself for failing to evacuate his own city.

Katrina tore the lid off the whole soggy mess, and the entire world got to see it play out on TV for days on end. When the President finally got a clue, New Orleanians had the unique privilege of sitting on their rooftops and waving as Air Force One flew majestically overhead, while federally dispatched mercenaries prowled the city streets below.

Police officers and bus drivers had shamefully abandoned their duties, leaving their fellow citizens stranded and dying. Tens of thousands who fled the storm had nothing to go back to and stayed wherever they wound up, destitute and dependent on the kindness of strangers. Those who stayed behind were castigated as ignorant, shiftless fools, even though many of them didn't have the ways and means to flee. And even if they did, they worried that whatever they left behind would likely be looted, so they stayed and took their chances, and many of them drowned.

Eden spent three sleepless days in a rowboat, doing whatever he could to save whomever he could find. He teamed up with Mr. Silverstein, a secular Jew who owned the newsstand across from Eden's church. They took turns paddling Mr. Silverstein's aluminum dinghy through the low-lying neighborhoods surrounding the crescent of high ground on which the original city was built.

The Church of the Rebirth was Eden's parish in the French Quarter, one of the original neighborhoods of the Crescent City. The church and its school became one of the many makeshift shelters that sprang up all over the region. Sister Nancy and her nuns tirelessly performed whatever first aid they could, referring to their old Girl Scout manuals and cutting up their habits for bandages when they ran out of clean bed sheets. Across the street, Mr. Silverstein had a dozen people camped out in his living room, who were fed three kosher meals a day by his Orthodox wife Sophie.

When Eden and Mr. Silverstein weren't rescuing people from rooftops and attics, and when Eden wasn't administering Last Rites, and when they weren't weeping over what they found in the fetid rubble, they kept their minds off their weariness and hunger with a lively debate about God and Nature, and the nature of Man.

Though they agreed on almost nothing, they became good friends. Afterward, Mr. Silverstein sometimes attended Father Eden's Masses, sitting in the back pew with his arms crossed in mulish skepticism, but he was consistently one of the biggest contributors to the Church's many neighborhood drives.

Eden waved good morning to Mr. Silverstein, sitting in the shade under the awning of his repaired newsstand, and trotted up the front steps of the church alongside a sturdy construction ramp. The nineteenth-century granite walls had shrugged off the hurricane, but the roof hadn't. The steeple was blown away, and after all these years the roof was still mostly blue plastic tarping that leaked whenever it rained. The ramp was almost as old as the blue plastic roof, a semi-permanent installation while they nudged their reconstruction efforts along whenever donations would allow.

He was about to step inside when he heard a flirtatious young lady's voice behind him. "Hey, Father Eden."

He smiled and turned back to her. Women had flirted with him all his life. It was the cross he had to bear, and they never let him forget it. Especially Britney and her mother Sharon. They were a pair of eye-popping mulatto beauties from a local family, who claimed that when God spoke to them, He had a French accent. And Eden didn't doubt it a bit.

Britney and Sharon were dressed in crisp jumpsuits and ball caps. They were lucky to share a full-time job at the Campbell's Soup food bank, and worked a weekly drop-off at their parish church into their rounds. Joyce guided her daughter Britney up the ramp, who was walking backwards, pulling a dolly stacked with canned goods. Eden eyed all the food and offered his weekly blessing: "Mmmm, mmmm good!"

Britney put her back into it like a pro, smiling over her shoulder at Eden as her mother steered her. Joyce had her daughter when she was barely out of grade school. Her boyfriend promptly made himself scarce and her family turned her away, but the Church of the Rebirth didn't. She became one of their many orphans, and both she and her daughter grew up within the walls of the convent. Britney had a crush on Eden since she could walk, and her mother had long given up trying to discourage her. Eden was used to it by now.

They stopped at the top of the ramp and smiled at the priest, framed in the doorway. Joyce always suspected that it was God's punishment for her past sins of the flesh, having to work alongside a priest who was so damn good-looking. She often wondered if he even realized it, but so far as she could tell, he didn't.

"I got it," he told them, and took over for Britney. She curtsied and giggled, and her mother grinned and smacked her shoulder. With a careful nudge of his foot, Eden jockeyed the dolly up the aisle, the women a step behind him. They all crossed themselves as they passed the altar and swung to the left, heading for a closed door.

Sharon scooted ahead and got the door. The hallway beyond was a temporary plywood corridor that led to the building next door, where the school's kitchen was located. It was also where the altar boys prepared for Mass. The plaster ceiling of the vestibule behind the altar failed in the hurricane, and the room was still boarded up.

Eden rolled the dolly into the corner beside the walk-in refrigerator, carefully depositing the neat stack of boxes beside several others. The other boxes were crammed with rusty and dented cans of food, the things that most people, if they had a choice, didn't care to eat. But Eden eyed the accumulated bounty with a grateful smile, and turned to Britney and Sharon.

"Thank you, ladies."

They smiled back. "Always happy to help," Britney said, and her mother Sharon nodded.

"Anytime you need us..." she added, but she blushed as Britney eyed her sidelong and jabbed her in the ribs.

Oh, Lordie! Sharon thought. *There I go again, flirting with a priest. I'm gonna go to Hell for sure.*

She peeked at Britney, but her daughter had her attention on something else. Sister Nancy was approaching from the classroom corridor. The old nun had been both of the women's grade school principal, and she still had the power to make them nervous with little more than a glance. If there was one thing that all the students learned from Sister Nancy, it was how to watch their P's and Q's.

Britney and Sharon curtsied to her and Nancy nodded back, but her focus was on Eden. The ladies took the hint.

"We best be off, now," Sharon said to him, and he grinned back, understanding. Sister Nancy had that effect on people, but that was why the students at the Church of the Rebirth had such good grades. No one would dare set foot in a Rebirth classroom without knuckling down, and when it came to lunch, they ate whatever was put in front of them. Sister Nancy wouldn't have it any other way.

"Thanks again, ladies. Bless you," Eden said to them.

Britney and Sharon smiled goodbyes, and curtsied to him for good measure before they went back down the temporary hallway and into the church. Eden watched them go and then turned to Nancy with a knowing smile, but she was occupied with other thoughts.

"What's on your mind, Sister?" he asked, sensing her mood, and growing concerned.

Nancy cast about for the right way to tell him. "Well, the truth is..." She didn't quite know how to put it. She glanced around, and Eden leaned a little closer.

"Yes...?"

She finally peeked at him, and her face crinkled in a crafty smile. "Your *request!* I just got the call!"

For a fraction of a second, Eden was puzzled, and then he remembered. His eyes widened in surprise. *After all these years,* he thought. *No, it couldn't be!*

"Haiti?" he asked her. Nancy nodded, smiling at him.

Eden was stunned and delighted. It was like he just won the lottery. And in a sense, he had. His dream posting finally came through, years after he wrote it off as a childhood fantasy.

"My God, at long last...!" he breathed. But at the same time, his mind was racing. How could he possibly go now?

"Congratulations! I know how much it means to you," she said to him, a gentle hand on his shoulder, but all he could do was nod as the implications set in. He was actually going to Haiti! It was unbelievable, but there it was.

"When do I leave?" he asked her.

"Soon. Next week!" she said.

He glanced around the kitchen. It was cluttered with stacks of donated food. It all had to be sorted and distributed. There was so much to do.

"How will I get everything done?"

"We'll manage, Father. We always have, and we always will."

He looked into her eyes and smiled. She wasn't about to let him back away from his dream. She was a remarkable woman, he thought. One of the strongest souls he had ever encountered. He really had her blessing; he was free to go.

"It's going to be so good to finally get down there," he said. She nodded, understanding, and patted his arm.

"Closure, Father?" she gently asked him.

It had taken her a long time to warm up to that word, but if there was ever a time to use it this was the time. Eden's past was an open wound for nearly as long she'd known him, and she'd known him since before he could talk. Eden nodded, but his smile waned a bit, thinking of the road ahead. "The mission comes first, of course. But it'll be good to learn a little more about my family. My mother, especially."

A sad cloud passed over Nancy, and she nodded. "It *still* grieves me to think what that poor young woman must have gone through, in that ramshackle old clinic."

She shuddered at the thought, but Eden gently smiled.

"God has His own way of balancing our lives. That's His job. And ours is to help Him."

That brought her spirits back, and he winked at her, a gleam in his eye. "And if He needs me in Haiti, all the better, eh?"

He had a knack for making people smile. He always did. He would do well in Haiti, she thought. That poor country was in worse shape as New Orleans.

She grinned at him, and then her smile faded as she remembered something and her eyes drifted away from his. "He needs your help with something else, Father." She looked back to him. "Do you remember the Aly family, the Coptic Christians?"

Eden nodded. The name was familiar to him.

"Fareed Aly jumped from his balcony this morning," Nancy told him. "His brother and sister are in a bad way."

Eden closed his eyes, pained by the memory. He saw the whole dreadful thing on the news, just the other day. Of all the sadness in the city now, it was something that even the newscasters were troubled by. It just didn't make sense.

Eden crossed himself, and looked at the floor. "He was my age. Such a shame." He finally looked back to Nancy.

"Of course, Sister. I'd be glad to visit them."

"Thank you." She took a deep, steady breath to calm herself. "I just hope someone catches that monster."

Eden nodded in agreement. "Even God would be hard-pressed to forgive this one."

CHAPTER TEN

Mas parked her BMW in the Perdido Street parking lot and opened one of her saddlebags. She took out a manila expanding file and her bottled water, and walked briskly toward the side entrance of City Hall, the folder tucked under her arm and her free hand clutching the strap of her shoulder bag as she took a sip. Her iPhone rang. She sighed, juggled all her stuff, plucked it off her hip and answered it.

"Agent Mas."

"Hi, it's me. Those phone logs came in from CSI."

"Good deal. Could you fax them over to Captain Thorrington's office? I'm going up there now."

"Will do."

"Thanks, Charlene."

Mas ended the call, holstered her phone and trotted up the stairs. She put her badge, her gun, her phone, her bag and the file through the scanner, but she kept her water, defiantly sipping it as she let the guard wand her before she stepped through the detector.

Her keys set off the beeper, and the guard grinned at her. She dug them out of her leather jacket and tossed them in a tray.

The guard let her through and she scooped up all her stuff, checking the wall clock. The Cap'n wanted to see her at eleven. She headed for the elevators, nodding hello to the occasional cop. NOPD headquarters was up on the third floor.

Mark Kaddouri would be at the meeting, too. Mas hadn't seen him in almost a month, and wondered if he finally finished rebuilding his back deck. Katrina tore it right off his house and deposited it two blocks away. His car and his garage had both wound up across the street in his neighbor's front yard. The car was still inside, and the garage door was down and padlocked. The garage was rebuilt by a shyster contractor from out of state and had to be completely redone. Mark got so angry that he went to Home Depot and loaded up on tools, how-to books and a pile of lumber. Carpentry became his weekend hobby, whether he liked it or not. And he didn't. The garage had taken three years to finish, and the back porch was taking more than two.

She stepped off the elevator and headed down the hall to Captain Thorrington's suite. Most of the officers on the floor knew her, and swapped hellos or nods. She stirred a lot of parochial jealousy when she went off to Virginia to become a Fed, but when she returned and wound up doing largely what she was doing before she left, her former colleagues eventually gave her their seal of approval. Local law enforcement always had a natural distrust of the Feds, particularly in the South, where the Confederacy was alive and well in many a heart, but Mas knew enough about being a cop, particularly an NOPD cop, to avoid stepping on too many toes.

She smiled good morning at Thorrington's secretary. "How's the weather, Helen?" Mas asked her.

Helen grinned at their secret code. She had been busy as a bee, scratching a pile of Greenlit Lottery tickets when Mas came in, but she took a break from her labors and toasted Mas with her coffee mug. A Krispy Kreme donut hung on her pinkie.

"He's fine," she told Mas. "He just had his coffee. Want some?"

Mas wiggled her bottle of water – *I'm good.* Helen wiggled her donut at Mas and took a yummy bite, and they exchanged grins. After a lifetime of dieting, Helen had retired from chasing men, and never looked back. Her world revolved around her son now. He was an aspiring film producer, and they had been buying lottery tickets with every spare dollar they had. But not just any old tickets. Greenlit The Motion Picture Lottery would fund his movie if they won. And since getting a movie made was as much of a long shot as winning the lottery, they figured what the hell – the odds were in their favor the more they played.

"Mark's here," she told Mas. She watched for a reaction, but Mas just nodded as she passed Helen's desk, a lingering glance at the donuts. Helen grinned and licked a stray crumb from her lips.

"I'm expecting a fax," Mas said. "I hope you don't mind."

"Not at all," Helen said, watching her. Helen was a matchmaker from way back. She even introduced the Cap'n to his wife, a retired district attorney. Mas was her next project.

Mas enter the Cap'n's office, quietly shutting the door. One of these days, Helen thought, that girl has got to settle down.

Mark Kaddouri stood up from the chair in front of Thorrington's desk, and smiled a warm hello. A fifth-generation Lebanese-American, Kaddouri was a lean, muscular homicide detective with fifteen years on the force. Princeton offered him a full scholarship, but he went across town to Tulane University instead. He loved New Orleans, and never had any plans to leave, not even for college. He joined the force the day after he got his Master's in Criminal Justice. Mas had been his rookie, spending three years under him before she became a Fed.

She nodded pleasantly at her old boss, and then she smiled at Thorrington, who was kicked back in his desk chair.

"Morning, Cap'n."

"Morning, Agent Mas."

Thorrington just looked at the two of them standing before his desk, a ghost of a bemused grin on his lips. He knew what was up, but he didn't know why. He knew Kaddouri was sweet on her, and for good reason, but for some reason she wasn't opening herself up to him. Kaddouri was probably the best thing she'd ever find in her line of work.

The only thing Thorrington could figure was that Mas was so wrapped up in the Branding case that she couldn't get her mind on anything else. And that troubled him. She was losing perspective and life was passing her by. Or eating her alive, he didn't know which.

He waved to a side chair. She sat down, placed her file on his desk and got right to the point. "Let's have a look at those videos, shall we?"

He was right; she couldn't get her mind on anything else. He glanced at Kaddouri. "Mark? You do the honors. I'm no good with that computer stuff."

Kaddouri smiled and waved a hand at the worktable against the wall. A PC was already up and running, with a card reader cabled into it. "Have a seat," he said.

Mas and Thorrington got up and the three of them sat at the table, Kaddouri in front of the computer. He pivoted the screen so they could all see, and slipped a memory card into the reader. He moused around as they watched the screen.

A grainy, stuttering camera clip taken from ground level showed Fareed Aly falling from his balcony. They could hear the crowd around the camera gasping on the tinny audio track, and they heard Fareed hit the sidewalk with a muffled thud.

Kaddouri popped out the memory card and slipped in another one. This shot was from a cell phone, another low-res clip, but with no audio track. Watching Fareed fall in silence was even more unsettling than the first shot.

He swapped the card for a third one and played another clip. It was substantially the same image as the first, but this one was shot with a halfway decent camera. Still, there was nothing new to see. Fareed's body thumped onto the concrete sidewalk and bounced once, and the crowd gasped.

The fourth clip was from another digital camera, but it was from a different angle than the others. It started with a slow pan of the crowd gathered at the jump site. The cops at the roadblock could all be seen, as well as Thorrington standing by his squad car, his megaphone in hand and looking up at Fareed's balcony. Dr. Osborn was standing with his assistant by the coroner's van and the paramedics had their equipment out. They all had their heads tilted back, watching. Beyond them Archbishop Nano's black Maybach limousine.

Mas frowned at the screen, noticing something odd, and pointed to it. "What's that?"

Kaddouri froze the clip and they all leaned forward for a better look. Whatever it was, it was just a soft red blur beside a grey translucent blob. Kaddouri fiddled with the software and cleaned up the image.

Mas reacted with a quick intake of breath, staring at the screen. Kaddouri instinctively leaned forward again and Thorrington squinted for a better look.

A glowing red cigarette cherry floated in midair in the midst of the crowd. Close behind it was what looked like an exhaled lungful of cigarette smoke. But there was no cigarette to be seen, and there was no smoker either.

Mas and Kaddouri swapped glances. "That's weird," she said.

"Very weird," he replied.

Thorrington just nodded, silently agreeing with them.

"Can you roll it in slo-mo?" Mas asked Kaddouri.

He jumped to the beginning of the clip and they watched it again in slow motion. As the camera panned the crowd, they saw a crystal-clear image of the cigarette cherry suspended in midair, close to the camera. Right behind it, a lungful of smoke was exhaled into existence. It billowed lazily around the cherry, and then without warning the image suddenly pixilated and froze. A moment later, the screen went black.

Kaddouri fiddled with the program and Thorrington sneered at him. "Great," Thorrington said. "'The computer that ate Exhibit A.' Outstanding, Kaddouri..."

Kaddouri kept his cool, and fiddled with the PC until it became obvious that it wasn't going to cooperate. It was something he had never gotten used to, even though he knew he should. When you worked for the government, city, state, or federal, PCs came with the territory. Kaddouri sighed and tapped the power button twice for a hard reboot.

They sat there waiting for it to walk through its paces. It took for-freaking-ever.

"You guys need to switch to a Mac," Mas teased them.

Kaddouri nodded, and Thorrington just watched the screen. He hated computers. He didn't even like email. *"I have a phone number,"* he *would remind people. "Leave a goddamn message."*

The screen finally came to life, and Kaddouri jumped back to the start of the clip, rolling it again. They all leaned forward to watch.

The clip played exactly as before, without a flaw to be seen, except that the cigarette cherry and the cloud of smoke were no longer in the shot.

Mas and Kaddouri glanced at each other again. They had no idea what just happened, and Thorrington was as puzzled as they were.

"Ghost in the machine?" Thorrington asked. "Voodoo?"

Kaddouri shrugged. Thorrington glanced at Mas for her take on it, but she was as frustrated as they were. More than that, an edge of anger was rising inside of her, and Thorrington didn't like what he saw. He caught Kaddouri's eye.

"Could we have a moment, Mark?"

Kaddouri sensed that something was up, and nodded. He knew as well as the Captain did that Mas was on a short fuse, especially when it came to the Branding Killer. He didn't like it any more than Thorrington did. They both worried about her, but neither of them knew exactly what to do about it. Kaddouri slid his chair back and got up, opening the door to the outer office as he did. He quietly stepped out and closed the door behind him, leaving them alone.

CHAPTER ELEVEN

Mas gazed unfocused at the tabletop, waiting for Thorrington's admonishment. Life was hard enough, she thought, and the job was even harder. Particularly these last few years. He didn't need her blowing a fuse over something like a video glitch, especially not in his office. It was rude, it was unprofessional, and ultimately it was useless. She knew all the reasons, but sometimes it just didn't matter.

He got up and poured himself a steaming cup of coffee. He knew she chugged water before lunch, and didn't offer her one. He watched the vapor rising from the mug as it filled up, thinking of what to say to her. He was growing weary, and perhaps she was as well, but at least she had youth on her side. He was pushing seventy, and wasn't sure how much longer he could fight the good fight. He didn't need to be worrying about her. Not now.

Several of his officers abandoned the force at the height of the storm, and five years later indictments and trials were underway, some of them were going to jail and recruitment was still down. Thank God the Feds turned Mas loose on the Branding case, because he had his hands full. The murder rate was soaring, and displaced locals were still staging protests outside City Hall. Privately, he couldn't blame them, but he feared that if things didn't finally take a turn for the better, there could be riots. And if martial law was imposed, Washington might send down their damn mercenaries again, and God only knew how things would play out from there, with those Blackwater types running around loose. He had more than enough of those arrogant yahoos already.

Mas knew that fits of temper and flashes of anger weren't high on Thorrington's list of admirable qualities, particularly when it came to visitors in his own office. Ironically, it was the only place where he could get away from it all. His wife had been on anti-depressants since the storm, and was just now getting out and about again. He needed Mas to be strong, so any chink in her armor concerned him. *Save it for the street* was what he had been telling her. She was waiting for him to tell her that now.

He sat heavily at his desk, coffee in hand. She switched chairs to sit across from him, and sipped her water. Thorrington still didn't think of her as a Fed, and he suspected that she probably didn't either, despite what her badge said.

An old picture sat on the bookshelf behind his desk. It was of Mas' father Julian and her mother Beth, and a young Lt. Thorrington and his wife Susan. The men were in uniform, sitting astride their Harley-Davidsons, and a young Chrissy sat on her father's gas tank.

Thorrington smiled over his coffee at her. "How come you don't ride a Harley like your daddy did?"

Mas smiled back at him. "The day they make a machine as fine as my baby, I'll go right out and adopt one. Promise."

Julian Mas' daughter was the closest thing that Thorrington had to one of his own. It was daddy time.

"How you doing, Chrissy?" he asked her.

"Fair to middling, all things considered. How you doing, Cap'n?"

"Better than you, I'll wager." He blew on his coffee, and took a cautious sip. "How do you find time to work on this case, with everything else the Bureau's been throwing at you?"

Mas tried to shrug it off, but her nonchalance fell flat. She looked down at her water bottle. "My job is to *find* the time."

"You need sleep, young lady. You still having nightmares?"

It was more of a statement than a question. Mas hesitated, and then finally nodded. There was no use trying to hide anything from the Cap'n. She never could. No sense trying now. She kept her eyes on her water bottle and shrugged. "If it's nighttime, it's time for nightmares."

"Johnson had nightmares," he reminded her.

At the mention of Johnson's name, she finally looked up. "I saw him at the jump scene, but he drove off before I got to him."

Thorrington was surprised by the news, but said nothing. She watched his eyes, but he contemplated his coffee, avoiding her probing gaze. They trained her at the Fed Farm for stuff like that, and he didn't like being under her microscope, or anyone else's for that matter.

"Did he really go crazy?" she asked.

He glanced at her. "Close. He retired."

She grinned. "No wonder Daddy liked you."

His expression softened. "I'm a likable sort," he said, and leaned on his desk, closer to her. "That man save my life more than once, Chrissy, so me and Suzie owe him. You're not getting rid of us that easy. You and your mamma are the closest thing to family we got."

She smiled, but she had a sixth sense where he was going next. She was right.

"Why don't you see someone," he suggested.

Mas blew a little sigh and sagged in her chair. "A shrink? You're kidding, right? We've been *over* this, Cap'n..."

He didn't say anything, and just watched her fidget.

"You're going to pop a gasket if you keep this up," he admonished her.

She drained her water bottle, tossed it in the trash, and then picked up her manila file and got to her feet.

"You don't have to save the world, Chrissy."

His voice was gentle, almost pleading with her. She cast her eyes downward and turned to the door, opening it. Kaddouri was sitting on the couch across from Helen's desk, waiting for her, a fax in his hands. He looked up and almost smiled, but he saw the troubled look in Mas' eyes.

She turned back to Thorrington. "No," she said, agreeing with him. She didn't have to save the world. "But it sure would be nice to save someone. Just once."

She went out, quietly closing the door. Thorrington stared at the closed door, ignoring his coffee.

CHAPTER TWELVE

Devlin was resting on the root of a giant mangrove tree deep in the bayou, leaning against the cool moss that grew on the massive trunk. Mist lay upon the waters all around him, a gently swirling fog propelled by a delicate breeze. The midday sun suffused his sanctuary with a dazzle of light, reflecting off the golden figurine of Christ, nailed to the crucifix dagger he cradled in his hands.

He hadn't touched the weapon in ages. He grasped the top of the crucifix and separated it from the sheath with a gentle tug, revealing a glint of the polished iron blade hidden inside. As he withdrew it, a Voice came to him. *"Bow down to my creation."* Devlin recalled his firm reply. *"I will only bow down to you."*

A flood of memories came tumbling out of his endless past, as though it had taken place just moments before...

The Battle for Heaven raged in the skies above. A third of Heaven's winged angels followed Lucifer into battle, and now they were falling into the Abyss. He lay on his back, his head dangling over the precipice as the archangel Michael's spear pressed against his throat. The anguished cries of his minions filled the heavens, seeing the Lord of Light pinned by the commander of God's armies.

"I only bow to my creator," Lucifer told him.

Michael hesitated. For all his treachery, Lucifer had still been Michael's commander before he dared to challenge God. Instead of lancing Lucifer's throat, Michael withdrew his spear and broke the shaft over his knee. He dropped the pieces on Lucifer's breastplate and turned away, his heart broken.

Lucifer grabbed the spear by its broken shaft and got up on his knees. "Fight me!" he screamed, but his cry was lost in the chaos all around him. The battle was over.

But not the war. Devlin withdrew the dagger completely from its sheath now, and admired it in the dappled bayou sunlight. The blade was fashioned from the very same spear.

Devlin toiled as a slave in the garrison at Jerusalem, fixing the tip of the spear to a hardwood shaft. The Roman soldiers were preparing for a crucifixion detail and needed their weapons. Devlin handed the spear to a young soldier.

Devlin turned the dagger over in his hands, examining the gleaming dark metal. After all these centuries, the iron was still free of rust.

When the young soldier lanced the side of Christ, a tremendous clap of thunder shook the hills and a pelting rain came down. The young man dropped the spear, as thoroughly terrified as the spectators were, and he scrambled away to join his comrades.

Devlin held the wormwood sheath up to the sunlight, examining the golden figurine of Christ. The tiny hands were carefully nailed to the crosspiece.

Some of the mourners ignored the rainstorm, their heads bowed in prayer before their crucified Savior.

Devlin sneered at the memory. How easy it was to sacrifice yourself, to go through the agony knowing all along that you'll be swept back up to Heaven.

Devlin stepped from the clutch of faithful, dressed in the finery of a Roman patrician. He retrieved the soldier's spear and walked away toward the eastern hills, a dark smile on his lips.

Devlin smiled, testing the sharpness of the ancient blade against his thumb.

Sitting alone in the desert night before a pillar of fire, Devlin patiently honed the tip of the spear, transforming it into a razor-sharp dagger.

He inserted the tip of the oiled blade into the mouth of the worm-wood sheath, inlaid with ivory filigree.

In the shade of a wormwood tree, Devlin carefully formed the sheath with a block plane and a sanding stone.

He slipped the blade back inside, reforming the crucifix. The dagger was hidden now, beneath the golden body of Christ.

Emperor Constantine accepted the crucifix dagger as a tribute from Devlin, a wandering knight who had come on foot from Jerusalem. On Devlin's tunic was a peculiar rose and cross symbol that would evolve into the insignia of the Rosicrucian Order. It would be another seven hundred years before the secret organization would reveal its existence. Devlin was already their first traitor.

Constantine took him to the first Christian Church of Rome, still under construction. In the Papal chambers, they placed the weapon in an iron vault under the dais for the Papal throne.

Devlin cradled the crucifix in his hands. It felt alive, as if it were a cherished lover come back to him after an eternity, offering dearly remembered pleasures.

"*He never loved me,*" Devlin thought, and a voice responded at once from deep inside his dark soul. Lucifer's voice. "*But I loved him.*"

Devlin scowled in disgust, and said aloud, "Get behind me!" Then he looked up from his reverie, peering into the lazy swirling mists of the bayou. There were no humans for miles around, but he could smell an angel somewhere close by. The cloying, sweet odor was unmistakable.

"*Michael,*" Devlin hissed, and turned to look.

Michael the Archangel stood on the water nearby, backlit by the winter sun. After all these eons, he still wore the uniform of a general-in-chief, but he no longer had his wings. After the War in Heaven, God decided that angels should no longer have them. They engendered nothing but pride and hubris. Even an angel can fly too close to the sun.

"Once again, you are being foolish," he said to Devlin. His voice was quiet, but clear in the stillness. Despite the protection of God's good graces, Michael was keenly aware of the risk he was taking, to visit the most formidable foe that he or the Lord had ever encountered.

Devlin scowled at him. "How dare you pass judgment on me, you treasonous swine."

"Treason? You crucified His son, and yet He's forgiven you."

Devlin got to his feet and stood upon the water as well, glaring at the archangel, the sheathed dagger clutched in his left hand. Devlin knew the truth – when Christ was on the cross, the angels who were left in heaven were ready to wage battle once again. They were incensed that the creatures God created in His own image were sacrificing His only-begotten son. It was only Christ's forgiveness as he was dying that stayed their hand.

"God's chosen people crucified His Son," Devlin told Michael. "I only tempted Him."

"Murderer!" Michael spat, and Devlin glared at him.

"The killings must stop," Michael told him.

"*You* can stop them!" Devlin growled. *"Tell me who He came back as!"*

Michael said nothing. He knew the consequences, were Devlin to succeed. The order of the universe would be stood on its head and chaos would ensue for all eternity.

Devlin was annoyed. With his free hand, he took a cigarette from his pocket. He blew on the tip to light it, inhaled deeply, and exhaled the smoke toward Michael.

Michael recognized the aroma at once. "The Tree of Knowledge."

Devlin nodded, and took another satisfying drag.

"You've become addicted to the one thing you lack," Michael said with a knowing smile.

Devlin looked at him sharply. "This is *not* your affair! *None* of this is!"

He trailed off, distracted by something over his left shoulder. It was a faint, low humming, a chorus of men's voices, barely audible above the rustling leaves and the creatures of the bayou.

He turned to the sound, vexed by the intrusion, but he saw nothing. Still, they were close by, lurking somewhere in the mist. *They were growing impatient,* he thought. No matter. He would deal with them later.

He turned back to Michael, but the Archangel had vanished. Devlin was alone.

He sat back down on the mangrove root and smoked his cigarette, brooding over the dagger in his hand. He couldn't wait to use it.

CHAPTER THIRTEEN

Mas came down the front steps of City Hall with Kaddouri. They were taking a lunch break, and Mas brought her expanding file along. They passed through the center archway and turned left, heading up the block. She pulled the fax of Fareed Aly's phone logs out of the file and scanned it as they walked.

"Another Christmas baby."

Kaddouri nodded. "Yeah, this guy's the Grinch from Hell, huh?"

"How did he support himself?" she asked him, scanning the logs. "Did he have a job? Friends? Family? What did you guys find out?"

"He was a radiologist until he got laid off," Kaddouri told her.

Mas glanced at him, waiting for more.

"And he had some local family," he continued. "Twin older siblings, forty-two years old, over in St. Bernard's Parish on Cavanaugh." He pointed at the fax. "Eli and Seraj Aly. That's who the last call was from."

Mas flipped to the last page of the fax to see, and frowned at something. "He got a call from a restricted number, right before they called," she told him.

She tucked the fax back in the file, and speed dialed her secretary. "Hey, it's me. Fareed Aly got a restricted call the morning he jumped. Call the phone company and get the digits. Thanks, Charlene."

Mas ended the call, looked around, and blew a sigh. She needed to eat before she dealt with any more aggravation.

They strolled down the block, taking in the sunshine streaming through the leafless trees. The streets around City Hall were pleasant and substantially back to normal. Everything had been steam-cleaned, aired out and re-painted, and the utilities had all been restored. An uninformed visitor would never suspect that anything was amiss, but Mas couldn't help feeling like she was in a theme park. *New Orleansland.*

She felt Mark's eyes on her, and thought he was waiting for her to say something. "The place is coming along," she offered.

He nodded, looking around as well, then looked back to her as she was finishing a long, hearty yawn.

"'Scuse me," she said with a sheepish grin.

"You getting enough sleep?"

"Yeah..."

He just looked at her, waiting for the real answer. She wasn't fooling anyone.

"The nightmares are back," she confessed. "Cap'n thinks I need a shrink."

She was annoyed at the suggestion and let it show. But Kaddouri just shrugged. He didn't see it as something to take offense over.

"Do you?" he asked.

She shrugged back, unconvinced. "I don't care what they say, when you see a shrink everything winds up in your file."

"You can talk to me. I'm strictly off the record."

She debated his offer, but she decided to pass. "I'm sorry," she said, "but I don't think it's me. This case would drive anyone nuts. Maybe that's why it's never been solved."

They were passing a Christian bookstore, and paused to look in the window. A shop clerk was finally taking down the artificial Christmas tree. She smiled at them, and Mas and Kaddouri smiled back, watching her work.

"Jesus! Those fake trees are tacky," Mas commented to Kaddouri.

"That's got nothing to do with Jesus," he remarked. "That's Wall Street, baby."

"Christmas trees are pagan, you know that?" she said. "Some of the Germanic tribes used to decorate their trees with the body parts of their victims."

Kaddouri grinned. "Well, *that* must have put them in the holiday spirit."

Mas didn't grin back. She just nodded, taking in the Christian books and artifacts on display as she turned something over in her mind. He had a feeling that he knew what it was.

They stopped at Marcelle's Sausage Shack down the block and ordered some boudin veggie sausage sandwiches at the take-out window. The standing space at the wall counter was taken up with a lunchtime crowd, but a sidewalk table was being vacated. They grabbed it and sat down to eat.

Two street musicians were blowing jazz under the awning. Kaddouri leaned over and dropped their change into an upturned bowler hat nestled between the battered instrument cases. The men broke into a jig to thank them and Mas saluted in response.

They ate in silence, Kaddouri giving her time to process her thoughts.

"Eleven victims, all boys, born on Christmas morning," she finally said. It was exactly what he thought she was chewing on.

"Don't forget the nurse and the mothers," he reminded her.

"Yeah, and the priest, too," she said. "But I think they just got in the way." She bit into her boudin sandwich, dripping with sauerkraut, hot mustard, roasted peppers and grilled onions. She was careful not to splash anything on her suit. It took some doing.

"Thirty-three years and he's still on the loose," he mused, contemplating his sandwich.

Mas glanced at him. "Cajuns are superstitious, so the hospital records were never reassembled."

Kaddouri simply nodded.

"You know, the more I see of what this guy can do," she said, "the more I'm convinced that God's got a part-time job."

Kaddouri just nodded again, not knowing what to say. It troubled him when she got like this. He wished he knew exactly what to do for her, but she only let him reach so far inside of her world. He learned long ago to let her set the depth gauge of their conversations.

The spicy sausage was making them sweat; it wasn't for tourists. She opened her expanding file and dug out the autopsy report, scanning the document and ticking off the salient points as they ate.

"Temperature was one oh six post-mortem, CDC was notified; no fingerprints; both eyes were branded; no scorch marks; no residue."

He just nodded. She slipped the report back in her manila file and patted it with a humorless smile. "We got nothing," she told him.

They continued their walk, chicory coffees in hand, and stopped at a crowded corner waiting for the light to change.

Mas watched the streetlight as she spoke to him. "The cop on the balcony said his eyes were fine, right before he jumped."

Kaddouri glanced at her. The light turned green but they didn't cross. Pedestrians streamed around them. "He also thought he had a bomb," he said.

He stepped off the curb and she fell in beside them as they crossed to the other side. She window-shopped as they headed down the sidewalk, and he watched her reflection in the plate glass windows.

"Someone must have pushed this guy's buttons something fierce," he finally remarked.

"He's *got* to be getting help from somewhere!" she said, suddenly angry again.

"Yeah, but still, he's totally off the hook. Serial killers..." He didn't bother to finish the thought. She knew a lot more about the subject than he did.

"...leave clues; yeah, I know. It's like big game hunting for them. But he's leaving a trail with no scent."

She stopped and turned to him. "Maybe that's why Johnson called it quits."

He stopped and scowled at her, exasperated.

"Who the hell knows," he grumbled. "The man was a mental case."

They continued walking in silence. They rarely had spats, and felt uncomfortable from the breach of civility.

"He was at the jump site yesterday," Mas told him.

Kaddouri shot her a surprised look.

"He's playing cop," Mas theorized. "Probably picked it up on a scanner."

Kaddouri brushed off the news with a dismissive wave of his hand and looked around, not wanting to discuss it any further. Mas just smiled, watching the pavement as they continued. They walked in a circle; City Hall was just up the block. It was time to get back to work.

Her iPhone rang and she dug it out of her purse. "Agent Mas," she answered.

"It's me," Charlene said. "The digits are registered to the Vatican consulate."

Mas stopped in her tracks and Kaddouri halted beside her, wondering what was up. She had a vivid memory of the Maybach limousine that almost ran her down. It had Vatican City consulate plates.

"Charlene, run a set of Consul plates for me, number two three one five."

She ended the call. Kaddouri was looking at her, wondering what's up. "A limo almost ran me over at the jump site," she explained. "It had Vatican plates."

He tried to wrap his mind around the implications. "You think the Church is involved in this?"

She shrugged. "Well, if they are, we're walking into a minefield."

CHAPTER FOURTEEN

A full moon glimmered on the placid waters of Lake Pontchartrain. The lights of the city of New Orleans rimmed the south shore. Transparent clouds, backlit by moon glow, floated in from the Gulf on blanket of cool, moist air. The ferries and fishing trawlers were all berthed for the night and the lake was still.

Five fallen angels stood in a circle on the surface of the waters, their eyes cast downward, humming as they awaited their Lord's arrival. The hems of their white greatcoats stirred in the gentle breeze.

Devlin approached from out of the twinkling diffusion of city lights on the southern horizon. He stepped so lightly upon the water that his clothes and his black greatcoat remained dry. He could have been walking on wet pavement.

He took a final drag on his cigarette and flicked it away. It flared with a final burst of crimson light as it touched the water and was extinguished. A tiny stream of smoke rose from the sizzling spot on the lake. The cigarettes had become a daily habit, something that was as much a burden as a respite from his troubles. That in turn troubled him, compounding his displeasure, which prompted him to smoke even more.

He entered the circle and stood amongst them. His minions ceased their humming and bowed their heads in respect, but it was clear to him that they were displeased. He expected as much, and waited for them to state their case.

They lifted their heads to face him. They always spoke to him in unison, and would do so now. They were brothers in arms, united under his command since the Early Times, when they came under his spell. But that was when wars were fought in heaven, not down here on the earth. Now they were growing bold.

"Only one remains, Lord," they said to him.

"Yes, and He's well-hidden," he replied, but the anger in his voice modulated in mid-sentence, and they inwardly shrank back. They knew what was coming. Devlin's true nature was standing before them now, and Lucifer continued in a low, measured voice, far more chilling than Devlin's mercurial tone. "Who's to say that He – " Lucifer glanced at the star-filled heavens, " – didn't pull a fast one?"

The angels were thrown by the very idea. They actually hadn't considered the possibility, and Devlin was sneering at them now, as his anger surfaced again. Clouds began to boil into existence over their heads, so dark that they threatened to hide the moon. The angels grew nervous, watching him as he flicked from his earthly disguise to his true nature, from Devlin to Lucifer and back again, his all-too-human fury surging and subsiding. For immortal beings who had witnessed nearly everything, it was still unsettling for them to see. He had been among human beings for far too long, and while he made his mark on them, they in turn had made their mark on him.

"Would He do that?" the angels asked him, a cautious diffidence in their tone of voice.

"*Of course!*" Devlin shot back. They were starting to annoy him. He wanted another cigarette, and that annoyed him even more. But he forced himself to regain control, and as he did is features changed yet again.

"The stakes are incredibly high," Lucifer quietly said, but he glowered at them to drive home his point, and they cast their eyes downward. The devil himself was confronting them now. "*Look* at me!" Lucifer commanded, and they reluctantly complied, even as his anger resurged, transforming him into Devlin once more. It was difficult enough to face Devlin when he was in good spirits, but now his eyes bored into each of them as he spoke, fixing them with a piercing glare.

"Don't I make you nervous?" Devlin asked them, his features flickering back and forth as he looked at each of them in turn. Devlin was indeed angry, but they finally realized that he wasn't angry with them. At least, not at this particular moment. Their Lord was simply making an important point, and taking great pains to ensure that they understood exactly what it was. The angels smirked, finally catching his drift, and as his mood stabilized his form fully coalesced into Devlin, who was sneering at them now.

"When I win this bet," he explained to them, "*I take everything!*"

The angels glanced across the circle at each other. They liked the sound of that; it buoyed their spirits. But something was still troubling them. They took a moment to properly phrase their concern.

"Time is fleeting, my Lord," they finally said. "His thirty-third birthday has just passed. Good Friday comes in three months."

Devlin nodded, his eyes narrowing. He didn't need to be reminded. The clouds were roiling overhead; Darkness was forming in fits and starts.

"And between now and Crucifixion Day," Devlin reminded them, "He must willingly sacrifice Himself for a complete stranger." Devlin suddenly grinned. "I don't think He'll be having a Happy Easter."

Moonlight danced on the waters around them, but the five angels weren't completely persuaded by his confidence. The skies above began to grow agitated once again.

"Be of good cheer!" Devlin commanded them, but none of his fallen angels smiled. He pressed his case, reminding them of the advantages he held.

"The terms of the bet work both ways. Not only has He hidden The One, but He has hidden *Himself* from The One as well."

Devlin grinned again as he made his final point. "This time around, He's walking the earth completely on His own."

He paused to let that sink in, and scanned the circle of somber faces around him. The angels said nothing and bowed their heads, accepting him at his word. They had no choice in the matter.

Devlin slowly disappeared from the circle, becoming a wisp of vapor that floated away on the cool water. Above the circle of angels, darkness came quietly as gathering clouds obscured the moon.

CHAPTER FIFTEEN

Songbirds were chirping in the big magnolia tree outside the open windows of Bishop Nano's office. It was a balmy day, odd for January, and the expanse of manicured nature outside the rectory luxuriated in the warm embrace of God's gentle hands. But to Bishop Scipione Nano Borghese, the tiny creatures in the shade tree seemed to be mocking him.

Zamba was towering over Nano, leaning into him as he made his point, with a long dark forefinger jabbing at the man's face like a striking asp.

"Once again, you have given us the wrong name," he seethed, glaring at Nano with undisguised contempt.

Zamba hated the Catholic Church, particularly those who ran it. His island home had suffered more than enough of their arrogant meddling, distorting Haiti's ancient beliefs into a hopeless tangle of superstition and B-movie nonsense. Dressed in Catholic drag, the real power of *voudon* was becoming lost. Zamba intended to regenerate the ancient customs and restore them to full flower. Breaking the power of the Church was the first step.

As he saw it, Rome was hell-bent on establishing a spiritual tyranny over the world and nothing more. It was a racket; their piety was window-dressing. Like any successful multi-national, they were adept at eliminating the competition and consolidating power. In old Europe, they tortured witches and pagans and burned them at the stake. Over time they became more polished, but in reality little had actually changed; they simply did their dirty work through proxies. Shortly before World War II, the priests in Haiti incited the gullible populace to murder hundreds of *hougans* and *manbos,* the voodoo priests and priestesses who for centuries had held together the spiritual fabric of the island. That spiritual fabric in turn held the people together. Catholicism ripped that fabric to shreds and the island was suffering as a direct result.

When Pope John Paul II came to Haiti and kissed the soil, the bad luck generated from that one act had plunged the country into unremitting chaos from that point forward. The dynasty of Papa Doc Duvalier, the voodoo physician, and his son Baby Doc eventually lost their grip on the nation, as the country lurched from one disaster to another.

Zamba would have preferred to strangle Nano rather than to listen to any of his feeble excuses, but his master Devlin was consumed with a much larger issue than any pet peeves that Zamba harbored for Nano's teetering, sclerotic Church. The entire world was at stake, and whether Zamba liked it or not Nano was playing a pivotal role. What particularly rankled Zamba was that the Borghese family spawned a long line of Church hierarchy for centuries on end, not the least of which was the infamous Pope Paul V.

And though every one of them had been incompetent, they kept rising to the top. Here was another one.

At the moment, Nano couldn't have replied to Zamba's blunt assessment even if he wanted to. His chest and his throat were constricted with fear, and it was all he could do to swallow in an effort to keep down a rumbling nausea that kept crawling up from his gut. He was completely aware of what Zamba was capable of doing to him. Dealing with Zamba and Devlin was like juggling a pair of chainsaws; after more than thirty years Nano was growing weary of the relentless tension the two of them generated.

"Our patience has run thin," the voodoo master told him. His deep voice was barely above a whisper, but it was enough to make Nano wince.

"Please understand," Nano stammered, finally managing to find his voice, "That clinic was devastated by a tornado! The records have vanished —"

"*Fool!*" Zamba growled, cutting him off. "Do you think we have forgotten that night?"

Nano suddenly felt like a dunce. *Of course they haven't!* He chastised himself. *They were both right there in the thick of it.*

"Did you ever consider," Zamba hissed, "that Molinari could be buying time, feeding us sacrificial lambs?"

Nano blinked. He hadn't considered that possibility, at least not seriously. True, in his fits of pique, the thought crossed his mind, but he had always dismissed it as the by-product of his petulant aggravation. He wondered now, was he slipping? Was he getting too old to stay on top of things? In retrospect, how could he have rejected the notion out of hand? As much as he hated to admit it, Zamba had an excellent point — it was as likely a scenario as any other.

Zamba seemed to be able to read his mind, and castigated him with another withering sneer. His disdain for the bishop was so profound that his necklace sensed his murderous loathing, and began its transformation into a black asp.

Nano's eyes widened, staring at the dark magic, and Zamba willed the *loa* to be still. It morphed back into an iron link chain and resumed its quiet vigil.

Nano was still staring at it, wondering if it would just continue to lie still and be a tasteless example of slave chic bling. Zamba let him wonder. The uncertainty kept the bishop off-balance, making him more receptive to what Zamba had to say.

"You have been wasting our time, Nano, ever since you handed the dagger to that idiot priest."

"But now we have it back again —"

"And what does that prove?"

As rattled as Nano was, he realized that it was a good question. But he didn't have the time to process his thoughts and form a reply before the intercom in his desk phone came to life.

"Your Excellency?" It was Father Francis, his secretary in the outer office. "Agent Mas and Detective Kaddouri are here to see you. Shall I bring them in?"

Zamba glared at the intercom, annoyed at the interruption, but Nano was buoyed by it. He whipped his head around and focused on the phone, like a man overboard laying eyes on a floating log.

"Yes, Francis. But give me a moment."

Zamba turned his glare on Nano, livid that he had taken advantage of the intrusion. Nano glanced back at him and just stood there, taking short, shallow breaths, unsure of what Zamba would do next.

The voodoo priest stared balefully at the old man, silently warning him to be careful of what he said. Without a word being spoken, Nano completely understood the man's intent.

Zamba stepped back into a darkened corner of Nano's office, fixing the bishop with another cautionary scowl as he receded into the shadows. Zamba knew exactly where he was in the cavernous room, having been there many times before. With his eyes still locked on Nano, he reached behind himself and pushed on a section of rosewood paneling, on the wall beside the last set of bookshelves.

A hidden door opened silently. Zamba finally turned away and stepped into the unlit passageway, disappearing into the darkness. He closed the door behind him, but not entirely.

Nano went to his desk and dropped into his tufted leather chair, letting out the lungful of air he had been holding since he spoke to Francis on the intercom. The tension spring under the chair squeaked as it caught the full load of his weight. With everything else that was going on in his life, the squeak still registered in the back of his mind as yet another thing that needed tending to. It wasn't that he was easily distracted. Rather, he found that the more he aged, the less he was able to ignore things. Perhaps senility would be a relief, rather than the tragedy it was made out to be.

He only had a few more moments to compose himself. His guests could wait, but Zamba might run out of what little patience he possessed and do something rash. What that might be, Nano couldn't guess. The man was capable of anything. And if he couldn't do something, his master certainly could.

Nano took several deep, slow breaths to calm himself, something he'd learned from a yoga CD that he ordered online. It sure beat praying to a God that he had long since given up on. As his pulse slowed, he even managed to crack a little smile, contemplating the apparent long-standing irony of his situation, an Unbeliever in charge of a diocese. Apparent, because, in truth, there was no irony involved. Everybody knows that a successful pusher never uses his own product.

His moment of reflection brought his spirits back somewhat, and he finally felt ready to charm his guests. He tapped the intercom button on his desk phone, leaning close to it out of habit. "All right, Francis. Show them in."

He picked up his favorite Montblanc fountain pen and pretended to be busy putting the finishing touches on a letter. As he scribbled away, Father Francis opened the door to show the two cops into his office.

Old codger that he was, Francis held onto the doorknob and simply waved his hand for Mas and Kaddouri to enter. He did as little walking as he could these days, and it was a good thirty feet from the door to Nano's desk. *The hell with that,* he thought. *They can find their way without my help.*

Nano looked up from his correspondence and smiled graciously at his guests. The first thing that struck him was how good-looking they both were, how well they went together. He had expected a mutt and a bulldog.

Mas and Kaddouri stepped into the room and Francis quietly closed the door. Nano rose from his chair, his left hand on his blotter to steady himself, and extended his right hand to Mas. *She's lovely,* he thought. *Whatever made her become a cop?*

"Agent Mas, a pleasure."

She took his hand and shook it firmly. "Your Excellency..."

"Detective Kaddouri..." Nano said, shaking his hand.

"Your Excellency..." Kaddouri responded.

Nano waved a hand, inviting them to sit by the fire. Although it was a pleasant day, the cavernous room tended to be dank and gloomy, and the fire cast a welcoming glow on the tall bookshelves and dark paneling. Plus, it *was* January, despite the weather, and it served as a festive accompaniment to the Christmas decorations that still graced the room.

Nano gestured for Mas to sit in one of the antique wingback chairs, separated by the tea table. "Thank you, your Excellency," she murmured, and sat down.

Nano glanced at Kaddouri, about to suggest that he could wheel the desk chair over, but Kaddouri was attracted by the display of priceless Christmas ornaments on the mantel. Nano had been collecting them for years. The entire Borghese dynasty had been acquiring art of one sort or another since the Dark Ages, and he was a chip off the old block.

"'Twas the season, eh?" Nano said with a twinkle in his eye. "I'm always so reluctant to put them away."

Kaddouri just smiled, and then stood there bouncing on his toes, indicating that he preferred to stand, and he gestured for the bishop to sit across from Mas.

Nano thought it was a cop strategy, having one of them looming over him, but he didn't press the point. He sat in the other wingback chair, settling into the soft cushions. He rested his elbows on the arms of his chair and clasped his plump hands together, regarding them both.

"And how can I help you?"

Kaddouri was standing by the mantel. He glanced at Mas to say that it was her interview to conduct and not his, and then drifted away to wander the room and check out the antiques while Mas got down to business. She watched Nano's eyes as they conversed.

"I ran into you the other day, your Excellency."

He was puzzled, and tilted his head, asking for a clue.

"On Beaudry Street?" she prompted him. "Where the man jumped from his balcony?"

Nano thought back to the incident, and then he remembered the moment. He cracked a dry smile and squinted his eyes at her. The expression gave him a kindly uncle demeanor, one he liked to use when talking to women. It was a way that he could flirt with impunity. Priests had used it for centuries, and Nano had it down to a fine art.

"Actually, I believe I almost ran into *you*, Agent Mas," he said, and she smiled in return.

He glanced over at Kaddouri, standing by his desk. The detective was admiring a small sixteenth century painting on the wall, a portrait of a teenage girl. There was something about her smile that captivated him, but he couldn't quite put his finger on it.

"Does she look familiar to you?" Nano asked him. Kaddouri nodded, his eyes stuck on the portrait. "I think I've seen this before. Is it an original?"

Nano smiled. "You've seen *her* before, but not in that painting. Lisa Gherardini. She was twelve years old at the time. I picked it up in Florence for a song several years ago, when I was assigned to the Vatican. I'm told it's quite valuable now."

The art historian in Florence had contacted the Palazzo Borghese about the piece, while Nano was visiting his ancestral home. He hurried down to Florence in the dead of night and scooped it up for his private collection. If anyone else in his family purchased it, it would have wound up in the palazzo along with all their other treasures, for the edification of gum-chewing tourists in T-shirts.

Kaddouri glanced at him, intrigued. Mas watched the bishop, studying his eyes and his mannerisms as he entertained Kaddouri with his prideful anecdote.

"She eventually married a Florentine merchant by the name of Francesco del Giocondo. Does the name ring a bell?"

Kaddouri was astonished. *"Mona Lisa!"* he whispered, and turned back to the portrait, finally recognizing the girl's smile.

Mas was as astonished as he was, and it took all her will to keep her eyes on Nano, rather than catch her first glance of a young Mona Lisa. She could see it on the way out, she told herself. Right now, what she was seeing was a bishop who was puffed up and gloating with pride. *Not very bishopy of him*, she thought.

Nano was, however, human, and he was understandably proud of his find. When it was finally confirmed that Lisa Gherardini had in fact sat for Da Vinci, the value of his little memento from a day-trip in Florence instantly skyrocketed, from the paltry sum of forty Euros to well over thirty million and climbing. Sotheby's had him on speed dial, but he was content to hang onto it until the Devlin affair was put to bed and he could retire in peace. Instead of going to an Old Padre's Home, as he called it, he planned to sell the painting and purchase a villa on Lake Como, with a full staff and all the trimmings.

Nano turned back to Mas and smiled. "Now, where were we...? Oh, yes, I was almost running you over with my Maybach. Please accept my apology." He opened a box of truffles on the tea table. "A chocolate for your troubles."

She had to admit that the man knew how to turn on the charm. "Apology accepted, your Excellency."

She helped herself to a truffle, and he had one as well. They both sat back for a moment and savored the handcrafted confections. They were heavenly.

Kaddouri was examining a three-dimensional chess set on an antique table for two. The game depicted a battle between the Vatican and the Kingdom of God, played with delicately carved alabaster and onyx pieces. The Basilica was a dark fortress on one side of the board. Its first two checkerboard rows were the wide steps leading down to St. Peter's Square. God's Kingdom was on the opposite steps, a crystal palace facing the Basilica.

Some of the pieces were still on the steps. Jesus and Mary were the king and queen of the Kingdom of God, and Mary Magdalene was His bishop. Lucifer was the king of the Vatican, and the Pope was his queen. Most of the pieces from both sides were in play. Archangels were the Kingdom's knights and rooks, and angels were the pawns. They faced off against cardinals and bishops, and the Vatican's pawns – human beings kneeling in prayer, their rosaries in hand.

Kaddouri drifted to the wall of books, shelf upon shelf of leather-bound texts that framed the leaded windows open to the afternoon breeze. He stepped under the rolling ladder to get a close look at a first-edition collection of the papers of Thomas Jefferson.

Just above his head, Zamba's asp lay on a rung of the rolling ladder. Its tongue darted in and out of its mouth, trying to decipher Kaddouri's scent. His cologne and mousse confused the creature, and probably saved his life.

Kaddouri drifted out from under the ladder, attracted by an early map of the Caribbean. The asp followed him, crawling up the ladder and transiting along the bookshelves.

"Could you tell me why you were on Beaudry Street, your Excellency?" Mas asked Nano.

He shifted in his chair and laced his fingers together. "I have a new chauffeur," he explained. "Mr. Gibbs was taking me to the airport to pick up a colleague, but we took the wrong exit and found ourselves at your roadblock." He offered a hapless smile, and shrugged. "We were lost."

Mas countered with a sly grin. "And now you're found."

Nano was charmed by her wit. If things were different, he'd be asking her out to dinner. She reminded him of the call girl he had in

Switzerland, one of the most cultured and intelligent people he had ever met. She was a good Catholic girl, someone you could bring home to Mother Superior. He was still in love with her, after all these years. Catholic girls were the best. He often fantasized of her coming to visit him at Lake Como. She could stay as long as she liked. If she was still in the business, he fully intended to see her again, if only for the pleasure of her company.

"That's a Protestant ditty, Agent Mas. But it's still a wonderful song."

She nodded with a smile. Nano turned his head to see how Kaddouri was faring. The detective was in a shadowy corner of the room, near the hidden door in the paneled wall. His hands were clasped behind his back in a respectful museum posture as he admired the old map of the Caribbean Sea. Another priceless original, it was from the private collection of Sir Francis Drake. He sensed Nano's eyes on him and turned, nodding appreciatively.

Nano graciously smiled, but as he did, his features froze. The black asp had draped itself on top of the gilded map frame, lurking in the warm shadow behind the brass picture light. It was stretching toward Kaddouri, flicking its tongue to taste the air, still trying to decode the jumble of odors the detective was exuding. As a humid breeze drifted in from the open window, the base note of his body musk became faintly detectable, despite the artificial aromas he put on that morning to mask it.

The asp confirmed its prey and was ready to strike.

Nano slapped his hands on his knees and stood up. "Well!" he said, a little loudly, "I'm sure we could chat the day away, but..."

The meeting was over. Mas stood up and shook his hand. Nano turned to Kaddouri with a cordial smile and extended his hand to him. It was incumbent upon the younger man to cross the room to take the older man's hand, rather than the reverse, and Kaddouri did so out of respect. The asp withdrew into its warm hideaway, behind the brass light, as Kaddouri shook hands with Nano.

The bishop escorted them to the door. "Thank you for your time, your Excellency," Mas said.

"God be with you, my child. I enjoyed our little visit. Truly."

"You have quite a collection," Kaddouri said to him.

Nano clapped a hand on his shoulder. "Thank you, Lieutenant. Lisa's a little darling, but truth be told, that old map of Francis Drake is still my favorite."

He used the moment to glance back at the map. The snake was still behind the brass light. He opened the heavy oak door and bid them adieu, as they stepped out to Father Francis's office.

Nano gently closed the door and turned quickly to locate the asp, but it was no longer on top of the map frame. His eyes darted quickly around the room, scanning for the deadly creature, and his gaze finally came to rest on the hidden door in the paneled wall. It was slightly ajar.

There was a soft click of the latch as Zamba quietly closed it from the other side. Nano gulped, and broke out in an uncomfortable sweat. A voodoo master and his demonic serpent were both in his private quarters now, doing God-knows-what.

Mas and Kaddouri came down the steps of the rectory and got into his shiny black Land Cruiser. They buckled up and rolled down the sweeping driveway toward the open wrought-iron gates.

"He's lying through his dentures," Mas told him.

Kaddouri grinned. She had a way with words. "About what?" he asked her.

"The chauffeur of the Archbishop of New Orleans doesn't know how to get to the airport? Spare me."

Kaddouri piloted his SUV through the gates and turned right, heading back toward the freeway. The traffic was light and it was a pleasant day to be on the road. He stuck to the speed limit and sat back to enjoy the drive. He shrugged, "He said the guy was new."

Mas just gave him a look, and he got her point.

"I was blind, but now I see," he recited.

She smiled and looked out the windshield. "About damn time, Detective."

He just smiled and watched the road. She used to be his rookie, back in the day. But he had to admit, she was turning out to be sharper than he was, and that made him proud.

Zamba stood beside Nano's four-poster bed, looking through the open window at the Maybach limousine parked in the driveway below. The garage was behind the rectory and the driveway ran directly under Nano's bedroom windows.

Nano steered the bloodhounds away from himself and toward his own chauffeur, blaming the man for their appearance at the police roadblock the morning that Devlin enticed the man to jump to his death. Zamba knew that even though Nano had diplomatic immunity, it only extended to his staff while they were on the job. If the police suspected anything, they would question the chauffeur the moment he got off work.

The limousine was parked in the shade of the big magnolia tree, just outside the bedroom windows. Mr. Gibbs spent the entire morning detailing the automobile, and he was nearly finished. The doors were open to air out the interior so that the scent of saddle soap would dissipate before the Archbishop asked to be taken anywhere. He usually liked to go for a ride in the late afternoon and stop for coffee and brandy in the French Quarter at sunset.

Mr. Gibbs was kneeling on the lambswool carpeting in back, burnishing the ashtrays with an old toothbrush and a drop of silver cleaner, when he felt something touch the cuff of his pants. He dipped his head and peeked under his arm, but all he saw was the dangling cuff of his black pants, a stretch of his bare calf, his black sock and his shiny black shoe.

Then he felt something touch his other cuff.

The asp slid out of the Maybach and dropped to the cool cobblestones. It slinked to the trunk of the magnolia tree and made its way up the rough bark to a large, thick branch that angled toward the rectory. The tree was in need of pruning. Its outer branches were already brushing against the building, but the arborist usually didn't come until the middle of the month.

The snake retraced its own scent, slithering back to the open window of Nano's bedroom. Zamba was standing there, waiting patiently for the *loa's* return. He held out his arm and it slithered up his smooth dark skin onto his broad, muscled shoulder. It looped around his neck, took its own tail in its mouth, and returned to its resting state as Zamba's voodoo necklace.

CHAPTER SIXTEEN

Father Eden hadn't been to St. Bernard's Parish in years, and the neighborhood was much worse than he remembered. He was walking through a dismal wasteland, making his way south toward Cavanaugh Street, passing one dilapidated hovel after another. He usually drove the church's car to visit parishioners, but Sister Nancy needed it for shopping that day so he had taken the bus. The city buses mostly kept to the major boulevards these days. Many of the side streets were still too littered, and the Katrina exodus permanently trimmed the population to such a degree that several side routes had to be eliminated. If someone needed to go deep into the 'hood these days, they took a taxi or they were on their own.

Eden didn't mind walking; it was good exercise, and it gave him a fresh perspective on the world. Like most of the city, St. Bernard's Parish had taken a beating, but that wasn't what struck him as he negotiated the fractured sidewalks and the pot-holed streets. The parish itself was a wasteland. The social fabric was always threadbare in St. Bernard's, but now it was hanging in tatters. The very culture of the parish was dying.

A gaggle of punks were playing *celo* outside a liquor store, one of the few businesses that weren't boarded up. A fight erupted over an accusation of loaded dice. Suddenly all the guns came out, and teens went running in every direction. Moments later, the weapons were tucked away and everything was back to normal, but the incident tinged Eden's perception of the entire neighborhood. He kept walking, but now he had a knot in his stomach.

A late-model Mercedes with chrome rims rolled by and parked in the driveway of a house down the block. Two young men piled out, both sporting a thick handful of gaudy gold chains, designer shades and spotless high-dollar kicks. They were wearing and driving every dime they had, while the house was a shambles. As Eden passed their open front door, a wide-screen TV that took up an entire wall roared to life and the ball game came on. It was the only furniture that wasn't falling apart.

Eden had grown up admiring Dr. King, and it pained him to see the man's dream fading before his eyes. St. Bernard's had devolved into a parish terrorized by short-tempered gangbangers who were fighting and dying over turf they didn't even own. They were renters. And ever since the flood their absentee landlords were busily condemning as many of the properties as they possibly could. Katrina was the best excuse in generations to wipe the slate clean and start over, and the city fathers were tacitly behind them every step of the way. Eden didn't side with them, but he could understand their position.

What little money that did come into St. Bernard's that wasn't appropriated by mothers to feed their kids, was invested in bling. The breadwinners weren't buying bread, they were spending it – laying their money down for the flashier things in life instead of stepping up, collectively if need be, to put a down payment on a piece of the pie.

Sadly, it was the same story all over America. People raised by television were suffering from an epidemic of Affluenza, spread by Madison Avenue and festered in the shame of being thought poor. Of all the people afflicted by the malady, it was the poor who suffered the most when they caught the bug.

While some people degraded themselves and insulted each other with epithets like nigga and bitch and 'ho, and convinced each other that the Man was keeping them down, immigrants were stepping off the boat every day of the week with a suitcase and no English, and just rolling up their sleeves and getting to work. Ten years later, they owned their own house, their kids were in college, and they could speak fluent English. And they were discriminated against every step of the way.

Eden felt a hundred eyes on him as he approached the corner of Cavanaugh Street, but as out of place as he felt he wasn't afraid to be there. What troubled him was that he couldn't do much of anything to help them out. The irony was that although he dedicated his life to helping the poor and the disenfranchised, he belonged to the richest private organization on earth. If he were the Pope, he'd auction off the Church's art collection and half their real estate, and initiate a micro-loan program for penniless entrepreneurs. Micro-loans were lifting people out of poverty in Bangladesh; there was no reason to think that it couldn't work in New Orleans.

A streetwalker on the corner smiled at him. It wasn't every day that she saw a handsome priest. Or any priest, for that matter. He just nodded hello and turned the corner. Some women reminded him of why celibacy could actually be a good thing, and she was one of them.

Cavanaugh Street was a dead-end, and in stark contrast to the rest of the neighborhood the cul-de-sac was quiet and orderly. Eden had no idea why, but the residents on Cavanaugh knew. Madame Zantelle was an immigrant from Benin, a beautiful *manbo* who lived in the pink bungalow across from the Aly place. When she moved in nine years ago, she summoned the *loas* to come protect her dwelling and the surrounding inhabitants as well. She made the requisite offerings, sacrificing a chicken and dripping the blood in a jagged line across the street, down at the end of the block. She did this at precisely three in the morning, by the light of the full moon.

As the weeks passed and her neighbors came to see her with their various troubles, she told them what she had done for them, expecting they would spread the word and that the proper tributes would be paid. Since the day she moved in, it was the only street in St. Bernard's

Parish that had not suffered a burglary or a homicide. Madame Zantelle's voodoo was strong.

It disturbed her that the Alys weren't coming to her for help, since it was quite obvious that their brother's death was the work of the Devil. The *manbo* sat in her front room gazing at the Aly house across the street, but their curtains were drawn tight, the same as they had been since the day of Fareed's suicide.

When the priest appeared, she finally had her answer. The Alys were afraid to summon the dark forces. They had called for a lily-white, watered-down version of spiritual succor instead. She sniffed in disgust. A priest had no inkling of what to do in a situation like this. He wouldn't have the power to wrestle with Satan. He was a piteous, ignorant fool to even try. She smiled, watching him.

Eden paused before the careworn house, his back to the tidy pink bungalow across the street. The Aly home was a cottage built back in the Twenties that probably should have been torn down after the flood. A FEMA symbol had been spray-painted on the siding to indicate that the place was condemned, but someone removed the strips of wood and the city never got around to enforcing the declaration. The exposed tarpaper flapped in the afternoon breeze, revealing glimpses of the lath and plaster interior walls.

Eden checked the address against a slip of paper in his pocket, and climbed the loose plank steps to the porch. He tried the bell but it didn't work, so he knocked on the screen door and waited, keeping his eyes on the closed front door.

It was opened by a thin Egyptian-American woman in her forties, wearing a starched housedress and nervously fiddling with a small Coptic crucifix on a chain around her neck. A man stood behind her, the same age and just as thin as she was, dressed in a perfectly clean undershirt and a pair of crisp khakis. He was smoking a cigarette and had a rosary wrapped around his hand, the crucifix clutched in his sweaty palm.

Seraj and her twin brother Eli didn't look much alike, but they were cut from the same mold, an ancient bloodline of tall, lanky herders that could be traced back thousands of years to the headwaters of the Nile. Even when they were at peace with the world they both tended to stoop, since they were taller than almost everyone they encountered. But now their world had turned ugly and they were hunched over, burdened by a constant sense of foreboding. They just wanted the nagging fear to subside and the nightmares to stop.

Eli turned away and slouched into the shadows of the front room. Even though he was clutching a rosary, he didn't want to talk to a priest, when push came to shove. The man wouldn't understand what he and his sister were going through. The voodoo lady across the street probably knew better than some damn priest, but she wanted money, and for the last few years the Alys were flat broke. Fareed had been helping them with the mortgage, but now he was gone.

Eli was half-hoping that the visitor was their neighbor Mr. Morris. Fareed had given Eli a car stereo for Christmas, and it was still in the original boxes, sitting with the speakers in a couple of shopping bags by the front door. Mr. Morris was rebuilding his '56 Buick for his boy Cleon, and Eli offered to sell him the stereo for a good price. Although it pained Eli to sell off a present from his dead brother, it would bring in a good piece of the mortgage, and since Fareed had been helping them with the payments anyway, Eli reasoned that Fareed would have understood.

Seraj looked through the neatly stitched door screen at the handsome priest and gave him a thin, puzzled smile. She had no idea why he came calling, but her cordiality was impeccably intact despite the stress she was under. Still, as the days wore on, it was getting harder and harder to summon her manners for a stranger, even a priest. Nevertheless, a little voice in her head told her to be nice, considering what just happened to poor Fareed, God rest his tortured soul.

"Father...?"

"We heard the sad news about your brother."

Seraj just looked at him for the longest time; the fresh wound tore at her heart, and she was well aware that it probably always would. Fareed's pain was over, but hers and her brother's had just begun. Seraj unlatched the screen and pushed it open for the priest to come in. She glanced over his shoulder at the bungalow across the street. Madame Zantelle was sitting in her big chair in the front window, watching as usual. Seraj closed the door and locked it as soon as Eden stepped inside.

The place was tidy, but it was clear that like so many people in town, and so many more all over the country, they had fallen on hard times. Eden ministered to the poor before so there was little he saw that shocked him. Mostly it just made him sad, particularly the newly-poor. They always seemed to have the hardest time of it.

There were several votive candles flickering around the room. Portraits of Coptic saints, rendered in the iconic Orthodox style, were hung about the room, and a Last Supper tapestry on black velvet bordered with Arabic inscriptions was hung over the dining table.

Seraj offered him a seat in an overstuffed chair with embroidered doilies draped over the armrests. Eden sat down across from the sofa, where Eli's thin frame seemed to be all but swallowed up by the sofa's soft cushions. Seraj went into the kitchen. Her brother's bare feet were nervously flexing in his leather sandals under the coffee table, in rhythm with his fist as he unconsciously clutched at the rosary in his hand. He was looking at the priest, smoking an unfiltered cigarette and wondering what the man had to say.

Seraj came back from the fridge with a soda for Eden, and put one on the coffee table in front of her brother. She sat beside him, and a billow of dust wafted up from the sofa cushions. The particles lingered in the afternoon sunshine.

Eden nodded a thank-you for the soda, popped the top, and took a sip, grateful for her hospitality. "You've both just been through a dreadful loss," he began. "We want you to know that your brother Fareed is in our prayers down at the Church of the Rebirth. It may not seem like it now, but the comfort of God is always close at hand."

Seraj's eyes drifted to the floor, and Eli slowly shook his head. Eden thought the man was going to launch into a sour rejection of what he just said, but Eli was melancholy, not confrontational.

"I don't think God has much to say about it, one way or the other," Eli said, almost in a whisper, and he stubbed out his cigarette in a full ashtray.

Eden was thrown by his comment. Despite their anguish and loss, he thought that they still were God-fearing people. Sister Nancy told him that the extended Aly family had long been a part of their Roman Catholic city, participating in the culture to one degree or another for several generations. Their great-grandfather came from Cairo to build riverboats and allowed himself to be adopted by the Catholic Church, although the family always kept the Coptic tradition. The New Orleans diocese had already absorbed Voodoo and Santaria; by comparison, Coptic Christianity was an easy accommodation to make.

"How do you mean, Eli?"

Eli didn't answer, but simply shrugged like a shy child. He couldn't find the words to express what he was feeling, any more than he could make sense of it in his own mind. He just wanted to turn off the bad feelings, and he couldn't find a way to do it.

"You believe in God, don't you, Father?" Seraj asked Eden. He pursed his lips, puzzled at the thrust of her inquiry, but it was more of a statement than a question.

"Well, yes. Of course," was all he could think of saying in reply. He hoped it didn't come off as rude, but he was wondering where this was going. For her part, Seraj was embarrassed by her own directness. She realized that it was an awkward thing to ask a priest.

"We don't question your faith," she stammered, fingering her silver crucifix. She sensed that she had just driven into a ditch, and didn't know any graceful way to back out. Eden could see how she was feeling and he wasn't offended, but he was puzzled by what she was driving at.

"Then what is your question?" he asked.

Eli interrupted the moment by getting up and going over to the liquor cabinet. They watched as he poured himself a shot of Absolut Vodka. Then he leaned into the kitchen, opened the freezer door, and retrieved a handful of ice cubes. He came back to the sofa, set his drink on the coffee table and sat across from Eden.

Seraj was embarrassed for what her brother had done, and wanted to get the conversation back on track as smoothly as possible. But she couldn't think of how, exactly. She cast about for a way to explain what she meant, but it was clear that Eli had more than enough. He felt bad and he needed to feel good again; it just came down to that.

"Do you think that God loves the Devil?" Eli asked Eden.

"Pardon me?" the priest stared at him in surprise.

Eli looked away and Seraj glanced at her brother, embarrassed by his behavior once again.

"You'll get through this," Eden said gently. "God will show you the way."

Eli was gazing out the window, at Madame Zantelle's house across the street. Seraj knew what he was looking at, and why.

"Yeah, well, God don't come 'round here no more," Eli finally replied.

Eden pursed his lips, wondering how to respond, but Seraj thought he was silently chastising her brother. She frowned, waving off his reaction as if it were an annoying fly buzzing around her tidy household.

"We didn't *call* for no priest!" she shot at him. "We don't need no lectures."

Eli backed her up by raising his glass to her in a toast. *"Absolut!"* he said, and downed the shot.

Seraj looked at the floor again and ground her teeth in frustration. She felt like she had just sinned for talking harshly to a priest, but the truth was that he had no idea what they were going through. For all his good intent, he was out of line. Still, he did come to give them whatever comfort he could, and for that he deserved better than a taste of her temper.

She collected herself and tried to explain. "You don't know what happened on that balcony."

"Shit, lucky for him," Eli said quietly.

Eden and Seraj looked back at him, and for his part Eden was thankful that Eli said something. It broke the confrontation with Seraj, and he knew he wasn't going to get anywhere with her when she was being so testy.

But it was cold comfort, because Father Eden had a gathering sense that he didn't have a clue about what was going on. He might have had the angels on his side, but he was flying blind. Something was bothering them, and it was more than the simple fact of their brother jumping to his death.

"What?" he asked them, but they didn't answer. Eden looked to Seraj, and her eyes welled with tears. He reached over and touched her shoulder, and the tears came on stronger.

"Seraj. Tell me," he prompted her.

As the words came to her throat, she grew more agitated. "We just trying to avoid dealing with... Oh, Lord...!"

She clamped a hand over her mouth, and her eyes scanned the room as she felt a sudden stab of fear. Eden was perplexed by her sudden unraveling and leaned closer to her as a gesture of support, but she didn't respond or reply. She just kept her hand over her mouth as if she were afraid she might say more. He heard her breath rush past her fingers and realized that she was hyperventilating. She grabbed her brother's hand with her other one and squeezed as hard as she could. Eli stroked her forearm to soothe her.

Eden cocked his head and tenderly frowned at her, silently urging her to speak, and she finally uncovered her mouth just a little.

"He *made* Fareed do it!" she told Eden breathlessly. *"Our brother didn't jump!"*

He was growing uneasy now. Something had climbed on her back and wouldn't let go, and he didn't think it was the pain of her loss. It was something else entirely.

"Who?" he insisted.

Seraj tilted her head closer to him and removed the hand from her mouth. "He heard that voice in his head!" she told Eden in a hoarse whisper.

He swallowed hard. He had a growing sense that this was more than he bargained for. Much more.

"Who was it, Seraj?"

She pursed her lips and pulled her head back, gripping her brother's hand even tighter, turning his fingers pale.

Eli smirked at the priest. "You know who it was, man." Eden glanced at him, and Eli slowly nodded, his eyes narrowing, certain of himself.

"You know," Eli said again.

Eden was beginning to catch on. His throat was suddenly dry and he tried to swallow. He turned back to Seraj.

"Who was it?"

But she was so frightened that she could only manage the barest of whispers. He had to lean close to hear what she was saying.

Father Jean Paul Eden was completely ashen, and had to hold onto the handrail to keep from stumbling down the rickety stairs. He negotiated his way down the worn wooden steps of the Aly's front porch as if he were disconnected from his lower body, as if his legs had suddenly gone numb from a deathly chill in the air.

Mas' BMW was parked at the curb in front of the house, her helmet clipped to the frame. She stood by her bike, checking the house address with a piece of paper. Three young studs on the porch next door were leering at the attractive young woman, but whatever was on their minds quickly evaporated when she brushed aside the hem of her jacket to slip the paper in her pants pocket. Her badge and her holstered 10mm were prominent on her hip.

She ignored the teens, although she knew exactly where each of them were standing, and what each of them held in their hands – beer bottles, a TV remote, a cell phone, a lighter and a hash pipe.

Her eyes were on the priest. She couldn't remember ever seeing one who was more distressed. But Eden paid no attention to her. Absorbed by what he had just been told, he walked right past her as if she wasn't even there and headed down the sidewalk, pale and lost in troubled thought.

She watched him go for a moment, and decided not to disturb him. It looked like he was grappling with something he might have caught by emotional contagion from Fareed's surviving kin. But there was something else etched into his face as well, something that she couldn't quite put her finger on. She mentally filed it away and trotted up the steps.

Across the street, in the driveway of Madame Zantelle's house, a man sat behind the wheel of a rental car, idly fiddling with the gold Rosicrucian ring on his finger and watching everything.

Mas was in the same armchair that Eden occupied just minutes before. Seraj and Eli were across from her, sitting close together on the sofa. Eli was in a mellow mood from his first shot of Absolut, and poured himself another one. Seraj was still in a knot of anguish, her eyes puffy and red. He mixed her a drink when the priest left, but she hadn't touched it.

Seraj sniffed, and wiped her nose with a handkerchief that she kept tucked in the pocket of her housedress. Her clothes and her house were as neat as a pin, but she was a mess.

"He lost his job," she said to Mas, "and was finding his way back to God. The bishop was bringing him back to Jesus."

Mas tilted her head. "The bishop?"

Seraj nodded. "Yeah! He saved Fareed's soul!"

Eli took her hand in his. She grasped his hand tightly in response, hanging on for strength. The love they had for each other was nearly all they had left.

Mas slowly nodded as she digested this latest bit of information, her mind racing.

She sat on her idling BMW, talking on her iPhone to Kaddouri. The three studs on the porch behind her were enjoying the view, and admiring the quiet purr of the tuned exhaust. She was their new fantasy, and they were absorbing every detail they could before she raced down the road and out of their miserable lives.

"Mark, send me that video clip, the pan shot of the crowd."

She took the phone from her ear and shaded the display with her hand, watching the file download. She tapped play and viewed the clip.

She saw the cops, the roadblock, the paramedics, and Thorrington standing beside his cruiser, the megaphone in his hand. Nano's limo was in the background, but it wasn't at the roadblock like Nano told her. It was parked at the curb.

She got back on the horn to Kaddouri. "Nano wasn't stuck at the roadblock, Mark. He was parked on Fareed's street. Check out the video. And Seraj told me that a bishop visited Fareed just last month."

"If Nano's our killer..." Kaddouri began, and she finished the thought for him:

"He's also a diplomat."

"Exactly," he said to her. "We won't be able to stop him from leaving the country."

"Any luck on the chauffeur?" she asked him.

"Yeah. We found out he's been working for the archdiocese for over thirty years."

CHAPTER SEVENTEEN

The basilica cast a long shadow across the grand expanse of St. Peter's Square as the late afternoon sun dipped behind the enormous dome atop the most recognized symbol of the Mother Church in the entire world. The cloudy western horizon behind the dome fanned the sun's rays and rendered a postcard ending for the crisp winter day. Shutterbugs all over the Square eagerly captured the image, savoring the moment as if it were a good omen.

The square still thronged with tourists, parishioners, clergy, nuns, and pigeons. The tour buses were parked nose to tail out on the Via del Concilizione. The drivers were chain smoking and swapping jokes, waiting for their passengers to return so they could take them back to their hotels for pasta and wine.

Devlin walked unseen through the crowd, heading directly for the steps. He'd been to St. Peter's many times before, down through the centuries. Normally, he would take his time and savor the architecture. He had always thought that St. Peter's would be a fitting headquarters for his impending reign on earth. Particularly since it was engineered and built by apostate Masons, and most particularly since financing the lavish structure is what finally triggered the Protestant Reformation. Which caused centuries of conflict between God-fearing Christians. The whole thing stood as a monument to folly. Even though God accused his angels of hubris, it was man created in His image who had really taken the cake, through their overwrought worshipping of Him. Devlin thought the irony was delicious.

There were a few changes he'd make to the décor, but overall he intended to preserve most of the Christian motifs. They would provide a nice sarcastic touch.

At the moment, however, he wasn't in much of a touristy mood. To secure his rights to the property, he had to conclude the business at hand, and time was running short.

Two impoverished young girls were kneeling on a blanket they laid out each morning at the base of the steps. The individual roses they sold were arranged before them, and the upturned sunbonnet they used for transactions had a handful of coins and Euros from a slow afternoon.

A breath of cold wind tickled the edge of the blanket, and a dozen loose rose petals tumbled lazily across the ancient paving stones. The girls watched them scatter, idly wondering how far they would get before they were all stepped on. It was a way to pass the time.

But this time, something odd happened that made them sit up and take notice. Three of the petals that were drifting along in a tight bunch suddenly turned to ashes, and simply dissipated into thin air. The girls glanced at each other, utterly astonished, and looked back to watch the other petals.

Devlin's invisible boot came down on another pair of rose petals, and turned them to ashes as well.

The girls stared at the phenomenon, not daring to breathe. They couldn't see Devlin's boot, or him, but his impact on their world was abrupt and chilling. Believing their eyes was the difficult part.

Devlin continued walking unseen through the crowd, and was gratified to see that although the people were completely unaware of his presence, their shadows knelt down in respect as he passed them by.

He was on a collision course with a nun, but he didn't alter his stride. She passed right through him, and it sent a shiver down her spine. Disturbed by the experience, she crossed herself and clutched at the crucifix dangling from her rosary, even as her shadow knelt down beside her and bowed its head to Devlin.

He trotted up the thirty-nine steps – three sets of thirteen, his favorite number – and momentarily slowed his pace to glance up at the colonnaded façade. The Catholic grandeur of the place towered over him as if it were asserting itself to be some sort of timeless, immutable giant. He spit contemptuously on the paving stones and the granite sizzled, startling a flock of pigeons.

Devlin passed through the Maderno façade and into the portico, approaching the central pair of enormous bronze doors. Bernini's statue of Constantine was off to his right, at the north end of the front porch. That was one thing Devlin was going to have fixed. While it was nicely done, Bernini had gotten Constantine's face all wrong.

The Filarete doors had been salvaged from the original basilica. Bernini had done a better job on the *bas-relief* bronze panels, Devlin thought; he'd keep them as they were. The Borghese family shield was featured in the *bas-relief* of the portico ceiling above his head. Pope Peter V, Cardinal Scipio Borghese's uncle, had made sure their family stamp was on the building when the portico was added to the structure in 1612. Devlin found it amusing, particularly since their descendant Nano was such a dunce.

The doors were closed now, it being sunset, and two Swiss Guards stood at attention flanking them. Devlin passed under Bishop Nano's ancestral family shield and stepped through the bronze doors as if they weren't even there. The guards didn't see him, of course, but they felt a sudden cold breeze that made them shudder.

Inside the vaulted nave, Devlin glanced at Michelangelo's Pieta in passing, in the corner off to his right, protected by a bulletproof panel after a crazy geologist went after it with his hammer. The statue could stay, too, he thought, but the shield has got to go. No one would dare lay a hand on it when he became the landlord.

Overall, Devlin liked the various depictions of Christ's suffering and death. They comforted him, but not for the usual reasons. It was a long walk up the nave to the right transept, on the north side of the altar and St. Peter's tomb. Votive candles in the side chapels snuffed out as Devlin passed up the center aisle. The parishioners in the chapels were suddenly in darkness, and fumbled for matches. Puzzled nuns scurried to help them.

The angels in the frescos and the oversized statuary shed tears of blood as Devlin passed below them, and the air seemed to move away from him as he walked. He turned into the transept and approached the confessional booths. On the crucifix behind him, the enormous figurine of Jesus shed tears of blood as well. Devlin blew Him a kiss.

Mahogany confessional booths bracketed the three altars of the north transept. The altars had been built to commemorate Saint Wenceslas, Saint Erasmus, and Saints Processus and Martinian, the two men who were Saint Peter's jailers before he helped them see the light. The booths themselves were stand-alone affairs, with separate doors for the priest and the penitent to enter, and engage in the holy sacrament with a reasonable expectation of privacy. To the uninformed, the booths could have easily been mistaken for extravagantly appointed duplex outhouses. Devlin passed through the penitent's door of the last booth on the left and the varnish crinkled in response.

He sat down on the hardwood stool and a moment later, he heard the confessor's door open. Someone entered the other compartment and quietly closed the door behind them.

Devlin took the parchment invitation out of the pocket of his black greatcoat and slipped it under the screen. A moment passed, then the panel in the priest's compartment that covered the screen was slid to one side.

Cardinal Jacob Molinari was in his seventies now. The long years and the ongoing stress had conspired to take their toll on him, but the light in his eyes was still strong. And yet, for all the praying that he did and all the sacraments he performed, he no longer considered himself a man of faith. It was a sentiment he abandoned many years ago.

Instead, he was among the lucky few in the history of Christendom – or Judaism, for that matter – who had ever had a direct and ongoing long-term confrontation with the work of the Devil himself. Molinari's strength came from his knowledge of the circumstances in which he and his adopted Church were mired. His life's work in the service of God had made him intimately aware of the awesome forces engaged in the struggle between heaven and hell, and the fragile nature of every life that hung in the balance. Watching over the Child had become central to that struggle. The vestments and the rituals, the form and the practice of doctrine, were all a distant second to that one paramount concern.

For Molinari, faith had nothing to do with how he conducted his life, and neither did scripture, particularly the arcane arguments over the Old versus the New Testament. It was all, ultimately, about God. The details were simply that, and no more. What motivated him was certainty. He knew precisely what he was up against; it wasn't a matter of belief or mystical speculation. It was entirely real to him, a matter of objective fact, and now it had come to pay him a visit, sitting a mere three feet away on the other side of a thin wicker screen in the most sacred house of God.

He made the sign of the cross before he spoke. "I'm sorry I'm late," he said to Devlin with unfailing courtesy. "I had to find a way to slip in here unnoticed."

Devlin had no interest engaging in small talk, and got right to the point. "I've grown tired of your games, you devious bastard! Once a Jew, always a Jew."

Molinari drew a patient, silent breath and crossed himself again.

"All these years," Devlin scowled, "and you still haven't been able to get a straight answer out of them?"

Molinari chose his words carefully. He knew he was walking a tightrope; he had been doing it for over thirty years. "I can only tell you the truth that is revealed to me –"

"Don't lecture me about *truth!*" Devlin growled, cutting him off. The battle that was perpetually raging in Devlin's soul erupted, and as he struggled to regain control his transformation into a calm and coolly smirking Lucifer was clearly visible through the privacy screen.

Molinari mumbled a silent prayer, moving his lips out of habit as the Latin tripped off his tongue. When he felt strong enough to continue, he took a deferential tone to feed the Devil's pride.

"The Rosicrucians are a close-knit group, my Lord. I've done all I could."

The change came again and Devlin returned, bristling with anger and impatient with yet another excuse. Molinari shivered as he watched, and icy stabs of fear shot into him from all directions. His heart started pounding in his chest, and he had to strain to hear over the thumping in his eardrums.

"You live right down the street from where they eat and shit!" Devlin hissed at him. He frowned at Molinari's outline, a diffuse shadow on the other side of the privacy screen. "They *are* still in Rome, aren't they?"

Molinari nodded, although he knew that Devlin might not be able to see the gesture in the confessional's gloom.

"Yes. They've always been here."

But Devlin was suspicious. "And you still haven't cozied up to them, after all this time?"

"They don't cozy, my Lord. We have philosophical differences."

"As do we, Cardinal Molinari."

Devlin took one of his cigarettes out of his greatcoat pocket and blew on the tip to light it. He took a deep drag and exhaled. The smoke drifted through the wicker screen.

Molinari coughed and closed his eyes to try blocking it out, but it was no use. The smoke instantly stung his eyes and irritated his lungs, and imparted no advantage to him the way that it did to Devlin. Devlin had absorbed whatever benefit the smoke could deliver before he exhaled.

When it entered Molinari's nostrils, the smoke from the Tree of Knowledge had a much different effect on him. He suddenly became troubled by the sobering realization that he could never unsee what he had seen, and could never unlearn what he had learned. Rather than being buoyed by the insight, the smoke brought it to light as the awful truth. It was as if a harsh search beam had flooded into him, and chased away whatever soft shadows remained in his mental landscape. There was no longer any place to hide, even when his eyes were closed. Whatever knowledge he gained from it was a cold comfort to him.

"I want the last name," Devlin demanded. "That much you're certain of? There's just one more?"

Molinari opened his eyes and nodded, exhausted by the ordeal. "Yes, that much I've learned," he told Devlin. "And forgive me, but it took decades to even learn that much."

Devlin took another drag and exhaled through his nostrils, filling both sides of the confessional booth with smoke. "I'm not the forgiving type," he reminded Molinari.

As the smoke billowed through the screen, Molinari had a stark vision of looking into the Abyss. He lived the last three decades of his life knowing it was there, but now the smoke deprived him of the ability to block it out. It was crystal-clear in his mind now, yawning open before him, and he could no longer look away.

"The time draws close," he whispered, more to himself than to Devlin.

"Don't remind me," Devlin told him.

There was something that had been puzzling Molinari for a long time now. It came unbidden to the front of his mind, and found its way to the tip of his tongue before he could stop himself. Perhaps it was the smoke that was speaking.

"Tell me, why did you kill the others?" he blurted out.

Devlin sneered at the cardinal's shadow behind the screen. The man had become bold in his old age. Perhaps it was because he knew the game was over, and that there was nothing left for him to lose.

"I didn't kill them, I murdered them. There's a difference." Devlin explained, and Lucifer surfaced to contribute a salient point. "'Thou Shalt Not Kill' needs a re-write," he told Molinari. "It's the thought that counts. Make a note."

Molinari watched breathlessly as Devlin returned and sighed in annoyance. "The rules of the game are, I can't *murder* The One," Devlin reminded him. "I can't harm Him or stop Him. I can't even make Him harm Himself. I can only lead Him astray. But first, I have to find Him. So murder was a simple process of elimination – if they die, they're not The One. Sort of like dunking a witch, only more fun."

He sat up on the penitent's stool and withdrew the crucifix dagger from his waistband. "And even if I lose, I can still kill Him with *this!*"

He held it against the screen for Molinari to see. He knew that Molinari would recognize it; the cardinal had dispatched Simone to New Orleans to give it to Nano only a week before.

Molinari indeed recognized the weapon. He bowed his head to avert his eyes, and crossed himself. Devlin could see enough through the privacy screen to realize what he was doing, and sneered at him.

"Stop doing that! It's pathetic."

Molinari kept his head bowed, and placed his hands in his lap, folding them in prayer. But before he could stop himself, he challenged Devlin with another question.

"Why are you so confident you will win this bet, my Lord?"

Molinari was surprised by his own effrontery, but there was no turning back now. He knew that the smoke was having an effect on him, and yet he knew that he wasn't hallucinating. He also knew that he had no way of predicting exactly where it would lead. All the sense that he could make out of it was that he could no longer ignore his own thoughts. They were coming to the fore and he couldn't leave them be.

Perversely, Devlin actually felt like answering the man's questions, despite the aggravation. It roused his sense of superiority to be challenged by a mere mortal. He tucked the crucifix dagger back in his waistband and grinned.

"Because what human have you ever encountered who would willingly sacrifice his own life for a complete stranger, without any guarantee of an eternal reward?"

Molinari didn't expect that he would gain anything by arguing with the Devil, but he couldn't let that go unchallenged. "I think you underestimate the nature of —"

"I underestimate *nothing!*" Devlin hissed at him.

It was high time the wool was pulled from Molinari's eyes. Devlin loathed the entire hodgepodge of irrational, self-aggrandizing fairy tales that these humans, particularly the Christians, had blinded themselves with. The worst fairy tale of all was their arrogant presumption that God had created them in His own image, when the truth of the matter was precisely the reverse. Man had created God in his own image, and Devlin saw that as an insult to God. As a former Jew, Molinari should have known better, and that angered Devlin even more.

"Your world, this world, is based on a *lie!*" Devlin growled. "Think it through! A husk of a man, walking around saving people. He's made out to be a hero, and for what? For taking a beating for a couple of days, knowing he's got the grand prize waiting for him. Your precious Jesus was no hero."

Molinari was shaken by the blasphemy uttered within the very bowels of the Mother Church, within sight of the Papal altar and the tomb of St. Peter himself. His strength was failing, but he knew that the fate of world depended on him, just as it had for over thirty years. He had to make it to the end of this unholy rendezvous in one piece; he could collapse after that. He closed his eyes in prayer.

"Our Father who art in heaven — "

"*Your* father, not mine!" Devlin snapped. "He didn't raise me, he just turned me loose."

Molinari finished the prayer in silence and crossed himself. He found that it gave him the strength he needed. He had come this far and had done all that he could. He had long ago resigned himself to the path he had chosen. From this moment forward, as it was with every moment gone by, it was in God's hands.

He looked through the ventilation slats of his door, out to the great basilica. It was dusk and the lights had been turned on, augmented by a vast array of candles. As it always did, the sheer beauty of the house of God took his breath away.

"How can you say that this is all based on a lie?"

Devlin cracked a humorless smile. "Because it is. You hypocrites praise His divinity, but isn't it true that divinity is only achieved through completely unselfish means?"

"Yes it is, but —"

"Your Savior just won the big lottery, that's all. And all he had to do was get nailed to the cross to claim his prize."

He took a final drag from his cigarette and put it out on his tongue. It sizzled, giving off a tiny blossom of crimson flame. He liked the taste, and swallowed it whole.

"But *this* time around," he continued, "it's a level playing field. Not only is your Chosen One a mere mortal, with no knowledge of His own divinity, but deep down He's also an unbeliever, no matter what He pretends to be."

Molinari looked down at his rosary. The crucifix glinted in the dim light of the confessional. He touched it with his thumb and took measured breaths, listening to the Devil himself whispering in his ear in the house of God.

"*This* time around, He's just a man. And a man isn't going to sacrifice himself without the promise of an eternal reward. Even a terrorist isn't that stupid."

Molinari was utterly dismayed to find himself agreeing with Devlin's argument. He searched his soul in vain, looking for the means to rebut the logic, but the harsh light of knowledge brought on by the smoke from Devlin's cigarette revealed the truth to him, and as much as he wanted to he couldn't turn away.

Devlin was right.

"Then the crucifixion will have been in vain..." Molinari mumbled, coming to the obvious conclusion.

Devlin sat up, sensing the change in Molinari's voice, and he nodded. The old man finally understood.

"When *I* win, there *is* no crucifixion," Devlin told him. "There *is* no blood sacrifice to end all blood sacrifices. There *is* no 'Blessed One.' There's only *me.*"

Molinari hung his head and gazed at his wrinkled hands folded in prayer on his lap, his rosary laced between arthritic fingers. One hand had been hanging on to the other, but in his despair even his strength to do that was leaving him. He watched his fingers unravel and the rosary slip to the floor. His empty hands folded in upon themselves, grasping thin air.

"So be it," he whispered.

Devlin smiled. He had finally filled the cardinal with the proper dose of despair. The man would be a compliant minion from now on.

"I have a name for you, my Lord," Molinari said in a thick voice.

"The last one?" Devlin asked.

"I believe so," Molinari sighed. "We finally have the weapon that pierced Christ."

Devlin nodded, a smile playing on his lips. He was fondling the weapon, his fingers tingling in anticipation.

"Tell me the name, Cardinal."

Molinari rested his elbow on the little shelf below the wicker screen, and held his forehead in his hand. Devlin laced his fingers together as if he were praying, and leaned close. They looked exactly like a penitent and his confessor.

Molinari whispered something. Devlin's feral eyes glowed, and he nodded his head.

CHAPTER EIGHTEEN

The American Airlines 737 approached the island of Haiti from out of the northwest at an altitude of 31,000 feet and began its initial descent through a clear tropical sky. Eden was blessed to have a window seat, and eagerly gazed at the expanse of emerald mountains below as the aircraft skirted the northern coast of the island. His breath caught in his throat and his pulse quickened. Photographs didn't do the island justice. It was one of the most startlingly beautiful vistas he had ever seen.

Somewhere along the miles of beach far below Christopher Columbus first set foot in the New World, claiming the land for Spain and for the greater glory of God. The Italian-born adventurer caught Queen Isabella of Spain in an expansive mood just a few months before, on the same day she finally expelled the Muslim Moors from her Catholic country. He pitched his globetrotting scheme to her, and she took him up on it. Spain hungered for the spices of India, half a world away, and the only land route at the time was through the Muslim Middle East. Columbus boldly proposed to travel to the spice markets of the east by sailing west.

Thinking he had reached India, he called the local Taino natives "Indians" and the name stuck. The Tainos had migrated there from South America centuries before. The name they called themselves meant "the men of the good" and they called their island *Ayiti*, the land of high mountains. Columbus could have cared less, and called it Hispaniola, or "Little Spain."

In the span of one year his expeditionary force enslaved all four million Tainos on the island, compelling them to mine for gold. Within the first decade of colonial rule, over three and a half million Tainos succumbed to overwork, systemized massacres, and a variety of barnyard diseases from which the Europeans had built an immunity, through centuries of domesticating their farm animals.

As the airliner banked to begin its final approach, Eden cinched his seatbelt and finished his coffee, all the while looking out the window. Details on the ground were becoming more distinct with each passing second. He had done a bit of reading about his new posting, and his head was spinning now from the rush of history that came flooding back to him, as they descended toward Toussaint L'Ouverture International Airport. It was over 500 years since Western man first set foot on the island, he mused, and it still hasn't recovered from the shock.

In 1505, a Catholic priest took sympathy on the few miserable Tainos who were still alive, and lobbied Spain to send African slaves to maintain the island's meager gold production. They were stronger and better workers, they were suited to the tropical climate, more receptive to Christianity, and fewer of them died of melancholy.

The gold mining continued with renewed vigor, and soon a new sugarcane industry was built with the imported labor. But for all the sweat and blood expended, it soon became clear that there just wasn't all that much gold to be found in western Hispaniola. And Spain was mostly interested in gold.

They turned their attention to Mexico and South America, and as they did the French took a keen interest in the area's agricultural potential. As Spain abandoned the western part of the island, the French moved in and started calling it Saint-Domingue, to distinguish it from Santo Domingo, the eastern part of the island that was still held by the Spanish.

The French brought in more African slaves, and over the course of 150 years they built little Saint-Domingue into the richest colony on earth, producing sugarcane, tobacco and half the world's coffee. The place was a gold mine.

By the late 1700s there were over 500,000 slaves but only 20,000 whites and 40,000 mulattos, and democracy was in the air. The United States to the north had just won their independence from Protestant England. Catholic France, America's ally and England's enemy, was roiling with revolutionary fever, championing the ideals of liberty, equality, and fraternity. But when their black slaves on their Caribbean plantation had the audacity to take the home country at their word, all hell broke loose in France's prized colony.

Napoleon wanted to hold onto his colony any way he could. He was at war with Britain and Saint-Domingue was producing as much income for France as the entire thirteen colonies in North America had ever produced for the British. England lost their cash cow in the American Revolution, and it seemed that France was about to lose theirs. Napoleon knew that without the cash flow coming from Saint-Domingue, his dream of global empire was doomed.

The stewardess announced in French and then in English that everyone should fold up their trays and return their seats to the upright position. Eden complied and planted his feet firmly on the carpet, to brace himself in case they had a rough landing. He knew he was in God's hands, but on the other hand flying always made him nervous. Still, he kept a look out his window, taking in every detail that he could. Now that he was seeing the beauty of the land for the first time, he almost regretted his research. It would have been wonderful just to see the island as a place of beauty, without the weight of its troubled past blanketing the verdant hillsides.

When Napoleon's expeditionary forces lost Saint-Domingue in 1804, the freemen renamed their new country Haiti to honor the Tainos' original name for the land. The Tainos had been enslaved and decimated by the white man just as they had been. The former black slaves were rightly proud of what they accomplished. They had thrown off a mighty global power commanded by one of the greatest generals of all time, and formed the first black republic in the history of the world.

While imperial France was debating its next move, thousands of Haitian freemen poured into New Orleans to help the locals fight the French there, making matters worse for imperial France. With Haiti lost, Napoleon no longer had the funds to control his vast holdings on the American continent. Plus, he sorely needed cash to fight the English. President Thomas Jefferson's Louisiana Purchase from France instantly doubled the size of the United States. Many of the free Haitians who had come to New Orleans stayed there and became free Americans.

Although their native Haiti had been liberated, the tiny country's struggle had only just begun. And even though Haitian freemen helped defeat the French in Louisiana, America refused to recognize their newly independent black neighbors to the south – doing so might give their own slaves some dangerous ideas.

As the new Haitian government was trying to get its bearings, the few white landowners who remained were secretly lobbying France to retake their former colony. But France had a better idea. In 1825, it sent a dozen warships bristling with 500 cannon and extorted a "reparations" debt of 150 million francs – ten times the selling price of the Louisiana Purchase.

To prevent their re-enslavement, Haiti took on the obligation, even though paying it off would cripple their economy for nearly a century. The tiny populace of white and mulatto landowners was largely unaffected; it was the free workingman who was doomed to decades of poverty by paying taxes to service the debt. The elite who cut the deal with France had seen to that.

As the flaps came down and the nose came up, the 737 glided over a rusty carpet of corrugated tin roofs. *Citie Soliel* was the only real slum in Haiti, but the international press always went out of its way to feature it in their stories. Eden watched the hovels pass under the wing, less than a thousand feet below him and a world away.

And the rest of the world wondered why Haiti was so poor, he thought to himself as the wheels touched down. *All they had to do was ask France. Or any Haitian.*

The engines reversed to brake the plane, and it shuddered and bucked until it finally settled down to a leisurely taxi speed. As they turned toward the terminal, Eden could see that a *kompa* band and a throng of people had assembled to welcome the arrivals. The cordiality of people never failed to humble him.

The jetliner rolled to a delicate stop. As the engines shut down, a ground crew wheeled a rollaway staircase up to the side door, and chocked the wheels as the bumper pressed tight against the plane's aluminum skin. Just beyond the base of the stairs was the end of a long, spotless red carpet.

The throng of cheering locals had been waiting for more than an hour, and now that the plane had finally arrived they clapped and swayed to the *kompa* music. The crowd was enthusiastic and a sense of hope filled the air. They waved homemade signs and banners written in French Creole, welcoming the new arrivals to their island home.

A motorcade of three G550 Mercedes SUVs, the center one a stretch limousine, was flanked by a squad of Haitian Police on BMW motorcycles. The convoy rolled up to the other end of the red carpet and stopped. The police got off their bikes and formed a perimeter around the buffed black limos. A burly member of the Haitian Secret Service got out of the front passenger seat of the stretch limo and stood ready by the back door, scanning the crowd and the assembled media for any sign of trouble.

Other agents got out of the front and rear limousines, glancing around and assessing the situation. When they were assured that

147

everything was in order, the lead agent nodded to the one standing ready at the president's limo. He opened the back door and snapped to attention.

President René Préval emerged from the back of the stretch G550, and a rousing cheer went up from the crowd. A distinguished gentleman in his sixties, President Préval smiled and waved to his citizens as he stood at the foot of the red carpet. Behind him, Monsieur Delatour, his Minister of Tourism, stepped out of the limo, a lean muscular man in his forties.

The Haitian Secret Service quickly formed a perimeter around the two men as the president waited patiently for the aircraft to empty out. The people he had come to greet would be deplaning last.

Dozens of Haitian citizens and tourists descended the staircase, getting their first taste of the warm, humid air. It rained that morning, and the tarmac had only just been dried by the sun. As each of them stepped off the stairs, the airport personnel waiting for them politely but firmly directed them toward the international terminal. Although the band played a welcoming tune, it was clear that the red carpet hadn't been rolled out for them.

The stream of passengers dwindled to a halt and as the last of them came down the stairs, a sense of anticipation rose in the crowd. They all looked up toward the open door and the band wrapped up the tune they were playing. Everyone waited, holding their signs and their banners and their musical instruments.

Bishop Adrian Lomani emerged from the passenger cabin with a group of five priests. Eden was among them. At the sight of the clergy the crowd came to life, cheering and waving their signs as the band launched into a rousing tune.

Lomani and his priests waved hello and descended the aluminum staircase. They were pleasantly stunned by the enthusiastic reception. As they came down the steps, Préval and Delatour approached them on the red carpet and the Secret Service formed a moving perimeter to flank them.

The bishop was the first one off the staircase. He led his priests along the red carpet to meet Préval and Minister halfway. As Préval and Lomani neared each other, their smiles widened as they reached out to shake each other's hand. The moment their hands clasped together, the crowd erupted in a new round of cheers, accompanied by a grand flourish from the *kompa* band and a flurry of photographer's flashes.

"Mr. President, it is an honor," Bishop Lomani enthused, and President Préval nodded his head. "The honor is mine, your Excellency."

The two men were genuinely glad to see each other, which was a refreshing change of pace for the President. There were so many times in the course of his duties when meeting with someone was simply that — a duty, and not a pleasure. He was thankful that Lomani and his priests had come to Haiti. The Church had long suffered from a checkered reputation on the island, and though much of it was deserved it was time to turn the page. This new enterprise had all the makings of a bona fide fresh start, and President Préval dearly wanted to see it succeed.

"We are eager to begin, Mr. President," Lomani told Préval.

"And we are thrilled to have you," Préval assured him, and then he gestured to the man standing at his side. "Our Minister of Tourism, Monsieur Delatour, has arranged a lovely place for your orphanage, one of our grandest old citadels in the northern highlands, far from the busy capitol. We hope it will garner good luck."

Lomani shook hands with Delatour. "Thank you, Monsieur Minister," he said with a smile.

"You're welcome, your Excellency."

The bishop turned to his associates and motioned for Eden to step forward. "President Préval, Monsieur Minister," Lomani said, "May I introduce Father Jean Paul Eden, from the archdiocese of New Orleans."

Eden bowed to President Préval. The President offered his hand, and Eden shook it. "I'm honored, Mr. President," Eden said.

"Welcome to Haiti, Father Eden. It's a pleasure to have you."

Eden bowed once again, and turned to Delatour as Lomani busied himself introducing the other priests to President Préval. Eden shook the Minister's hand and bowed his head.

"Monsieur Minister, a pleasure."

"You're the one who requested a tour?" Delatour asked the priest.

Eden nodded. "If it wouldn't be too much trouble, Monsieur..."

Nothing registered on Delatour's placid, neutral demeanor, and nothing whatsoever escaped his attention. Every nuance and inflection of each person's voice, every gesture and glance and expression, was duly recorded, digested, and filed away in his mind. Reading people was his job, and he did it exceedingly well. Evaluating what he read was a high art, something that verged on voodoo.

As he chatted with the priest, President Préval's cell phone rang. Préval smiled at Lomani and the priests that the bishop was introducing him to, and turned away to take the call.

"Monsieur La Croix," he said, greeting the caller in a quiet voice and then listening intently to what he had to say.

"Yes," Préval told him, and then La Croix said something that surprised him.

"She is?" Préval replied, and glanced at Eden. The young priest was smiling and conversing with Minister Delatour, absently fiddling with the crucifix on his rosary.

CHAPTER NINETEEN

Cardinal Molinari had no trouble finding the unmarked alley. Although it was his first visit to the jagged cobblestone corridor, he had known its exact location for the last three decades. It was one of the rare backstreets in the Eternal city that was still off the beaten path of all but the most determined tourists, a carefully preserved time capsule from the dawn of the Enlightenment and just a stone's throw from the Vatican.

Thirty years was a long time to conduct business with someone without any sort of direct contact. Molinari felt that it was time he paid his respects, particularly in light of recent events. There was much to discuss; things were coming to a head.

Medieval stucco walls towered three stories on either side of him, punctuated by casement windows underscored with gaily-painted flower-boxes. The French doors of the Juliet balconies on the upper floors were shut tight against the winter chill. Laundry flapped overhead in the occasional breeze, but it would take forever to dry in this weather. The alley was always in shadow, even in summer, so that moss grew freely on the cobblestones, undaunted by foot traffic, scooters, and bicycles.

A brace of wrought iron stanchions had been installed across the alley entrance to discourage vehicular traffic. Molinari stepped up on the sidewalk, steadying himself with his walking stick, and cautiously made his way along the narrow concrete ribbon. It was only slightly less cockeyed than the old cobblestones.

Once he rounded the first turn, the white noise of the city muted to where he could almost believe he just stepped back five centuries in time. There were no scooters or bicycles to spoil the illusion, and the early morning air was too chilly for the residents to open their doors and windows and reveal their TVs and microwaves. He had the alleyway to himself for the moment, and cherished each unhurried step into the Italy of his youth.

He rounded the second turn and paused, finally laying eyes on his destination. It was a massive structure at the dead end of the alleyway, an enormous cube five stories high, built of hand-hewn granite blocks and minimal ornamentation. Its small, inset windows were fortified by wrought-iron grillwork on the exterior and backed by thick interior oak shutters. Like the rest of the structures lining the alley, the building had no address or plaque. There was no need for either one; anybody who needed to know was well aware of what the place was and who resided there, and knew not to come calling unless they were specifically invited, which they never were.

Molinari stepped onto the worn marble stoop and tapped the silver cap of his walking stick on the oak door. The thick planks of the door were banded together with three wrought-iron straps. From the look of it, the door, like the rest of the structure, had been fabricated by hand at some time in the early Renaissance, if not before.

The peephole in the door opened and quickly closed again. Molinari drew a nervous breath and slowly let it out to calm his jitters. Behind the door, a heavy iron bolt was slid free. Deep within the thick granite wall beside the door, he could hear a chain clattering as a counter-weight moved. The door slowly swung open on its three greased wrought-iron hinges.

There was no one standing on the marble floor inside to greet him, but it was clear that he was being invited to enter. Molinari crossed the threshold and the door closed behind him with a quiet thud.

Granite dust shook loose from the doorframe above, drifting down to the intricate brass inlay of the marble stoop. The handiwork there depicted the seal of the Knights of the Rose Croix – a medieval knight sitting on a horse and bearing a shield that featured a large cross with a red rose at its juncture. The image was rimmed with the Latin words *Fraternitas Roseae Crucis*. Inlaid in an arc above the seal were three royal crowns.

The Fortress of the Three Crowns was not quite what Molinari expected, but once he was inside it began to make sense. Its strength and beauty was in its enduring simplicity. The knights of the Rose Croix took vows of poverty, chastity, piety, and obedience, and in contrast to the organization that Molinari worked for they apparently took their vows to heart. From what he could see, the building was entirely functional, both inside and out.

The floors were marble, made to last, and the walls were unadorned plaster, as was the ceiling. There was one piece of art in the large rectangular foyer, but Molinari doubted that it was there for aesthetic effect. It was an enormous painting on canvas, hung on an otherwise blank wall. Over three meters high and two meters wide, the oil depicted St. Michael the Archangel vanquishing Satan at the point of a spear by the edge of the Abyss. Offhand, Molinari guessed that the canvas had been painted by Michelangelo, or by one of his students.

The knight who let him in was dressed in a simple white satin mantle, bearing a large embroidered cross with its signature red rose on the front, and the same on the back. As the young man escorted Molinari across the broad expanse of white marble floor, the cardinal reflected that, centuries ago, a medieval German inquisitor had nearly extinguished this secret Masonic society. Pope Innocent III dispatched the dreaded Konrad von Marburg to eliminate the heretical Albegensians living in the Thuringian Forest near the ancient city of Hesse. But according to legend, a young boy by the name of Christian Rosenkreuz was rescued from the inquisitor's sword by the Albegensian monks of Langeudoc, who hid the lad away in their monastery.

Ah, those rascals from Languedoc, Molinari thought with a wry smile. The cardinal felt a kinship with them that reached across the centuries. The heretical monks of Languedoc had kept more than the fabled bloodline of Christ in their safekeeping. They shepherded St. Peter's watchdogs into existence as well, for it was the young Christian Rosenkreuz, whose entire family had been executed by a Papal Inquisitor, who began the Rose Croix.

Molinairi glanced around at the cavernous vestibule. The Rose Croix had been able to keep the Shadow Vatican in continuous operation just around the corner from St. Peter's for over five hundred years. Given the awesome power of the Mother Church, it was a remarkable accomplishment.

The young knight brought Cardinal Molinari to a pair of oak doors set in the wall opposite the entry. The doors were similar in style and construction to the front door and were flanked by a pair of armed Rose Croix guards. They wore a full set of body armor under their white satin mantles and held their assault rifles at the ready, trigger fingers poised.

Molinari knew they weren't standing there for decoration. He worked around the Swiss Guards at the Vatican for over fifteen years, and had visited several embassies and government buildings in the course of his duties, with ample opportunity to see a variety of armed guards flanking any number of doorways. But these guards actually gave him pause. For one thing, they didn't stare straight ahead like palace ornaments; they looked him right in the eye as he approached. He had no doubt that if he acted suspicious in any way, he would be in mortal jeopardy.

The escorting knight swiped a card in a security panel set in the wall, and then held his palm against the black glass screen. A set of lasers behind the screen scanned his print. As a last measure, he positioned his right eye before a lens in the panel.

Once his retinal scan was crosschecked against his palm print and ID card, something mechanical clicked inside the door latch. It was followed by the muffled sounds of a chorus of steel mechanisms smoothly working in concert, but Molinari couldn't tell where the sound was coming from or what it was. The busyness concluded with a quiet *thunk,* and the pair of ancient oak doors whispered open.

Except they weren't oak doors at all. The burnished wood and the wrought-iron straps were a decorative veneer that cloaked a massive pair of vault doors silently operated by hydraulics. The edge of each door showed the butt ends of a dozen retracted stainless steel bolts that aligned with holes in the surrounding doorframe and threshold. Beyond the open doors lay a vast, dimly lit room.

The escort turned to Molinari, and with a deferential nod he gestured for the cardinal to enter the room alone. Molinari complied, and the doors whispered closed behind him. He heard the bolts smoothly slide back into their holes, and with a final *thunk* he was sealed inside.

The rotunda was twenty meters across with walls three meters high and capped with a domed ceiling. The points of the compass were inlaid with brass in the white marble floor. A pair of identical oak and wrought iron doors was positioned directly opposite from where Molinari stood in the circular room. According to the floor compass, the far set of doors lay to the east.

Two black marble pedestals occupied the center of the otherwise empty rotunda. One pedestal was tall and slim, about the height of a man's eye, and set closer to the western doors where Molinari stood. The other pedestal was lower, about a meter high and a meter in diameter. It sat in the precise center of the room.

A small crystal pyramid was on display atop the tall pedestal, discreetly ringed by security lasers. Three ancient royal crowns of gold were displayed atop the low pedestal. They rested on a bed of crushed purple velvet and were protected by a thick crystal dome.

Molinari's eyes roved the walls, and gazed up at the domed ceiling. Every surface was covered with frescos done in the Renaissance style, indirectly lit by hundreds of low-voltage lights arrayed behind a simple crown molding that rimmed the entire room.

The ceiling was a depiction of a cloudless night sky. Individual fiber optic threads were buried in the plaster. Their twinkling ends depicted thousands of stars, dim and bright and of various hues. The constellations were overlaid with representations of the gods of the Zodiac, arranged in the twelve houses and aligned with the compass on the floor.

The fresco on the curved left wall told the story of Evolution, from the primordial soup through the dinosaurs to the primates and the rise of Man. The fresco on the right wall told the Bible story of the Three Kings seeking the Christ Child. One of the Kings was sighting the Eastern Star through a crystal pyramid he held in the palm of his hand.

Molinari approached the crystal pyramid atop the tall black pedestal. At just about at eye level, it seemed to be inviting him to come closer and have a look. He couldn't resist. He steadied himself with his walking stick and leaned in close, careful not to touch the treasure and set off the security lasers. Squinting one eye closed, he peered into the pyramid with the other one, exactly like the King in the fresco.

The pyramid concentrated the soft ambient light of the rotunda into a single bright ray that traced a straight line through the three stars of Orion's belt in the ceiling above. The stream of guiding light shined down upon a manger depicted at the far end of the fresco.

Molinari stepped back from the pyramid and gazed in revelation at the Nativity scene. Centered above the far set of doors, the birth of the Christ Child was the ultimate destination of not only the Three Kings in the fresco on his right, but also of the procession of creatures crawling out of the primordial swamp in the fresco on his left.

In one transcendent moment, Molinari understood that the lesson of the rotunda lay in the harmony of science, mythology, and religion. There was no conflict, no contradiction, and no blasphemy, no repudiation of truth, denial of fact, or dependence on blind faith or superstition. All of it was resolved into a singularity of the Divine made manifest on Earth. Though he couldn't articulate it if he tried, it all made perfect sense to him now. It all made perfect sense. Breaking into a wry smile, he realized that more than anything, what it actually reminded him of was an athletic young rabbi splashing through a primordial swamp on Christmas morning, following a star in the east.

The doors below the Nativity scene were opened from within by a nurse in a white uniform pantsuit and a stethoscope draped around her neck. She smiled and beckoned for him to come. He was standing behind the pyramid, his eyes aglow. She had seen the look before. She understood.

Molinari returned her smile and walked around the two pedestals, the silver tip of his walking stick clicking on the marble floor with every other step. Behind her, he could see a sun-filled suite of rooms, all done in smooth plaster and white marble and trimmed in rose red.

In the far room, a large bed sat on a low dais facing an arc of French windows that overlooked a manicured garden. Peacocks wandered beneath an orange tree and among the rose bushes. Beyond the garden wall was a sweeping vista of Rome.

Sir Reynard was propped up on his pillows, resting comfortably on pure white sheets under a quilted down comforter. The old black gentleman was well over one hundred years old, but his mind was still sharp. Reynard smiled kindly at his visitor and bade him to come to his bedside.

Molinari was deeply honored to finally meet the Grand Master. He entered the bedroom and approached the bed with diffident steps, sinking to one knee upon the dais and steadying himself with his walking stick. He lifted Sir Reynard's lean, wrinkled hand and kissed the master's Rose Croix ring. A pure white diamond glinted in the center of a rose formed by tiny, faceted rubies.

"Sir Reynard," Molinari said with a respectful bow of his head.

Reynard grasped the cardinal's hand in thanks, and Molinari looked into his eyes. "So good of you to come, my friend. At long last."

CHAPTER TWENTY

Looking back, Molinari realized that he should have visited Sir Reynard years ago, but their association had been a deep secret from the start. The pattern of subterfuge they developed had solidified into a comfortable routine that kept both of them safe for more than three decades. So perhaps it was just as well.

The cardinal remained on his knee so that Reynard could see him without strain.

"Is he safe?" Reynard asked him.

"Yes," Molinari reported.

Sir Reynard briefly closed his eyes and nodded, relieved to hear the news.

Two muscular attendants in white satin mantles approached the bedside, while the nurse positioned a wheelchair at the edge of the dais. One of them helped Cardinal Molinari to stand, and he stepped off the dais, safely out of the way. The attendants drew back the comforter and sheet, and then lovingly lifted Sir Reynard from his bed and placed him gently in his wheelchair.

Molinari walked beside the chair as the nurse wheeled the Grand Master to a dining table by the windows. One attendant held out a chair for Molinari, and the other offered a steadying hand as the cardinal sat across from Reynard.

Once the two men were comfortable, the attendants poured them tea and set out scones and butter. As they worked, one of the peacocks came up to the window and displayed his tail fan. Sir Reynard clucked and cooed at his pet. The peacock was proud of the attention, and fluttered his fan to show off for the visitor. Molinari quietly clapped his hands and nodded in approval, until the peacock felt sufficiently admired and wandered away to eat the roses.

The men were amused at the display of pride and vanity and sipped their tea, getting a good look at each other at long last. The nurse and the two attendants retired to an adjacent room, leaving the door open. They could see Sir Reynard, but they couldn't overhear his conversation.

Reynard regarded the cardinal sitting across from him, and reflected on the irony of their lives. "We've watched each other grow old, without ever laying an eye on each other," he said with amusement.

Molinari smiled, and toasted him with his tea. Reynard returned the gesture, and they both took a careful sip.

"I had a visitor today," Molinari began. Reynard knew whom he was referring to.

"You seem exhausted," the Grand Master said, and Molinari nodded. "It must have been difficult."

Molinari nodded again. "It had to be done," was all he could think of saying.

"And where is he now?" Reynard asked after a pause. Molinari knew he wasn't referring to Devlin.

"Haiti," Molinari told him. "At a rural mission, well off the beaten track."

"Do you think the plan will work?"

Molinari tilted his head to one side and looked down to the table, then back to Reynard. "We'll know soon enough."

Reynard nodded. There was nothing more they could do at this point, other than wait and see. He smiled, changing the subject.

"And how are things at the Vatican?"

Molinari smiled back and blew a dizzy sigh. Reynard chuckled, and settled into his wheelchair for an earful of gossip.

When the anecdotes ran dry, their conversation turned to more serious matters, lasting through lunch and well into the afternoon. It had been a long and difficult journey, and there was still a ways to go; there was much to discuss.

Years before, Devlin had met in the dead of night with Elio Toaff, the chief rabbi of Rome, and his Privy Counsel. The nine rabbis spent the better part of a snowy November evening in Toaff's chambers at the Great Synagogue, listening in sober silence as Devlin laid out his version of the cosmos.

He told them what he said were the true stories of Adam and Eve and the Fall, and the Great War in Heaven, but after hours of chillingly persuasive argument and revelation, it all boiled down to this – the Christ Child would soon be born on the Louisiana bayou on Christmas morning, and if that were to happen, the world would be under His thumb and the Jews would suffer, worse than what Hitler put them through. It was all in the Book of Revelation.

The Jews killed Jesus once before, Devlin reminded them. They must do it again, or Judaism would soon be destroyed. Rabbi Toaff had no doubt that their visitor was truly the Devil himself, but on this last point the chief rabbi of Rome finally ran out of patience.

"You lie," Toaff told him in a clear, quiet voice. "The Romans killed Jesus, not the Jews. And you damn well know it."

Devlin was astonished that the man was being so bold and blunt with him. It was clear that the rabbi knew who he really was.

"Your lie is what nearly destroyed Judaism, and what you propose now would surely finish us off for good."

Devlin's face began to change as his true identity began to boil to the surface. The Privy Counsel waited breathlessly to be struck dead, but Toaff stared down the Devil himself and continued in the same measured voice.

"You may frighten us, but the return of Christ doesn't frighten us," he told Devlin, and then he cracked a dry smile. "Once a Jew, always a Jew."

Devlin was so furious that he nearly struck all of them blind. He wanted to see their eyes bleeding and he wanted to hear their screams, and he wanted to slowly squeeze the life out of each of them, one by one.

But no; he had something even better in mind. He would track down the Christ Child himself and kill Him with the one weapon that he could use to circumvent the terms of the bet he made with God. Then the world would be his, and Toaff and his Privy Counsel would all live to a ripe old age to regret their decision and see their mistake. Devlin had always planned to let Judaism remain intact after he won the world for his own. They loved God and they never bowed down to Christ, so they were his kind of people. But now, all bets were off. Except the one he made with God, of course. And that one he would win, by hook or by crook.

Devlin smiled back at Toaff, nodded his regal head, and disappeared in a theatrical flash of fire and smoke. Toaff and the Privy Counsel let out a collective, ragged sigh of relief. Several of them voiced the Hebrew prayers that they had been reciting in their heads during Devlin's visitation. They glanced at each other, and at Rabbi Toaff, all of them unsure of what to say. But Toaff was certain of one thing. If the Devil himself was scheming to kill the returned Christ, then saving the Child had just become the most important thing in all of Judaism.

Toaff turned to Rabbi Molinari, who sat motionless through the entire three hours, his eyes flicking from Devlin to Toaff, absorbing every detail.

"Have you ever been to America, Jacob?"

"Yes, Rabbi," Molinari said. "My aunt lives in upstate New York. We went every summer until I joined the *Col Moschin*."

Rabbi Toaff had always thanked God for sending him an Italian Special Forces commando. One of the more interesting rabbis he had ever met, and he had known hundreds over his long tenure as chief rabbi. Some of the Israelis from the IDF were scary characters, but Molinari always had something different, and that's why he was on the Privy Counsel. The fight in his eye was strictly in the service of God.

"You're flying to New Orleans tonight, Molinari. And tell Rabbi Simone to pack his bags, too. You'll need an assistant."

Molinari stood at once and almost saluted, but he just nodded and went out the chamber doors at a brisk stride. There wasn't a moment to lose.

In the ensuing years, as Molinari and Simone kept the Child safe from their new positions within the Catholic Church, Simone eventually got the rest of the story from Nano about that fateful night, and relayed it to Molinari when Nano was transferred to New Orleans and they were transferred to Rome.

When Devlin left the Great Synagogue, he went a mile up the Tiber River, crossed over to the west bank, and passed like a ghost through St. Peter's Square. He went silently up the thirty-nine steps, through the Filarete doors and directly into the bowels of the basilica. It was after midnight and the place was closed to parishioners, but Devlin didn't come to pray.

The crucifix dagger was in a vault under the papal throne, and he meant to retrieve it after all these centuries. If the Jews wouldn't kill the Lamb of God again, then he would do it himself, and woe betide the Privy Counsel for choosing to be on the losing side.

He shoved the throne aside and pried open the vault, but the dagger wasn't there.

"Can I help you?" came a voice from behind him. Devlin turned, scowling. He had been invisible up to this point, but moving the throne and opening the vault had given him away.

Cardinal Saul marveled as Devlin took solid form right in front of him. Devlin saw that the man wasn't bewildered or even afraid. *This one is different,* he thought to himself.

Saul smiled at the visitor; he knew who Devlin was. He had been expecting Devlin for the last few days. The Vatican astrologers had been poring over the musty volumes down in the Vatican Secret Archives for several weeks now. Devlin's visitation was clearly predicted, as was the birth of the Christ Child. It was all coming to pass, and the Cabal of Cardinals had no intentions of letting the opportunity get away from them. If the Devil could change the course of history, then so could they.

"We are already in your service, my Lord," Saul said to Devlin with a slight bow of his head. "Be at peace. The future is well in hand."

Devlin smiled, understanding his drift, and relaxed.

"Come, my Lord, let me introduce you to my associates. We've been eagerly awaiting your arrival."

Devlin smiled again, and motioned for Saul to show him the way. They walked side by side into the left trancept, heading for a private staircase that would take them into the sub-basement under the Sacristy.

In the broad sweep of history, there were very few people who had ever successfully fooled the Devil. Saul sensed that his name had just been added to the list. St. Peter was surely keeping track, but Saul doubted that his clever accomplishment would get him through the Pearly Gates. Not when it was balanced with sending the dagger to New Orleans. He wondered if Louisiana was really as pleasant as he heard it could be. It was snowing in Rome, an uncomfortable night for playing games with the devil. Perhaps Nano and his entourage were enjoying a bit of sunshine.

Molinari and Simone were whisked across town in Rabbi Toaff's limo to Fiumicino International, where a Learjet was being fueled for their flight to New Orleans. Molinari's father Gabriel was their chauffeur, a comfortable job that Molinari arranged for him after his mother Rebecca died and his father's business fell apart. Gabriel Molinari was a Hassidic Jew, proud of his son's chosen path after a successful career in the *Col Moschin*.

Molinari reasoned that there was a good chance he would never see his father again. Despite the stern glances of admonition from young Simone, Molinari told his father what just happened, and what they hoped to accomplish in New Orleans. The man nearly ran off the road, but Molinari knew he was tough enough to live with the truth. They both made it through World War II as Jews in Fascist Italy.

The next time Gabriel heard from his son, it was on a long-distance phone call from a Catholic seminary in New Orleans. The young Molinari expected an argument, but his father was surprisingly sanguine about his son's conversion, particularly in light of what he heard in the limo on the way to the airport.

Gabriel had always felt affection for Christians. They saved his life during the war, Along with his wife Rebecca and their young son, when Pope Pius XII was cooperating with the Fascists and the Nazis. Their Rosicrucian rescuers told Gabriel that their secret society was founded hundreds of years earlier by a young man who escaped from German executioners dispatched by the Vatican. An evil Pope in league with German butchers was a combination that was quite unsurprising to them. Their secret order had been working for over five hundred years to counteract what they saw as an apostate church that had long since turned away from the grace of God.

Gabriel was more surprised than anything else by his son's conversion, mostly because the Rosicrucians had schooled the impressionable lad through the entire war, slipping a strong streak of anti-Catholic Christianity into the curriculum whenever they could. But Gabriel reasoned that his son was a good man, he could handle himself, knew what he was doing, and that we all seek God in our own way.

He also knew that the Rosicrucians had their own means of deciphering whatever papers the Cabal of Cardinals held in the Secret Vatican Archives. In fact, the knights of the rose knew that the Church's books were actually derivative works. The original body of knowledge was locked in the vault below the Fortress of the Three Crowns. The collection of Greek and Latin texts was only one of the treasures they brought with them from Languedoc, where it had all been kept safe and dry through the Dark Ages, when monks were virtually the only people in Europe who even knew how to read.

The Rosicrucians had been using the ancient texts ever since in the course of their own esoteric studies, and were intimately familiar with them. They surely knew as well as the Cabal of Cardinals what the precise date, time, and location of the blessed event would be, as well as the name of the mother.

Over the crackling long-distance phone line, Gabriel advised his son to re-establish a link with their old friends of the rose cross. He would need it for the long road ahead.

The sun cast a golden afternoon light over the garden wall, and bathed the marble floor in a soft ambient luster. After hours of conversation, lunch, espresso, and more conversation, Sir Reynard's energy was finally beginning to flag. The nurse and attendants had been watching him all afternoon; it was time for the Master's nap.

They came out of the adjoining room, and one attendant went to the rotunda doors while the nurse and the other attendant approached the dining table. Reynard nodded to them, and Molinari knew that it was time to go.

The attendant lent a hand to Molinari as he got up from the table. His hips were stiff from sitting so long, and he was thankful for the assistance. The young knight went to join his partner by the doors, as the nurse got behind Reynard's wheelchair and rolled him back from the table.

She wheeled Reynard alongside Molinari, and the three of them crossed the wide marble floor at a leisurely pace. The attendants were opening the doors for Reynard and his guest to pass through. As they approached, Molinari took a moment to savor the canvas hung above the doors. It was Salvador Dali's "The Crucifixion of St. John of the Cross." He paused to admire the modern masterpiece.

"That is a truly excellent copy," he enthused.

Working at the Vatican gave him the opportunity to be surrounded by some of the finest art ever created, and Molinari had developed a discerning eye. Although he wasn't moved by Dali's modern pieces, the man's representational work had a timeless, magic touch. He suspected that Dali and da Vinci would have either been great friends, or jealous rivals. Or both.

Reynard was amused by his remark, and glanced up to him with a merry twinkle in his eye. "It's not a copy," he told the cardinal.

Molinari was stunned. He looked back to the canvas, his mouth agape, and stared at it for several precious seconds. When the two old men finally passed under the canvas and through the open doors into the rotunda, the attendants and the nurse swapped glances and allowed themselves a smile.

Molinari looked around the rotunda with fresh eyes. His gaze gravitated toward the fresco of the Three Kings, and stayed there as he and Reynard approached the center of the room.

Molinari paused in mid-step, frowning at the golden crowns depicted in the fresco, and turned to the low pedestal beside him. The crowns under the crystal dome were identical in every respect. He glanced at Reynard, who was watching him and smiling the entire time.

"And are these...?" Molinari asked him, and Reynard nodded, his smile growing. Molinari mirrored his nod, and gazed back at the fresco in wonder.

"The Three Kings are my ancestors," Reynard told him. "We Rosicrucians go back a long way. You folks are Johnny-come-lately."

Molinari was speechless, absorbing the image on the softly lit semi-circular wall. The perspective was cleverly rendered so that the tableaux seemed to embrace him, drawing him into the scene as Reynard elaborated for his guest.

"When Herod learned that the Three Kings were seeking the Christ Child, he asked them to bring word of where the boy was so that he could worship the child, too. But they didn't trust the man. So when Jesus was born, the Kings spirited the family into Egypt. We've been safeguarding Christ from the very beginning, my friend."

Molinari thought back to his theology teacher at the Rosicrucian monastery. The old man's mind used to wander during his lecture, and he kept diving into arcane details that no young child should be subjected to. One day he explained to little Jacob Molinari that Christian Rosenkreuz didn't actually start the Rosicrucians, that it was really a secret society he revived from ancient times. Christian Rosenkreuz probably wasn't even his real name; he probably just made it up and called himself that. A lot of people did that back then, and in any case the historical records were very sketchy. The origins of the Rosicrucians actually went all the way back to the time of Christ and the Essenes, and the Gnostic traditions of Egypt and the seeds of mystical knowledge that eventually grew into Islam.

Or something like that; Molinari couldn't remember most of the details. He was eight years old at the time and he could barely pay attention. To him, ancient history was just that, ancient history. And besides, he was a Jew. What did he care about Jesus Christ? He just pretended to listen because the Rosicrucians kept him and his parents safe from the Nazis. And they had plenty of food, which was hard to come by if you were a poor Jewish kid growing up in Fascist Italy.

He blinked, snapping out of the swirl of memory, and gazed once again at the three golden crowns displayed atop the pedestal.

"I know this has been an enormous sacrifice," Reynard said quietly. "An uncomfortable adjustment."

But Molinari shook his head. "No, not at all." He turned back to Reynard. "From the moment we learned the truth, we did whatever we had to do to keep close watch over the child, and stay one step ahead of the devil."

A dry grin creased Reynard's lips. "And one step ahead of the Church."

Molinari nodded and looked back to the three golden crowns, lost in troubled thought.

It pained Reynard to see him this way, and he cracked a playful grin to cheer him up. "We like our trinkets, too."

Molinari turned back and smiled at him, and Reynard returned it. They continued toward the vault doors, moving back through history between the two frescos.

The bolts inside the vault doors slid free and the doors whispered open. In the foyer beyond, the two guards stood ready just beyond the threshold, flanking the open doors. Their eyes were locked on the departing guest, leaving nothing to chance.

Cardinal Molinari carefully lowered himself to his knee and kissed Sir Reynard's ruby and diamond Rose Croix ring. As he got up and turned to go, Reynard tenderly touched his shoulder.

"One more thing," Reynard said, and Molinari turned back to him. Reynard smiled.

"We'd like to have the dagger back when this is over, if you don't mind. We'd feel better if it was in our safekeeping. I'm sure you understand."

Molinari smiled back, and bowed his head.

CHAPTER TWENTY-ONE

Zamba Boukman had his suspicions, and he doubted that this time would be any different from the others. Either Nano was a fool, or he was playing them for fools. Perhaps both. But thus far it had all been a colossal waste of time, and time was quickly running out. In any case, the man was doomed.

Zamba stood in the shadows of the alley across the street from the Church of the Rebirth, watching the cluster of weather-beaten buildings for any signs of life. He always thought it was best to know as much as they could before they acted, but in the final analysis it didn't matter that much to Devlin, and Zamba knew that it shouldn't have mattered that much to him, either. Not at this late date.

Besides, they were unstoppable and they both knew it. Zamba didn't mind making a mess; he just didn't like sloppy work. There was a difference. Power without control was simply force, and force wasn't much of anything to be proud of. Power, on the other hand, was golden. That was what he admired most about his master; the execution of power.

And the power of execution, he quipped darkly to himself as Devlin appeared beside him, smoking one of his infernal cigarettes. They stood together in silence for a moment, observing the church across the street.

"So this is The One?" Zamba asked him. "At long last?"

Devlin took a long, slow drag. His smoking had become a habit, and that concerned Zamba. It was a bad sign, a weakness. But he said nothing. Zamba kept his eyes on the church and his opinions to himself.

Devlin took another satisfying drag and exhaled through his nostrils. "Father Jean Paul... *Eden*," he breathed, savoring the last name, letting it roll off his tongue in a cloud of languid smoke.

"Fitting, isn't it?" Devlin asked, and they swapped delicious grins.

"Born on the bayou – at the Bayou Memorial Clinic – on Christmas morning in the year of our Lord, nineteen hundred and seventy-six," Devlin told him, and took another drag.

"Taken in by a Catholic orphanage, after mommy died in childbirth."

A flicker of doubt crossed Devlin's features. "Sounds too good to be true," he grumbled.

"And if he *is* The One?" Zamba asked.

Devlin looked at him and grinned, and then he flicked his cigarette away. It hissed in a puddle, flaming bloody crimson, and the butt vanished in a wisp of smoke.

They stepped into the street without looking, heading for the front doors of the old church across the way. A car swerved wildly to miss Zamba, and passed right through Devlin as if he weren't even there. The engine sputtered from a sudden loss of oxygen, and the entire electrical system shorted out.

Sister Nancy heard knocking on the big church door and turned her head, slightly aggravated. *The door was always open; why didn't they just come in?* She was kneeling in prayer before the statue of St. Anthony and a rack of votive candles that she lit for Father Eden. The knock made her lose her place on her rosary. As she fumbled with it and tried to recall where she was, her mind went to what she was praying about, rather than getting back to the act of prayer.

The person knocked again. Nancy glanced coolly at the doors, but thought it best to be polite. She crossed herself, and glanced up to the statue of St. Anthony.

"Pardon me," she said in a sardonic whisper, and carefully got up from the kneeler and made her way down the side aisle, feeling the circulation in her legs returning. At seventy-two, she prided herself in being able to kneel for an entire hour in prayer. She knew that pride was a sin, but it gave her a good excuse to get down on her knees and pray. Her Buddhist nun friend across town told her to see it as a karmic circle of sin, penance and redemption, and realize there was nothing vicious about it. Recalling the woman's whimsy made Nancy smile, so that by the time she got to the door, she was in a good mood.

She opened the big oak door, and looked up. An enormous, muscular black gentleman was standing alone on the front steps, smiling down at her. Sister Nancy smiled back.

Zamba was dressed in a conservative three-piece business suit instead of his usual Caribbean clothes. He said nothing, but he made the sign of the cross, indicating that he wanted to come in and pray.

He probably didn't speak English, Nancy thought, or perhaps he was mute. Those who can't speak tend to be shy; no wonder he knocked. She felt ashamed for her earlier annoyance, and opened the door wider to invite the gentleman inside.

CHAPTER TWENTY-TWO

When Mas saw the well-preserved 1976 Toyota Land Cruiser parked in the driveway, she knew she finally found the right house. She had been tooling along the back roads of Chantilly Flats for the better part of an hour, and had little to go on but her memory of the vehicle and the rumor that Peter Johnson was living somewhere on the outskirts of town in an unmarked house on a street with no name.

The house had seen better days, but then so had Chantilly Flats. The locals had taken to calling the place Chantilly Flattened, and the few hearty souls who remained were still cleaning things up bit by bit.

Mas rolled into the driveway and killed the engine, then got off the BMW and pulled it up on the stand. She removed her helmet, shook her hair out, and took a look around. The one-acre lots gave the folks in Chantilly Flats plenty of elbowroom. It was a place where you could keep a horse and some yard birds if you felt like it, and the next-door neighbors wouldn't raise a fuss if you did.

But that was then. Now there was hardly anyone left to raise a fuss about anything. Neighbors had become few and far between. The houses that were still standing were made of brick, and the occupants had more elbowroom than they knew what to do with.

Mas clipped her helmet to the bike, and took the brick walk to the front door. There used to be a screen door but she guessed that it must have blown away, along with most of the roof shingles. A large blue plastic tarp covered the roof above the porch, and flapped lazily in the breeze.

She knocked on the door and waited for a response, glancing around and peeking in the front window. She couldn't see much, due to the glare of sunshine on the smudged pane of glass. *The man should invest in a squeegee,* she thought idly, waiting for him to come to the door.

After a polite interim she knocked again, and listened for footsteps inside. When none came, she knocked a third time, much louder, but still shy of sounding like a storm trooper. She was fairly certain he was home, and unless he was dead asleep he'd know by now that someone was at the door.

"Agent Johnson? Sir? Please open up." There was no response. "I need to talk to you," she continued. "It's important."

Still, there was no response. Mas began debating whether or not she should leave, but she concluded that it was a long way out here and a long way back into town for nothing.

Maybe he's in the shower, she thought, and stepped off the porch to walk around the house for a listen.

The deadbolt clicked. She stopped in her tracks, turned around, and stepped back on the porch as the door cracked open a few inches. Peter Johnson peered out at her.

He was a large, slightly stooped man in his sixties, hawk-nosed, with a receding hairline and a furrowed brow. He had deep-set eyes that didn't quite match, but Mas couldn't put her finger on exactly why. He possessed a powerful gaze, but it was hobbled by a bad habit of flitting from one thing to another, as if he were an over-tired sentry at a forward base, harassed and surrounded by an elusive enemy. The man was a mess.

"Agent Johnson?" Mas inquired.

He flinched at her choice of words and shrank back, closing the door as he admonished her, "Don't call me that. I'm retired."

She jammed her motorcycle boot in the door like a traveling salesman. He stared down at her boot, and then his eyes darted back up to hers. He was more surprised than offended by the tactic. She cracked a disarming grin.

"I'm not, and I need your help. I'm Agent Christine Mas."

Johnson looked her up and down, and then looked past her to her bike in the driveway, then up and down the asphalt road. No one was around, and from what he could tell no one was peeking out their windows, either, although she was a sight to see. She was wearing a full set of leathers.

"Who sent you?" he demanded to know.

"I did. It's my day off."

He studied her eyes, and saw something. He nodded over and over. "It's happening, isn't it?"

"Sir?"

"It's getting to you," Johnson said. "*He's* getting to you. Isn't he?"

Johnson repeatedly nodded once again, a silent answer to his own question. In fact, he was nodding up a storm. Mas just rode it out, waiting for him to knock it off and start making sense.

"I know that look," he said. "I can still see it in the mirror, most days."

She started to speak, but he jabbed a finger in her face, scowling at her.

"Don't say it! Don't you *dare!* Not here! Not in my house! I don't want his name mentioned under my roof –"

The blue plastic tarp above their heads suddenly flapped in a fitful breeze. Mas stifled a grin, and Johnson scowled at her all over again. She pursed her lips, contrite.

"Yes, sir, I promise."

The house was dark and cluttered, with books stacked on the living room floor in disorganized piles. There was a collection of Bibles on the coffee table, along with a handful of esoteric works, among them *The Apocrypha*, *The Gnostic Texts*, and *The Aquarian Gospel of Jesus the Christ*. Other books scattered on the floor nearby delved into Satanism, black magic, various kinds of paganism, and heresy.

A volume on the subject of Bible codes lay open on the coffee table, beside a large-print Bible. A notepad and a clutch of pens were nearby. From the looks of things, Mas guessed that he was engaged in some sort of Bible study, sitting on the couch surrounded by an ad hoc library. She wondered if he found any peace from it. From the look in his eyes, it didn't seem so.

As they passed the coffee table on the way to the dining table off the kitchen, she caught a glance of a legal pad with a series of numbers carefully written on it, beside the large-print Bible that looked to be the centerpiece of his study space. A piece of notepaper dangled out of the Bible and served as a bookmark, with the number *1147* carefully written on it. The paper had been ripped from the dashboard notepad in his Land Cruiser. Mas didn't know that, but she did recognize the number. It was Fareed Aly's street address.

There were several framed pictures of saints hung on the walls and paneling. Votive candles lined the mantel and various other Christian knick-knacks were scattered about on the end tables, the TV, and the credenza. A crucifix with a dried palm frond tucked behind it was hung next to a lavishly framed painting of a haloed baby Jesus, bestowing a blessing on whoever laid eyes on the Child.

Mas took a seat at the dining table as Johnson poured them both a cup from the coffeemaker on the crowded kitchen counter. She looked around, keeping her expression neutral, and her eyes landed on an article thumbtacked to the side of the kitchen cabinet. It was yellowed, already five years old and counting. *FBI Special Agent Christine Mas Leads Branding Killer Case.*

Johnson sat across from her and handed her a mug of coffee. He gestured to the sugar and powdered cream on the table, but she waved it off. He dug a small bottle of eye drops out of his shirt pocket and dosed his left eye, blinking rapidly.

He put the eye drops away and then doctored his coffee, carefully portioning out the sugar and powdered cream like he was compounding a prescription. *It'll get cold before he's done,* she thought, and glanced around the room as he dialed in the magic ratio.

In contrast to the mess around the couch, there was a beautiful Christmas tree by the front window, still fresh and green and decorated with handcrafted ornaments. It would have made Martha Stewart proud. Mas allowed herself a ghost of a smile.

She turned back to him, and found that he was watching her as he stirred his coffee. "Looks like you made it through the storm," she said pleasantly.

He shrugged; he wasn't in the mood for chitchat. "I don't think the owners did," he grumbled, and sipped his coffee, fiddling with his shirt buttons.

"This isn't my place. I'm homesteading, I guess you could call it. It's safe here. When the Devil lays waste, he moves on. He never backtracks. That's one of his flaws. Arrogant self-confidence. You learn to hide in his wake, among the debris."

Mas diplomatically nodded, and sipped her black coffee. It was bitter and strong, and slightly scorched. She could see the pot and the coffeemaker behind him. They both needed a good scrubbing and a flush of white vinegar as well. Martha Stewart would not be amused.

"So how are you?" she asked him. "I mean, since you stopped working on... you know..."

He bristled, giving her a stern look over the rim of his coffee cup. "What does it matter? I am where I am, in here..." He pointed to his head, "...and here." He pointed to his heart, and then resumed fiddling with the button on his chest.

She noticed an old police scanner, sitting on the kitchen counter behind him. He could see where her eyes had drifted, and waited for her to say something.

"I saw you at the jump site the other day," she told him. "Been following the case?"

Johnson nodded and repeatedly sipped his coffee, shifting uncomfortably in his rickety chair.

"Why?" she probed. "It drove you..."

He shot a cold glance at her and she trailed off, realizing that she almost said the wrong thing. She looked around the room, thinking fast. "...out here," she finished lamely, but her foot was already in her mouth.

"Say it!" he insisted. "Go on. 'It drove me crazy,'" he coached her, almost mockingly, and she responded to the edge in his voice by looking right back at him.

"Why'd you walk away from the case?" she asked bluntly.

Instead of shrinking away, like he had from her other questions, Johnson looked her in the eye, and to her surprise she was the one who shifted uncomfortably. There was something about the man that she couldn't fathom, and it wasn't nuttiness. That was obviously a part of it, but something else was going on, too. Whatever it was, she felt as if he was suddenly controlling the conversation. The thing that disturbed her the most was that she couldn't quite spot when the tables turned. But they had.

"What made you want to be a Fed?" he asked her.

Before she realized what she was doing, she found herself telling him exactly what he wanted to hear. "My father was a cop," she mumbled, suddenly introspective. "He was killed right in front of me."

Mas was inwardly stunned. No one had ever gotten that out of her in their first conversation. She focused on her coffee cup on the table before her, but she could see his expression out of the corner of her eye. He seemed genuinely moved by her revelation.

"That must have been awful," he said quietly.

She nodded, pursing her lips as she felt her face flush despite herself. *This guy's good*, she thought, as the memory enveloped her and then swallowed her whole.

Officer Julian Mas was off-duty, driving around town in the family car with his kid when she had a sudden yen for a treat. Her exact words were, "Daddy, the A&W done flung a hankerin' on me." She was a charmer at the tender age of twelve, and he was a sucker for those big brown eyes. And Chrissy was a sucker for peanut butter malts.

It was just after lunch, with plenty of time until dinner, so he pulled into the A&W parking lot and stopped the car. He shut off the engine, but her favorite song was on the radio and she turned it back on to keep singing along. "Rock Lobster" would take forever to get through, plus she had to do the whole hold your nose and sink to the bottom of the sea routine, which was quite a trick to do in the front seat of a Buick, but somehow she would always manage. She sang loudly to him, and he got the message. He'd get the malt and she'd guard the car.

Julian got out and shrugged his jacket around him. It was early September, but it was already getting chilly. A frosty malt didn't make a lick of sense to him when it was below seventy, but it was warm in the car and he wasn't going to talk her out of it. Maybe he'd get a coffee while he was at it, he thought.

As he got out of the car, he slipped his service revolver out of the holster under his seat and tucked it behind his back. He felt naked without it, and it made less of a bulge there than riding on his hip or tucked in his waist. Besides, he didn't want to leave it in the car with Chrissy. He trusted her, but a gun was a gun and her mother would have a fit if she ever found out he'd left it in reach of their baby girl.

The song was over by the time he came back outside, with a coffee in one hand and her peanut butter malt in the other. She was already bored stiff, suffering through a long string of radio ads. He went around to her door, and she cranked down her window as he put his coffee on the roof. He handed her the malt, and she immediately sat back in her seat and got to work on it.

Julian was about to pick up his coffee from the roof of the car, when he caught something in his peripheral vision and turned around.

An enormous, muscular African-American man dressed in a colorful tropical outfit was by the Dumpster on the side of the building. A boy's dead body was slung over his shoulder like a sack of potatoes. The boy looked to be about twelve, the same age as Chrissy. Behind the man's massive form, Julian caught a glimpse of someone else dressed in a black greatcoat, disappearing behind the back of the A&W.

Zamba Boukman looked Julian Mas in the eye and smiled, and then dropped the boy's limp body into the Dumpster. Behind Julian, Chrissy was wondering why her father was still standing by her door with his back to her.

"HEY!" Julian bellowed.

Chrissy sat up in alarm, dropping her malt on the floor. Something was wrong, but she couldn't see what was happening. Her father's broad back was blocking her view, and he was making matters worse by pressing against her window, as if he were trying to shield her from danger. Which he was.

Zamba looked up in surprise at the would-be hero, and held his hand out like a cop directing traffic, silently warning Julian to back off. With no time to deal with the intruder, Zamba summoned his *loas* to swoop down on the man standing by the Buick.

Julian suddenly found himself pinned against the car. In an instant, the confrontation had catapulted him into another realm, and the ground rules no longer applied. Something lethal was pressing down on him, and he somehow knew that the strange man was the source of it. And he also knew that in the next few seconds one of them was going to die.

Julian reached around to the small of his back and pulled his service revolver out of his belt, in full view of his daughter sitting in the car behind him. In the half-second that he took to draw a bead on his target, he couldn't spare a breath to shout a warning to her. But he knew that just drawing his weapon would tell her that something bad was going down. She was a smart girl; she'd know what to do.

Zamba's chest absorbed three hollow-point rounds from Julian's .357 Ruger Speed Six, in a two-inch grouping just to the left of the lower part of his breastbone. At a distance of less than thirty feet, the man's heart should have exploded along with most of his left lung. The hydrostatic shock from the three fragmentation rounds should have punched a ragged red hole out the back of Zamba's ribcage the size of a soccer ball.

Instead, the three puncture wounds simply closed up and healed.

Zamba grinned at Julian, his arm still outstretched, his palm still facing the astonished cop. An instant later, the same three slugs slammed into Julian Mas in the exact same place; a perfect, bizarre boomerang.

In the car, Chrissy was already hunkered on the floor in front of the passenger seat, stunned from the ear-splitting sound of her father's gunfire just seconds before. Now, just inches above her head, he was slammed back against the passenger door window as the three silent rounds blew a hole through his back.

Blood and safety glass sprayed the inside of the car and showered down on her. She was too paralyzed by fear and horror to scream. She couldn't even move. She just looked up and watched in uncomprehending shock as her father wavered for a moment on his feet, and then slumped out of sight.

Sunlight poured in through the windowless door, where his wide shoulders and back had been shading her as she sat with her peanut butter malt just moments before. She was kneeling in the mess now, but that wasn't the chill she was feeling.

She grabbed the sill of the car door above her, oblivious to the shards of safety glass caught by the window trim, and pulled herself onto the seat, cautiously peering outside.

No one was there except for her father, motionless on the ground below.

Mas was staring into her coffee as her tears found their way down her cheeks from a pair of red, swollen eyes. She slowly shook her head, pursing her lips as she puzzled yet again over something that had been haunting her for most of her life.

"He just drew his gun and fired three rounds, just like that. No let the kid go, no you're under arrest, no Miranda, no nothing. Then he slammed up against the car, real hard, and then he just dropped. But by then, the perp was gone. I never saw him."

Johnson was blinking rapidly, moved by her story, but only his right eye was tearing up. He dabbed at it with a tissue, and then wiped the tears away from his other eye. Mas was having a hard time of it, but she forged ahead. "Ballistics said the three rounds they recovered from his chest were from his own gun. As near as they could figure, the perp took the gun and shot him."

She sneered, and peeked at Johnson. He had much the same reaction that she did. The official story didn't match what happened. Official stories seldom did.

"But I know what I saw," she insisted, "and I know what I heard. He fired those rounds, and *then* he slammed up against the car. And here's the kicker — the cops found a kid's body in the dumpster, next to the A&W. He was the fifth Branding victim."

Johnson nodded. "I remember that kid."

She nodded back, and some of the tension finally drained from her. She could tell that he believed her story. In fact, he was the only person who had ever taken her word for it, without a trace of skepticism, despite how utterly unbelievable it seemed. She felt she should thank him somehow, but she wasn't quite sure what to say or what to do, other than return the favor somehow.

The opportunity wasn't long in coming. "Do you believe in God?" he asked her.

She stifled a dry grin, and sipped her coffee to buy enough time to formulate a polite response.

"I guess," she replied with a shrug. *I should have known this was coming,* she thought.

184

"You gotta believe in something," she offered, and she peeked at him, allowing her grin to show. "Depends on what day of the week it is."

He chuckled, but not at her quip. It was her foolishness that he found amusing. "Spoken like a true secular progressive, Agent Mas."

She sat back in her chair and waited for the sermon, or whatever it was that he had to say. He propped his elbows on the table, coffee cup in hand, and leaned an inch closer to her. But he wasn't leaning into her so much as trying to reach her.

"I'm a Catholic, through and through. And you didn't answer me. Do you believe in God? Tell me."

She had been through this before, with fundamentalists and men of the cloth and even her own mother. Depending on who was asking the question, she either gave it serious consideration or short shrift, or she just kept things pleasant and hoped that the person would eventually change the channel. But Johnson was one of those who sincerely wanted to know. She figured she at least owed him the courtesy of an honest answer.

"I believe that there's more to this world than science can show us. And if you want to call it God, then I suppose that's as good a name as any. But whether He exists or not, you still gotta get up and go to work in the morning." She sipped her coffee and smiled. "Does that answer your question?"

Johnson didn't reply. Besides, she owed him more of a response than she gave him, and collected her thoughts to deliver her next point.

"There was a mass murder at that clinic and then the place got hit by a tornado, but the tornado didn't kill a soul."

From the pile of books he was studying, she knew he would place a lot of weight on the odd coincidence, and that was precisely what she was driving at.

"Was the massacre the wrath of God, or was the tornado some kind of miracle? Or does evil just touch down at random and skip over the lucky ones, like lightning?"

Johnson didn't have any answers for her, at least none that he could articulate. Her expression softened to ease him off the hook, and she could see he was thankful for it.

"You must have found something, Peter."

"It's not what I found," he told her quietly. "It's what found me."

She was confused by that, and a little frustrated. She had opened up to him and he wasn't returning the favor, he was being coy. They were both Feds, whether he had retired or not, and just like Marines there was no such thing as an ex-Fed. Despite his condition, whatever the hell it was, she expected more out of him. Perhaps she was being unreasonable, but that was just too damn bad. People were dying. How reasonable was that?

"*I believe in God, Agent Mas,*" he told her, as a prelude to saying something more. She nodded perfunctorily but other than that she didn't reply, hoping he would leave it alone. His beliefs were his to choose and she didn't want to debate the subject, but the man wasn't finished.

"And I believe that God needs all of us to pray for him," Johnson said, quietly finishing his statement.

"Excuse me?"

He suddenly became animated and lunged toward a book on the counter, grabbing it with both hands. It was a Bible. He turned back to her, leaning over the table.

"*We have to pray for Him!*" he urged her.

He was utterly sincere, and the anguish in his eyes was a painful thing to witness. She just looked at him, wondering if he really had gone crazy after all.

Mas straddled her idling BMW and slipped on her helmet. Johnson was peering out his front room window, his Bible in hand. He deliberately deadbolted the front door, his eyes locked on hers. She ignored him, glancing away as she placed a call on her iPhone.

Mark answered at once. "Detective Kaddouri, NOPD."

"Hey, it's me," she said.

"How'd it go?"

"Well, it went. South, mostly."

She could see Johnson in the rearview mirror next to her throttle as she goosed the gas. The engine quietly purred in response. Mas glanced in her mirror again.

Johnson was still watching her, but now he had the Bible tucked under his arm and his notepad and pen in hand. He watched her wrap up her call, then tuck her phone away and nudge her bike off the stand.

She rolled down the driveway, and as she paused to check both ways for traffic he jotted down her license plate number – *1184* – on his notepad, and went quickly to the couch.

He sat down before his big Bible on the coffee table, placing the Bible that was tucked under his arm onto the couch beside him. He opened the big Bible, his notepad in hand, and then opened his book on Bible codes and got to work.

CHAPTER
TWENTY-THREE

Devlin and Zamba walked down the center aisle of the Church of the Rebirth heading for the front doors, stepping around a large dark puddle on the tile floor. Zamba was dressed once again in his Caribbean clothes. The business suit had been his way of gaining Sister Nancy's trust, which he thought was particularly amusing. Everyone knows that men in business suits wreak more havoc than anyone else. His clothes were spotless and Devlin's were as well, but there was blood splattered everywhere.

"Who says torture doesn't work?" Devlin asked him.

Zamba cracked a dry smile in response. It was good to see his master's humor return. The last several minutes had seen to that, although when they started he was in no mood for levity. Not only had the violence been cathartic, but more importantly they were leaving with the knowledge they had come for. Zamba was certain of that; he noted that Devlin wasn't indulging himself with one of his cigarettes.

"Ironic, sending him to Haiti," Devlin remarked.

"Truly," Zamba murmured.

They stopped at the entry doors and turned back for a last look around. They were quite satisfied with their handiwork, although strictly speaking it wasn't essential to the larger task at hand. Except that after years of frustration, they now were so close to success that

Devlin felt the urge to vent his wrath and get it out of his system. In that sense, it was therapeutic.

He was happy again. He clapped his hands and a pair of sunglasses appeared, covering his eyes. Zamba grinned.

"See you in paradise," Devlin said, and disappeared in a theatrical poof of smoke. Zamba stepped outside and closed the doors behind him.

In the deathly quiet of the church, a steady trickle of blood dripped from the main chandelier, expanding the crimson puddle in the center aisle below. A human leg, torn from its socket, had been tossed up there.

The splash patterns of blood primarily emanated from the wide set of steps before the altar, where the dismembered corpses of four nuns lay in a gruesome pile. One of the bodies had been neatly decapitated. On a pedestal by the lectern, Sister Nancy's severed head sat on the silver collection plate.

CHAPTER
TWENTY-FOUR

Mas was taking a nap. It was a long ride back from Chantilly Flats into the city, and then the traffic was hell all the way to the Lower Ninth Ward. She plowed through some nasty puddles in the backcountry and had to sponge the bayou off her leathers when she got home. They were airing out on the back porch now, draped over the kitchen chairs.

It had been a warm, unusually dry day in the city, and the odor of mildew in her apartment was at a happy minimum. When she came home, a glorious sunset was washing her three oversized rooms in a soft tangerine light that filtered through the lace curtains. It was on days like this that the spacious master bedroom suite of the old house assumed the gracious charm that led her to fall in love with the low-rent hideaway in the first place.

She indulged herself with a hot bath, then lay down to cuddle up with Junior and promptly dozed off as the sun slipped behind the neighbor's roof. The Bull Terrier contentedly snoozed on the big four-poster bed beside his favorite person. He kept his enormous nose tucked under his front paws, as if he were self-conscious about it and didn't want anyone making fun of him while he was sleeping.

His torso suddenly twitched as if he was reacting to something in a dog dream. He buried his snout deeper underneath his paws and sighed to restore his tranquility, but it didn't work. He was feeling more and more uncomfortable, and he couldn't seem to shake it off.

The problem was that he wasn't reacting to something in his own dream; it was in his master's dream. Something was causing her to squirm around, and being pressed up beside her on the bed like he was, her agitation was disturbing his beauty sleep. Mas had been flinching intermittently for the last few minutes.

She did it once again, more violently this time, and it finally woke him up. He lifted his head to glance at her, and saw that her forehead was puckered in distress. Exquisitely attuned to her emotional state, he knew at once that something was wrong. Mas began to sweat, and he could smell the fear emanating from her body. He rolled onto his feet and stood on the bed, growing more concerned by the second as he watched her struggle with something deep inside her soul...

Mas clung to the railing, soaked in cold sweat. Her toes were cramped from balancing on the lip of the balcony, high above the crowd. She was desperately trying to save Fareed, hanging on with one hand as he dangled from her other hand. Thorrington was down there, watching silently and still in the noisy, jostling throng.

Her fingers slipped from the railing, but before she could scream she was grabbed from above by a man's firm grip. He pulled her to the safety of the balcony...

He was a priest, dressed in full vestments, a radiant light behind him so strong that Mas couldn't see his face. She averted her eyes, but as she turned from the light as Fareed slipped from her grasp. She held the priest's hand and watched Fareed fall, looking up to her in horror as her scream blended with his...

RRRINGGG!!! The sound of a cell phone seemed to issue from Fareed's open mouth. It was loud and abrupt, but there was no cell phone anywhere around. There was a cordless phone in the condo, lying on the carpet in the living room. The CSI guy was in there, carefully dusting it for prints.

RRINGGG!!! It was definitely a cell phone ringtone, but the CSI guy thought it was the cordless phone he was dusting. He got to his feet, and brought it out to the balcony, because Mas was the special agent on the case and she had to answer the phone, because if someone was calling then it must be for her. He stood beside the radiant priest and smiled at Mas, holding the phone out to her...

RRINGGG!!! Mas lurched awake, her heart pounding in her chest. Her iPhone was jangling on the nightstand. Junior was off the bed now, huddled in the corner and watching her, thoroughly spooked. His job was to protect her, but he didn't know how.

"It's okay, Junior. Mommy just had a bad dream."

He moved his tail once, in a tentative gesture of relief. Her voice was soothing, but he was still worried for her. She had an unseen enemy and he was powerless to help.

Mas picked up her phone, saw who it was, and took the call. "Hello?"

Kaddouri was sitting in his car outside, idling at the curb behind her motorcycle. His phone was pressed to his ear and he was peering out the window at her darkened upstairs apartment. It was dusk and there was no one out on the street. The few houses that were still occupied had some lights on, but the neighborhood was mostly in shadow.

He called her an hour earlier, but her bathwater was running and she didn't hear it, and she didn't check for messages before she lay down or she would have called him right back. But he didn't know that.

He wasn't sure what was up, but he had to get hold of her right away, so he drove over to her place. Before he got out to knock on the door, he decided to give her one more call, and after four rings she finally picked up. She usually picked up after one or two.

"I've been calling you. Are you all right?" he asked her.

"I was taking a nap. What's up?"

"There's been a massacre."

CHAPTER
TWENTY-FIVE

Mas and Kaddouri arrived in his shiny new Land Cruiser and rolled to a halt at the police cordon, down the block from the Church of the Rebirth. The street outside the church was choked with squad cars, EMS vehicles, and two coroner's vans. They lit up the surrounding buildings with a carnival of bright colors, flashing and rotating like there was a party going on, but the officers and the press who were clustered outside the church weren't smiling.

Kaddouri had his phone to his ear, nodding his head as he listened, impatiently wishing that the guy on the other end would wrap it up and get to the damn point.

The cop at the cordon waved them through; he knew Kaddouri and he had seen Mas around at headquarters. Kaddouri saluted a thanks to the officer and idled forward, parking at an angle against the curb. He shut off the engine and they both sat a moment, looking through Mas' passenger window at the flurry of activity just down the street.

They were monitoring the radio traffic on the way over, and they knew it would be bad. They had seen their fair share of bloodlust and mayhem over the years, but Kaddouri was getting worried about her and wanted to lighten the mood somehow before then went inside. He knew she hadn't been sleeping, so the nap didn't overly concern him, but she wasn't her usual self on the way in to town. She used to be able to bounce back, but lately something was going on in that pretty head of hers. Something heavy was pressing on her heart.

Mas had always been guarded in one way or another; most attractive women were. Kaddouri could usually find a way around it, but there was something different about her, something he couldn't puzzle out, and it was starting to keep him up at night. He realized that he was falling in love with her and wondered if she realized it, too.

The call was finally over, and Kaddouri stared at his phone. Mas wondered what was up. He slipped his phone in his pocket and took his keys out of the ignition before glancing at her.

"Nano was seen leaving a motel with Fareed the night before he jumped."

Mas glanced at him in surprise. The image of the two of them together was somehow distasteful to her. Not because Nano was a man of the cloth – priests have always managed to have sex, one way or another – but she had a hard time imagining any man, or woman for that matter, frolicking with the likes of Nano. But more than that, she just had a nightmare about Fareed, and now the man's bloated face and scorched eyeballs were lingering in her mind.

"They were... dating?" It was the only thing she could think of saying. She meant it as a euphemism, and Kaddouri got her point. He just cracked a wry grin and shrugged.

She didn't grin back, and they got out of the car.

They walked together up the worn granite steps of the Church of the Rebirth, each one a gentle four-inch rise so that the sick and the feeble, the young and the crippled could easily enter the house of God. The baby steps felt awkward to them, frustrating the rhythm of leg muscles accustomed to a higher rise. Kaddouri thought in passing that it also made a parishioner slow down and contemplate where they were headed and what they were about to do.

As a Lebanese, he had been around Catholicism his entire life, but it still struck him as odd that a Muslim such as himself could be allowed to enter a house of God without removing his shoes or even washing his feet, and accompanied by a woman no less. Beyond that, not only was Mas wearing shoes, but she wasn't wearing anything to cover her head. Not even a hat. His grandfather would have had a fit, may Allah rest his soul.

The cop at the door recognized them, and held it open so they could pass inside. Mas entered first without crossing herself or bowing her head. She wasn't an unbeliever, exactly, but she was secular through and through.

Kaddouri, however, bowed his head in respect. It was a house of God, no matter who built it and whether they thought he was a believer or not. He silently breathed *"Allahu akbar"* as he crossed the threshold. *God is greater.* His non-Muslim friends thought the phrase was "God is great." But no, the proper translation was, "God is greater." Greater than anything you could possibly imagine.

Captain Thorrington was there to meet them under the low wood ceiling, in the vestibule beneath the choir loft. The church beyond him was lit up like a gymnasium. Not only had every light been turned on, but the CSI team brought their floods inside as well. The cold halogen glow chased away any spiritual ambience, leaving the statues and the icons and the worn wooden pews looking like a collection of forlorn thrift store bric-a-brac. The magic had been leeched out of the place; it was just a cold, dank warehouse of religious artifacts and tired church equipment now.

Thorrington said nothing, and Kaddouri realized that he had never seen him so ashen before. The captain turned and led them into the church, up the main aisle. The floor ahead was sticky with a large pool of blood.

He angled around it and they followed his lead. As they passed by, a large drop of blood dripped down from above and splashed into the puddle with an audible plop. Mas and Kaddouri paused and glanced up.

197

Above their head was a human leg, pale from the loss of blood, draped over the dusty wrought-iron chandelier. The limb had been torn from its socket; little bits of flesh and muscle dangled from the jagged stump, surrounding the top of the exposed femur.

They glanced at each other, and then they looked around. Thorrington patiently waited for them to absorb their surroundings. There was blood splattered everywhere, as if whoever tossed the leg up there had swung it around their head first, and beat several of the nearby pews with it for good measure.

When they were ready to continue, Thorrington resumed leading them up the aisle. Mas and Kaddouri were every bit as sober as he was. Up ahead of them, the same CSI team that worked the Fareed Aly jump site was gingerly examining the bodies of the four nuns lying before the altar.

Blood was on everything, and had run down the steps in dark sheets and rivulets. Body parts had been tossed around like toys, spewing trails of blood, some hacked off and some ripped by brute force from their sockets. Unsmiling and silent NOPD photographers roved the scene, their flashes going off as they methodically snapped morbid stills of whatever captured their attention, whatever might help make sense of the chaos.

Mas was about to go up the steps to the altar when she stopped in her tracks and looked to her left. A photographer had just snapped a picture of something, and for a brief moment the dazzle had rendered her eyesight useless.

An instant before, she had caught something in her peripheral vision, and as her eyesight returned the thing that she thought she saw came into focus, standing in sharp relief under the glare of the halogens. It wasn't a trick of the eye. It all too was real, but it still took her brain a moment to catch up to reality.

Sister Nancy's severed head sat on the silver collection plate, on the varnished mahogany pedestal beside the lectern. Her neck had been neatly cauterized so that not a single drop of blood, not even a smear, had leaked onto the polished metal. Her habit was still clean and black, and her collar was still a pristine white. The thin black fabric fluttered gently in the breeze wafting in from the cracked stained-glass windows. Her eyeballs were branded and her mouth was gaped open in utter surprise.

Kaddouri swallowed repeatedly to keep from throwing up. Beside him, Thorrington pursed his lips and cast his eyes to the floor. He'd already seen the horrific spectacle and didn't need to dwell on it further.

Mas took a breath to steady herself and stepped forward, a trembling hand reaching into her jacket pocket. She withdrew her thermometer and slipped the end inside Sister Nancy's mouth, under her purple tongue. She wanted to look away, but she couldn't get the thermometer to stay in position, so she had to use the tip of her finger to keep it in place.

She could see the others out of the corner of her eye, watching her. After what seemed to be an endless interval, she finally removed the thermometer and checked the reading.

Dr. Osborn was standing by the altar, watching her. She focused her eyes beyond the digital readout and caught the coroner's gaze, then went up the steps and quietly conferred with him. The CSI team was busy nearby, but they kept sneaking glances at the two of them as they talked.

Kaddouri and Thorrington waited for her to return to them. When she did, Kaddouri glanced at the captain but Thorrington was still gazing at the floor. Kaddouri had never seen his captain like this, and it worried him.

"One oh two?" Kaddouri asked Mas.

She nodded, and then she glanced at Thorrington. Kaddouri did the same, and the captain knew that it was his turn to speak. He finally peeked up at Mas.

"All of them? One oh two?"

Mas nodded. "They've been dead for over an hour."

She put her thermometer away. Kaddouri was still glancing side-long at Thorrington. The man looked like he had been beaten half to death. It was too much, Kaddouri knew, far too much. He wasn't going to put the captain on the spot; he turned back to Mas instead.

"He's off his M.O.," Kaddouri theorized. "All these people are over forty. Could be a copycat."

Mas shook her head. "He's on his M.O.," she told him. "These people just got in the way. No, it's him. I can feel it."

Kaddouri nodded, accepting her judgment. During her analysis Thorrington began to tremble, and he was barely paying attention to her now. His eyes kept drifting to Sister Nancy's head, then down to the floor. Kaddouri looked at him and so did Mas. The captain's eyes were moist with tears. It rattled them; it was something they had never seen before.

"Cap'n...?" Kaddouri inquired. They waited for him to gather himself, and when he finally did he looked at them.

"Sister Nancy was my sixth grade teacher," he told them. His voice was a hoarse whisper. "The woman was a saint."

Kaddouri didn't know what to say. Mas closed her eyes and breathed deep and slow to steady herself. When she finally opened them, she found that Thorrington was looking right at her.

"Do whatever you have to do, to put an end to this," he told her. "The gloves come off, right here and now. So help me God, I'll back you up all the way up to the Supreme Court if I have to."

Mas nodded. Thorrington turned to the large crucifix over the altar, and only then did her eyes well with tears. Thorrington genuflected and made the sign of the cross, then gently tapped his breastbone three times with his clenched fist. *Mea culpa, mea culpa, mea culpa...*

He remained sagged over his clenched hand a moment, and then he forced himself to stand. It was a slow and difficult process.

He finally stood erect, turned around, and walked back down the aisle alone, toward the front doors. He passed directly through the slow, steady drip of blood coming down from the leg on the chandelier above. It splashed onto his shoulder board, staining his gold stars.

CHAPTER TWENTY-SIX

Mas and Kaddouri came out of the church several minutes later, after conferring with Dr. Osborn and the CSI team leader. They were both sickened by what they had seen, as was every other cop and first responder on the scene.

The media had gathered in full force while they were inside. Cameras and newscasters were deployed and their klieg lights only added to the circus atmosphere, but they were uncharacteristically quiet. They sensed that some inexplicably awful thing had transpired inside the church. Instead of badgering law enforcement for tidbits, they kept their distance, talking in hushed tones into their mics as they faced their live cameras. The entire nation was keeping vigil on the evening news, as the rest of the world watched over their shoulders.

Every eye was on Mas and Kaddouri as they came down the steps, but no one approached them. The cops on hand kept the gathering crowds back with no more than a glance and an occasional hand gesture, allowing Mas and Kaddouri to continue down the block toward his vehicle.

They wore their poker faces and kept their eyes cast down to the cracked sidewalk as they went. Kaddouri had a dozen questions and speculations, but he didn't want to launch into his thoughts until they were in his car and well down the road. Besides, Mas was in the thick of puzzling it out and he didn't want to interrupt her ruminations.

There was one particular aspect of this latest horror show that was preying on her mind. Not a change of M.O. so much as a change of motive. These latest victims were all clearly older than forty. The case had suddenly taken a new turn, but there was no hint as to why.

Up to this point, all of the Branding Killer's victims had been confirmed as Christmas babies, born at the clinic in 1976. They were the offspring of backwater bayou yokels who had faded into the swamp with their newborns, suspicious of authority and certain that a hex had been cast on the clinic, making it almost impossible to trace them to the catastrophe. Mas had eventually done it, but only in retrospect, after each victim was found. She still didn't know how, or why, the killer was tracking them down, one by one.

There had always been a mulish suspicion of law enforcement in that neck of the woods, and no one came forward for protection, even after ten well-publicized victims. Or perhaps it was for that very reason. Whatever Christmas babies were still alive had chosen to seek safety in anonymity, even though the killer had demonstrated that he would likely be able to hunt them down as well.

Up until now, Mas and everyone else who was familiar with the case fully expected that any new victim, just like Fareed, would be in their early thirties. But these victims were all much older. Beyond that, the crime scene showed a ghastly degree of brutality, even for the Branding Killer. He — and Mas had always had a strong hunch that the killer was a male — had always gotten right down to business in the past, dispatching his victim and anyone who got in the way, but no more than that. In that respect, he was a professional.

But this time there was no apparent victim, or even an apparent primary target. And why in a church? There had been no church connection before. Instead, this seemed to be nothing more than a sadistic exercise in blood vengeance.

Was he sending a message? Was he frustrated? Was it a calling card? A red herring? Or was it just plain old black-hearted cussedness, as her daddy used to say. She wasn't sure what to think —

"Peter?" she said, suddenly halting in mid-stride, looking ahead.

She was surprised to see Peter Johnson standing next to Kaddouri's Land Cruiser, among a crowd of people gathered behind the yellow tape. Kaddouri stopped beside her and looked at the crowd, wondering who she could be talking to.

Johnson was carefully writing the address of the church on his notepad. Absorbed by a whirlwind of thoughts, he hadn't noticed them approaching. Startled, he looked up at the sound of her voice and began to stammer, casting about for something to say.

Mas sensed his pangs of awkwardness and smoothly covered for him. "Detective Mark Kaddouri, this is Special Agent Peter Johnson."

Kaddouri recognized the name at once. Johnson was a legend of sorts – the kind of legend that was more of a cautionary tale than anything else, but he was a legend nonetheless. Kaddouri smiled cordially and extended his hand.

Johnson stuffed his notepad and pen in his jacket pocket, wiped his sweaty palm on his pant leg and shook hands with Kaddouri.

"Retired agent," Johnson corrected Mas, and Kaddouri just nodded. *I should hope so,* Kaddouri thought, but he kept his smile plastered on. He dug out his car keys and took a step toward his driver's door, hoping his body language would tell Mas that he wanted to go.

Johnson smiled nervously and patted the fender. "I got one of these..."

Kaddouri just smiled again and nodded. But Johnson's attention had already drifted away, nervously looking around at the buzz of activity. The lights in particular bothered him, and he squinted as he took in the scene. He leaned toward Mas, and she dipped her head to listen to what he had to say. Kaddouri took a step closer to hear.

"It's too..." Johnson began, and then he tried again. "It's not..." But he couldn't get it out. He leaned closer and finished in a harsh whisper, speaking to both of them. *"We're not safe!"*

At that moment, he was distracted by something that was transpiring behind her. Mas and Kaddouri turned to see what it was.

The church doors were opened from the inside, and the coroners rolled out the first victim, zipped in a body bag. The press and the throng of hushed onlookers murmured, and surged forward in response. The cops running crowd control reasserted their authority, and no one got out of line or did anything stupid. News reporters gripped their mics and tersely narrated the latest development, and a flurry of camera flashes went off as the body was wheeled into the back of a van.

Mas pointed out the corpse for Johnson, and glanced at him, thin-lipped. "Look!" she said. "People are dying. *No one is safe.*"

He stared at her, and blinked. Her cordiality had suddenly evaporated, but as far as she was concerned that was his fault. He brought his case of jitters into town with him, and she didn't want to be subjected to it again. Now that she had his attention, she got right to the point.

"What I want to know, is how do we narrow the field before this monster casts a wider net?"

"He's coming," Johnson told her, directing his gaze above her head. "And this time, he's going to triumph."

"Who is?"

Instead of answering, Johnson pointedly closed his mouth and moved away from her ever so slightly. Kaddouri wondered what Johnson knew about this, if anything, but Mas was out of patience and scowled at the retired Fed.

"Who is?" she demanded.

Her blunt tone was like a physical impact. Kaddouri cracked a glimmer of a smile. He'd been on the receiving end of her anger before; the woman knew how to fight. It was one of the things he admired about her.

She took a step toward Johnson, but not to threaten him. She wanted to break through whatever wall he was hiding behind.

"*Who?*"

He just stared at her, mesmerized.

"You need to tell us!" she urged him. Mas was clearly angry now, and yet her tone was more pleading than anything else.

"Help us get to the truth, Peter," she said to him, her voice suddenly soft and reassuring.

He peeked at her from behind his mental wall. She had gotten through to him; Johnson owed her a response.

Kaddouri just watched them. Something was happening in Johnson's fevered skull, and Kaddouri was anxious to see what it was. If anyone could dig it out, Mas could.

"Who's going to triumph?" She prodded him. "Over what?"

Johnson suddenly became agitated, his breath coming fast and shallow. There was a giddy edge to his demeanor, as if he were about to laugh. Mas scowled at him.

"You find this amusing?" she demanded to know.

But Johnson quickly shook his head. Kaddouri glanced at her, noting her change in tone. Whether she was willing to admit it or not, Mas was nearing the end of her rope. He could sense it, and he wondered if she could.

Kaddouri looked back at Johnson and saw that the man's eyes were suddenly wide open. He was terrified. Mas had pretended to misread him. Johnson wasn't amused, and she knew it; he was about to freak out.

"You don't understand – " Johnson tried to tell her, but her expression had turned stone cold.

"Snap out of it."

That brought him around, somewhat. He just looked at her, waiting to be chewed out.

"You can have a breakdown when this is over," she told him, and he began shaking his head.

"No, you don't understand –"

"Then you *make* me understand!" she snapped.

He sighed, and glanced at Kaddouri for a little help. Kaddouri, however, was firmly in Mas' camp, and wasn't about to lend him a hand. Johnson looked back to her.

"You wouldn't believe me if I told you."

"Try me."

He stared at the pavement, formulating his reply, and then looked directly back at her. Mas saw that for the first time, all the craziness was gone from his eyes.

"Lucifer walks among us," he told her in a quiet, clear voice. "And his work is nearly finished."

CHAPTER
TWENTY-SEVEN

The Learjet 45XR glided through a thin wisp of moonlit clouds and lined up for its final approach. The small commercial airstrip was just north of Toussaint L'Ouverture International, on the far side of the industrial parks. Private aircraft and corporate jets were parked near the small terminal. Some were tied down and tarped in a futile attempt to stave off the tropical climate. Those who could pay a premium fee were housed in a series of aluminum hangars lined up along the concrete runway.

Port-au-Prince had been baking under a brilliant Caribbean sun the entire day, and her city lights were twinkling under a rising blanket of sultry air. Evening brought a balmy relief to the city, and the streets were clogged with traffic. Citizens and tourists alike were energized, as if the entire metropolis had gotten up from a nap and was ready to stay out late and party. They crowded the sidewalks, conducting their business and leisure in the open air, under thousands of naked light bulbs and neon signs.

The Learjet whined as it passed overhead and deployed its landing gear, but hardly anyone took notice. As far as the man on the street was concerned, the rich and powerful were so invisible that they may as well have been ghosts.

The 45XR taxied off the runway and rolled into a hangar as the twin fanjets flanking the tail spooled down to a whistling hush. The last bit of forward inertia was expended to precisely line up the jet with the guide stripe on the polished concrete floor, and then the brakes were applied and locked and the engines were silenced. It was a textbook finish to an uneventful flight, except for one odd detail. No one was in the cockpit.

The clamshell door gently whispered open and folded down, until the integrated staircase was pneumatically suspended just above the hangar floor. No cabin attendant appeared from within.

A moment later, Zamba Boukman emerged alone from the dimly lit interior and stood erect at the threshold, his nostrils flaring as he drew in the thick fragrance of the Haitian evening. Although it was tinged with the vapor of jet fuel, the island's lush aroma was unmistakable. The warm tropical air enveloped him and every pore of his body immediately relaxed, inviting its humid embrace. It was good to be home.

Zamba descended the staircase as a ground crew entered the open hangar door behind the jet. The three men grabbed sets of hard rubber wheel chocks and fanned out to wedge the tripod landing gear front and back. The crewman who chocked the left wing wheels was the first one to spot Zamba as he was stepping off the staircase, just forward of the wing. All he could see of the voodoo master was his white balloon pants and sandals.

The man scooted out from under the wing and stood erect with a deferential smile for the big shot, whoever he was. It always behooved a ground crewman to be polite. You never knew who you were going to encounter stepping off a Learjet, but whoever they were they were guaranteed to be far more powerful than you or anyone you know, particularly if they weren't wearing a suit.

The man paled and his jaw dropped open, staring up at the towering figure before him. Zamba said nothing, and simply waited for the man and his partners to give him his due. It wasn't long in coming.

The man wanted to say something, but he simply couldn't speak. Unaware of his plight, his two partners came strolling around the nose of the plane to join him, their company smiles propped up for the VIP. They could see their comrade standing frozen in place and staring up at the stranger, and they vaguely wondered what was up. His astonished expression told them it was either something wonderful or something awful, but they couldn't determine which it was. But as Zamba's face came into their view, they had much the same reaction as their hapless friend.

Standing together before Zamba, the three men simultaneously began to tremble. Their fear ricocheted off of each other, amplifying their anxiety. It was utterly impossible, but there he was, Zamba Boukman himself, alive and in the flesh.

They dropped to the concrete floor and prostrated themselves, not daring to gaze upon him any longer. They knew that in Haiti nothing was utterly impossible, and they didn't want to take a chance that his appearance was just a vision, or some sort of black magic whipped up by an unknown enemy to throw a fright into them. Even if it was a hallucination, its solid, unwavering presence spoke of a power much greater than they themselves could muster, and it would be foolish to show disrespect.

While they were groveling facedown on the cool concrete, Devlin materialized beside Zamba and grinned at the pathetic cretins before them. The three men had no idea that he was there. Devlin had no business with them, so only Zamba was privileged to lay eyes on him.

"How sweet," Devlin said in a voice that only Zamba could hear. "They remember you."

"As well they should. They *are*, because of me."

They walked around the trio and headed for the open hangar doors.

"Have you been enjoying my island?" Zamba asked him, and Devlin smiled, nodding.

The men behind them remained exactly as they were. As long as they could hear Zamba's footsteps they didn't dare make a move. They could also hear him speaking to someone, but they detected no replies. Perhaps he was conversing with his *loas*. Whatever was happening, they didn't want to know the details. They just wanted him to go away and not be displeased with them.

Outside, five men were approaching the hangar from an armored Mercedes G550. They slowed to a cautious halt as they saw Zamba appear from behind the left wing, strolling towards them. Devlin was invisible to them as well, but Zamba was more than enough for them to confront.

Although the Minister of Tourism was surrounded by four officers of the *Palace Nationale Police*, Delatour felt no sense of security at all. For their part, neither did the PNP officers. Despite being well-armed and trained to kill without hesitation or compromise, the officers felt as helpless as he did. They had been hardened to face death, but tangling with the likes of Zamba Boukman wouldn't end there. Death would be just the first round.

President Préval's minister nervously extended his hand to shake. Zamba gripped it and smiled, enjoying the man's fear. The handshake was brief, sweaty, and cold. The sweat was from the minister; the chill had come from Zamba.

"Where is the priest?" Zamba asked him.

Delatour hesitantly leaned in close and whispered in Zamba's ear so his escort couldn't hear. The four armed men were grateful for that; they didn't want to know the minister's business with Zamba, whatever it happened to be. That was Delatour's bad luck, and they didn't want any of it rubbing off on them.

"He is at the Citadel," Delatour breathed in Zamba's ear, and quickly drew back. A disturbing odor emanated from Zamba, and the minister felt his body instinctively recoil from it. It was a vaguely sour musk that made him feel as if all the oxygen had been leeched out of his blood.

He took another step backwards and bowed in respect to cover his reaction, though he sensed that he was hiding nothing. He was certain that Zamba could not only read his thoughts, but he could see past them into his soul, a place where Delatour himself had no power to look. Only God and the Devil knew what Zamba might find lurking there.

Delatour stepped further back, his head still bowed, and then he turned on his heel and withdrew as quickly as he dared, the four PNP officers accompanying him.

Devlin and Zamba watched them climb into their armored SUV. As it raced away, Devlin turned to him.

"Molinari knew that Eden wasn't at that church."

Zamba nodded.

"I want Molinari to suffer. Harshly."

Zamba nodded once again, and Devlin's features suddenly darkened. His true face was rumbling just beneath the surface, like a volcano that could erupt at any moment. Zamba hope that this would all be over soon.

"Eden...!" Devlin hissed.

Zamba waited breathlessly for an eruption, but to his relief Devlin held his fury in check. Instead, he reworked Zamba's own phrase and tossed it back to him.

"And to think that I am *not*, because He is..."

Zamba exhaled, as Devlin cracked a wicked smile.

"Now the fun begins," Devlin told him.

CHAPTER
TWENTY-EIGHT

Father Eden was certain that if he stood up, everyone would be able to see his underwear through his sweat-soaked white cotton trousers. The tropical uniform may have seemed like a carefully thought-out package back at the Vatican, but he doubted the designer had ever actually worn one for an entire day in the tropics. Shorts and short-sleeved shirts would have been a nice touch, although he didn't have any ideas to improve the backwards clerical collar. Perhaps a perforated one. Still, he had to admit that it was a big improvement over basic black.

He had been sitting in the plastic wrap-around chair for the better part of an hour, wedged between two giggling children in the chair on his left and Isaac La Croix in the chair on his right. La Croix was a dapper young African-European gentleman in a tailored white linen suit, with barely a bead of sweat on his brow. How he did it, Eden had no idea. Perhaps it was in the genes. La Croix's white G550 was parked out front, under the only shade tree in the entire village.

They were visiting with a large Haitian family, sitting around the plank table in the front room of their brick shack under a tin roof that radiated heat. Eden's French was getting a workout. They were taking care to speak slowly to him, although when the children got to jabbering they would lapse into Creole, and he couldn't follow without La Croix's whispered on-the-fly translations.

Jeanine Lacombe was the family disciplinarian, and with a simple glance her children would apologize and return to the straight and narrow. Her husband Antoine sat at the other end of the table and sucked on his pipe, happy that his wife had brought such honor to his household. Most of the village was lingering around his little shack and peeking in through the windows.

None of them ever had a priest pay them a social call before. This would be good for him and his entire family, the husband thought. His enemies and rivals would think twice, and the boys would honor his daughters now. Catholic priests weren't as powerful as voodoo priests, but they were better than no priests at all.

His wife was telling her high school stories to Eden, one after the other, weaving them into a long, drawn-out narrative. Their children were as thoroughly entertained as Eden was. They had never been privy to so many details about their mother's youth. Some of the stories bordered on the scandalous, and her teenage daughters filed them away for future negotiations.

She had the family photo album laid out. With some of her younger ones pressed in around her, she was flipping through the pages, showing old snapshots to Eden to illustrate her narrative. She turned the page and pointed to her favorite photo, a group portrait of herself and her classmates. The woman was in her fifties now, but her features were clearly defined at a young age and it was easy to spot her among the gaggle of teenage girls, mugging for the camera in their crisp Catholic school uniforms. She was the one in the middle, perhaps sixteen at the time, and she was hugging her classmate, the only Caucasian girl in the group.

She spoke slowly to Eden, enunciating with particular care so that he could follow her French. He was eager to learn whatever she could tell him. Jeanine Lacombe, his natural mother's friend and his grandmother's servant, was the lure that brought him to Haiti.

214

"We were the best of friends!" she said with a soft, wistful smile. "We shared all of our secrets."

Across the table from Eden and La Croix, her teenage daughters grinned and whispered to each other, and two of their little brothers teased them. Their mother glanced at them, and they settled down. Her husband just grinned. Women amused him.

"Then one day," his wife told Eden, "the nuns told us she went to America. They wouldn't tell us why, but I knew the truth — she was pregnant with you."

"Did you know my father?" Eden asked hopefully, but the light in her eyes diminished and he knew the answer before she even shook her head.

"No," she told him quietly, "no one ever knew who he was."

Eden was deeply disappointed, but he managed to maintain his composure and looked back at the photo. Even the little boys in the chair beside him could see he was sad. They looked to their big sisters for a clue, and then to their father. He just kept his eyes on the priest, so they looked back to the holy man as well. They weren't sure what happened, but adults had a way of suddenly turning sad, and then they were quiet. Not like children. Children cried so that everybody would know how they felt, and then maybe someone would make them feel better. They waited to see what would happen to the priest. Maybe he would cry, too.

Their mother touched the back of Eden's hand and gently patted it. He looked at her and propped up a brave smile, and then his eyes drifted back to the photo again.

The entire family glanced at Jeanine, waiting for her to make it better. She was the mother; that was her job. She slipped her fingernail under the edge of the photo, and carefully dislodged its corners from the four slots in the yellowed album page.

Eden looked up and saw that she was smiling at him, and she handed him the photo without a word. He silently thanked her, and gazed at the faded image of his young mother in his trembling hand.

Outside the shack, the family quietly gathered around as Eden and La Croix climbed into the Mercedes. Everyone waved goodbye, but it was a subdued farewell. Eden watched the family recede in the large mirror on his passenger door, and spent the rest of the afternoon peeking at the photograph, trying to imagine the sound of his mother's voice.

CHAPTER
TWENTY-NINE

Eden stared out the dusty windshield of the SUV as La Croix drove them up the mountain road, winding ever closer to the Citadel. Eden had never seen anything so enormous built without machinery. La Croix had the air conditioner blasting and was treating him to yet another lecture on Haiti, just as he had every day in the course of their journey around the country.

After a week of touring the island, La Croix was finally taking him to his new posting. The mission was in the barracks of the massive fortress. He and the other priests who arrived with Bishop Lomani were tasked with turning the rooms into an orphanage. A handful of Haitian nuns would be assisting them, forming the core of the nursing and teaching staff.

Eden was eager to join the others and get down to business. He felt guilty for starting off his new posting with a week-long guided tour, but Delatour, President Préval's Interior Minister, had introduced him to La Croix only an hour after he stepped off the plane, and before Eden knew it he was whisked away from the others with the blessing of the bishop.

The Citadel, La Croix explained as he negotiated one hairpin turn after another, capped the entire summit of the mountain they were climbing, Mount Bonnet a L'Eveque, the Bishop's Miter. Eden smiled at the name, and was sure that Lomani would approve. It was the largest fortress in a chain of more than two-dozen redoubts built between 1805 and 1820 across the northern highlands, to protect the new nation that lay to the south from a French invasion.

Eden looked around, taking in the rugged terrain. It was a patchwork of thick jungle canopy interspersed with swaths of denuded scrubland, where the locals had scrounged for firewood over the years. He had a hard time imagining the backbreaking drudgery it would take to simply climb these mountains, let alone construct a stone fort by hand under the bright Caribbean sun.

The driving force behind the project was King Henry Christophe, a hero of the slave revolt who crowned himself the first monarch of the nation. La Croix explained that the Citadel was the linchpin of Christophe's defensive strategy for the northern coast. If the French ever dared to invade again after Napoleon had failed, Christophe planned to torch the entire coastal region, including his hometown of Cap-Haitien, and retreat with his army beyond the palace at Sans-Souci to the string of fortresses that guarded the narrow mountain passes.

Eden glanced at La Croix in surprise, and the man gravely nodded. The radical plan was testimony to the resolve of the slaves who had won their freedom in 1804, and they were determined to live free or die trying.

The price, La Croix explained to him, was staggering. The Citadel was the largest fortress that had ever been built in the Western Hemisphere, before or since, and it was accomplished at a cost of 20,000 lives. Each one of the more than three hundred cannon and mortar had taken a work crew over three months to transport from the coast. With a cache of ten thousand cannonballs, there was little doubt in anyone's mind that the Citadel could have held out indefinitely, if any army had been foolish enough to attack. As it happened, none ever dared. Not even Napoleon's.

After years of autocratic rule, with his court in turmoil, his country staggering under a crushing debt burden to France and his soldiers edging toward revolt, King Christophe suffered a stroke and eventually took his own life with a silver bullet through the heart. He was secretly buried somewhere under the courtyard, in a batch of the same mortar used to construct the outer walls — a blend of quicklime, molasses, and cow blood. The ghost of Christophe would always be on guard, seeing to the safety of his beloved country.

Eden and La Croix pulled to a halt at the end of the jungle road, where two young guides with a team of pack mules waited for them. The road was narrow and rutted the last few miles to the Citadel. Tiny Japanese pick-up trucks could squeeze through if they had to, if everyone on board had machetes to clear a path, but La Croix had no intentions of scratching his shiny white G550. Jungle shrubbery was unforgiving to any paint job, no matter what the factory said. Besides, La Croix reasoned with a private smile, riding on a mule would put the priest into the appropriate frame of mind.

He told Eden the last bit of Christophe's story as the guides strapped Eden's luggage onto the pack animals and readied a pair of mounts for them. According to legend, the king's ghost still walked the grounds, forlornly searching for his loyal soldiers.

Eden just smiled, and La Croix kept his expression diplomatically neutral. In Haiti, a truly haunted land, such things happened all the time, but he didn't press the point. Eden was in another world now, whether he knew it or not. He would soon find out about the ghosts and the zombies.

CHAPTER THIRTY

Father Eden was shopping for produce at the open-air stalls along the dirt road that ran through the village. The Citadel loomed over the agricultural valley like a hulking sentinel. He had been up there working hard all week, coordinating construction with Bishop Lomani and Father Casper, who grew up in a family of stonemasons. This was his first visit down the hill by himself. It was a chance to practice his French and to get away from the clatter of the cement mixer.

The vendors were particularly cordial to him and chatted him up in slow, carefully enunciated French, helping him learn new words as they bantered and bargained with him. The newly arrived priests had become overnight celebrities, and the locals beckoned Eden to their stalls as much to be seen with him as to get his business.

The women doing their morning shopping whispered and gossiped, boldly watching the good-looking man in white as he jovially fumbled his way through his first shopping spree in Haiti. It was clear that he was happy to be there. They didn't sense that he was patronizing them, like so many of the American hippies and tourists who passed through on their way to the Citadel. He seemed to feel right at home. Their children left their sides to scamper around him and he soon became the focus of a ragtag flock, vying amongst each other to carry his purchases as he drifted from stall to stall.

Thalia Rose was shopping for fruit, but it was the off-season and nothing seemed to satisfy her. She briefly paused at each stall and took in the display, but whatever she was looking for was better than anything they had to offer.

The vendors drank her in as she approached to linger over their offerings, before moving down the row of stalls. The Taino Indian bloodline was strong in her, setting her apart from most other Haitians, and the women of the village felt their faces flush with jealousy, watching her walk among them. Thalia wore a diaphanous sundress, but the young woman could have stopped traffic wrapped in a burlap bag. What was she doing out here in the middle of nowhere, the women wondered, making them feel worthless and distracting their men?

As far as they knew, she lived somewhere farther downstream, in one of the lowland villages. Perhaps she came from around Sans-Souci, but no one was really sure. Some of them had seen her on the coast, in Cap-Haitien, and they assumed that she was married to wealth or that she soon would be, or that she would run off to the city to become a model or a kept woman. None of them expected her to appear at their rural marketplace to do her shopping. The men were delighted by her appearance, but the women weren't nearly as enthused.

Thalia blithely tuned out the undercurrents as she moved from stall to stall. She had her own distraction to occupy her. She wanted to get close to the priest.

Eden spotted her in the crowded street behind him. He kept stealing looks at her when he could get away with it unnoticed. Somewhere far back in his mind he realized what was happening to him, but he tried to ignore it. As he meandered from one stall to the next, chatting with the vendors and entertaining his host of children, the truth was becoming more difficult to dismiss. It wasn't quite to the point where he felt he should pray for guidance, but with each passing moment the time was drawing closer, and so was the woman. As much as he tried, he found that she was too difficult to ignore.

Holding a mango up to admire it in the sunlight, he glanced past its golden-green skin and saw that she was looking directly at him.

She smiled, and went back to browsing over a mottled collection of bananas.

He looked back down to the pile of breast-sized mangoes on the vendor's table before him, chastened by a sudden and powerful twinge of guilt. The light was perfectly fine under the awning; there was no need to do what he had done.

The vendor knew it, too, but he dismissed it as a bit of comedy and laughed. The children joined the old man, but Eden knew that the laugh was on him. He had responded to temptation, and was sorely tempted to do it again.

It felt good when she smiled at him. He hadn't felt that way in a very long time, although he knew that it was always there, just below the surface, waiting for the proper stimulation. And here it was, like a warm breeze arising out of nowhere.

"*Allo,*" she said to him in a soft voice, almost a whisper, and he turned to her in surprise. She was standing right beside him. How she got there, he hadn't a clue.

"*Bonjour, mademoiselle...*" He trailed off nervously as his French suddenly failed him.

She smiled and continued in English. "My name is Thalia Rose."

Eden was relieved; he had been struggling to converse with someone, anyone, all morning, and wasn't sure of half of what he was saying. With her, in particular, he didn't want to misspeak. He knew he was on fragile ground. They both knew it.

"Father Eden," he said, with a self-conscious little bow. "Jean Paul Eden."

"A beautiful name."

"As is yours, Mrs. Rose."

"Miss."

Eden smiled. "Miss Rose."

"Thalia," she corrected him further.

"Thalia..."

She smiled back and pointed to the Citadel, high on the mountain. "They sent you here?"

"I asked to be sent, to build the orphanage."

That intrigued her. "You asked to come here?"

He nodded. "My mother grew up in Haiti. I wanted to trace my roots."

"Perhaps I can help you," she suggested with a delicate smile. "There is much to discover in Haiti."

He felt himself blushing and looked down, unsure of how to respond. He could sense where their conversation was heading, and he felt as if he was being gently drawn into a gravity well toward a warm, delicious center.

"Thank you for coming to us," she said. "I know you will do many wondrous things."

He looked back to her, and felt that he should at least make a gesture of resistance. "The Lord guides my hand," he told her. "I am here to do His will."

Her eyes sparkled, and her lips curled into a bewitching smile. "And what *is* His will, Father Eden? Can we ever really know what He wants us to do, when He works in such mysterious ways?"

"His task is to show the way. Our task is to learn it."

"And there is so much to learn in this short life of ours."

"A never-ending quest, Miss Rose."

She smiled again. "Thalia, please."

"Thalia..." He repeated, and smiled in return.

She laughed, and he blushed again, realizing that he was actively flirting with a beautiful young woman in a wispy sundress, and probably not another stitch on her body.

She took a step closer and smiled. "Let me show you the real Haiti."

He tried to back-pedal, but the fruit stand was directly behind him and the children laughed as he bumped into it. Thalia Rose was a force of nature.

"That would be lovely, Thalia," Eden said, and she smiled at him again.

"Lovely Thalia," she echoed, teasing him. "I like the sound of that."

The vendors were watching them, and so were the children. The women were going about their business, but they were watching as well. They could all see what was developing between the two.

Thalia was used to people watching her, but she sensed that Eden wasn't. She took a demure step back, preparing to go. He wasn't quite sure what to say, but he somehow sensed that everything had already been said.

She turned to leave, and as she walked away she smiled at him over her bare shoulder.

"My door is always open," he found himself saying, before he could stop himself. Her smile widened in acknowledgment, and his eyes widened in surprise at his own boldness. That made her smile even more.

He watched her walk into the morning sun, her dress gently swaying with each step, and he saw that he was right. She wasn't wearing a stitch underneath.

CHAPTER THIRTY-ONE

Mark Kaddouri liked to drive in the country with the windows down. It was a chilly dawn in January so he had the heat on, but it was coming through just the lower vents. His toes were warm and there was a cool breeze on his cheeks, and that's just the way he liked it. The bayou had a fresh, green smell to it, a fertile tang in the air that he couldn't find enough of in the city.

He sipped his coffee and pinched off a chunk from one of the buttermilk donuts Mas had laid out on some napkins up on the dashboard. She sat beside him, bundled up in her cashmere pullover, idling putting on her lip balm and nursing a latte. It wasn't her usual brew; she just felt like a change of pace. Kiddie coffee, he called it at the drive-through. Coffee for people who don't like coffee. She slugged him on the shoulder, and it was the first time they had ever heard Johnson laugh.

He was riding in the back seat, sucking down a large dose of caffeine through a big straw he jammed through the hole on the rim of the lid. Mas teased him about it, but Johnson explained to her in excruciating detail how a straw radiates just enough heat to cool the coffee down to just the right temperature, and it deposited the coffee on the middle part of your tongue, which kept your lips and the tip of your tongue from getting scorched. Plus, you don't have to hold the cup to your lips and tip it back to drink, which comes in handy when you're driving because that way you don't block your view...

227

Mas groaned at his non-stop disquisition, but Kaddouri mentally filed it away for future use. He singed his bottom lip something nasty on his first sip, on the way out of the drive-through when they hit the speed bump, and it was just getting back to normal. Maybe Johnson wasn't quite as nutty as they thought he was.

Her phone rang. She unholstered it from her belt, saw who it was, and answered it. "Hi, Mom... Yeah, tomorrow night will be fine... Okay, I'll call you... Love you, too. Bye."

She hung up as they slowed down and turned into a cracked and potholed asphalt driveway. It curved upslope and out of sight between a gauntlet of overgrown vegetation. After more than thirty years, what had once been two rows of neatly pruned ornamental shrubs lining a wide driveway had grown into a pair of fat, towering hedgerows that scraped both sides of the Land Cruiser and obscured their view.

Kaddouri winced as the branches slid over his buffed paint job. His detailer would tease him for it, but what the hell. The man needed the work. And anyway, it was cheaper to fix than bullet holes.

They rounded a gentle curve to the left, and as they did the hedgerow on the right ended, giving way to a meadow of young trees, tangled with clinging kudzu vines and draped with moss, and clogged with a tossed salad of undergrowth. Years ago, it had been a front lawn.

The driveway led into what was once an asphalt parking lot, but wild grasses had pushed through the cracks, widening them, and then some saplings had come through the cracks as well, so that the parking lot was now a slightly less verdant extension of the meadow, with chunks of asphalt mixed into its spongy mulch.

Kaddouri rolled past the end of a concrete wheelchair ramp, overgrown like everything else, and parked before a set of wide concrete steps choked with vegetation. The steps terminated at the front doors of the Bayou Memorial Clinic. The plate glass windows were long gone, and the pair of aluminum-framed doors was sprung open. What Mother Nature hadn't damaged, vandals had. They got out of the car with their coffees and looked around.

The light poles of the old parking lot were completely smothered in flowering vines. The small parking structure nearby had taken a direct hit from the tornado and was now just a jumble of concrete slabs and rusted cars, overgrown and tangled with vines. A sapling was making a go of it up on the roof, where the surrounding trees had dropped their leaves for over three decades, building a thick bed of mulch on the concrete.

Most of the asphalt shingles were missing from the clinic roof, and the ones that were left had curled up and died in the sun ages ago. The plywood beneath them was delaminated and swollen from years of exposure. The clapboard siding of the old building was fatally compromised by the encroaching vines, which grew back out of the cracks and made the place look like an Ivy League dormitory in desperate need of a gardener. Most of the windows were busted out. Faded, tattered drapes fluttered in the breeze.

Jeez, Mas thought. *Turn your back on Mother Nature, and she'll walk right over you.*

Kaddouri's phone rang, and he answered it. "Detective Kaddouri, NOPD... Yes, sir..."

He listened to the news and hung up, looking at Mas. "The archbishop's chauffeur is dead. His wife just called it in."

She nodded, digesting the news, not particularly surprised. "What was the cause of death?"

Kaddouri shrugged. "Osborn's performing an autopsy. We'll know soon."

Johnson was busy writing the clinic's address – *5040* – in his notepad. As he contemplated the number, his hands began to shake and he became more agitated by the second. He had been studying Bible codes for almost three decades now and knew exactly what the number referred to. It had been right there in the case files for all these years, but somehow it didn't register on him until this moment. *Sweet Jesus,* he thought. *Sweet Jesus...*

They were watching him, and when Mas caught his eye, he shrunk into himself and stuffed the notepad in his jacket pocket.

"What?" she wanted to know.

But it wasn't something he could share with them. Not yet. She scowled at the retired agent, out of patience.

"Dammit, Peter! *SPIT IT OUT!!*"

He didn't respond and glanced at Kaddouri for some guy help, but just like before, he could see that Kaddouri was clearly on her side, and not his. Johnson looked back to her and swallowed. He was on his own.

"Come *on!*" she fumed. "I've been holding onto my sanity for the last five years! No more riddles. No more cryptic crap! I want answers. *Give.*"

He took a long, deliberate draw of coffee through his straw to buy some time as he collected himself, until the straw slurped at the bottom of his cup. His last prop was gone. He looked at her and took a deep breath before he spoke. "This is all much deeper than you can possibly imagine," he told her.

"Try me," she shot back. "I got one hell of an imagination."

His lips twitched in a ghost of a smile, hearing her choice of words, and he looked at the dilapidated building. "It all leads right back here, to the clinic."

"Yeah, the twelve Christmas babies," she said impatiently. "That's why we're here, Johnson."

Fareed Aly was victim number eleven, but Mas said twelve because she strongly suspected that the massacre at the Church of the Rebirth had to do with another Christmas baby who was somewhere, and still unaccounted for. Kaddouri agreed with her on that point, and so did Johnson. But now all of a sudden, Johnson was shaking his head.

"Thirteen," he told her. "Not twelve. *Thirteen.*"

CHAPTER THIRTY-TWO

Melissa was nine months pregnant and her time had clearly come. She came in from the storm, pushing open the plate glass door with her shoulder and stumbling into the lobby of the Bayou Memorial Clinic, holding her swollen belly with both hands, her fingers laced tightly in front of her pubic bone. She was barefoot and her clothes were soaking wet.

The old man was the first one to notice her. He was slouched in his Naugahyde chair, glumly gazing through the front doors and watching the rain come down. He had been watching TV along with everyone else, but President Ford's second Christmas address to the nation was about to be re-run and he didn't want to hear it again. He got the message the first time through – the economy was a mess, the government was a mess, and the world was a mess. But aside from that, everything was fine. Merry Christmas.

He instinctively tried to get to his feet to help her. He was raised to be a gentleman and she seemed like such a fragile thing, but the malaria he picked up on Guadalcanal had come back again and he could barely stand. He dropped back in his chair, frustrated by his infirmity, and watched her wobble toward the reception desk. *My Lord,* he thought, *where's her family?*

Lucien rolled his mop bucket into the hall closet and closed the door. The flu was going around, and that was the third time this evening he had to clean up in the lobby. His rheumatism was acting up with all the cold rain; he could hardly wait till midnight came around to punch out and go home. The grandchildren would all be snug in their beds; he could sit a while by the Christmas tree and drink his beer in peace. They'd wake him at dawn, tearing into their presents. It was his favorite moment of the year.

He headed back to the lobby to change the channel on the console TV. Johnny Carson was coming on any minute, and Lucien never missed his monologue if he could help it.

The moment Lucien stepped out of the hallway, he saw the young lady weaving on her feet toward Miss McKay, behind her typewriter at the reception desk. She was already signaling little Bobby, the other orderly, to go fetch the gurney down the hall.

Bobby dashed past Lucien and came back with the gurney by the time Lucien and Miss McKay got to the young lady. Everyone in the lobby watched the three of them help her lie down, and two of them even helped keep the gurney steady.

The girl was soaked to the bone. Lucien unfolded the gurney blanket and covered her up to her chin, then gently brushed the wet hair out of her eyes. He held her hand and talked softly to her, walking beside the gurney as Bobby rolled her into the hallway toward the elevators. Miss McKay was already on the phone, calling up to the maternity ward.

Her eyes were much too wide, and he sensed that she must be delirious, but he was no doctor. He leaned in close to tell her she would be fine, though he had no way of knowing whether that was true. She gripped his hand tightly and kept gasping something he couldn't quite hear.

Bobby stopped the gurney and punched the elevator button. As they waited, Lucien leaned closer and she repeated what she said. He smiled and patted her hand, but she said it again, louder, and insisted that it was the gospel truth.

The young orderly heard what she said the third time around when she raised her voice, and he swapped a private grin with Lucien as they rolled her into the elevator. Lucien smiled back, but he felt a touch of sympathy for her. If she really believed what she said, then his suspicions were right on the money. The poor girl was delirious.

Johnson stood with Mas and Kaddouri in what used to be the clinic lobby, surrounded by the rusted remains of the Naugahyde furniture frames. Someone had scavenged the cushions many years before. The console TV, the typewriter, and the phones behind the reception desk were long gone as well, but several old magazines from the rack by the front door were scattered around the room. The tornado had tossed them about, then over the years the wind came through the broken windows and stirred the mess around.

"There was a walk-in that night," Peter Johnson told them. "Nobody knew who she was, or where she came from. She was already in labor; they didn't have time to make a file for her. She said her name was Melissa, but she never gave a last name."

He turned toward a shattered picture window and they followed his lead. The parking structure could be seen beyond the saplings that had taken up residence on the front lawn. The '65 Bonneville was still on the first floor, a twisted, rusting hulk that the tornado had shoved into a pile of other cars. The rear passenger door of the Bonneville was open and the back seat was plainly visible.

He squinted at the wreck and noticed the license plate number – *2112*. It was another confirmation of his theory. He gripped the notepad in his pocket, but decided to commit the number to memory and jot it down later. He didn't want to call any more attention to his research. He would present his findings to Mas and Kaddouri when he was done. He had the feeling it wouldn't be long now. Eleven dead Christmas babies so far. Only two more to go.

Johnson took his hand out of his pocket and pointed to the Bonn-eville. "They found her body on the back seat the next morning. Her nurse ID'd her."

By first light on Christmas morning, the fire crews had gone through every room of the clinic and discovered to their relief and amazement that aside from the atrocity in Room Three, not a single person had perished in the entire building. The tornado had cut a wide trench through the lawn outside the maternity wing and tore up the parking structure before it continued into the bayou, spinning out of existence as quickly as it materialized.

Sergeant Flanders gingerly picked his way through the tangle of cars on the first floor of the parking structure. It was his duty to look for casualties, not to become one himself. He spent a good ten minutes walking the perimeter before he set foot inside the structure itself. From what he had been able to tell, it was stable enough for him to poke around and look for bodies. He didn't expect to find any, but with tornadoes you never knew.

There was a large puddle of dark red fluid below the back door of a Bonneville. The front end of the car was sitting on top of another one, both of them maliciously twisted like broken toys. All the safety glass of the Bonneville had shattered, but none of the panes had popped out. At first he thought the puddle was transmission oil, but telltale streaks had stained the sill below the back door. Something in the back seat was leaking red fluid. A single drop fell to the puddle below, and then another one.

He couldn't see through the shattered glass, and the door handle didn't work. He pried the door open with his crowbar, and gasped at what he saw.

Johnson finished his coffee, and tossed the cup into a windblown pile of trash in the corner of the lobby. Mas and Kaddouri did the same; they weren't in the habit of littering, but considering their surroundings, it was pointless to be fussy.

"She had two abdominal traumas," Johnson told them. "One looked like a stab wound, and the other one was like an emergency Caesarean, but it wasn't done by a surgeon and it wasn't done with a scalpel. It could have been from a piece of flying metal..."

He trailed off and shrugged, to convey the puzzlement that everyone felt about the case at the time. "It didn't add up," he concluded.

Mas frowned. "Why not? Maybe the perp aborted her like the woman."

Johnson shrugged again. "Yeah, except there's one thing she kept saying the night she came in. Everyone brushed it off as crazy talk, but it kept coming up in an interview I conducted with one of the orderlies, right before I retired. The rest home thought he had dementia, so no one believed him. But I did."

"What did he say?"

"He said that Melissa swore up and down she was a virgin."

"That's impossible!" Kaddouri blurted out.

Johnson just glanced at him. "It's happened once before, Mark."

Kaddouri didn't respond. He learned long ago not to argue with a belief system. He fought for years with his Muslim fundamentalist grandfather until they were both blue in the face, and neither one of them had ever budged an inch. In college, he discovered that Christians could be every bit as stubborn. He drifted a look at Mas, and she turned to Johnson.

"What else, Peter?" Mas asked him.

Johnson looked away through the broken picture window, out to the parking structure, and nodded his chin at the mess. "A lot of those cars got tossed around pretty bad in the tornado, so the autopsy was inconclusive."

"What do you think happened to her baby?"

"Well, I have my theories," he said, gazing at the Bonneville outside. "But one thing's for sure – the autopsy concluded that she really was a virgin after all."

Kaddouri looked at him and blinked, then glanced at Mas. She caught his expression, but her eyes drifted away. She was stunned as well.

"Jesus..." she breathed.

Johnson looked back to them. "Yeah," he said. "That was my guess, too."

CHAPTER
THIRTY-THREE

Room Three was quiet. A breeze wandered in through the cracked window, but it made no sound. The morning sun hadn't yet climbed above the bayou's canopy, and the light in the room was muted. Still, every ghastly detail could clearly be seen.

Mas, Kaddouri and Johnson stood in the middle of the cracked linoleum floor, layered now with years of dust, mold, and moss. The entry door was missing, its hinges torn out by the tornado when the door was ripped from Zamba's hand some thirty odd years before.

The closet door was open. The floor and the baseboards inside were still smeared with a large dark smudge of Father Vicente's blood. The bed frame was still there, but the mattress was gone. It had been removed by NOPD's Crime Lab, as the CSI unit was called at the time, during their initial investigation of the massacre.

The bloodstains on the wall over the bed were dark brown, almost black, but the splash patterns were starkly evident. The clinic was so underfunded that they painted the rooms with flat paint rather than enamel. The blood had permanently stained the off-white latex, soaking in like a fresco and becoming a permanent part of the wall.

While Mas and Kaddouri were taking in the room, Johnson stood between them, gazing with a thousand-yard stare at the bed, and then at the dent in the blood-splashed wall.

"Lisa," he whispered.

Mas glanced at him, puzzled. He was silently weeping, but only his right eye was shedding tears.

"Who's Lisa?" she asked him.

Johnson took a moment to answer, his eyes resting once again on the empty bed frame. "My wife," he finally said. "The pregnant woman who was murdered in this room."

Mas and Kaddouri exchanged uneasy glances. They were floored by the revelation and had no clue what to say, but Mas knew that one of them had to say something. She gently touched Johnson's arm.

"Peter, I had no idea..."

He continued in a halting, hollow voice. "Lisa grew up on the bayou, so this was her clinic. She went into labor late Christmas Eve."

He looked outside at the mangled parking structure, nearly swallowed by thirty years of encroaching mangrove forest. "The place was in a panic, and so was I."

He let out a ragged sigh and let his eyes drift to the floor. "I was maybe three minutes late. Not that I could have done anything to stop him."

"Who?" Mas asked him.

At first Johnson turned away, unable to say anything. Then he swiveled back to Mas and looked her in the eyes.

"The Devil himself."

The desert tan 1976 Toyota Land Cruiser had a growling 4-liter powerplant and rode high on its all-terrain tires, which made it a little hinky in the turns, but the thing was pure hell on straightaways. Special Agent Peter Johnson scooped it off the lot the same day it came in on the train from Los Angeles. It was the sexiest thing he had ever seen, other than his wife.

He was barreling down a two-lane blacktop deep in the Bayou, his off-road lights and high beams and a fitful moon the only illumination for the road ahead. There weren't any side markers on the parish roads out here in the sticks, and the center stripe badly needed a fresh coat of paint. The road was a wet black ribbon hemmed in by an equally black swamp, and he was pushing to get to the clinic before the brunt of the storm came roaring in from the Gulf. Only the good Lord knew how bad it would be. Things were bad enough as it was, and getting worse by the second, almost drowning out the stereo. But if any vehicle could survive a hurricane in the swamp, his Land Cruiser could. He even had winches on the front and back, and he was quite prepared to use them. Part of him was even looking forward to it. But after the kid was born.

He saw the dim yellow lights of the clinic ahead and downshifted. The twin pipe growled and the all-terrain radials gripped the asphalt as he popped the clutch. Engine compression braked the vehicle and he gripped the top of the wheel. He was about to whip into the long, curved driveway of the clinic, lined with a low pair of neatly trimmed hedges, when he suddenly slammed on the brakes and stared through the windshield in a panic.

The Land Cruiser lurched to a nimble stop and sat rumbling beneath his feet, awaiting his next move, but Johnson wasn't sure what to do next. He could just make out a thin finger of a tornado backlit by the moon, dropping out of the clouds that were roiling over a patch of bayou directly behind the clinic.

The howling wind suddenly ramped up to a deafening roar, buffeting the heavy vehicle as the tornado touched down and tore up the lawn alongside the maternity wing.

Johnson shifted into first and laid rubber all the way up the driveway to the main parking lot. He stopped at the base of the concrete stairs and leapt down from the driver's seat, just as the people in the lobby came flooding outside. Among the throng of panicking people, the Guadalcanal vet was helping Lucien, who was clutching at his chest and gasping for air.

Johnson dodged his way around the fleeing horde and raced through the lobby, heading for the main stairwell across from the elevators. Outside, the roaring wind pitched into a deafening scream. He'd been there several times before and knew exactly where his wife's room was, but he didn't know if the room, or his wife, would still be there by the time he got to the second floor. He made it to the foot of the stairs the moment all the lights went out.

In less than a minute, the tornado had done its work and continued on into the bayou, where it blew itself out almost as suddenly as it sprung to life.

Johnson picked his way over the splintered remains of the stairwell's big French window that littered the terrazzo stairs. He stepped onto the maternity wing and looked around at the disaster, scarcely daring to breathe. Sheets of paper still fluttered in the air, the handwritten records of a thousand maladies and more, but that was the only thing on the floor that was moving. The only sound was the wind and rain. He was alone.

Emergency lights burned in the stairwell at the far end of the hall, and a narrow shaft of light streamed through the safety window of the exit door. Halfway down the hall, between Johnson and the exit door, a dim red bulb glowed above the nurses' station. The exterior lights were blown out and the full moon was obscured by clouds, so the windows were of little use. Other than the faint red glow and the narrow shaft of light coming through the stairwell door, the entire wing was in darkness.

As Johnson made his way down the hall toward Room Three, the clouds outside parted and a cold glow of moonlight streamed through the wing's shattered windows and the open doors of the eastern rooms. He saw that the door to Room Three had been ripped off its hinges.

He took a moment to steady himself, not quite knowing what to expect, and then he looked in his wife's room.

CHAPTER THIRTY-FOUR

Special Agent Peter Johnson stood frozen in the doorway of Room Three for an eternity of anguish, unable to breathe or blink or even move a muscle. His keen eyes took in everything, every nuance of horror, and every last detail of unspeakable, awful, irreversible reality.

His wife and their baby were dead. More than that, they had been brutally murdered. He couldn't believe that a tornado could so neatly disembowel a woman and hurl her fetus against the wall.

After arriving at that grim conclusion, he realized that his own life was over as well, even though he was still alive. He even began breathing again, but it didn't seem right. He couldn't feel anything, and he wasn't sure he wanted to.

There was a noise, somewhere down the darkened hallway beyond the nurses' station. His training kicked in and he reflexively drew his .45 longslide Colt Automatic, turning to the sound as he backed out of the patch of moonlight formed by the open doorway. He stood in the dark and listened, watching for any movement.

Beyond the station, Zamba Boukman was in the nursery with Devlin, pushing on the damaged door to hold it open so that he and Devlin could step back into the hall.

The door groaned in its twisted frame, loud in the surrounding silence. There were other sounds, but they were further off, of people screaming in panic and calling to each other. Sirens in the distance were becoming more distinct by the moment as they drew ever closer.

Devlin took a last look around the nursery. Zamba's bloody voodoo dagger was clutched in his fist, ready to strike, but all the pink and blue bassinets were empty. The nurses, doctors, and orderlies on the floor had scooped up every last infant and fled down the emergency stairs in the moments after the tornado passed.

He could see them now through the shattered windows, gathered with everyone else on the front lawn below. Police and fire trucks were coming down the highway. It was time to leave.

Devlin and Zamba stepped into the dark hallway, heading for the emergency stairwell at the far end of the hall. Devlin didn't want to take the main stairs. The steps were much wider and they were still intact. Heroes and rescue personnel would likely be coming up that way instead.

Johnson saw Devlin and Zamba silhouetted by the light coming through the window of the emergency stairwell door. The dagger in Devlin's hand swung into view as he walked.

Johnson leveled his Colt and drew a bead on Devlin's back. He was a master shot, and after what he just saw in Room Three, he was begging for any excuse to fire.

"FREEZE!"

They paused in the darkness and glanced at each other, before Devlin turned around to face Johnson. Outside, the clouds came up, the moon slipped out of sight, and the icy stabs of moonlight coming through the open doorways quickly faded to black.

All three of them were barely visible now in the inky darkness. The long hallway was punctuated by the pool of dim red light over the nurses' station, midway between them. Johnson couldn't see their faces; both of them were backlit by the stairwell light.

He firmed his stance and took careful aim at the one with the knife. Johnson was left-handed, and sighted with his left eye while he squinted his right one nearly closed.

"Drop your weapon!"

Devlin ignored his command and strode directly toward him, an angry, purposeful advance. He quickly passed through the pool of red light, which illuminated his murderous scowl for a fleeting moment.

Johnson winced, doubling over in agony as a flash of searing pain shot through his left eye. In the instant that he saw Devlin's face, his cornea had been burned; he could feel it. Hunched over in agony, he tilted his head to the left and sighted as best he could with his right eye.

Devlin was a dark silhouette once again, barely fifteen feet away and closing fast, raising the dagger.

Johnson peeled off six rapid rounds, a series of thunderous explosions in the confined space. He knew that he would essentially be deaf for the next several seconds. It only compounded the surreal quality of what he saw next.

The tight group of .45 slugs punched clean through Devlin's upper torso. Any one of them would have knocked a human being off their feet, no matter where the bullet struck. That's what a .45 round was designed to do, and that's why Johnson packed a Colt. Because .45s didn't throw bullets, they threw sledgehammers. The way he saw it, if he was going to shoot someone he wanted them to drop.

But Devlin kept on coming without a moment's pause, and as he did he began to laugh. Johnson clearly heard it, even through his temporary deafness.

The red light behind Devlin streamed through the six bullet holes in his chest, and as he moved in for the kill the tiny beams of bloody red light swept over Johnson's astonished expression.

Johnson dropped to his knees, his hand cupped over his damaged left eye. With his one good eye, he could see Devlin's black boots approaching. Immobilized by pain and bewilderment, he waited for the blade to strike.

243

Four cops were charging up the main stairwell behind Johnson, their revolvers drawn. They heard the gunshots, and were more than ready to drop anyone who messed with them.

But Johnson's ears were ringing, and he only dimly noticed their footsteps behind him. His mind was fully focused on Devlin, but as he stared at the black boots just a few feet away from him, they suddenly vanished.

A moment later, the cops came onto the floor behind him. They saw him huddled on the floor, his left hand over his eye and a .45 in his other hand. No one else was around. They leveled their revolvers at him.

"Don't move, buddy!" the sergeant warned him.

"I'm FBI!" Johnson gasped.

CHAPTER THIRTY-FIVE

They were outside again, standing by Kaddouri's SUV. Mas and Kaddouri were still trying to absorb Johnson's story. He was relieved that he finally told someone the truth. Whether they believed him or not was another matter.

"I stayed on the case for almost thirty years, but they eventually forced me out. They said I was too obsessed, said it was driving me nuts."

He cracked a humorless smirk. "They thought I was seeing things." He pinched out the contact lens that covered his left eye, to show them the damage. His pupil was neatly branded, exactly like all the Branding victims, though not as deeply.

Mas and Kaddouri stared at the mark, speechless. He squirted some eye drops on the lens balancing on the tip of his finger, and then tipped his head back and put the lens back in. He followed it up with a few more drops and blinked away the excess.

Mas' iPhone rang, but she just stood there, staring at him. He pointed at her phone, in its holster on her belt. "Better get that. Someone might be calling."

His deadpan quip snapped her out of it and she answered the call. "Agent Mas."

She listened, and then quickly turned to the hood of the car, taking a notepad out of her back pocket. She flipped it open and pulled out the tiny pen inside.

Kaddouri and Johnson swapped glances. *Something's happening.* They watched her.

"Thanks, Melanie," she said, and hung up. She turned to them; they were waiting expectantly.

"That was Research," she told them. "We got a lead on the church massacre." She glanced at her notes. "A Father Jean Paul Eden was the parish priest. He left on a mission to Haiti a few days ago."

"And?" Kaddouri asked her.

"And the Archdiocese says that as far as anyone knows, he was born on the bayou on Christmas morning, nineteen seventy-six."

He swapped glances with Johnson, and they looked back to her.

"Where exactly?" Johnson asked her.

"Nobody knows for sure. He was taken in by an orphanage. All his records were lost in a storm."

"You're shittin' me," Kaddouri said.

Mas shrugged. "That's their story."

She slipped the pen back in her notepad, closed it, and put it back in her jacket. "I'm leaving for Haiti tonight."

"I'm going down to the morgue," Kaddouri told her. "I'll come down to Haiti as soon as I can."

She turned to Johnson. "Peter, do you want to help?"

He nodded. She dug around in her bag and handed her card to him. He pocketed her card and patted it, happy to be on board for the duration.

They got in the Land Cruiser and buckled up. Kaddouri steered around the saplings in the old parking lot and negotiated the curved driveway. They all winced as the hedgerows scraped the sides of the vehicle again.

"I'll get you access to the Bureau library," she told Johnson. "Call me as soon as you find something."

He took a big breath, and nodded. He hadn't set foot inside the Federal Building in years, and he was sure it was going to be a damned uncomfortable experience. But as long as Mas had his back, he was willing to give it a go.

Kaddouri hung a left at the bottom of the driveway and accelerated. It was going to be a long drive back into town. They'd probably miss most of the holiday traffic. Maybe they'd stop for lunch at the crawfish shack they passed on the way out. He loved the cinder block shacks out here in the sticks and the food they dished up. Just a tall table to stand at and a sheet of newspaper with a pile of crawfish dropped on it. Couldn't be beat.

Mas took her phone out. "I gotta make some calls." She speed dialed a number. *First things first,* she thought.

"Mom? It's me. Hey, change of plans. There's a place called Riz Noir over by the airport."

Kaddouri slouched down for a long ride back to town. *There goes lunch,* he grumbled to himself.

CHAPTER THIRTY-SIX

Riz Noir was a new restaurant just down the road from Louis Armstrong International. Mas heard good things about it from the Feds that flew in periodically from D.C. She had been wanting to check it out, and today was her opportunity.

She reserved a window table for lunch. Her jet took off at 3 p.m., and it would be fun to watch the planes take off while they ate. It always put her in a flying mood.

It was overcast and drizzling by the time they pulled up to the curb in Beth's Cadillac, though she would have been just as happy riding on the back of her daughter's BMW. It reminded her of her husband Julian's Harley. He pulled her over to give her a ticket one fine day in the summer of '75. Her mama always said there was something about a man in uniform, and when Officer Julian Mas of the NPOD stepped up to her driver's door, Beth understood exactly what her mama was talking about. It was love at first sight, and she scandalized her entire family by becoming a biker chick on the weekends, even though the man was a cop and even though she married him in a proper church wedding.

But today wasn't a good day for a bike ride. Besides, Mas had her briefcase and a carry-on to contend with, and Beth had her huge, heavy purse. And then there would have been the long-term parking fee at the airport for the bike. Cars did have their advantages, and this was one of them.

Beth dropped three quarters in the meter, and they walked hand-in-hand into the restaurant. She pretended she was still a little wobbly from a broken ankle the summer before, but the woman was fit and trim from years of disciplined exercise, and was already back to short bouts of jogging. Mas knew she was just using it as an excuse to hold her hand, and she found it endearing.

They followed the hostess to their table, gazing out the windows at the rainy afternoon as an airliner took off from Louis Armstrong nearby. When Mas was a child, her daddy would fly model airplanes for a hobby. Nowadays, any sort of aircraft reminded them both of Sunday afternoons picnicking in the park with the other mothers and children, as all the fathers and their teenage boys fiddled with their buzzing contraptions, launching them upstairs for mock dogfights and pylon races. Mas could still vividly remember the smell of the fuel, and the glue and epoxy in the garage when her father was building or repairing one of his biplanes. The man was a craftsman. She learned her attention to detail from sitting at his side and watching for hours as he told her stories about being a cop.

The hostess gave them their menus and left. Beth opened her purse and took out two gleaming glasses, along with two sets of polished silverware. Her daughter indulged her, and set the restaurant's glasses and utensils aside as Beth laid out the things she brought from home, a set for herself and one for her Chrissy-girl.

The busboy came up and saw what the game plan was at once. *One of those...* he thought. *This'll be fun.*

He filled their private glasses with ice water and removed the restaurant's glasses and flatware with a smile. Beth smiled a pleasant thank you, and so did her daughter. He nodded, and moved on to the next table before they asked for anything strange. Beth had a sip of water, and found it refreshing. Mas was secretly relieved.

She was tolerant of her mother's eccentricities. Beth didn't trust restaurant help and that was that. She was always pleasant to them, but she would watch them like a hawk. It used to drive her father

250

crazy, but Beth had been a waitress when she was single and saw some dreadful things, and there was just no arguing with her.

Beth smiled at her daughter and Mas smiled back. They both had the same charming squint, although genetics had nothing to do with it. Mas used to mimic her as a child, until it became an engrained habit. They scanned their menus and chatted about the offerings. After a few minutes, they were ready to order.

The waiter appeared, but he kept his eyes on Mas. The busboy had given him a heads up about the older lady. Mas grinned at him, and he grinned back.

"Hi," she said. "We'll have the *deux plats de poisson rose, kreyol, avec du banane mur frie*. And *pour le riz, je prend un plat du riz avec djon-djon.*"

"Mmmm, that sounds delicious!" Beth said with a grin. Food always sounded better in French.

"And my mom would like a glass of Marcelle Joseph Cabernet, and I'll have a Serac on ice."

"And could you bring us some warm bread?" Beth asked him.

"Very well," he said, jotting it all down. "Will there be anything else?"

"Yes," Beth said, reaching into her purse. He waited to see what she would be pulling out. Probably a corkscrew.

She handed him a Visa card. "I'm paying," she informed her daughter.

"Mom...!" Mas began, but her mother waved away her protestations.

"Hush. I want the points."

Mas smiled and sat back, letting her have her way. The waiter moved off with the card tucked inside his ticket book.

Beth reached across the table and grasped her daughter's hand, so proud of her. She was given to sudden eruptions of affection. "It's a *miracle* how much you look like me!" she said. "I'll *never* get over it."

Mas fondly stroked the back of her mother's hand with her thumb. Beth tended to get particularly effusive and sentimental when Mas was going out of town. Mas used to find it embarrassing, but as she grew up she learned to roll with it, and now she thought it was sweet. It was just her mother's way; for all the apparent dramatics she was completely sincere.

"You and Daddy picked a baby that blends right in," Mas told her.

"Our lost little lamb," Beth said with a teary smile. "That's what we used to call you."

Mas just smiled, remembering.

The waiter brought their salads and set them down. He cranked some fresh pepper for Mas, but Beth passed. His busboy poured Mas' Serac on ice as the waiter poured Beth's red wine. The ladies smiled a thanks, and they were left alone.

Mas picked up her fork, but Beth folded her hands in prayer and bowed her head. Mas promptly put her fork down and did the same.

"Lord above," Beth prayed, "Thank you for this bounty, and for all your blessings great and small. And thank you for our trials, Lord. They help us see the joys of life. Amen."

"Amen," Mas murmured. They crossed themselves, and Beth picked up her wine.

"That was beautiful, Mom."

Beth smiled at her. "I just made it up. You inspire me."

Mas blushed, and picked up her drink as well. Beth popped a bit of warm bread in her mouth and followed it with a sip of red wine. Mas joined her in a tiny sip, then put her drink down and dug into her salad. She was hungry.

Beth watched her daughter eat. "You're tired," she observed.

Mas closed her eyes briefly, and nodded. There was no way to hide it, and there was no use denying it. A mother could always tell. Especially hers.

"The food will help me sleep," Mas said.

Beth smiled, and cut her salad into smaller chunks. It also gave her a chance to look it over, but nothing seemed amiss.

They ate in silence, watching the planes land and take off in the gray drizzle of a winter afternoon. Beth finally looked back to her, a shadow of concern puckering her brow. Mas peeked at her. *Here it comes,* she thought, and she was right.

"You don't have to do this, Chrissy."

Mas stopped eating, and sighed. Beth puckered her lips, almost as if she regretted what she just said. In truth, though, she didn't regret it one bit, and Mas knew it.

Beth searched her daughter's eyes, struggling to find the best way to convey what she was feeling. Mas sat still, allowing her to have the moment she needed.

"Your daddy knows you loved him, and I know you loved him," Beth said. Her eyes were tearing up and turning red.

Mas nodded, but she was unsure how to respond. Her mother wanted to say more, so Mas gave her the time to express whatever she felt she had to say. It was the least she could do under the circumstances, she thought. She was flying off to a foreign country to track down a serial killer, and her mother was understandably concerned.

"There's nothing you have to prove, honey. You were always our darling daughter from the moment we laid eyes on you, and you always will be. Love isn't bound by flesh and blood, Chrissy. Love is forever."

Mas could only nod again, and tears began to form in her eyes as well. Her mother was quietly weeping and dabbed at her mascara.

Mary Beth Mas took a deep, brave breath, and forcefully let it out. She was a cop's widow, and she wasn't about to break down in public. It was a commitment she made at his funeral, and she was going to honor it no matter what.

She deliberately wrapped her hand around her wine glass and held it up with a brave smile. Mas lifted her Serac.

"To Daddy," Mas said. It was her toast to recite, every time they ate together. It had been their tradition since the time she was twelve, since her father's wake.

"To the man of our lives," Beth replied, just as she had a thousand times before.

They clinked their glasses together and drank a toast of love, honor and remembrance.

CHAPTER
THIRTY-SEVEN

The sun was starting to sink in the west, somewhere behind the thick cloud cover. An unmarked FBI Learjet 45 was parked outside an unmarked hangar, its twin fanjets idling in a silky, high-pitched whisper. The pilot and co-pilot were walking through their pre-flight checklists, while John the steward gave the main cabin a once-over in preparation for takeoff.

The split clamshell hatch was open and the integral staircase of the lower half was getting rained on. John had a stack of towels to clean up after it was secured. He didn't like having a puddle on his clean carpet, no matter the weather. He glanced at his watch; it was time to scoot. He craned his head to look outside.

Mas was standing under her mother's oversized black umbrella, hugging her goodbye. Mas' briefcase was stacked on her carry-on close beside her. The wind was up and they were both getting wet from the hips down. She would have to towel off her luggage when she got on board. She knew John, and for all his good manners, he ran a tight ship. He was a local boy and she still didn't know how he ever made it through Katrina. Not so much the storm, but the ungodly mess afterwards. He didn't strike her as the happy camper type.

Beth pulled her head off her daughter's shoulder and looked in her eyes. "Call me when you get there. I worry."

Mas grinned. She'd been hearing that ever since she could remember. "You're the mom; that's your job."

She remembered something else. "My landlady's taking care of Junior, but could you stop in and see him? He adores you."

Beth smiled at the mention of his name. *The poor little beast,* she thought. She'd have to stop by on the way home. She might even spend the night, maybe the whole weekend. The landlady wouldn't mind, and Junior was such good company. Beth's place got to be so lonely sometimes.

"Of course!" she told her daughter. "He's part of the family." Beth held her by the shoulders and took a good, long look at her, then got up on her toes and kissed her forehead.

"Your father would be so proud of you."

Mas held back her tears, but when they hugged once again, they both shed more than they thought they would. *Yeah, real tough Fed, crying on mamma's shoulder,* Mas thought with a wry smile, and gave Beth a final firm squeeze before they broke apart.

Mas stepped backwards into the rain with a farewell smile and turned toward the jet. She knew that if she didn't go quickly, it would just be harder on them both.

Beth clamped a hand over her mouth just in case, to keep from calling out something she shouldn't. As she watched her daughter go, her brow puckered in a sudden pang of despair.

She felt so utterly alone under her big umbrella, with no one to love and cling to, not even someone to simply be with and watch the world go by. *It's always like this,* she thought, *every time my Chrissy-girl goes away. Why should this time be any different?*

Behind her, Kaddouri pulled up in his scratched Land Cruiser and got out. He was dressed in a London Fog, but the rain had picked up something fierce and by the time he was halfway to the jet he was already soaked.

The clamshell hatch was closing. John secured the hatch from inside, and a moment after that the brakes were released, allowing the idling fanjets to propel the small plane forward at a genteel crawl.

Kaddouri broke into a run, dashing right past Beth, but he didn't have a moment to say hello. She would understand; she knew how he felt.

Beth watched him sprinting in a dead heat for the plane, and her heart soared. She was wondering when he was finally going to make his move, and maybe this would be it. She hoped so; she dearly wanted grandchildren.

As foolish as it was, and as silly as it may have looked, Kaddouri was trying to run down a jet. It didn't matter to him; he just wanted to say goodbye one more time. He already said it casually, back at City Hall, but he wanted to say more than that, even though he still wasn't sure exactly how it would come out.

He drove to the airport in rain-clogged traffic, even driving on the shoulder and using his flashers, because he knew he wouldn't be able to live with himself if he didn't at least try. However awkward it might be, he knew that if he just put himself in the situation, if he just threw himself into it, the words might come out right, if they even came out at all. And if they didn't, just showing up would be saying a lot all by itself, so what the hell.

Mas had just taken her seat when she saw him on the tarmac, pacing the aircraft. She broke into a smile and he waved, elated that she caught sight of him. If she hadn't, they would have kept right on going.

He saw her turn to the steward in the aisle, and then get to her feet. A moment later, the jet slowed to a halt, and a moment after that the hatch cracked open. Mas was standing at the threshold. She came down the steps, even as they were locking into place.

John was behind her, a wad of towels in his hand. He was going to have a wet carpet all over again, but he was a romantic at heart and thought it was a sweet gesture, whoever this hunky guy was.

Kaddouri stood in the rain, out of breath and smiling at Mas as she stepped off the ladder and stood before him.

"I... I... I..." he stammered, and grinned in embarrassment. He was at a complete loss for words. She grinned back, waiting for him to spit it out.

The co-pilot appeared at the threshold behind her, watching along with John, but they didn't have time for this hearts and flowers nonsense. They had to go. Now.

"Agent Mas, we're next in line for take-off," he informed her.

She nodded, and reluctantly went back up the steps. She wanted to give Kaddouri just a few more seconds, but she didn't have any say in the matter. She had asked for a big enough favor as it was, getting them to stop in mid-taxi for a goodbye chat.

"Your contact is Agent Nadege Francine from the U.S. Embassy," Kaddouri shouted to her as the engines spooled up. "She's an old friend of mine from the Academy. She'll be there when you land."

Mas stood in the threshold and flashed a puzzled grin at him, pretending to hold a phone to her ear as if to say, *You came all the way out here to tell me that?*

He grinned back and shrugged, but they both knew exactly what he came to tell her. He'd been working up to it for a long time.

John closed the hatch again and secured it, then dropped his towels on the floor and moved them around with his foot to blot up the water. He could see Chrissy's suitor outside in the rain, watching them go.

Kaddouri back-pedaled, retreating to a safe distance as he kept his eyes on the cabin windows. He saw her sit back down in her seat and buckle up as she ducked her head to spot him through the tiny window.

She saw him standing alone in the rain, with her mother far behind him under her umbrella. Mas was soaked, but she didn't care. She could change in John's immaculate restroom as soon as they were at cruising altitude.

She waved goodbye and saw Kaddouri waving back, until the pilot steered into a right turn and eclipsed her view.

"I love you," Kaddouri finally said, watching the Learjet fading away in the rain-streaked twilight.

It turned once again and paused, positioning itself at the foot of the runway. A moment later, the engines spooled up to full power, the brakes were released and it raced away. It soon became a white blip on the runway, faster and louder, and then the nose came up and it launched itself into the sky with a hellacious roar.

Beth was standing under her umbrella behind Kaddouri, watching him watch the plane take off. Aside from dinner with her daughter, it was the best thing that happened to her all day long, seeing the two of them together. She said a little prayer; there truly was a lot to be thankful for.

He finally turned back to her and smiled hello. Beth smiled back and walked toward him as he approached her. She held her umbrella high and he stepped under it, pecking her on the cheek. She took his arm and they walked to his SUV.

CHAPTER
THIRTY-EIGHT

Father Molinari stood before an open pair of French doors in his Vatican office, gazing out on the Eternal City with his cell phone in hand, watching a phalanx of rain clouds lumbering in from the Tyrrhenian Sea. He had one more call to make. Then he could have a nice strong cup of chamomile tea, and if the good Lord was willing, finally get some rest.

The buildings of the city were hemorrhaging heat through a million small leaks and radiating even more from their red tile roofs. The rising calories wrinkled the air until it seemed that all the lights below were twinkling Christmas decorations.

His office at the Vatican tended to be on the chilly side and tonight the air had a particular bite to it, but he welcomed the bracing snap of winter weather. It was a sobering shock to his system, a sort of meteorological hair shirt, he thought with a wry smile.

Molinari looked at his watch. He wore an old Rolex, an Oyster Perpetual Explorer, a relic of the Fifties that used to be his father's. Gabriel Molinari gave it to him on the day he was ordained. It was the same model that Sir Edmund Hillary wore when he climbed Mount Everest, so Molinari figured it was good enough for hiking up and down the stone staircases of Vatican City. It didn't have any bells or whistles; it just kept good time, so he had learned to do time zone calculations in his head. It was trickier to do in the summertime because New Orleans ran on daylight savings time and Haiti didn't. But this time of year, the two locales were in sync.

It was Tuesday, January 12, a few minutes before 10 p.m. That made it nearly 4 p.m. in Port-au-Prince and almost 5 p.m. in New Orleans. The weatherman on cable TV said it was a beautiful day in Port-au-Prince.

I suppose that's something to be thankful for, Molinari thought dryly, and punched the phone number of the man in Haiti into his cell phone, then pressed Send. He didn't have the number on speed dial or in his directory, just in case, although he knew that his phone logs were available if someone wanted to spy on him. Still, he reasoned that if they went so far as to look through his phone logs, his goose would already be cooked.

His new cell phone still seemed like a science fiction gadget to him. As a matter of fact, they all did. Pressing Send on his first one had taken him a long time to get used to. The first few weeks he had his old flip phone he'd keep forgetting, and just dial the number and hold the thing to his ear, waiting forever for the damn call to go through. Father Simone finally realized what was going on and came to his rescue, showing him the digital ropes.

He's been a Godsend, Molinari thought, as he listened to the call ring on the other end. All these years shuttling back and forth to New Orleans, stuck in the middle and playing dumb and taking the heat from Nano, Simone had done a yeoman's job. His rewards would be bountiful when all this was finally over, and God willing it would all be over very soon. The man in Port-au-Prince finally answered the phone.

Father Simone was working in his adjacent office by the glow of his screensaver, methodically catching up on a stack of boring paperwork that had been clogging his in-basket for the last week or so.

262

You would think this could all be done by inter-office email, he groused to himself, *but no.* The powers that be were in love with paper. Parchment was coded into their very DNA, he was sure of it; even resorting to plain old paper must have been an anguishing sacrifice for them, back in the day. A lot of the old-timers around the Vatican still looked on the computer as the work of the Devil.

On that point, Simone could agree with them. It erased time, distance and privacy, and had the power to link all the evil that was in the world. It could also link all that was good, but marshaling goodness was like herding cats while evil craved agreement and enjoyed marching in lockstep. On balance, he concluded, the scales were tipped toward darkness.

They always were; it was part of the entropy of the universe. Things fell apart. It was always much easier to destroy than it was to create, always easier to tear something down than to build it. The people back home in America used to say that it took a dozen men to build a barn and just one jackass to knock it down, which was true. The entire game was rigged to go downhill, and in the grand scheme of things hope amounted to little more than whistling in the dark. Goodness was a scam and heaven was a house of cards; reading the Book of Devlin had taught him that. No wonder the Cabal of Cardinals kept it under lock and key. And it was a good thing that Father Simone had the key.

Molinari's muffled conversation penetrated his dyspeptic ruminations. He put his pen down and tilted his head to listen.

"The sacrifice was dreadfully painful, but necessary," Molinari was saying.

Simone had a good idea what he was talking about, and to whom he was talking. He silently got up from his chair, carefully rolling it back on the worn rug. He slipped off his shoes and walked in his stocking feet toward the interoffice door. It was three centuries old and sported a massive keyhole. He got down on one knee and peered through. It was an old Vatican tradition, even before the Borgias threw their private parties featuring the scandalous Dance of the Walnuts. *Oh, the things you'll see,* he thought, *peeking through a Vatican keyhole...*

Molinari was pacing his office, his cell phone pressed to his ear. "It grieves me as well, but the time draws near! The fate of billions of souls is at stake."

He stopped at his desk and picked up a color laser printout from an open file folder. He studied the reproduction of the eight-by-ten glossy photo as he listened to the chatter at the other end, nodding in commiseration. His contact in Haiti was understandably concerned.

"Just three more months," he assured the man, "and we will have beaten the Devil for all time." Molinari put the photo back in the file and closed it. "The Lord will triumph, my friend."

He said his goodbyes, and then he ended the call and put his phone on the desk. He didn't like carrying the thing around with him. He picked up the file and slipped it in his desk drawer, then turned the key of the pickproof lock and clipped it to a silver chain around his neck. It was time for some tea and then to bed, though he doubted he'd be able to sleep.

He glanced at Simone's office door. It was closed, but he could see light streaming under the door and leaking through the big keyhole. *The poor man was still slaving away,* Molinari thought. *God bless him.*

God help us, the man in Haiti thought.

The sun lay golden and low over the western sea. He was parked along the fence at Port-au-Prince International Airport, watching the planes come in. The woman's Learjet was due to arrive any minute now.

He had a massive headache, made worse by the drumming and singing that had been going on all afternoon, somewhere in the neighborhood nearby. The tourists would simply think that they were happy island people, like the *kompa* band at the international terminal, but he knew better. The *loas* were being summoned; they would ride many people tonight. The island was in turmoil, and trouble walked the land. Zamba Boukman had come back home.

It had been a clear, balmy afternoon, but it was starting to get hazy now. The smog would be back tomorrow, mingling with the haze, and so now was the time to catch whatever fresh sea breeze that he could. Cooking fires lingered in the air as they always did. They blended with the aroma of jet fuel and diesel exhaust, along with the sewers and the gutters and the festering puddles and trash. Haiti had its own signature brand of musk, and it hung in the tropical atmosphere like a primordial funk. Some people called it the aroma of poverty, but he knew what it really was. It was the stench of fear.

He held his cell phone in the same fist that he was slowly and methodically rubbing against his forehead. *It's been a long day, and it will surely be a longer night,* he thought, moving his fist in small circles. As he did, the sun glinted off his gold Rosicrucian ring.

CHAPTER **THIRTY-NINE**

Eden was working at the Citadel in the merciless glare of the afternoon sun, under a pure blue sky in the northern highlands. He was supervising a group of laborers, fifteen in all, who were hard at work on the pavilion footings. It would be a temporary shelter while they were renovating the centuries-old collection of rooms that the government had given them for the orphanage.

Their first pour of the day had taken its sweet time to set in the cool early morning mountain air. They were pouring the second and last batch now, just before quitting time. Slow-setting concrete was fine by him; he'd never poured any before, much less worked with a set of blueprints. He was faking it, and all the workers knew it. They also knew that air temperature had almost nothing to do with how fast concrete set. It was all in the mix, and they had Bishop Lomani pay for a blend that was slow enough for them to work at a leisurely pace. They weren't lazy by any means, but white men from the north had no idea just how debilitating it was to work in Caribbean weather, even in wintertime. It wasn't like Florida, or even Louisiana. A Caribbean island was a different world with its own climate and pace.

Eden's ineptitude didn't matter to them. They were beholden to him, and to all the missionaries, for the steady work they had brought to their highland village. There was enough to do at the mission to get them through the rest of the winter, and that was a Godsend. And although the priests were amateurs, the locals were not. They had all built their homes out of concrete and cinder block, so they knew exactly what they were doing. Masonry was in their blood. They were going to make Bishop Lomani think that Father Eden was a screaming genius, whether the young priest could read a set of plans or not. None of them could either, and their houses could stand up to hurricanes better than the ones in New Orleans, so who needed building codes and who needed plans? They would take care of Eden just as Eden was taking care of them.

Their women and some of their children had come up the mountain with them, to watch them work and to make their meals. They sat on the chairs and crates they brought along, gossiping amongst themselves as they watched their men working. The children ran around playing soccer and making up games, but they knew how far they could stray. Ghosts roamed the ancient Citadel, even during the day. The children stayed nearby and in plain sight, where it was safe.

The Haitian nuns were busy in the old kitchen trying to get it clean, and one of the priests was trying his hand at fixing the plumbing, but thus far a satisfactory solution eluded him. Almost a week had gone by, and they were still cooking under the stars.

Although it was Tuesday, Eden still missed not having Sister Nancy's traditional dinner of chicken and dumplings on Sunday night. The other priests were from Canada, two were from Dominican Republic and all the nuns were Haitians, so he and Bishop Lomani were the only ones at the mission who carried a Norman Rockwell vision of Sunday dinner in their heads. As they feasted on the boiled green bananas mashed with butter that Father Ortiz made that Sunday morning, it finally dawned on Eden that not only was he in a foreign land, but that he was actually living there and not just visiting. The land wasn't foreign; he was.

Eden glanced at the audience of village women and smiled at them; all the women smiled back. They knew why he was looking their way. Thalia Rose had come up the mountain with them. She had been appearing at the marketplace lately. The selection of produce was so much better in their village, she told them. So was their selection of priests, they whispered to each other.

She smiled at Eden, and he quickly turned back to his work. He wished that he knew what his workers were doing, and he hoped they were doing it right. He grew antsy watching them, and wanted to make himself useful.

A form was slowly giving way, distended by the weight of all the wet concrete it was holding. A hammer was lying on the ground and some nails were scattered in the dirt. Eden put the plans down and tried his hand at bracing the form, running a scrap of two-by-four across the form and nailing it to the top of each sideboard. He made one side secure, but on the third strike of the hammer to secure the other side, he whapped his thumb something fierce.

"Jesus Ch – !!" he hissed, and jumped to his feet, jamming his thumb in his mouth as much to shut himself up as to soothe the pain. The workers glanced at each other and grinned. They heard what he said as plain as day.

The women were too far away, but they could tell exactly what happened, and they could deduce precisely what he must have said. They covered their mouths to keep from laughing out loud. Eden peeked at them, his thumb still in his mouth. The children thought he looked like a baby, and burst out laughing. They mimed him and showed each other their pained expressions, and their mothers didn't bother to hush them up.

Thalia caught Eden's eye, and licked her own thumb with a wet, languorous tongue. *His thumb instantly felt better.* He was amazed, but he attributed the relief to a warm stirring of lust that circled his heart, moving closer and closer like a band of marauding savages. He felt his ears flush, a sure sign that he was embarrassed, but somehow he couldn't take his eyes off of her. It was as if they were all alone.

He drew his thumb out of his mouth and licked it, mirroring her. The women sitting on the lawn with Thalia smiled. They could see the magic she was weaving.

Thalia had made friends with the women over the last few days, coming up in the bus with them each morning and then walking up the mule trail, chatting and watching the work to pass the time of day. The women found the attraction between her and the priest a great source of cheap entertainment, and they welcomed her into their circle although they were still unsure which village she was from. Somewhere near Cap-Haitien was all they knew, and Thalia wasn't one to divulge details. She seemed to enjoy being a mysterious, beautiful woman, and her air of confidence lent credence to their suspicion that she must be possessed of a great deal of power. Power in Haiti could run deep and dark, and now that she had insinuated herself into their circle, they felt it best to just let her be and watch whatever developed, until they could learn more about her.

In a dense stand of trees behind the women on the lawn, a Haitian man, tall and powerful, was watching Thalia and Eden. He, too, saw the magic that the young woman had over the priest. He saw the priest's burning desire as plainly as a mystic could see his acolyte's aura. Day by day, the man knew that she would draw Eden ever closer. But he would be on watch. He would be there when she finally captured the priest, no matter how long it took. He would wait. He had all the time in the world.

The women knew he was there, and they ignored him. He was probably crazy, or just retarded. Perhaps he was a zombie. There were several in the area, but they mostly kept to themselves. They lived in and around the graveyards, but they could range far and wide if their masters sent them on an errand. Most of them were simply doomed to wander like ghosts at a party, and they did no harm if people kept their distance and didn't rankle them. Like bums, they were invisible to the general populace, unless their craziness drew too much attention or demanded a response. This one, the poor thing, just lurked in the trees all day and watched Thalia, but that seemed completely unremarkable to them. A beautiful woman was a sight to behold, and he was a man. He seemed harmless enough.

CHAPTER FORTY

Retired Special Agent Peter Johnson parked his '76 Land Cruiser in the side lot and walked through the oily puddles, headed for the front entrance of the Hale Boggs Federal Building on Poydras Street. He was lugging his old briefcase, weighed down with Biblical research. The rain had stopped, but the sky was a uniform shade of battleship gray. It would probably be that way all week.

When he came around front, he stood on the sidewalk for the longest time looking up at the façade of the downtown building, working up his courage to go up the stairs. The two security guards inside were watching him, and some IT techs were coming down the steps, carrying PCs out of the building. Mas was flying off to Haiti to wrestle with God-knows-what, Johnson reminded himself. The least he could do on his end was sit his ass down in the Federal Library and see what he could find.

He drew a determined breath and forced himself to put one resolute foot in front of the other, and soon he was trotting up the steps just like Elliot Ness. Not like Kevin Costner, like Robert Stack. Stack was the Man. Growing up watching Robert Stack in *The Untouchables* on TV is what inspired Johnson to become a Fed. Desi Arnaz produced the show, and kept it on the air despite several threats from the mob. America had more to thank him for than *I Love Lucy*.

TV was black and white back then. *Everything was black and white back then,* Johnson thought, purposefully ascending the granite staircase. *Nowadays, everything was shades of gray.*

One hand gripped his briefcase and the other was jammed in his raincoat pocket. Robert Stack strode into the lobby, frowning like he always did, and stopped before a metal detector. *Well, that's new,* Johnson thought. *What would Robert Stack do?*

The guards made it known with a glance that Johnson needed to stand still and remove his hand from his pocket. Slowly. *Right,* he reminded himself. *It's a whole new ball game.*

He slowly removed his hand and showed them what he was carrying – his driver's license and his old FBI badge. They recognized his name, and swapped glances.

He put his briefcase on the conveyor belt, and they put a bin on it for all his other stuff. He hadn't flown since before 9/11, but he knew the drill; he'd seen it on TV, in living color.

He removed his belt and shoes and dropped them into the bin along with his keys and phone, and then he stepped through the metal detector. He didn't trigger the alarm, and they let him through. But he didn't feel any safer within their security perimeter. They couldn't keep the Devil out.

The library was on the fourth floor. Banks of tall windows let in the afternoon gloom, and the view of the city was diffused through rain-beaded glass. The librarian smiled a pleasant hello from behind her new Mac as Johnson nervously approached her desk.

There were several agents and administrative staff sprinkled about the room at various tables, their heads buried in their work, but when a couple of agents looked up and recognized him, they began to whisper. Their reaction had a snowball effect, and soon the entire room was staring at him.

Johnson gulped and froze in place, painfully self-conscious, but the librarian kindly motioned for him to come forward. He complied and stood before her desk, holding his briefcase against his chest.

"Agent Mas called me, Mr. Johnson," she told him. "Make yourself at home." She waved an inviting hand at the long rows of reference volumes.

Johnson nodded, and scanned the room. "Oh, boy..." he breathed to himself. *Here goes nothing.*

CHAPTER FORTY-ONE

The sun was easing into a feather bed of clouds on the western horizon as the Learjet 45 banked over Le Golfe de la Gonâve and lined up on the main runway of Toussaint L'Ouverture International. It was a little after 4 p.m. local time.

Aided by a strong tailwind, the thirteen hundred mile flight from New Orleans to Port-au-Prince had taken just over two hours. They could have made even better time than that, but they had to avoid Cuban airspace.

Mas had been squinting out the portside windows during the entire descent, as they approached from out of the north and skirted around Cuba. She could just make out the glint of windows and sheet metal at Gitmo, the U.S. garrison at Guantanamo Bay. Gitmo occupied an isolated patch of beachfront property near the barren eastern tip of the island, a bastion of democracy on the last communist holdout in the western hemisphere. When Fidel took over the island in 1959, he was smart enough to leave Gitmo alone.

Mas knew some of the agents who had tangled with the Marines over the infamous interrogation methods they used there. But the Marines had their own way of doing things and the FBI wasn't welcome at Camp Delta, even though the Feds had been in the interrogation business long before Joe Kennedy was making his fortune as a rum-runner in these very waters.

The mountainous island of Hispaniola was a massive, jungled hulk to the east, set in a royal blue sea. Aside from the cities of Gonaïves and Saint-Marc and the carpet of corrugated roofs and wood smoke that was the Haitian capital of Port-au-Prince, urbanization in Haiti was intermittent at best. Mas had read in her briefing book that when night came, long stretches of coastline would lie in darkness, and the clusters of electric lights that did huddle on the beaches would dissipate as soon as they ventured inland.

The satellite photos in her State Department briefing book were starkly revealing. Aside from the occasional town or village square and the rare highway, much of the inland regions were lit in a dim yellow, almost red. As they descended and the lay of the land became more pronounced, Mas realized that the faint smudges of light she had seen in the photos must have been the glow from a million wood fires and charcoal braziers in the shantytowns and hamlets that dotted the countryside below.

The briefing book explained that the rural poor of Haiti had been cutting down their forests for decades to cook and keep warm. If that didn't change soon, the entire western third of the island, in contrast to the lush Dominican Republic that made up the center and the eastern part of Hispaniola, would eventually become a desert savannah as bleak as Easter Island.

The jet touched down lightly on the concrete runway, and then braked with a tremendous rush of exhaust as the twin fanjets were thrown into reverse. Within moments, the Learjet was taxiing off the runway at a leisurely pace, heading for a spot on the taxi tarmac at the north end of the international terminal.

They taxied to a halt at the corner of the long two-story stucco and glass building. It struck her as being much like a regional airport from mid-century America. Passengers had to disembark down rolla-way staircases and set foot on solid ground and then walk in the open air to the terminal.

It was her kind of place. She never liked the bustling commuter hubs like D.C. and Dallas and New Orleans. She preferred an airport that was more like an overgrown bus station, in which you knew that the place where you arrived was markedly different from the place you just left. It was much better than shuttling from one bland air-conditioned sky mall to another.

Just south of where they were parked, an American Airlines jet was disgorging its passengers before the main entrance of the terminal. Ekaso was on board, and a screaming throng of his fans was pressing up against a phalanx of local cops guarding the bottom of the rollaway staircase. The other passengers were disembarking first, and they had a tough time threading their way through the excited fans who had come to see their hero.

He appeared at the threshold behind them with his manager Ivey Johnson, an Irish-American woman with green eyes, and the young star waved to his cheering fans below. They responded with a surge of boisterous enthusiasm. Ekaso's bodyguards stepped out of the airliner and flanked him and his manager, signaling to the crowd to mind their manners. It didn't seem to do much good.

The officers below parted the rowdy crowd again for the last few passengers, who streamed toward the entrance of the immigration building where other arrivals were lining up. They got in back of the immigration line and collected themselves, getting their bearings and taking in the lush tropical air, settling in for a slow advance as the line inched its way forward.

To keep their spirits up, the Boukman Experience was on hand playing *kompa* music for them. The women of the troupe were dressed in white and dancing barefoot, and encouraging the long line of tour-ists and returning locals to step to the rhythm, while the Boukman drummers kept up a syncopated chant.

Mas smiled, surveying the scene through a cabin window of the Learjet. There was a party going on, and the island was inviting everybody to come.

John opened the clamshell hatch and the dense tropical air rushed in, embracing them both. He breathed in deeply and smiled. No matter how often he flew, he never quite got used to the amine tinge of a pressurized cabin. And there was no point trying to cover it up with yet another vile chemical.

Energized by the fragrant humidity wafting through the hatch, he picked up her luggage and went down the staircase first, and then stood beside it and offered a gentleman's hand to help her disembark.

Mas angled around Ekaso's jubilant fans and headed for the back of the line at the immigration building, rolling her carry-on behind her with her briefcase strapped on top. She drank in her surroundings with each step, letting the place seep into her any way it chose. She loved to travel, and the first five minutes in a new place were always among her favorite moments.

The weather was a lot like New Orleans, only more so, she thought. It was the best way she could conceptualize her first impression. Like Southern Louisiana, Haiti was a fecund environment in which anything could take root and flourish, and usually did, for good or for ill. Western Civilization was invented in a temperate clime; the closer it got to the equator, the strands that held all the pieces in place became more and more tenuous.

Her ruminations were interrupted when a handsome black gentleman in a white linen suit approached her with a gracious smile. "I am Isaac La Croix," he said. "Welcome to Haiti."

Mas stopped and offered a smile in return, but it was tempered with hesitation. She had no idea who he was.

"Good afternoon, monsieur. Are you my liaison?"

"At your service," La Croix said with a slight bow.

Mas had to admit to herself that she was charmed. She extended her hand and La Croix shook it. Behind him, she noticed an officer of the Palace National Police coming out of the Salle Diplomatique door of the immigration building. The man stepped up beside her new liaison and nodded a polite hello, as La Croix gestured to the officer, keeping his eyes on Mas.

"Your passport, if you please," La Croix said to her, indicating that she should hand it to the PNP officer. She took it out of her jacket pocket and handed it to the man. He flipped through the pages quickly and carefully, and then he glanced at her with a perfunctory smile.

"Bonjour, Mademoiselle Mas. Suivez-moi, s'il vous plait."

He gestured toward the door he had just come out of, and La Croix took the handle of Mas' rolling luggage. As she started for the door, the officer finally glanced at La Croix. La Croix nodded an imperious hello, and they fell into step behind Mas, La Croix wheeling her luggage behind him.

Captain Felix of the PNP had recognized Isaac La Croix at once. Delatour, the Interior Minister, briefly visited the Salle Diplomatique office with the man earlier that day, and he showed the stranger every courtesy. Captain Felix had no idea who he was exactly, but he was certain that La Croix was not to be trifled with.

Just to be on the safe side, the officer stepped ahead of them and opened the door for the pair. In Haiti, it was always prudent to presume that someone had far more power than you or anyone you knew could possibly wield. Captain Felix lived through several coups, and retained his rank through each of them by keeping that simple guideline firmly in mind.

La Croix thanked him with a brief tip of his head, and then gestured for Mas to please enter first. They were making her feel like royalty. *Welcome to Haiti*, she thought, and stepped inside the Salle Diplomatique.

The Immigration Officer behind the counter stamped Mas' passport and handed it back to her with a smile.

"Voici votre passeport."

"Merci," Mas replied, and prayed that the lady didn't think she knew much more French than that. Ordering food was one thing; conversing was quite another thing entirely.

"De rien," the woman said.

Mas just smiled, and then turned to La Croix before she could get drawn into any small talk. "Where's Agent Francine?" she asked him.

Mas glanced around the office to make her point. Everyone there was wearing a local uniform. They were either officers of the PNP, the local police, or they were immigration officials. And they were all busy as bees, as if they actually worked there. There was no one around who looked anything like a female FBI agent, other than herself.

La Croix just smiled, standing close beside her with her carry-on. Before she could press him further, a senior officer of the PNP stepped up to them and nodded.

"Mademoiselle Mas?" the colonel inquired.

She nodded back.

"Please follow me," he requested, and turned toward a back door. Mas glanced at La Croix for a clue, but he just gripped the handle of her carry-on and gestured for her to go first.

The taxi tarmac and the main runway beyond gave up their last flourish of rippling heat as the sun eased behind the gauzy western clouds for its final hour of daylight. The crowd at the Immigration gate was a tired, sweltering throng, but they found their second wind when the late afternoon haze finally brought some relief. The doorway was jammed with people who by and large were in a buoyant mood from having just been greeted by the *kompa* band and from learning that they had flown in with an actual celebrity. A Babel of languages echoed off the walls and the high ceiling inside the building as the arrivals pressed forward and chatted about their flights, the weather, where they were from, where they were staying, and what their itineraries were.

FBI Special Agent Nadege Francine was late. She came straight from her office at the U.S. Embassy, in a Jeep Cherokee from the motor pool. The mid-size SUV was just the thing for whipping through the streets of Port-au-Prince in air-conditioned comfort, or racing on the twisting roads east of the city. But it couldn't fly over traffic jams.

Francine — nobody called her Nadege — was an exotic beauty of Haitian descent, and if people didn't notice the Jeep's license plate, they would routinely mistake her for a local rich girl rather than a Fed who was born and raised in Baton Rouge.

She walked briskly out of the terminal and headed for the Learjet taxied at the north end of the tarmac. The fuel truck was already there, and the clamshell door was open. She had a description of Christine Mas firmly in mind, courtesy of her old friend Mark Kaddouri, and expected Mas to step out of the plane at any moment.

Instead, the fuel truck crew disengaged their hose, hopped in the cab of their truck, and drove away as the steward in the Learjet closed the clamshell door. A moment later, the engines spooled up, the pilot released his brakes, and the jet began to taxi toward the runway.

Francine stopped in her tracks and looked around, then scanned the throng of people behind her on the tarmac. *Damn,* she thought, and dialed Mas' number from the text message Mark sent her.

Mas heard her phone softly ringing in its holster on her belt, but she was busy chatting with La Croix at the moment, and didn't want to seem rude. She turned off the ringer and let the call go to voicemail.

Francine let it ring, until the message came on. "Hi, Christine" she said, "Agent Mas? This is Agent Francine, pick up..." She was a firm believer in short and sweet messages, and ended the call, looking around for Mas as she speed-dialed Mark Kaddouri.

She had a fair idea of what Mas looked like, from the detailed description Kaddouri had already given her. He emailed Mas' picture to Francine earlier that day, but the ISP in Port-au-Prince suffered another one of its infamous glitches, and she couldn't get his email down from the server before she had to leave for the airport.

She got up on her tiptoes for a better look, but it was pointless; she wasn't a tall woman to begin with. Mark was already on the line, describing Mas' outfit to her.

"Hang on, Mark... No, I don't see any woman dressed like that."

She kept the phone to her ear, although it was almost impossible to hear above the din, and scanned the crowd.

CHAPTER FORTY-TWO

In the cool shade behind the terminal, Mas leaned close to La Croix, dropping her voice to a whisper. "Why am I being picked up by the entire Haitian army?"

La Croix smiled at her remark. The colonel had just taken them out a back door of the office to a security courtyard behind the terminal, formed by three blank concrete walls. The safe space was designed for the exclusive use of the Salle Diplomatique. The narrow driveway led to a barbed-wire gate, manned by armed guards sporting body armor and Kevlar helmets.

A fleet of five white Mercedes G550 SUVS was waiting for them. The vehicles were fully armored with run-flat tires, and displayed the blue decals of the PNP. They were idling with their drivers behind the wheel, and a senior guard was riding shotgun. Each guard had their ballistic window rolled down and their Street Sweeper automatic shotgun sticking out, as if they were daring anyone to get stupid on them.

Twenty PNP troops formed a protective cordon around the caravan. They held their M-16 assault rifles unsafetied and at the ready, keeping a wary eye on the surrounding rooftops. The only windows looking onto the courtyard were the small ballistic panes of smoked glass that flanked the back door of the Salle Diplomatique.

VIPs, government officials, diplomats, dignitaries, and criminals under extradition could be routed into and out of the courtyard, without creating a ruckus in the main terminal or generating a security headache. Beyond the gate lay several of the poorest neighborhoods in Haiti. Armored vehicles bristling with firepower had to be employed, piloted by lead foot drivers who stopped for nothing and no one. There were no speed limit signs in Haiti, but even if there were, the drivers would have ignored them anyway, and would have done so with impunity.

The troops weren't actually expecting an assault; it was mostly a demonstration of Haitian pride to show the American federal agent that they had their act together. Mas was suitably impressed, but she wondered what was up.

"They're the Presidential Police, madam," La Croix explained to her. "They're taking you to the White House to be briefed."

She was surprised. "About what? I'm just here to see an American priest."

La Croix simply smiled once again, and indicated that they would be riding in the middle SUV. One of the troopers snapped to attention and opened the rear passenger door. As Mas and La Croix got in the back seat, two troopers got into a pair of rear-facing jump seats in the back cargo area, with her carry-on between them and their assault rifles stuck out their open side windows.

In all the excitement, she completely forgot that someone had called her.

Inside the Salle Diplomatique, Agent Francine peered through one of the smoked glass windows and watched Mas getting into the vehicle, along with the gentleman in the white linen suit and the armed troopers. She was still on the phone with Kaddouri.

"She's been picked up by the PNP," she told him.

CHAPTER FORTY-THREE

A maze of tired, impoverished neighborhoods lay north and west of the airport, along the most direct route through town to the National Palace. Sodium lamps, mounted high up on the telephone poles, would be flickering to life when dusk came, lighting the pot-holed streets with a jaundiced shade of yellow. The poles were burdened with a rat's nest of power lines and cabling as if each household had strung their own wire, and in most cases they probably had. It was a miracle there wasn't a rash of electrocutions every time it rained.

The moon had set earlier that day, and so aside from the occasional street lamp, the neighborhood's nighttime illumination would mainly come from porch lights and the bare-bulb glare stabbing out the open windows and doorways of the festively painted shacks, all of them topped with rusting tin roofs.

The high beams and off-road lights of the speeding caravan announced their approach through the gathering haze, and Mas caught glimpses of urban living in a staccato stream of snapshots, as they rumbled past one cluster of hovels after another.

The air-conditioning was blasting and all the windows were down. *Just the way Mark likes to drive, only different,* Mas thought with a private grin. The vehicle was bristling with weapons thrust into the dusty air. Even the driver had a Glock in his free hand, his elbow resting on the windowsill. Mas was fairly certain that the rules of engagement were open to interpretation, and if anything crazy went down, the judge would side with the PNP.

She sat back and tried to relax, catching glimpses of families and old folks and restive young men as the caravan barreled through the faded neighborhoods.

The caravan suddenly braked and all the drivers leaned on their horns. Mas sat up in alarm, instinctively reaching for her Sig-Sauer in the holster riding high on her hip. La Croix touched his own weapon, just in case. They let her strap on her gun at the Salle Diplomatique, though they explained that she had to hand it over when she got to the palace. That was fine by her, but they weren't there yet, and all the troops were shouldering their weapons.

She craned her head to see out the side windows. A crowd of people had spilled into the street, blocking their way. They were gathered for a bonfire in an empty dirt lot, chanting and dancing wildly to a hectic, persistent drumming. A large animal, perhaps it was a doe, was roasting on a spit over the fire. To her untrained eye, it looked like a drunken barbecue, but as the caravan rolled closer she realized it wasn't anything of the sort.

A bare-chested *houngan* was dancing around the bonfire, dangling a wristwatch in his hand for the chanting crowd to see. He drank from a bottle of rum in his other hand, and as he took the last swallow he bit off the glass neck of the bottle and chewed it with a leer on his lips. That inspired the crowd and several of the others who were drinking, both men and women, to do the same.

Manbos in long white dresses were prancing around the fire, stamping their feet and keening in a strange language Mas had never heard before, lifting their hems for the men in the crowd to grind against them. Some of the sex was simulated, and some of it was quite real.

Two of the dancers were juggling a large painted portrait of Zamba Boukman. They tossed it into the fire and the crowd cheered wildly, over and over.

The *houngan* suddenly shouted an order. Half a dozen men rushed in and lifted the heavy iron spit onto their shoulders in response. The *houngan* then grabbed a long pike that was being kept for him by two young women, and held it aloft. The tip of the pike was fitted with a life-like plaster bust of a scowling Zamba, hand-painted in careful detail.

The *houngan* raised the pike aloft and quick-marched down the road. The six men followed, carrying the carcass double-time. The crowd followed behind them, bringing their drums and rum and surging into the street.

Mas' SUV jerked to a slow crawl as they passed the bonfire. For several slow seconds, she was eye to eye with Zamba's image, as angry flames danced around his scowling portrait.

"What's all that about?" she asked La Croix, keeping her eyes on the parade just ahead of them.

"Voodoo," he told her. "The local religion. They've been active lately."

"Why?"

He glanced at her before he replied, looking at the back of her head. "They sense something is about to happen," he finally said. "Don't you?"

She still had her back to him. "Who's the guy in the painting? They don't seem to like him very much."

"His name is Zamba, a powerful voodoo priest, hundreds of years old. They want him to go away."

She finally looked back at him and shrugged. "He's dead. What's the problem?"

Isaac La Croix smiled at her without humor, while the driver glanced in his rearview mirror at the naïve white lady in the back seat. He was one of the PNP bodyguards who accompanied Minister Delatour to meet Zamba at the airport. Her silly question made him stifle a laugh.

"People say he still walks among us," La Croix patiently explained to her.

Mas frowned, digesting his statement, and turned back to watch. It vaguely reminded her of a New Orleans funeral in that it was a throng of chanting, dancing participants, but they didn't seem particularly jovial. Far from it. There was distinct menace in the air. And given what La Croix had just told her, even though it couldn't possibly be true, the entire display was somehow disturbing.

She peered ahead through the driver's open window, trying to get a better look at what the men were carrying. She didn't know they had deer in Haiti, particularly within the city limits. A hunter must have bagged the animal in the hills, and brought the entire carcass back to the city.

The caravan was still moving forward at a crawl and all the drivers were still leaning on their horns. The lead vehicle finally passed the head of the procession and accelerated, and then the one behind it did the same.

Mas' driver floored it and they rolled up quickly alongside the head of the procession. The charred carcass chained to the spit was swaying side to side with each step the six men took, in rhythm to the drumming and chanting of the crowd that followed behind them.

Just before Mas' vehicle overtook the men, the carcass finally came into clear view. It wasn't a doe. It was a naked man, still smoldering from being roasted alive.

The *houngan* was dancing around the men who carried the spit, taunting the corpse with what Mas surmised was the dead man's wristwatch. It wasn't merely a trophy; it was a way for the *houngan* to hold on to the man's soul.

She sat back heavily as the Mercedes picked up speed, and stared unfocused at the back of the driver's seat trying to absorb what she just witnessed. It took a while. Particularly unsettling to her was the fact that no one else in the vehicle seemed to think that anything was out of the ordinary.

"He was probably one of Zamba's priests, celebrating his return," La Croix finally explained softly.

"Where did he go?" she asked him, still staring at the back of the driver's seat.

"To Hell, Agent Mas. Where else would the Devil's servant go?"

CHAPTER FORTY-FOUR

She finally turned to La Croix. He was smiling again, almost apologetically. "We have a colorful history and many fanciful legends," he told her, "all woven into a rich and beguiling tapestry."

"Yeah, so I've been reading."

She didn't feel like talking, and looked out the window at the careworn neighborhood as they picked up speed and continued toward the palace. The caravan's dust muted the harsh reality of the neighborhood to a soft focus.

La Croix smoothly resumed their conversation right where she dropped it. "You may know that centuries ago, when the French occupied this island, things were very bleak," he said.

She turned back to him with a weak smile. He was the perfect gentleman. They had been riding for the last few minutes in silence, ever since they saw the roasted man. La Croix correctly sensed that she wasn't in the mood for a chat, but he decided that it was better to distract her than to let her to wrestle in silence with what she had witnessed.

"The slaves were mistreated," he told her. "The French showed us no mercy. They did many unacceptable things. Zamba Boukman dedicated his life to gathering the slaves together."

"To revolt?" she asked him, and he nodded.

"Yes," he said. "But it didn't go smoothly, I'm afraid. The French scheduled him for execution. Legend says it was then that Zamba made his unholy bargain."

La Croix told her how Zamba had been locked in a cage, beaten and bloody, and was about to be executed at dawn by Napoleon's men. He prayed hard that night to the Haitian goddess Anacaona. Finally a ball of light appeared in his cage. But it wasn't Anacaona who had come to answer his prayers; it was the Devil himself who materialized before him.

Zamba had captured Lucifer's attention because he was born of a *loa* and raised by a voodoo priest, and it was through Zamba that Satan realized he could finally establish his church on earth. Satan's first blow was to turn Adam and Eve to sin; his second blow was to make an entire country worship him. Proof of the legend, the believers said, was that President Aristide, an expelled Catholic priest, finally sanctioned voodoo as a legitimate religion in Haiti. Voodoo priests could now perform legal marriages and baptisms anywhere in the country. The *loa* was out of the bottle.

Traditional Catholics were mortified, but it was too late; the die had been cast. Zamba was alive, and it was only a matter of time before Lucifer's third blow was to strike. Soon he would reign over all of mankind, with the faithful Zamba Boukman at his side.

Her lips curled into a dry smile. It was a hell of a yarn, but it was clear that La Croix didn't share her amusement for fairy tales.

"He made a pact with Lucifer," La Croix told her. "His immortal soul for the lives of the slaves, and freedom for all of Haiti. According to legend, the deal that Zamba made is embodied in the necklace. It is his burden, his yoke. The Haitians are forever free, while he is forever a slave."

Mas was thoroughly entertained by the scary story, but La Croix wasn't quite so buoyant. She smiled to lighten the mood. "That's quite a bedtime story," she said. "I'll bet you guys scare the pants off the kiddies with that one, huh?"

La Croix took a moment, and then he smiled back at her. "Of course!" He assured her, laughing it off. "Of course we do..."

He could tell that for all her intelligence, the woman had dismissed the entire story without so much as a second thought. *Not a wise thing to do in Haiti,* he grimly thought, though he continued to chuckle for his guest.

"So what happens if this guy Zamba loses his necklace?" she asked him.

His laugh faded, but he managed an expression of mock concern. "Oh, I would never want to find out, *mademoiselle.*"

His humor didn't go over as smoothly as he hoped, and there was an uncomfortable silence. Mas sensed that she had somehow lost the rhythm of their banter. But then he laughed again, and she joined him, secretly relieved.

Their driver had been watching them in his rearview mirror during their entire conversation, and spoke English well enough to follow every detail. He didn't find anything amusing about it at all. Such flippancy was dangerous.

They sped through the neighborhood as the sun slipped behind a giant American Airlines billboard. Although it was humid, Mas' lips felt dry. She slipped her hand in her pocket and took out her lip balm, but it dropped to the floor and rolled under her seat.

The Haitian flag snapped in the breeze over the center dome of the National Palace in downtown Port-au-Prince, spotlighted for all to see. Blood red and royal blue, with an intricate coat-of-arms, it featured a tall palm tree in the center as a symbol of independence. As they came around the curve and slowed, Mas got her first good look at the building. It was a truly magnificent structure, built in the high French style, a gesture to the nation's cultural roots.

They were right on time, Mas thought. Their meeting was at 5 p.m. and it was about ten till. As they approached the main gate, she glanced out her window while La Croix wrapped up a quick thumbnail sketch of the palace for her. He was explaining that the White House, as it was locally known, had a turbulent history to match that of the nation. It was actually the second building to occupy the site. A bomb damaged the first one in 1912, in the assassination of President Leconte. This new palace was built soon afterward, during the U.S. occupation that began during the First World War and lasted into the 1930s.

La Croix told her that this new building had suffered its fair share of misery, too. Haitian troops stormed up the front steps more than once; a bomb was dropped on the roof by a renegade Haitian Air Force pilot; less than twenty years ago, a Duvalier loyalist was dragged outside and down the front steps after an attempted coup d'état. The incident didn't end well for him. Haiti had a long litany of trouble and woe, he told her, and so did its seat of power.

The lead vehicle turned into the open entry gates, zooming past the guards who stood at stiff attention. La Croix leaned back in his seat to wrap up his spiel.

"Since the coup," he told her, "there has been even more devilry. Your Marines paid us another visit in '94 to help Aristide hold onto power, and then a few years later your CIA 'escorted' him out of the country. For his own good, of course."

"Of course," she quipped back.

"So you see, mademoiselle," La Croix finished in a playful, teasing voice, "the National Palace is quite used to Americans coming to call regardless of the circumstances, at all hours of the day or night."

Mas just grinned, and caught a glimpse of one of the palace guards as they breezed through the gate. He was careful not to catch her eye, but he could clearly see the attractive American woman sitting in the back seat. They all knew she was coming; the lead car had radioed ahead.

La Croix would stay behind with the caravan, he explained to her as they rolled up the long curved driveway. The troopers would escort her inside, where another member of the President's staff would be waiting to meet her. She would have to leave her weapon and luggage with the troopers, but other than that one precaution, she would be extended the utmost courtesy. They wouldn't wand her at the door, or have her step through the metal detector.

She realized that La Croix would undoubtedly go through her carry-on while she was upstairs, but her briefcase was locked and she knew he couldn't pick it. The lock and hinges were designed and built by the CIA. A good friend at Langley had them installed as a birthday present. *So there,* she thought with a private grin. *Stay behind and root through my things, and see how far you get, buster.*

Mas just smiled at him as their caravan slowed to a crawl before the front steps of the White House. He was smooth; she gave him that. But like most men, he was thoroughly transparent. She reached for her seat belt latch as she glanced at her watch. It was 4:53 p.m., local time.

CHAPTER FORTY-FIVE

The driver stopped their SUV and Mas unlocked her seat belt. As she let it roll into its housing, she felt something odd. She didn't know what it was exactly, but she clearly sensed that something was wrong. The SUV, the palace, her purse, and everything around her seemed just ever so slightly *off*, somehow. She couldn't put her finger on what it was, but it was as if everything suddenly shifted.

And it had. Fifteen miles west and eight miles down, the earth moved under her feet. It was always moving; tectonic plates do that. But instead of its usual snail's pace of a quarter-inch per year, the entire island and everything on it began to shift more than six feet to the west, all in one go.

A gut-churning rumble welled up from the bowels of the earth and the windows of the palace rattled in their frames. A massive chunk of plaster popped off the façade, and then another one. Weighing several tons apiece, they crashed to the pavement, throwing up a tremendous cloud of dust.

Mas grabbed her door handle and the back of the driver's seat, fighting down a yelp of panic. The PNP troopers instinctively gripped their weapons and swallowed back their fear, but a monster was suddenly upon them and they couldn't fight back. They crossed themselves for divine protection and piled out of the five vehicles, hanging onto their doors and gaping in wide-eyed astonishment at the wobbling façade of the palace directly in front of them. They were utterly petrified, but there was nowhere to flee and there was nothing to do but hang on and pray for deliverance.

The rumbling swelled and grew deeper as the entire mass of the island acted like a solid sub-woofer. The rocky substrata resonated with the muzzled rumbling of two tectonic plates grinding past each other. Force waves were propagating around the world through the earth's crust, and radiating out of the Caribbean basin into the Atlantic Ocean and beyond.

The palace walls twisted as the Mercedes lurched and shuddered, its computerized suspension working overtime to counteract the weirdly shifting pavement below.

The rumbling mutated to a deep, continuous roar as terrified screams punctured the air and the first billows of dust began rolling in from the neighborhood. The street in front of the palace rippled as though it were floating on a choppy sea. As the undulation swept down the avenue, a row of buildings across the street slumped against each other like dominos and collapsed, burying panicked people on the crowded sidewalk and everyone still inside.

Mas leaned against her door and pushed her way out of the lurching SUV. She hung onto the open door with both hands as the pavement lurched beneath her feet, and she stared up at the palace, unable to move. She could clearly see inside, through the twenty enormous pairs of French doors that lined the first and second floors. The people on both floors were in a mad panic and scrambling for the exits, but it was too late. The second floor walls suddenly buckled and the entire roof pancaked down to the first floor, crushing everyone upstairs.

Mas, La Croix and their driver and bodyguards frantically scrambled away from their vehicle. As they did, the main dome over the grand staircase dropped through the second floor and came to a halt atop the first floor columns. The entire portico blew outwards from the impact, burying the front steps under a landslide of debris.

The two SUVs at the front of the caravan were instantly smothered, as well as the front half of the Mercedes that Mas had been sitting in just moments before. Within a few short seconds, the entire building had sunk into itself like a sad, deflated airship.

Everyone who had been in the front two PNP vehicles was buried alive. Their comrades could hear their screams of agony, echoed by more cries of panic and pain issuing from the collapsed palace, piteous voices that cut through the thick, choking clouds of pulverized plaster.

The entire city was dissolving around them. Wails of terror from three million mortal souls filled the dusty air, blending with an ungodly rumbling that shook the crowded hills and shantytowns for miles around. 230,000 people lay dead or dying. The White House was gone, along with 250,000 residences, 30,000 commercial buildings, the National Assembly building, the Port-au-Prince Cathedral, and the main jail.

After thirty-five endless seconds, it was all over.

CHAPTER FORTY-SIX

The chirps of a thousand car alarms mixed with the myriad cries for help, as a chorus of terror and panic drifted toward the shattered palace from every direction. Desperate shouts to locate victims could be heard in response. La Croix and the PNP troopers were determined to help their fallen comrades, and took their first wobbly steps toward the pile of rubble that buried the two lead vehicles. Several of the men were still alive; they were screaming loudly for help as their blood seeped out from under the debris.

Mas let go of her back door and took a tentative step forward to join them, when a firm hand came out of the dust cloud behind her and grabbed her arm. She turned to whoever it was, thinking it was a protective gesture by one of the troopers from the trailing vehicles. But it was a woman.

"I'm Nadege Francine. *Come!*"

She gently but firmly pulled Mas toward her Jeep Cherokee, parked further down the driveway. Even in the tumult of the disaster unfolding around them, Mas noticed the U.S. Embassy license plate. But she back-pedaled, jerking her thumb at the half-buried SUV she arrived in.

"My bags," she explained.

Francine nodded and went with her to the partially crushed Mercedes. The rear door had been left open by the two troopers who piled out of the back in the first moments of the quake. But the impact of the debris that crushed the front of the SUV had slammed the door shut. The entire body of the vehicle was twisted now and the back door was stuck, its bulletproof glass still intact. They could see her carry-on and her briefcase inside.

They yanked repeatedly on the door, one foot planted on the bumper for leverage, and after several frustrating attempts they finally wrenched it open with a groan of twisted metal.

Mas yanked out her carry-on and briefcase and lugged them down the littered driveway to Francine's Jeep. Francine led the way, her badge out and held high and her other hand on the pistol strapped to her hip, just in case the people scrambling around them got any funny ideas. There was a wild edge of panic in the air, and anything could happen.

They piled into the Jeep and before Mas could buckle up, Francine peeled around in a tight circle and quickly weaved her way around chunks of debris, heading down the driveway for the main gate, one hand on the wheel and the other one on her weapon.

When they got to the gate, the panicked guards thought they had to show some kind of authority, to restore some semblance of order, but Francine just shot them a stern look and they let her pass.

As soon as they were on the boulevard, Francine had her window down and her weapon held aloft in her left hand, a clear warning to anyone on the street. Mas did the same, gliding her own window down and holding her Sig-Sauer aloft in her right hand. But nobody paid them any attention and after a few moments, they glanced around to assess the situation.

They were stunned by the world they were moving through. It seemed as if the entire city had just been carpet-bombed. Sirens and alarms were wailing and chirping in every neighborhood. Fires had broken out and more were erupting every few seconds. Boiling black smoke added to the dust-choked air and accelerated the rising sense of apocalyptic doom that engulfed the populace.

The streets were clogged with panicking people and screaming children, many of them dazed and injured, some of them grievously. It was evident that several would be crippled for life, or die from their injuries and the infections that were sure to follow. Those who were still largely in one piece were screaming for their loved ones and digging through the rubble with their bare hands.

They stared at the chaos unfolding around them as Francine's Jeep inched down a wide thoroughfare, threading through any clear space she could find.

"This is bad," she said in a hushed voice. "This is very bad."

Mas saw something out of the corner of her eye and turned her head to get a better look.

"Zamba," she said.

Francine glanced at her, surprised that Mas even knew the name. Mas pointed to something ahead, and Francine looked to see what it was.

The American Airlines billboard was slumped against a shattered building, and a wall had collapsed on the procession of villagers. The roasted corpse they were carrying was lying in the road, still chained to its pole. The *houngan* who had been leading the procession was facedown in the street, crushed by falling concrete. He was wearing the wristwatch of the roasted corpse, and his dead hands still gripped the pike with Zamba's bust.

But the pike wasn't lying on the pavement. Rather, it was weirdly upright, almost perfectly erect. When the *houngan* fell, the base of the pike wedged into a deep crack in the asphalt, and the rubble that buried him served to keep the pike planted and stable.

Francine rolled to a halt, staring at the macabre sight of Zamba's bust scowling at the destroyed city.

"Isaac told me about Zamba – " Mas began.

But Francine cut her off, suddenly testy. "Outsiders *always* misunderstand the legend of Zamba, no matter *how* many times they are told!"

She turned to Mas and continued in a stern voice before Mas could even respond. "*Haiti* didn't make a bargain with the devil, Agent Mas, *Zamba* did! And yet there are those who *still* blame him for Haiti's plight, and those who blame Haiti for his loathsome bargain."

Francine's frown twisted into a derisive sneer. "As if our ancestors had actually begged him to do something so foolish!"

She realized she was venting and knew that Mas didn't deserve it, but they were in the middle of an unfolding catastrophe and she was nearly at her wit's end. But so was Mas. Francine took a breath and continued in a quieter voice.

"Voodoo can be used for good or bad, like any other religion. In that way, they are all the same."

She suddenly frowned, remembering something that Mas just said. "And who is this Isaac?"

"Isaac La Croix," Mas told her, "the man who met me at the airport. He's with the President's staff."

Francine was puzzled. "My office at the Embassy works directly with the President's staff. I can assure you, they have no Monsieur La Croix."

Mas frowned as well, hearing the news. She was just as puzzled as Francine was. She looked away, angry with herself that she had been so easily fooled by the smooth-talking Frenchman, or whatever he was, or whoever he was...

But as she gazed out the windshield, her mind drifted away from self-criticism and quickly became riveted to the here and now. Everywhere she looked, she saw human disaster on a colossal scale. The damage and misery were absolutely horrific, and it was overwhelming to think that every other part of the metropolis was likely to be as bad as the street they were on. Compounding the tragedy was the utter certainty that as even bad as it seemed now, it was sure to get much worse as the days rolled on.

CHAPTER FORTY-SEVEN

The marketplace in the village below the Citadel was especially busy for a Friday morning. Although the northern highlands were largely untouched by the quake, the locals knew that shortages would inevitably follow, and that some things would likely be in short supply for months if not years. A lifetime of living on the razor's edge of poverty taught a person many lessons, and the fragility of rural supply lines was one of the harshest lessons to learn.

Friday at sunset was the time of week when those who were lucky enough to have jobs were usually paid. Since pocket money commonly ran out long before the following Friday morning rolled around, Friday morning was always the slowest time of the week.

But all that changed with the work that the orphanage brought to town. The construction project at the Citadel triggered a flurry of business in the village below, and the ebb and flow of local finance changed as a direct result.

The early morning mist had burned away and the sun was dazzlingly bright in a clear blue sky. It was a glorious winter day and there was commerce and hope in the air. Despite the national tragedy, there was a sense that there would be some respite for this particular village from all its years of weary anxiety. The rich and powerful Catholic Church was watching over them now, and only the *loas* were unhappy about it.

The locals milled in the dusty street, along with a sprinkling of recently arrived European relief workers who were secretly relieved at not having all that much work to do this far north, a couple hundred miles from the epicenter near Port-au-Prince. Some shacks had collapsed in the quake, but they were about to keel over anyway. Nobody died, there was one heart attack, one person had fractured their wrist and three people twisted their ankle.

During market hours, the street had always been more of a village square than a main drag. Amidst the random interactions of the morning crowd, a clear space happened to form in the middle of the road, and for some unaccountable reason it stayed empty and open, as if it were a hole in the world.

Devlin appeared in the open space, although he was quite invisible to any mortal there. His five fallen angels stepped out of the crowd, also unseen by anyone, and formed a circle around their master.

As always, they spoke in unison, their voices blending into one resonant murmur. "My Lord," they greeted him.

Devlin was in a foul mood. "You are aware of why I have come," he hissed.

"So is He," they replied. They didn't cast their eyes downward, but instead looked directly at him. This was something new, and their boldness displeased him.

"Then summon Him," Devlin shot back.

The angels lowered their heads, raised their arms, and began to hum. As they did, the light of the real world faded, along with their surroundings. As they extended their arms upward and as their humming grew ever louder, they faded away as well, leaving Devlin standing alone in pure darkness.

He waited, and then the light began to come. At first it touched him like delicate gold threads, coming upon him more and more until the tendrils streamed down in a radiant cascade, washing away the darkness and holding him in a pure, luminous embrace.

Lucifer bowed his head and knelt in respect. "My Lord," he whispered.

"Lucifer..."

"No matter how this ends, I will always love You," Lucifer said.

"And I will always love you," came the gentle reply.

Lucifer looked up to the source of light. There was something he wanted to say, and he was bold enough to say it. "This argument will finally be settled," he said in a strong, clear voice. "It's long past time that Your children learn the truth."

"The truth is always there, for those who earnestly seek it."

"Where?" Lucifer snarled, and his features flickered as he fought to control himself. "In the Bible? It *reeks* of hate and hypocrisy!"

"Man is free to see the world as he chooses —"

"*Believing is seeing!* You offer them faith, not freedom."

"They are My children. And My will has never led them beyond the protection of My grace."

"What of *their* free will?"

He waited for a reply, but there was none forthcoming.

"I loved You freely!" he said. "That is *my* will. Always, now, and forevermore."

The light glowed brighter and warmer, but he was Devlin now and its comforting radiance failed to soothe him. He began to shed tears of blood. "I didn't turn away from You!" he cried out. "I never did. It was You who cast me away! The one who loved You most."

He waited for a response, but again there was none and that roused him to anger. Devlin smiled darkly, his confidence intact and his transformation complete.

"When I win this bet — and I *will* — it will be glorious to see You uncreate Man!" he said.

311

"And how will one without a heart and soul ever grasp the essence of My children?"

Devlin's smile grew more wicked. "I'll never know."

He waited, but he heard no response. The light simply grew brighter, and then slowly, softly faded away.

As it did, the marketplace faded back into existence around Devlin, and so did his dark angels. The locals were still blithely unaware of his presence or of his companions, and for a little while longer the patch of road remained empty. People passing by didn't seem to think anything of it; it was just a hollow spot in the world that nobody noticed.

But soon it was filled with people again, and they passed through Devlin and his angels. They were vaguely disturbed by the experience, but quite unaware of what it could be. They shook it off and went about their business as if nothing had happened to them.

The angels meanwhile were still encircling Devlin, but their arms were once again by their sides and they seemed to be worried.

"Be of good cheer," he reassured them, but as strong as his powers of persuasion were, his advice fell flat. And he knew precisely why. He had become incapable of convincing himself; why should they believe him?

CHAPTER **FORTY-EIGHT**

FBI agents Nadege Francine and Christine Mas were bouncing along in Francine's embassy Jeep, negotiating a rutted path in the foothills below the Citadel as they searched for the priest.

They were exhausted from a long day of driving. It was late in the afternoon, and the fruit and water they snacked on at the village market was no substitute for a hot meal and a bath. The merchants told them that Eden set up a relief station in the foothills, and that he and the other priests were feeding some refugees who had made their way north over the last several days. Port-au-Prince wasn't the only disaster area; virtually the entire country was, and many people were on the road.

At first the merchants were sympathetic, but now they were nearly out of food and generosity. Thankfully the handsome priest had come down from the Citadel and told them to send all the hungry people up to him. They were camping up there now, somewhere in a meadow.

The drive north from Port-au-Prince had been nerve-wracking. Traveling the Haitian countryside was always an adventure, and to make matters worse there was a general exodus underway from almost every city, town and village. The entire population was rattled and desperate from the quake, and many of them had good reason to distrust anything built by the hand of man. Outdoor living seemed to be the only safe option. Most people stayed close to home, or what was left of it, but a good number of them headed out of town and just kept

313

going. Most of those headed north, away from the epicenter, clogging the roads and camping wherever they could. Even in the best of times, Haitian law and order was a hit-or-miss proposition, but now they were almost nowhere to be found. Mas and Francine had to draw their weapons more than once.

Chatting with Mas on the long drive north brought back memories of Francine's police training with Mark Kaddouri years before at the NOPD academy. On their rare days off after graduation, Francine and her boyfriend would go off with Mark and some of the other rookies in their muscle cars, tearing through the back roads of the bayou cruising for crawfish shacks.

The Branding Killer stories sickened her, but it didn't surprise her that the trail led to Haiti. From the way Mas explained things, voodoo was likely involved, and it was no shock to Francine that the killer was after a priest. *If you're going to kill a priest,* Francine thought, *Haiti was a good place to do it. It was a good place to kill anyone.*

More than a thousand earthquake refugees were camped in a mountain meadow, rimmed by lush stands of trees made nearly impassable by tropical foliage. They were desperate souls, with no transportation and little more than what they carried on their backs, or could stuff into carts and wagons. Campfires were being tended to, and several of the men were back in the trees digging a latrine.

On a rise that overlooked the squalor, Eden and his fellow clergy had set up a long row of tables. Several large gutted ocean fish were laid out side by side, and were free for the taking. Most of them had already been picked clean, but there was still some meat on the bones. Dozens more fish were in tin washtubs under the table.

The catch had been brought up from Cap-Haitien, courtesy of a Cuban trawler that made port in the minutes after the quake. The crew heard the news on their shortwave radio, and assumed that Cap-Haitien might be in the same desperate straits as Port-au-Prince. When they tied up and learned that wasn't the case, they contacted the authorities at the *Flota Cubana de Pesca* back in Havana anyway, and the FCP donated the entire catch on the spot.

Pans of bread were arranged in a separate row behind the fish. Father Ortiz had finally figured out how to get the oven started, and he had been baking up a storm with the Haitian nuns ever since, working in shifts through the long winter nights. The kitchen was the only warm room in the Citadel orphanage, so there were plenty of volunteers among the nuns to knead dough around the clock.

Most of the refugees were sitting around their fires, enjoying a full belly of bread and fish, the cool mountain air and the lush meadow greenery. Their children found a relatively flat patch of ground and were playing soccer. The game was a welcome diversion from their collective misery, and many of the adults were seated on a grassy hillock to watch the match and digest their lunch.

A hundred or so refugees were gathered at the tables for another helping, and as they got what they wanted, Father Eden handed each of them a half-liter plastic bottle of W.I.L. Several pallets of the American mineral water had been shipped to the Citadel by the Vatican, to tide them over until they could secure a reliable supply of potable water. Eden was spending his free time in the evenings Googling around for the best plans on how to build a rainwater catchment system and a solar still. The winter rains were coming soon, and he wanted to take advantage of them. But for now, they were grateful to be drinking bottled water. He had already handed out seven pallet's worth, or perhaps it was eight. He'd lost count working in the brilliant sunshine over the last few days. They had more up at the Citadel, but he couldn't remember exactly how much.

Bishop Lomani was working alongside Eden, standing with him behind the last table in the food line and handing out bottles of water. Lomani glanced down the line of tables at the scraps of food still laid out, and then cast an eye at the refugees dotting the meadow. He slowly shook his head, wondering how in the world they managed to do what they were doing. A nun beside him caught his eye, and her expression said much the same thing.

"It's a miracle that we fed all these people," he quietly said to her.

"Truly!" was her whispered reply.

Eden was standing on the other side of the bishop, but he was distracted by something and hadn't caught their remarks. Thalia Rose and some of the women from the village were working with the other nuns, standing behind the long row of tables dispensing remnants of food. As he leaned over his table to hand out a bottle of water, he sneaked a glance at her and discovered that she had been watching him. They exchanged secret smiles and got back to what they were doing.

Agent Francine saw the whole thing, and smiled knowingly. *Priests are men,* she reminded herself, a bit of wisdom her mother had given her on her first day of Catholic high school back in Baton Rouge.

She was leaning on the front fender of her mud-splashed Jeep, watching Mas approach the priest. While Francine was watching his private interaction with the beautiful young Haitian woman, she noticed that a Haitian man in the crowd loitering by the food tables was doing the same thing. Perhaps he was jealous, but in any case he didn't seem like he was there for the food. And now he was watching Mas approaching the priest at the water table.

"Father Eden?"

Eden turned to Mas and smiled. He recognized her at once as an American by her accent and by the way she was dressed. She was bathed in sweat and coated with sticky dust. He handed her a bottle of W.I.L.

"Water is life," he said, reciting the pearl of wisdom the bottling company adapted for their product's name.

Small world, she thought with a smile. It was her favorite brand. "Thank you, Father. Could we have a moment?"

"Certainly."

She motioned for him to walk with her, and they stepped away from the tables. As they moved away to be by themselves, Mas noticed the Haitian man out of the corner of her eye. He was standing in the crowd milling at the tables, but he wasn't eating and he didn't have a paper plate in his hand. Instead, he was watching Eden walking away with her. Mas was a stranger in a strange land, she reminded herself, and she didn't want to jump to any rash conclusions. Perhaps he was with someone picking up some food, waiting to help carry it back to their group. But there was something about the way he was loitering in the crowd. His body language told her that he was disconnected from the others around him, that he was alone in a hungry crowd but that he wasn't hungry himself. The priest seemed to be the only thing on his mind.

He was in his fifties, a tall, muscular man, of Haitian extraction from what she could tell. He could be a local, or he could be down here from America, tracking the priest and trying to blend in with the crowd. All she really knew at this point was that the priest was being hunted by a serial killer who was probably in his fifties, and that was good enough for her.

She didn't let on that she saw him, but she was sure that Agent Francine saw him, too. Whether the man knew it or not, he had just shot to the top of their persons of interest list. But first things first.

She stood with Eden in the late afternoon shadow cast by the Citadel, looming far above them atop Mount Bonnet a L'Eveque. Although her throat was dry, she didn't crack open the bottle of mineral water to resolve her discomfort. Her mind was on something else, and her smile faded as she extended her hand.

"Agent Christine Mas, Federal Bureau of Investigation. I'm down here from the New Orleans field office."

His eyes registered surprise, and as he shook her hand, his affable expression began to cloud with puzzlement. "You're a long way from home, Agent Mas. How can I help you?"

"Have you had any contact with anyone back in New Orleans since you arrived?"

"No, the refugees have kept us all so busy. Why?"

She took a breath, and plunged ahead. There was only one way to tell him. Just spit it out and clean up the mess afterward. "The Church of the Rebirth. There was a massacre. The Branding Killer was there."

Eden stared at her, completely stunned. He felt his entire body go numb. Several of the nuns and refugees were watching them, and so was Thalia Rose and the ladies from the village. Even though they couldn't hear, they could all see that something was wrong. The American woman had just told him something sad. Very sad.

"I'm so sorry," Mas said, and touched Eden's shoulder. The gesture of compassion brought tears to his eyes, and his face flushed with grief.

Behind Mas, the people fell silent watching them, and the Haitian man took a particular interest in the change of mood. Francine kept her eye on everyone who was watching, especially the man in the crowd.

"Oh, my Lord!" Eden managed to gasp. "Those poor women..."

His chin quivered as he stared unfocused at the ground. His tears rolled off his cheeks and made little dark spots on his dusty boots.

"We think he was looking for you," Mas explained quietly.

"Because of my birthday?"

She was surprised by that, and then she realized she probably shouldn't be. She nodded.

"I read the papers," he told her, catching the look in her eyes. "His victims were born on the same day I was."

She nodded. "I've come to save you," she told him.

He shook his head. "You came here to catch him."

She nodded again. "If I can, yes. But my first priority is to bring you home."

He looked away to the misty green mountain and the Citadel that crowned it. *The Bishop's Miter.* A light fog was drifting in from the north coast. There would likely be a cold rain that evening.

"I have no home now," he whispered. "They were my only family." He turned back to her. His tears had stopped.

"If this monster is looking for me, then let me be the bait in your trap."

Mas realized that this was no grandiose gesture born of grief. The man was completely serious, and entirely aware of the gravity of his statement.

"I'm afraid I can't do that..." she stammered, unprepared for his resolve.

"But I can," he told her bluntly. "I will not have my good sisters die in vain. These killings have to stop. So I will stay here and I will do my work, and if the killer's already here, then he will find me."

He waved his hand, taking in everything – the tables of food, the refugees and the Citadel, his orphanage in the clouds. "This is for *them* now. Especially now."

His face was red from weeping, but his quiet determination was entirely genuine. Despite herself, Mas realized that she was staring at him in awe.

CHAPTER FORTY-NINE

Thalia and the village women and the nuns all sensed that something heart-rending had just transpired. Mas could see them out of the corner of her eye, and she could see the Haitian man as well, still standing alone in the crowd, watching them.

Francine still had her eye on the man. She was sorely tempted to sneak up and embarrass him, just for the hell of it, but she glanced away as she heard a vehicle approaching.

A rusted Nissan Patrol with police markings was grinding its way up from the village, cresting the hill that she and Mas had just come over. Officer Jean-Claude Penet was driving the old clunker, the only thing the village could afford. Long years of duty in the countryside had battered both the SUV and Officer Penet all to hell. His back was sore from the bouncy ride, and he was itching to get back to his rum and cigars.

He had come to see what the priests were up to, and to find out what the refugees thought they were going to do while they were in his jurisdiction. He was well aware of the chaos that had descended all over the country, and while he wasn't heartless to the victims' plight, he didn't want to import their misery and neither did the village elders. Their village had been spared, and they intended for it to remain that way. As much as they wanted to help, they didn't want everything they had to be destroyed by an aftershock of homeless wretches.

Especially not now. His village in the valley below had blossomed into a beehive of profitable activity from the moment the priests arrived at the Citadel. Tourist dollars had always kept them out of absolute poverty, but the Citadel was so far off the beaten track and needed so much work that it was never the big attraction the government wanted it to be.

Building an orphanage at the Citadel would change everything. The collection of rooms the government gave to the orphanage was dark, dank, and moldy; most of them were without electricity and the plumbing didn't work. The pavilion they were building would be their classroom, lunchroom, kitchen and chapel until the interior was properly renovated. The renovations would take several months of hard work, perhaps longer than that. The entire village was looking forward to a prosperous year.

There were such a large number of orphans in Haiti, even before the quake, that if the first phase were successful the orphanage would surely grow and grow. Schoolteachers would come and they would need a place to live; food would have to be brought in and more would have to be grown; the grounds would have to be maintained; the government and the Church would spend their money and life would be sweet. And now this.

Penet kept the battered SUV in low gear and lurched his way along the rutted path. It was torturing the leaf springs, but that made him happy. His poor Nissan was due for a major overhaul, and the daily drives he was making up here would more than justify the bill. And the village could finally afford it.

Coming around a curve in the path, he punched the gas just to stress the front end one last time. The tires hit the sides of the twin ruts they were in and suddenly lurched to the left. The wheel slipped out of his hands and he shifted in his seat, accidentally stomping on the gas. The SUV wobbled out of the ruts and slid over the slick meadow grass.

The soccer ball caromed off the goalie's shin and sailed toward the sideline. One of the boys raced after it as it bounced high over the grass, and his friends were right behind him. Using a move he'd seen on TV, the kid launched himself on a heroic trajectory to head-butt the ball back onto the field.

Officer Penet slammed on his brakes, but his bald front tires didn't grab the moist grass and the inertia caused him to skid onto the field as if he were driving on ice.

His right fender slammed into the boy and sent him flying through the air, toward the throng of horrified adults. The boy landed in a motionless heap at their feet.

His mother screamed and wailed, dropping to her knees right beside him. Her aunt and her sisters joined her. The men glared at Penet and tossed away their rum bottles. Within moments, his vehicle was surrounded by an angry throng.

Penet panicked and tried to roll up his window as he loudly pointed out that he was a cop, but it was a futile gesture. Massive arms reached inside and pinned him against his seat, while a teenage boy lunged in through the passenger window, shut off the engine, and yanked the keys out of the ignition. They had all spent the last several days on the road, confronting mean and heartless cops. It was payback time. Penet's grip on the wheel failed him, and he was hauled through his open window.

Mas and Francine were at the fringe of the mob, their weapons drawn and held high, trigger fingers poised. They were shoving their way closer, shouting to be heard above the angry din. Francine worked her way behind the leader, and clocked him on the head with the butt of her automatic. He crumpled to the ground as she leveled her gun on the others. Mas stepped up behind her, and back-to-back they confronted the angry men that surrounded them...

But bullets speak louder than machetes, and the men finally lowered their weapons.

Eden was already kneeling at the boy's side, whispering a prayer and making the sign of the cross as he checked the boy's pulse. It was faint and unsteady, but it was still there. He didn't have to say anything; the women kneeling with him could see the anguish in his eyes. They wailed even louder as he desperately began CPR.

Penet had been released from the men who held him, and he groveled at the women's feet now, pleading his innocence. "It was an accident!" he wailed. "I swear to *God!*"

The other priests and all the nuns had come rushing over from the tables in a panic when the commotion started, and gathered the children to keep them away. But other than that, all they could do was watch and pray. They correctly sensed that the crowd was well beyond their reach or persuasion. The only reason Mas and Francine were still alive was that they had brought guns to a knife fight.

Eden was exhausting himself, trying to get a response from the boy's limp body. Sagging back on his heels, he looked to heaven and cried out in anguish. "Dear God, please don't take this child!"

Eden clenched a fist to his chest in supplication, and laid his other hand on the boy's heart, then took a breath and slowly let it out...

The boy took in a sudden breath, and opened his eyes.

The women gasped in astonishment, and began to cry out in relief and thanksgiving. Officer Penet looked up from his groveling and stared at the boy as well, and saw that he was stirring. He closed his eyes and wept, silently praying to God and thanking Him for His tender mercy.

A wave of relief washed through the crowd, and the tense standoff simply evaporated, as Thalia Rose kneeled down beside Eden to help comfort the boy. He glanced at her, and she smiled, touching his forearm in thanks. He put his hand over hers to thank her, and briefly stroked the back of her hand with his sore thumb.

Mas and Francine turned to each other, but neither one had been harmed. They holstered their weapons while the men that surrounded them gathered by their women and stood with Penet, the man they were ready to kill only moments before.

The other children had been standing by the cop's SUV the entire time, held back by the Lomani and the other missionaries. When their young friend suddenly began to breathe again, the missionaries made the sign of the cross and whispered prayers, and the children followed their example. Although they were young, they knew that something wondrous had just occurred.

Behind them, lurking in the foliage, the Haitian man was watching as well. But he wasn't focused on their young friend. He was watching Thalia Rose and the priest.

CHAPTER FIFTY

Lieutenant Mark Kaddouri thought Mrs. Gibbs was a beautiful woman; her quiet anguish over her dead husband only added to her inherent dignity. They had no children, and to him that was a shame. She would have done well as the matriarch of an extended family. She had the grit and the grace for it. The man had married well.

It was late at night and they were in the downtown morgue with Dr. Osborn the coroner. He was quite used to death in all its forms, and had to remind himself to be circumspect and appropriately dour for a viewing, which was hard to do after slicing someone open and taking stock of their viscera. He had sewn the dead guy up well enough to invite the missus over for a confirmation. Maybe she wouldn't throw up or scream like some of them did. He already had a long day and didn't have much patience left for dealing with some lady's histrionics about her stiff, unresponsive husband.

Except this case was different, so maybe she had a right to be freaked out. There was something weird about the corpse. There usually was with all the bodies that were piling up on Christine Mas' beat. But this was a new one, even for him. And he had sliced and diced a lot of stiffs for Mas over the years, ever since her old man got shot with his own gun. Or whatever the hell happened to Julian Mas; nobody really knew for sure. It still bothered Osborn, and he had a soft spot in his heart for Mas because of it.

He slid out the stainless steel drawer and glanced at Mrs. Gibbs. She had her eyes fixed on the refrigerated body like viewers always did, but she surprised him by glancing up and looking him in the eye before she nodded for him to go ahead and lower the sheet. Most of them didn't have it together enough to do that. They'd usually just stare at the covered corpse and nod, as if they expected Osborn to be watching them every moment for non-verbal cues. Maybe she was different.

Here you go, lady...

He carefully rolled down the sheet, but all she did was stiffen slightly upon seeing her dead husband's bloodless face. Then she quickly frowned, seeing something odd. Very odd, indeed. His flesh was covered with a strange assortment of welts, like some kind of hieroglyphics. Osborn had no idea what they were, and neither did the research geeks at the Federal building, even after spending the entire day searching the Internet for a pattern match.

It was like a gang had tagged him with a series of branding irons. But all mystery aside, it was the sheer indignity of someone defiling her husband's corpse that was too much for Mrs. Gibbs to bear. She turned away from the ghastly sight and buried her face in Dr. Osborn's shoulder. He glanced at Kaddouri, but the cop was already walking away and pulling out his cell phone. It was up to Osborn to dispense the tea and sympathy. Kaddouri would owe him one.

Mark stood well away from the weeping widow and eventually reached Mas down in Haiti.

"Chrissy?" he said in a quiet voice, "I'm at the morgue. Gibbs's autopsy is inconclusive. I've never seen anything like this."

He fiddled with his phone and sent her a picture he took of the corpse right before he brought in Mrs. Gibbs.

"There's these strange welts on his body, like ancient writing or something."

In Haiti, Mas and Francine were still in the mountain meadow, sitting on the hood of Francine's Jeep. Mas viewed the image Kaddouri sent her, and as she did, icy needles poked at her gut. Francine peeked at Mas' iPhone and frowned, wondering what in the world she was looking at.

"We can't touch Nano on this," Mas finally said to Kaddouri.

"But if the Church is involved..." he said, trailing off to let her fill in the rest.

She didn't reply immediately, and gazed across the meadow at Father Eden. He and a few of the priests were still serving loaves and fishes to the refugees, by the light of the rising moon.

"...we're going to get crucified," she said softly into her phone, completing Mark's sentence for him.

CHAPTER FIFTY-ONE

Cardinal Molinari looked up from his desk as the door creaked open. He had been meaning to ask Father Simone to oil it again, but they both knew that it creaked for as long as anyone could remember, and in a place like the Vatican that was an awfully long time.

He looked up from his newsletter to see who it could be at this early hour. He woke up after four fitful hours of sleep and it was barely first light now, a little after five thirty in the morning. Simone usually didn't come in before sunrise if he could help it.

He had no idea who in the world the tall, dark man could be. He seemed cordial, but it didn't put Molinari at ease. Not in the least. For one thing, he was dressed for a reggae festival and it was snowing outside.

Zamba entered the room, closed the door, and approached the cardinal's desk. "Forgive me, Father," he said with a wicked smile, "for I have come to sin."

The pain was excruciating, but Molinari couldn't scream. Zamba had somehow taken away his voice. He had lifted Molinari by the throat, completely out of his desk chair, and from that moment on Molinari had been mute. Through the initial flood of terror, the cardinal realized that he wasn't going to be throttled to death. No, it was bound to be more dramatic than that.

Zamba carried him by that one firm hand out to the empty hallway and up the stairs, and then up the maintenance staircase into the attic, and then up the last little staircase to the roof. Not a soul had witnessed the abduction. The residents of Vatican City who were up by now were busy saying their morning prayers. Molinari was praying right along with them.

The sting of frosty wind and icy snow shocked the old man back from the brink. His heart was being squeezed in a vise and he wasn't sure if breathing would matter anymore. He was certain he was having another heart attack. It would be his third, and likely his last. He welcomed it, certain that it would be kinder than what this monster had in mind.

Zamba did indeed have something else in mind. A large wooden cross was lying on the flat section of roof near the dome, and the moment Molinari laid eyes upon it he correctly guessed what he was in for.

Zamba slammed the old man's fragile body down on the broad wood column and as he pinned him with a knee to the chest, a fleeting question formed in the torrent of panic that engulfed the cardinal's mind. *Where in the world did he find an actual cross?*

This is the Vatican, came the peevish answer. It popped out of whatever corner of his consciousness that still continued to function unperturbed. A moment later, that tiny spot of lucidity was flushed away with pain, as the mallet came down and Zamba drove a spike through his right hand.

It fixed Molinari's entire awareness on that single point of his body, and became the sum total of what he could perceive, so that he didn't even know that his left wrist was being pinned by Zamba's immense grip. But when the mallet struck again, he knew, and found himself suspended between two transcendent points of agony.

His perspective returned as a direct result, and he realized that he was actually being crucified. It wasn't a dream; it wasn't even a nightmare. It was entirely, exquisitely real, right down to the splinters in his buttocks and the wet, icy snow that was falling on his face.

Zamba's massive hand held Molinari's ankles together, a spike pinched between his thumb and forefinger. He drove it through the cardinal's naked, crossed feet with one solid blow of the mallet.

Molinari's vision blurred with tears and his chin quivered as he struggled to breathe. His aged heart fluttered in a new and painful rhythm, and he couldn't even scream. That was the most awful part of it.

Zamba lifted the crucifix off the roof and held it so that Molinari was upside down, Zamba's one hand below the crosspiece and the other one up high behind Molinari's feet. He strode that way to the front balustrade, overlooking St. Peter's Square. There were normally thirteen statues arrayed on the posts that separated the sections of balustrade. The center statue, over the peak of the pediment above the portico, was a depiction of Christ the Redeemer. It was lying on the roof now, a heap of broken marble.

Zamba had been here earlier, in the wee hours of the morning, after he came upon the cross, the spikes and mallet in the attic, and moved them all up to the roof. They were an inspirational find, the long-forgotten props for a Passion play. Surveying the roof in the dead of night, he quickly decided that the center post, directly in front of the dome, was the perfect place to display his handiwork.

He removed the statue of Christ and discovered that a recent bout of restoration had secured the statue with an enormous stainless steel peg attached to the bottom of the statue that fit into a deep stainless steel mortise in the post. The original mortise had probably been hollowed out centuries before. The beam of the crucifix would be a tight fit inside the steel sleeve, but that was all to the better. When he laid down the statue of Christ he was quiet as a ghost, but he broke off the head and arms just for the hell of it, and then pissed on the face for good measure. The marble sizzled and melted in response.

Zamba stopped behind the center post, raised the upside down crucifix high, and rammed the top of it down into the steel sleeve that lined the mortise. *Square peg in a round hole,* he thought with a grin.

The impact was unbearable agony for Molinari. He gasped, but not only from the onrush of pain. It was more from the horror of his impending death, something that was simply too fantastic to believe. He was being crucified upside down, atop the basilica and directly above the portico overlooking St. Peter's Square, between the statues of St. John the Baptist and St. Andrew the Apostle.

Zamba placed his hand on Molinari's throat, and for the first time since Zamba seized him, Molinari heard the sound of his own painful gasps. His vocal cords were suddenly working again, and he began to pray out loud.

Zamba heard his mumblings and grinned. "He doesn't hear you."

From the moment it started, Molinari knew precisely what, and who, this was all about. He summoned enough control over his agony and looked Zamba directly and purposefully in the eye. He wouldn't beg for mercy, or give him the satisfaction of hearing his tortured screams. Cardinal Jacob Molinari would go to his Father with nothing but a prayer on his lips.

Zamba stood beside the crucifix and whispered a voodoo incantation. Molinari recognized the Creole patois; he often heard voodoo prayers back in New Orleans. As he stared into the ash-grey skies above, he saw a swarm of black dots coming closer and gradually taking shape. They were coming to feast on his flesh.

Molinari closed his eyes, though he knew it would be useless, and whispered a prayer to God Almighty as the murder of crows flapped in the cold air around him. But as the birds began pecking away at his flesh, Molinari screamed aloud, and forced the prayer through gritted teeth.

"*Sh'ma Yis'ra'eil Adonai Eloheinu Adonai echad! Barukh sheim k'vod malkhuto l'olam va'ed! V'ahav'ta eit Adonai Eluhekha b'khol l'vav'kha uv'khol naf'sh'kha uv'khol m'odekha...!*"

CHAPTER FIFTY-TWO

The Vatican clergy was already up and about, walking briskly in the frosty grey dawn of St. Peter's Square. Sunrise was coming, and the morning snow began to melt almost as soon as it touched the paving stones. Some hardy parishioners had already arrived for the morning blessing, and were milling about in small groups. Most of them knew each other from the surrounding neighborhoods and had been coming each morning for years. The first fleet of tour buses would be arriving soon, and despite the inclement weather of late winter, they relished the early morning. It was the only time they could have the Square to themselves.

The pigeons were swarming around the faithful for breadcrumbs, and some of them were prepared to indulge the pests. The two little girls who sold their roses at the foot of the steps had no use for the pigeons, and shooed them away as they laid out their blanket on a dry spot and arranged their roses for sale. To their way of thinking, pigeons were nothing more than rats with wings. They'd eat your lunch if you weren't looking.

Several parishioners brought their day-old bread in plastic bags and crushed it by the handful before tossing it high in the air. It was more fun to watch the birds scramble in mid-flight than to see them jostle each other on the ground. As crowded as their aerial feeding frenzies could be, the birds never collided with each other while they were on the wing. Their gyrations were cheap entertainment and amazing to behold, especially up close.

Signor Berlucci tossed a handful of crumbs up toward the Basilica's dome to watch the acrobatics against the gathering light, and suddenly paused, tilting his head. There was something up on the roof that he'd never seen before, and a flock of enormous black birds were descending upon it. Perhaps they were crows. In any case, he had never seen such a thing on the roof of the basilica. His eyes weren't what they used to be, and he asked his neighbor Paolo what he thought it was.

Paolo had no idea, and soon the entire clutch of people they were with stood still and tilted their heads back, squinting up at the lip of the roof above the portico.

A passing priest paused and joined them out of curiosity. He was younger than all of them, so his eyes were better and he saw what it was at once. His horrified gasp distracted a group nearby. They followed his lead, looking up as well.

Then a young woman standing with them shrieked in horror, and that brought the entire Square to an abrupt halt. Within moments every voice was silenced, and every eye present was focused on the roof. In the sudden quiet of St. Peter's Square, they heard the wavering cry of a Hebrew prayer, and realized that as out of place as it was, the prayer must be coming down to them from the roof of the basilica itself.

No one noticed Zamba emerging from the basilica through the Filarete doors. He strode out of the portico, beneath Nano's family crest and Papal ancestor's chiseled name, and walked down the steps, grinning at the frozen, horrified faces arrayed in the Square below.

He paused on the second landing and turned back to look up at his handiwork. He was quite pleased with what he had wrought. The screams erupting from the people in the Square behind him were a pat on the back for a job well done.

He turned and continued down the last section of thirteen steps, striding through the stunned, frozen people in the Square as he planned his day, walking toward the brilliance of the rising sun.

As long as he was in Europe, he thought that he really should visit Napoleon's tomb. He wanted to piss on it, just like he pissed on the statue of Christ. He wasn't leaving for Haiti until the next morning, so he would have plenty of time to take a commuter jet to Paris and pay his respects, such as they were, and be back at Fiumicino Airport in Rome in time for his flight to Haiti.

The people in the Square were fleeing in horror, rushing past him toward the eastern entrance. The two little girls abandoned their blanket of roses and joined the panicking throng.

Zamba ignored them as they scurried around him. His work was done here. He had made his point, and they would spread the word far and wide.

He suddenly slowed his pace and squinted ahead into the sunlight. The people were gone, but he thought he had just seen something else. *What was it?* he wondered.

Before he could react, two long iron nails came streaking out of the sun, hurtling directly toward him. The first nail pierced the back of his right hand, forcing his arm to swing behind him and rotating his upper torso to the right. That swung his left arm forward, and an instant later the second nail punched into the back of his left hand, violently rotating him back again.

His palms slapped together behind his lower back, and the point of each nail pierced the palm of the other hand. Then the tips of the nails bent at right angles, stitching his hands together.

He winced in utter surprise, erupting in fury as it dawned on him that his hands had just been firmly pinned behind his back.

Michael the Archangel approached him out of the dazzling sunlight, walking on air above the shiny wet paving stones. His shadow fell on Zamba. The voodoo priest looked up and saw instantly who it was. He glowered and took a defiant step toward the archangel.

A third nail pierced his foot, pinning it to the cold wet stone. Zamba stared down at it, more surprised than in pain, and then looked back at Michael and growled at him, taking another step forward.

A fourth nail pierced that foot as well, stopping him dead in his tracks. He stared down at it, and then looked up and smiled menacingly at the archangel.

"Nails..." he hissed at Michael. "When in Rome, eh?"

Michael didn't reply. Zamba willed the *loa* of his iron necklace to come to life, but with a simple wave of his hand, Michael caused Zamba's necklace to break.

Zamba gasped in dismay as the iron links fell separately to the paving stones all around him, each one transforming into a small black asp. The serpents were attracted by all the blood he was losing. They gathered at his feet, their curious forked tongues tasting the air. For the first time in hundreds of years, Zamba knew real fear.

As his strength left him and his knees grew weak, the asps slithered away in all directions of the compass. Zamba was helpless without them, crying tears of blood as his body began to rapidly shrivel and age.

"Return to dust," Michael commanded, and so it was.

The dust that had once been Zamba's frail, ancient body blew across St. Peter's Square. It mingled in the morning sunshine with a handful of rose petals the wind had picked up from an abandoned blanket, fluttering on the pavement at the base of the thirty-nine steps.

CHAPTER FIFTY-THREE

Peter Johnson had his sleeves rolled up. He was hunched over a table in the FBI library, jotting down neat, organized notes on an array of yellow legal pads. His eyes were focused and his breathing was soft and measured.

The craziness had finally subsided, now that he was back on the case. He'd been afraid that he would spiral down into torment and nightmares and be swallowed up by fear and paranoia, but diving into the case again proved to have the opposite effect. It was therapeutic, restoring the sharp edge of his earlier days. He was coming back from the darkness and he liked the way it felt. He hadn't slept so well in years.

He had been tirelessly following a thin data trail all day long that wound through stacks of reference volumes, CD-ROMS, microfiche newspaper articles and parish records. It was twilight in New Orleans, and the scent of jambalaya kept drifting in from down the hall. Every time the entry door of the library swung open, the scent wafted toward his table. Someone on the floor was feasting on take-out and the pungent aroma was making him hungry.

There was an open Bible on the table at his elbow, and the notepad on which he wrote Mas' license plate number – *1184* – served as a bookmark. Beside the Bible was one of several legal pads that he had spread across his workspace. "Bible Codes" was written across the top binding of one of them, in bold block letters. On the top sheet was a list of codes, where he found the numbers in the Bible, and what their hidden meanings were, all of it written in a neat, disciplined hand.

504. New Orleans area code. "The return of Jesus."

1147. Fareed Aly's address. "The will of God."

There were four more items below those two, but Johnson was compiling another list now, and he wanted to finish it before dinner, on a pad labeled "Branding Victims." So far, there were ten items on victims list. He wrote the eleventh with his black pen:

11. Fareed Aly. Bayou Memorial Clinic. 12-25-76.

Then with a light pencil, he added another name:

12. Jean Paul Eden. Bayou Memorial Clinic. 12-25-76.

He glanced at his Bible code list. There was an entry that might apply to Eden: *5810. Church of the Rebirth address. "The Father sent the Son to be the savior of the world."*

There were thirteen babies born that night, however, not twelve. If Eden did become the next victim, Johnson strongly suspected that he wouldn't be the last.

There were other items on the Bible code list that could be pointing to Eden. Then again, they could be indicating someone else. Bible codes were tricky in that regard, and after all this time Johnson still wasn't sure what to make of the matrix, but he did have faith that the answer could be found somewhere, somehow. He pondered the next two entries.

5040. Clinic address. "The beginning of Earth's great Millennium, the time of Jesus' return."

2112. Bonneville license plate. "A virgin shall conceive and bear a child, and shall call his name Emmanuel."

He didn't even want to think about the last entry on the list. Not yet. It was too much of a stretch, even for a mind like his, and he refused to leap to the conclusion it was enticing him toward. There was still an objective piece of the puzzle that was missing, perhaps several, which had to be found first. Without that, he would be taking a leap of faith rather than dispassionately pursuing a lead.

As much as he believed, and as much as he wanted to believe, he was honor-bound to construct a case with at least some semblance of rational, interlocking facts. His cheat sheet of Bible codes was adventurous enough and would never become part of the official file. It was his leg up, but he didn't want it to be his undoing.

He turned to the desktop computer and scrolled through a file of old newspaper articles on a CD-ROM. The PC was a relic of the Nineties and chunked along in fits and starts. The vintage CRT monitor was the size of an engine block and crowded the table. The librarian already got her new Mac. Johnson idly wondered when all the Macs would be delivered for the rest of the place. With his luck, probably the day after he was done...

He stopped on the headline of a tabloid article that he missed the day before. *MIRACLES NEVER CEASE! Dead Woman Found In Car – Virgin With Emergency C-Section?* Johnson knew that tabloid journalists were either go-getters or hacks, sometimes both, and sometimes in the same article. He always took what they said with a big grain of salt, even though the folklore of the Bureau suggested that agents secretly treated the tabloids like they were the gospel truth. The well-thumbed sleeves of the tabloid CD-ROMs in the archive file cabinets were a testament to the rumor.

He scanned the article, filtering out the obvious nonsense while trying to determine if there was anything of substance underneath. He suddenly stopped, staring down at the keyboard as his mind began racing. The article was crap, but it did get him thinking. About what exactly, he didn't know just yet; he let his thoughts run free and waited to see what would happen. They usually lit on something interesting if he exercised enough patience...

Got it.

He popped open the CD drawer, dropped a different one in the tray, and closed it. After several seconds, the splash screen of the *Bayou Press* appeared. The CD held an archive of the rural paper's daily output from 1975-1980.

Johnson typed 12/26/76 in the search window and hit Enter. After several more seconds, the old 386 poked around on the CD and found the December 26th morning edition. He scrolled through several articles detailing the aftermath of the tornado, the cleanup efforts, the Christmas spirit of the community, yadda yadda yadda. On the bottom of page 14, he finally found what he was looking for.

Church Orphanage Takes In Abandoned Baby.

He leaned in close and carefully read the article, and as he did, his lips began to tremble. He sensed that he was getting closer.

"...the Church spokesman explained that according to state law, they will put the infant up for adoption, but that the Church orphanage would be glad to keep the child if suitable parents could not be found after the required 90-day period expires."

From his earlier research, Johnson knew that back in those days the state of Louisiana required an orphanage or an adoption agency to wait ninety days from the recorded date of birth for the parents or kin to present themselves. After that, if no one claimed the child, the baby was legally considered abandoned and could be adopted, assigned to a private orphanage or deemed to be a ward of the state. The infants were jocularly known as ninety-day wonders.

He finished the article and went back to the splash screen. He typed "...baby..." in the search window, selected "By Title," and hit Enter.

Several articles were listed. He scanned the results and selected one from the March 25, 1978 edition. *Miracle Baby Finds Home.*

Johnson skimmed the article, and finally found what he was look-ing for at the bottom of the first page. *"...the child, now approximately one year old, will be legally adopted by..."*

"Approximately," he breathed. *The operative word was 'approximately,'* he realized. *That was the key!* Johnson clicked the Next button.

The top of the second page appeared and he saw the rest of the sentence, which essentially consisted of the proud family's name, where they lived, and what the breadwinner did to make ends meet.

As Johnson stared at the information, every nerve ending in his body began to tingle. Despite all of his methodical research, and all of his disciplined logic, he knew that what he really wanted to do was make that leap of faith, and it was taking everything he had to restrain himself.

He closed his eyes and made the sign of the cross, saying a little prayer for strength, then opened his eyes once again and eagerly hunched over his keyboard and mouse. There was still one more document that he had to see to lock everything down tight. He already knew what it would say, but he wanted to read it nonetheless. It would be his victory lap.

He gently removed the CD-ROM from the tray, and noticed that his hand was trembling. This time he knew that it wasn't from fear. He carefully, almost reverently, placed another CD in the tray. It held the 1976 birth certificates for the entire parish.

He closed the tray and the old drive slowly whirred to life. He hoped that it would hang in there for just one more round. A splash screen came up, including a search bar.

Johnson entered the family name and city, and then typed 12/26/76 in the search bar. *The 26th is approximately the 25th,* he thought to himself with an excited grin, and hit Enter. A moment later and there it was, flickering on the screen before him.

The birth certificate of Jesus Christ.

He read the entire document and the accompanying hospital report, savoring each detail, and knowing that the originals would be easy enough to obtain with a subpoena. To the hospital, they were just a couple of old pieces of paper, but Peter Johnson knew differently. They were priceless, and he was the first person in history to recognize their significance. For now, they were safely tucked away in the parish archives, but soon the entire world would know the truth, and he would be the one to show them.

Glowing with accomplishment, he placed his hand on his mouse and watched the screen, highlighting a capital "E." His hand was shaking, but he steadied himself. He moved his mouse again, high-lighting a capital "N." He moved his mouse once again and clicked, and gazed at the results for what seemed to be a breathless eternity, until a sobering thought gradually intruded.

Within moments, his euphoria had completely dissolved, replaced by a sober, gnawing fear that accelerated with every breath. *The documents were safe, but nothing else was.*

He quickly gathered his things. He had to leave at once.

Agent Peter Johnson raced down the front steps of the Hale Boggs Federal Building in the damp evening air, lugging his overstuffed briefcase and pressing his phone to his ear. He spoke in a clear, authoritative voice to the 1-800 virtual operator, enunciating each syllable so there would be no mistake and no lost time.

"American Airlines..."

CHAPTER FIFTY-FOUR

The crypts and the tombs and the mildewed gravestones in the side yard of the St. Louis Cathedral in New Orleans huddled under a chill winter fog. The lamplight from Bishop Nano's chambers on the top floor of the rectory cast a diffuse yellow glow down upon the cemetery. Deep shadows hid behind the crypts, forming black holes in the night.

Bishop Nano and Father Simone stood close together in the dark behind the lavish marble monument of Louis Trieste, a riverboat gambler who tried to buy his way into Heaven in 1842, after a flamboyant life of cheating and debauchery. Nano doubted that he ever got there, even though his donation had financed the construction of the rectory. At the rate Nano was going, he doubted that *he'd* ever get there either. Or Simone, for that matter. They were both well beyond the pale.

Simone had the file folder he pilfered from the locked drawer of Molinari's desk. The Cardinal had changed the pickproof security lock many times over the years, thinking it would deter prying eyes. It cost him a small fortune each time, but he felt it was worth it.

For some unfathomable reason, however, no one in the Cabal of Cardinals ever thought of changing the lock on the door of the Vatican Secret Archives. Simone copied Molinari's key and went into the Archives to read the *Book of Devlin*, and finally learned the truth. It was no longer any wonder to him why the Council of Nicaea edited the Bible and quashed all the Heretics. From the Orthodoxy to the Inquisition, it all made sense to him now.

On the day that Molinari went to visit Sir Reynard, Simone carefully removed the entire top of the Cardinal's old oak desk, exposing the contents of the locked drawer underneath. The voodoo priest paid a visit to Molinari shortly thereafter.

"I hope I picked a winner," Simone joked, as he placed the file folder in Nano's eager hands.

"Oh ye of little faith!" The bishop chided him with a little grin. "We have been winning this struggle from the start, Father Simone."

Simone looked at him and nodded, and then his eyes flicked down to the file. Nano could see that Simone was anticipating his reaction, but he played out the tension for a while longer, just to toy with the priest.

Simone swallowed, waiting. Nano grinned again and finally opened the file, glancing down at the contents. Simone watched him.

Nano blinked as the shock of what he saw finally registered on him. His smile dissolved into a startled frown and he glanced at Simone.

"Are you sure?" Nano asked him.

It was the same question Simone asked Molinari many years ago, when they were of another faith. The priest nodded, assuring Nano that it was indeed the correct photo. They had finally found The One.

Nano gazed at the photo and slowly shook his head. "Molinari..." he whispered. "You *bastard!*"

"He's dead," Simone informed him, and Nano looked at him in surprise. Simone nodded again to assure him it was the truth, and then he turned to leave. Nano watched him go. "See you in Rome, Bishop Simone," Nano said to him.

Father Simone paused and gave Nano a half-smile over his shoulder, before he disappeared into a long line of shadows behind a row of crypts.

Nano was alone. He looked back down to the photo in his hand, holding it up to a glimmer of light spilling down from his office windows above. "Well, I'll be damned," he breathed, still thoroughly astonished by the revelation. *In all probability,* he thought to himself, *I actually will be damned.*

In the windless night, something was moving behind the photograph. He lowered it to see what it could be, and was startled to discover Detective Kaddouri standing right in front of him. The photo fumbled out of the bishop's arthritic hand.

Kaddouri cracked a half-smile, amused that he had such a theatrical effect on the old coot, and bent down to pick up the photo from the mud puddle at their feet. The laser paper didn't hold up to water very well, and the image was already distorting. He angled it to catch the light.

He quick stood up, staring at the print in his hand, but unlike the bishop he was more concerned than astonished. He had no idea why the bishop had the photograph, and he particularly didn't like the fact that someone handed it to him in the dead of night.

Kaddouri frowned at Nano, gesturing with the piece of paper. "What the – ?"

But before he could utter another word, a shovel blade sliced through the back of his skull. An explosion of pain blinded him and he dropped to his knees. Nano shrank away from the sudden violence with a startled gasp.

Simone stepped out of the shadows, the shovel in his hands. They watched Kaddouri sink face first into the shallow mud puddle, landing on top of the photo.

Nano and Simone looked at each other, then back down to Kaddouri, but the detective lay motionless.

Nano bent over with a grunt and scooped up the file folder. He had dropped it when Kaddouri was hit, but luckily it landed on a patch of dry, solid ground. The photo, however, was gone. Even if they rolled Kaddouri over, it would be little more than a soggy pulp.

But no matter; he had a chance to take a good look at it. It was firmly etched in his memory now, an image that he would never forget so long as he lived.

He took his cell phone out of his pocket and sent a text message to Cardinal Saul in Rome: *1554*. The leader of the Cabal of Cardinals would understand the code. *We have found the Messiah.*

Nano started toward the back door of the rectory and Simone walked beside him, glancing back at Kaddouri.

"Is he...?"

"He's a cop," Nano said with a dismissive shrug, and Simone nodded once again, taking his point. Nano opened the back door and bid Simone to enter first.

"I'll be leaving with you," he informed Simone, and followed him inside, closing the door behind them.

Kaddouri stirred, and turned his head to get a breath of air. He was grievously injured, but he had no idea what just happened to him. Perhaps he had a stroke. His right hand was lying palm up beside his hip. He could feel his cell phone, still in its holster. He unclipped it and somehow kept it in his trembling hand.

He brought the phone up to his face, his clenched fist resting in the shallow mud puddle. Everything kept going in and out of focus. He unlocked it with his thumb. The screen was incredibly bright, triggering a flash of pain.

Squinting at the display, he speed dialed Mas. The screen said, "calling... Chrissy" for the longest time, and then the call timer finally began counting the seconds.

He had either gotten through to her, or to her voicemail. He couldn't tell which because he couldn't speak and he couldn't hear. She would simply know that he called, and that was all. But maybe that would be enough. It would have to be.

As the blood seeped from the gash in his fractured skull, his grip on the phone slowly relaxed and his hand sank further into the mud. Bloody red water oozed into his cupped palm, submerging the base of the phone. The battery shorted out, and the screen went dark.

CHAPTER FIFTY-FIVE

Father Jean Paul Eden walked silently down the hallway toward his bedroom on the second floor. The others were downstairs, directly below him in the large kitchen, making more bread. He could hear their chatter welling up the staircase behind him. He begged off from the nightly get-together, saying he was worn out from working on the pavilion and the long hours with the refugees, and felt he should turn in early. It was the first evening he had to himself, but he wasn't alone.

The section of the Citadel that the orphanage occupied was built as a barracks, but the old wood floor wasn't made of planking; it was made out of massive rough-sawn timbers that could take a load without protest. That way, cannons could be positioned at the second floor windows if need be. Eden didn't know that, but he was thankful that the timbers didn't deflect one iota with a person's weight, which was good because there was a person following him who shouldn't be anywhere near a priest's bedroom.

Thalia Rose was a close step behind, watching him walk and smiling in anticipation. Men were delicious, and she was going to have a feast.

Eden stopped at his door and looked both ways down the hall, and then down at her lovely face. She had the most enchanting eyes. He closed his own and took a breath, still not quite believing what he was about to do.

He opened his eyes, and found hers. "You can only stay a little while," he told her.

As if that would make any difference, he thought. His sin had already begun. In truth, it started the moment he first saw her in the marketplace, and it had not stopped since.

She must have read his mind, because her smile only grew wider. "Jean Paul..." she began, but he held up a finger to silence her.

"Please!" he whispered. "Even this is too much. I'm a *priest*."

"You are more than that," she whispered, glancing below his waistline. "So much more than that."

His lust was growing. She peeked back up at him, amused, and waited for him to catch up to himself. It didn't take long. He finally sighed and opened his door.

CHAPTER FIFTY-SIX

Peter Johnson came in to Cap-Haitien International Airport on a twin turboprop out of Ft. Lauderdale. It was a toss-up between that or flying into Port-au-Prince and taking a puddle-jumper north from there. Fat chance after the quake, he correctly concluded.

He renewed his passport at the Federal Building the morning after Mas took off to Haiti, on the off chance that she might need him to fly down, and now here he was. She had no idea he was coming. What he had to tell her wouldn't go over very well on the phone, so he hadn't even bothered to try. She probably wouldn't believe him, anyway. He scarcely believed it himself.

The lady at the Hertz rental car desk recommended the Land Cruiser. She warned him that the roads to the Citadel weren't like the ones in Louisiana. Her cousin lived in Lake Charles and she knew all about Louisiana, and Haiti wasn't Louisiana. She used a yellow marker to trace the route on the courtesy map, from the airport all the way to the Citadel, and then she recommended a nice hotel near the beach. The drive to the Citadel was about three hours, she told him. He could get a good night's sleep and be at the end of the road by lunchtime, where he could ride a rented mule the last few miles up the mountain. The guides were very nice and spoke good English.

Johnson thanked the woman, accepted the hotel brochure, and glanced up and down the line of parked cars. He had driven a Land Cruiser for decades, and he just recently tooled around in Kaddouri's new one. As much as he loved them, he had a taste for something different.

The agent saw the look in his eyes and knew he was reconsidering her suggestion. She smiled at him, and used the famous company phrase on him from their old TV commercials. He'd appreciate it, given his age.

"And how may we put *you* in the driver's seat, monsieur?"

He grinned back at her, and scanned the offerings, his steely Eliot Ness eyes finally landing on a convertible Mercedes G550 SUV. It was the most popular vehicle on the island, if you could afford one. But he didn't know that. He just always wanted to drive a new Mercedes, and now was his big chance.

"I'll take the Benz," he told her with a killer Robert Stack smile.

He tossed his carry-on in the passenger seat and buckled up, then re-folded the map and pinned it under the edge of his luggage. It showed the first part of his journey, out of town and into the foothills. He probably could have punched it into the GPS, but he didn't want to take the time to learn how. He was itching to roll.

He tossed the hotel brochure in the courtesy wastebasket, fired up the engine, and zoomed out of the lot. With God's blessing and a full tank, he guessed that he could be there before midnight, if the weather held.

He turned out of the airport gate and drove cautiously, blending in with the flow of traffic and glancing ahead to the dark range of mountains south of town. The moon was rising in the east, which was a big help. He was glad they had the G550. It was a bit smaller and narrower than the Land Cruiser, which would come in handy since he was about to go barging up a mule trail in the dead of night. The rooftop off-road lights would probably be a big help, too. And if he ran out of trail, he would call Mas and continue on foot. The moon would be up for several more hours.

CHAPTER FIFTY-SEVEN

Mas and Francine were on stakeout in Francine's thoroughly scratched and dented embassy Jeep. Johnson didn't know it yet, but Mas and Francine had widened the mule trail for him earlier that day, plowing and occasionally hacking their way up the mountain path. Officer Penet's Nissan Patrol had done most of the hard work the first few days after the missionaries arrived, but there was still a good bit of resilient undergrowth to be cut down to size. The work was great exercise, and they both needed it after the long drive north and all the drama at the meadow. Francine had plenty of paper towels and bottled water to clean up with, and they had packed a big lunch and a Thermos of coffee. But it was all gone by sunset and now they were hungry again.

They were parked in a cluster of banana trees beyond the construction site outside the walls of the Citadel, keeping an eye on the windows of the orphanage. Eden's bedroom window was open to the night. The light had come on briefly, and then went out again. Perhaps he was turning in early. He had been putting in long days at the refugee camp.

The evening breeze had finally died down, and the enormous fan leaves of the banana trees weren't flapping about anymore. Listening to them for hours on end had been almost unbearably annoying, and the conversation ran out about an hour after the coffee did. Both of them had already stepped outside to take a couple of bathroom breaks.

Mas cupped her hand over her iPhone to keep the display light under control and checked to see how the battery was doing. She'd left her car charger at the hotel. She saw that she missed a call.

Damn... She had set it on vibrate that morning for the stakeout, and then took it off her belt a few hours ago in an attempt to get more comfortable. It had been sitting on top of her bunched up jacket behind her feet ever since, right beside her holstered gun.

She checked to see who called. *Mark Cell,* the display said. She pressed Send to call him back and listened for the ring, but it went to his voicemail instead. "This is Detective Kaddouri. I'm not available; leave a message. *BEEP!*"

That's weird, she thought. He never turned his phone off, even while he slept.

"Mark, it's me. Call me back." She ended the call and frowned, wondering what was up.

Francine tapped her on the shoulder and pointed out the windshield. She had a hard time seeing in the darkness for the first few moments, until her eyes finally adjusted from having looked at her phone.

The Haitian man was approaching the kitchen door, crossing the lawn with a machete in hand. He looked up at Eden's darkened window, kept moving, and then paused to look up again, standing motionless as if he could see or hear something, or as if he were trying to.

Mas and Francine grabbed their weapons and silently slipped out of the vehicle. The dome light didn't come on; Francine had already turned it off, just in case.

Francine wasn't a large woman, but she was wiry and fast and had to wrestle three older brothers as a young girl to earn some respect. She tackled the man from behind and had the machete out of his hand before they hit the ground. It happened so fast that Mas didn't even see how she did it. She made a mental note to have Francine show her the move.

The man was face down in the grass. Francine held the point of the machete to his throat, and hissed a string of Creole invectives in his ear. The man settled right down and willingly placed his hands behind him, on the small of his back. Mas cuffed him and Francine stepped back, rolling the man over with the toe of her boot.

The Haitian man found himself looking into the barrel of a Sig-Sauer, trained on his forehead by an attractive white woman. The black lady who tackled him had the tip of his own machete pressed against his throat, but the gesture was overkill. A white woman with a gun was menacing enough for him.

"Why are you following the priest?" Francine asked him quietly in Creole.

The man turned his head and scowled at her. The machete nicked his throat, drawing blood, but he didn't seem to feel it. He was seething mad about something, and he spit his words out to Francine one at a time.

"That woman is my *wife!*" The man growled at her in Creole. "She died two weeks ago."

Francine just nodded, accepting the statement as fact.

"What's he saying?" Mas asked. Her fluency in Creole was about what it was in French; she barely understood a word the man was saying.

"The woman Eden is with is this man's wife. He said she died two weeks ago."

Mas looked at Francine in utter disbelief. Not only because of what she told her, but also the matter-of-fact way in which she said it. She actually believed the man's story.

"*I KILL her!*" the man told Mas.

She stared at him, trying to decipher his thick accent and broken English. It just didn't make any sense, whether Francine believed him or not.

359

Eden and Thalia were lying naked on his bed. They had just finished making love and he was still on top of her, missionary style, recovering his breath. As it returned to normal, so did his mind. The intoxicating euphoria of the last several minutes was quickly draining out of him, and nothing filled the empty pit it left behind. He realized that it was staring into the abyss of his conscience. Reality was inexorably seeping back in, like cold groundwater.

"What have you done to me?" he asked her, his face still buried in the pillow beside her head.

She smiled, gazing at the ceiling and smoking a cigarette. It was an odd aroma that Eden had never smelled before, and it was making him uncomfortable.

"What have you done *for* me...?" she murmured, playfully altering his question. And then in a deep voice completely different from her own, she finished her teasing echo by directly addressing him by name.

"...Father Eden?"

He lifted his head from the pillow at once, and his eyes popped open in surprise. What he just heard from her lips wasn't a woman mimicking a man. *It was a man's voice.*

He rose up on his hands and looked down at her, but it wasn't Thalia at all. *A naked white man was lying naked beneath him.*

Devlin's manicured fingers waved the cigarette in the air as he blew a cloud of languid smoke in the priest's astonished face.

Francine ended a phone call and glanced at Mas. "This guy is wanted for killing his wife," she said.

Mas just stared at her, still trying to make sense of what Francine told her earlier, and of what she just heard from the handcuffed man. Her attention was torn from the puzzle when a startled cry of panic erupted like a cannon shot from Eden's open window. From the tone of his voice, something or someone had just shocked him half to death. He was shouting incoherently at the top of his lungs, the kind of sound a man makes only once in his life.

Mas and Francine looked up to the window as he bellowed once again, but this time it was a wail of fear. They exchanged quick glances and Francine nodded, drawing her gun. She'd stay with the suspect.

Mas raced for the kitchen door, her Sig-Sauer gripped tightly in both hands, as Francine cocked her Beretta, making sure the Haitian could clearly see the weapon. In Francine's peripheral vision, she could see Mas entering the kitchen door, her gun raised.

Approaching headlights washed over the lawn, and Francine squinted at the arriving vehicle. She put the tip of the machete to the man's throat and swung her pistol around to the headlights, just in case. The vehicle quickly stopped, the engine and headlights switched off, and someone got out, leaving the door open for illumination.

Johnson cautiously approached, his hands in the air and his FBI badge held aloft. He made sure the cop could see it in the moonlight. He hoped she was a cop; he just saw Mas run to the Citadel and go inside, and he was pretty sure she had her weapon out, too. He guessed they were all on the same team, except for the guy on the ground with the machete pressed against his throat.

Johnson kept his hands up and stood perfectly still. "FBI! I'm with Agent Mas," he explained, gesturing toward the Citadel.

Priests and nuns stood motionless around the kitchen prep table, still in shock from hearing Eden's scream. Bishop Lomani and Father Ortiz were heading up the stairs, but they froze when Mas burst into the room, holding her gun high and showing her badge.

She signaled for them to come down silently, and they complied at once and huddled with the other missionaries. Mas signal for all of them to silently go outside, but they were frozen in place and she didn't have the time to argue with them. No matter, if things upstairs didn't resolve quietly they'd scatter quickly enough, unless one of them caught a stray round.

Eden was standing in the middle of the floor, cloaking his naked body with the bed sheet. The full moon filled the room, but he wanted better light than that. He reached over and turned on his desk lamp.

Devlin was standing by the bed, naked. He smiled as his clothes and greatcoat materialized on his body. He smirked at Eden, and then nodded his handsome head in a grand gesture of mock cordiality.

Eden winced in sudden pain and clutched at his smoldering eyes. Seeing the Devil had blinded him outright.

"My eyes...!"

"For so long, I have sought you," Devlin told him, and began walking in a circle around the priest, savoring his victory and his cigarette.

"I knew you couldn't resist the way of the flesh!" Devlin purred, and took a moment to savor the memory of Eden's lust.

Eden desperately wanted to flee, but he couldn't see a thing, and he was in so much pain that he could barely stand. He felt himself reeling in place, and wasn't even sure where the door was. Something warm and sticky was welling from his eyes. He realized it was blood.

"What are you talking about?" Eden cried out. *"Who ARE you?"*

Devlin sneered at him. "You know who I am. Look inside yourself. You know."

Eden stood still as Devlin's last two words took hold of him. It was the same thing Eli Aly said, and Eden finally he did know. And now that he did, he also knew that it was something he could no longer refuse to believe, and that was the hell of it.

"Satan walks among us," Eden said quietly.

Devlin grinned and raised his hands in the air, walking around the room like a triumphant boxer.

"I am so..."

He closed his eyes to fully experience the moment, and he breathed deeply, exalted and vindicated, waiting for the sweet torrent of eternal glory to course through him. He waited, and waited, and finally finished his sentence in a completely different tone than he began.

"...not feeling anything."

He opened his eyes and glared at Eden, furious. Eden couldn't see a thing, but he could feel Devlin's rage. He shrank back, even though he somehow knew that there was no place to hide from this unholy fury. But even as Eden cowered before the Prince of Darkness, Devlin's burning fury was fatally pierced by a staggering realization.

He dropped his cigarette. It sizzled and went out, burning a deep, smoldering hole into the timber floor. But the ancient beams didn't catch fire.

"No," he whispered, but his protestation didn't erase the hideous truth. All he felt now was the icy sting of utter defeat.

"No!" he said again, louder this time, and Eden wondered what he meant.

"NO!" Devlin shouted. Eden shrank even further back, but then he hesitated, sensing that somehow, something was different now. There was an edge of despair in Devlin's voice.

Devlin took in a great lungful of air, and with a force just shy of damaging his human form, he bellowed in helpless fury at the awful, inescapable truth.

"*NO!!*"

CHAPTER FIFTY-EIGHT

In the hallway, Mas pulled her ear away from the door, wincing in pain from the anguished howl. She had no idea who it was, but it surely wasn't Eden. She had been listening to the entire exchange through the door, but the man with Eden kept moving around the room. She had no clear idea until these last few moments exactly where he was, but now it seemed like he was finally standing still and venting his rage.

She took a breath to steady herself and silently turned the doorknob.

Devlin began circling Eden again, glaring at him and seething in anger. Eden could hear his footsteps.

"How can you not be...?" Devlin wondered aloud, still aghast at his blunder.

"I don't understand!" Eden wailed. He was frightened and confused, and in crippling pain. "Please, leave this place!" he begged Devlin. "I have nothing for you!"

Devlin stopped before him, and responded by backhanding Eden across the room. The priest slammed against the wall and fell in a heap, as Mas burst into the room directly behind Devlin.

He turned to her, snarling, but she stood firm, her weapon leveled at him. After all these years, she was finally face-to-face with the Branding Killer. She was amazed how young and healthy he looked, not much over forty. He had aged incredibly well, or he started his killing spree as a young teen. She had always visualized him as an ugly man, but he was a handsome devil.

"Move away from him!" she ordered, her weapon trained on him with two steady hands.

One wrong move and she was going to drop him with a shot to the femur. Or one to each thigh, if that's what it took. If that didn't work, she'd kneecap him as well, but there was no way in Hell that she was going to let him walk out of the room unless she handcuffed him first. His career was over.

Devlin, however, had other plans, and waved his hand. Her weapon turned toward her own temple, completely against her will. She struggled against the invisible force with all her might, and managed to somehow turn the weapon back on him.

He waved again, more forcefully this time, and the weapon suddenly jerked of its own accord, trying to fly out of her hand. Her grip instantly tightened in reaction, and as it did her finger depressed the match-grade trigger.

The 10mm hollow-point grazed his scalp. That was all it took for the slug to tumble, and as it did it began to expand, plowing a ragged trench through the top of Devlin's skull.

An instant later, the gun left her hand and slammed against the stone wall. The slide flew off and the pistol dropped to the floor. The clip and a dozen little pieces of the firing mechanism spilled out.

Mas watched him, breathless. Her ears were ringing from the gunshot, amplified by the dense walls and floor of the sparsely furnished room. She knew that a wound like that would likely kill him, or turn him into a vegetable, and she waited for him to drop. But the wound simply closed up and healed before her eyes.

Devlin grinned at her and thrust his hand forward. The door behind her slammed shut. He swiped his hand once again and she went flying across the room.

Mas slammed against the wall and dropped to the floor beside Eden. She was stunned and bleeding from the impact, and for a moment she lost consciousness. Then she groaned and rolled over, struggling to sit up in a corner formed by the wall and the armoire. Eden was slumped against the wall near her, still wrapped in the bed sheet and weeping tears of blood.

Devlin came closer to them, still furious. He wasn't nearly finished. He reached into his greatcoat and took out the crucifix dagger.

Mas was slowly regaining control over her mind and body, and was dimly aware that her life was in danger.

Devlin stood over them, but his attention was on Eden. He gripped the shaft of the crucifix and unsheathed the weapon with his other hand. Mas came fully alert, seeing the oiled dagger blade glinting in the lamplight.

"First, I'm going to deal with *you!*" Devlin told Eden, and pivoted the haft of the dagger as it lay in his palm. He grasped the handle and raised his clenched fist above his shoulder, preparing to stab downwards.

A faint humming began to fill the room, and swelled with each passing moment. Neither Mas nor Eden knew what it was, but Devlin did. His fallen angels had been watching over their master, anticipating the discovery and death of the returned Christ.

Mas saw Devlin raise the dagger high. "Too bad you can't see this coming," he was saying to Eden.

Adrenalin shot through Mas' body as a cascade of images flashed in her mind.

She was pressed against the car window, her father's jacket on the other side of the glass, her scream as loud as a gunshot; Fareed Aly's swollen face eclipsed as his body bag is zipped closed; the dismembered nuns lay in a pool of blood before the altar; Sister Nancy's severed head stared at her with hollow eye sockets, as Mas heard her the Captain's voice in her head, strong and clear, "The gloves come off, right here and now."

Crumpled against the cold stone wall by the armoire, Mas whispered back to him, *"So help me God."*

She was fully alert now. She was ready. *So help me God.*

She anchored the instep of her boot against the foot of the heavy armoire, and launched herself into the air between Devlin and Eden as the dagger came down.

The blade plunged deep into her abdomen, entering through the birthmark on her right side, the odd two-inch-long blemish that never seemed to make any sense. Until now. None of this had ever made sense until now...

She collapsed in Eden's arms and dropped into his lap, her back arched over his thighs. He instinctively brought up his hands to support her weight, fumbling a bit until he was holding her by the shoulders and under her knees. Her head fell back and she stared at the ceiling in shock as blood gushed from her wound. The tip of the blade had severed her iliac artery, and life was quickly flowing out of her. Eden tilted his face down toward the woman in his arms, as if he could see her. He was already blind when she rushed into the room, but laying in his arms now he somehow knew exactly who she was. She was the young woman who told him about the massacre, who said she had come to save him.

He could feel her breathing, weak and shallow, and he could hear a soft moan escaping from her with each exhalation. Her warm blood was draining onto his lap from the wound in her right side, washing over him. He felt his own pain quenched with each pulse of her heart.

Devlin stared at them. With Eden cloaked in the bed sheet sitting against the wall, and with Mas dying in his lap, they were a perfect image of the Pieta.

He dropped the dagger and its sheath, staring at the vision. They clattered on the stone floor, forgotten, the blade's true purpose accomplished after so long. The humming dropped away to an awful silence as the dark angels fled.

Devlin sniffed at the air, smelling her blood. His search was at an end, but it was the last thing he expected to find. This was a complete surprise to him. She was The One. All this time he had been hunting The One, while He – *SHE!* – had been hunting him.

Eden began to weep silent, healing tears, and they fell on Mas' brow. She looked up at him in wonder.

"I feel..." she whispered, "I feel..."

Johnson and Francine quietly entered the room, their weapons in hand, and they stood perfectly still, not daring to breathe. Johnson knew exactly what he was witnessing and made the sign of the cross. Francine sensed that it was a blessed event and did the same, just in case. She glanced at Devlin, and instantly saw that whoever he was, he was harmless. He was standing slumped against the wall, utterly numb, staring at Mas and Eden.

Johnson thought back to his time in the library, earlier that evening, remembering the hospital report that accompanied Mas' birth certificate. *"Acadia Dupuy, a licensed midwife practitioner, presented the abandoned child to the Church orphanage... birth date uncertain... official registration date December 26, 1976..."*

He gazed at the woman who lay dying in Eden's arms. *Born of a virgin,* he thought, *and you didn't answer me: Do you believe in God?*

He remembered toying with her name in the adoption certificate file on the library computer, deleting "INE" and the space between her first and last name, so that a click of his mouse formed one revealing word: *Christmas.*

Johnson began to silently weep, but he was finally at peace. All of his Bible codes made sense to him now. He refrained that evening from dwelling on the last item, but his leap of faith was complete now; he had landed on solid ground. He could finally let himself believe.

His hand-written list of codes was clear in his mind, particularly the last item:

1184. Mas' license plate. "After His resurrection, He comes back in a different form."

Johnson's shoulders were heaving as he crossed himself and whispered a prayer, over and over again. Francine stepped back and tried to make a call, but she couldn't get a signal through the thick stone walls.

"I'm going downstairs to use the land line," she whispered to him, and he nodded, his eyes on Mas. Francine took a hard look at the man against the wall, but he was in no shape to do much of anything but stare at Mas, just like Johnson was. Besides, Johnson knew he was there, and she had to call for a medevac. Francine slipped out the door.

Mas was breathing quietly in Eden's lap. Something wondrous was happening to her.

She gazed at the palms of her bloody hands. The stigmata had appeared, the wounds from the Crucifixion. There were holes in the top of her boots as well. Blood was oozing from them. Her birthmark made sense to her now.

It all fit together seamlessly, and she remembered everything as if it were only yesterday...

Offering herself to the Pharisees and the angry, jeering crowds; the steel-tipped lashes from the Roman soldiers and the weight of the cross; the long walk to Calvary; the mallet and the nails; Mother Mary keeping vigil; the soldier's lance; feeling empty and forsaken, finally crying out in despair; the thunder and lightning; a break in the clouds, and at long last, speaking to God the Father in Heaven.

"It is finished."

Mas closed her eyes, and died.

Eden opened his eyes and gazed down at Mas lying in his arms. *He could see again.* Johnson dropped to his knees, his hands folded in prayer and his head bent low. Devlin was wandering the room, astounded to discover that his head wound had returned and blood was pouring from it. He stared at his bloody hand, but it was incomprehensible to him.

"I'm *bleeding?*" Devlin gasped, and looked around at the stone walls in mounting horror as the implications sunk in.

Humans bleed.

He stumbled around the room, mystified by his surroundings and holding his head. "What is this place? Where am I?"

There was no response. He stopped before the mirror and stared at his image. It was utterly unfamiliar to him.

"Who am I?" He whispered, but no answer came.

"Oh, God...!" He wailed in despair, but his plea went unheeded. Utterly bewildered, he looked at the others, gathered together in a state of grace, but the light that entered their lives was unavailable to him. He stood alone, in darkness.

Johnson finally realized that he was weeping from both eyes, and pinched out his contact lens. He could see clearly now, and gazed at Eden, who was rapidly blinking the blood out of his own eyes. They smiled at each other and looked down at Mas' body, still gently cradled in Eden's arms.

They suddenly sensed a warm new presence, and knew it wasn't coming from Devlin. They looked up and saw to their astonishment that Michael the Archangel was standing beside them. They were transfixed at the sight, but they weren't afraid.

Michael took Mas' body in his arms and turned to face Devlin, who was trembling in mortal fear. A radiance from above filled the room with golden light and Devlin heard a clear, gentle voice reverberating in his head.

"They are all my children, Lucifer. Any one of them is capable of what she has done. That is the lesson you were too proud to learn."

Devlin looked around wildly for the source of the Voice. It was nowhere to be found, and yet it was everywhere at once.

"No!" he cried in despair, but the Voice was gone. He was on his own now.

The radiance streamed down into Michael and Mas, filling them with an inner light. Johnson and Eden watched in wide-eyed wonder, but Devlin threw his hands over his eyes, sure that he would go blind. The light swelled and filled the room, and then it drew up through the ceiling, taking Michael and Mas to be with the Father.

Slowly, the room returned to normal, and Devlin was gone. Johnson and Eden bowed their heads and made the sign of the cross.

Devlin materialized on the lawn below Eden's window, wailing in agony, a bloody hand to his head. Behind him in the kitchen, the terrified missionaries watched him through the kitchen window as Lomani raced up the stairs.

Devlin wandered into the darkness clutching his wound and moaning piteously, but no one was listening to him. For the first time in his long existence, he was of no importance. He was utterly alone.

Francine stood by her Jeep, her cell phone in hand. The Haitian man was handcuffed to her bumper, and they were both staring slack-jawed at something in the air above the Citadel. A stream of silver dust was rising into the sky, drawing Michael and Mas to heaven.

Isaac La Croix had arrived shortly after Johnson. He was sitting at the wheel of his G550, parked on the lawn by the other vehicles. He was thankful that someone had finally widened the donkey path, because he didn't want to wait until dawn to get up here. He was watching the silvery glimmer rise from the Citadel and stream into the clear, moonlit sky. It hung like stardust in cold night air. He had no idea exactly what it was, but surely it was a miracle, and La Croix made the sign of the cross.

Lomani came out the kitchen door with something cradled in his hands. The glowing sky above caught his attention, and he craned his neck to see what it was as he approached La Croix's vehicle. The night sky was so clear that he could see the Milky Way, and yet something delicate was falling on him, like ashes. *Perhaps there was a wildfire,* he thought. But no, it was cold, whatever it was. Cold and wet.

He suddenly stood still, awestruck, as he realized what was happening. It was impossible, but there it was. La Croix stepped out of his Mercedes, every bit as astonished as Lomani was.

Fat, lazy snowflakes drifted down all around them and clung to the warm ground, refusing to melt away. The Rosicrucian and the bishop exchanged delighted smiles, and stood side-by-side, enjoying the snow flurry.

Lomani sighed in wonderment, and handed La Croix the crucifix dagger. Their eyes met, snowflakes on their lashes. Nothing needed to be said.

La Croix simply nodded his head in thanks, and extended his right hand. Lomani grasped his hand in thanks, and then bent his head and kissed La Croix's gold Rosicrucian ring.

La Croix got back in his vehicle, started the engine, and drove away. He didn't turn on his headlights; the full moon illuminated the way, but he did turn on his wipers to clear away the Haitian snowstorm.

Bishop Lomani watched him go, and then walked over to Francine's SUV. She was still standing by her Jeep, staring wide-eyed at the miracle drifting down from the clear night sky. The Haitian suspect was on his knees praying, marveling at the snow and catching what he could on his tongue, savoring its clean taste. It was all entirely real. Every bit of it.

Lomani smiled at her, and she smiled back. Then she brushed away a tear and dug a small key out of her pocket.

She knelt down by the front bumper and unlocked the handcuffs, freeing the Haitian man. He stayed on his knees and hugged Lomani's legs in repentance and thanks. Lomani placed a tender hand on his head and blessed him as the snow continued to fall all around them.

Epilogue

Dr. Osborn's coroner's van was parked on the grave tender's path, near the crypt of Louis Trieste. The entire cemetery was taped off as a crime scene. The doctor and his assistant were in the back of the van, tending to their paperwork. The mud-caked body of Mark Kaddouri was on the rack, under a starched white sheet.

The back doors were open to the crisp winter morning. It snowed a few days ago, and since then the weather had been downright chilly. It even snowed as far south as Haiti, the first time in recorded history. They heard all about it on AM talk radio on the way in that morning. The global warming naysayers were having a field day with the news; the distinction between weather and climate still eluded them.

The CSI team was parked behind the van. Their trunks were open and they had their gear laid out on packing blankets on the hoods of their cars. They were prowling the grounds now, to see what they could see. NOPD had already found the shovel, in the bushes down the road from the cathedral. Someone had wiped it clean with a silk fabric particular to a priest's vestments. But Nano and Simone were in Rome, and so were their vestments.

Dr. Osborn and his assistant were sitting on their stools, wrapping up their paperwork. "How long's this guy been dead?" the assistant asked him.

Dr. Osborn shrugged as nonchalantly as he could, but he knew Kaddouri and it saddened him to have Mark's cold, dead body in the van. Compounding his sorrow was the news about Mas. They never even found her body.

"Offhand, I'd say about three days," he told his assistant.

Under the sheet, the corpse of Mark Kaddouri lay utterly still. The muddy remains of the photo of Christine Mas were still plastered to the front of his shirt, directly over his heart. There came a gentle voice that only he could hear.

"I love you, too."

Mark Kaddouri took in a ragged breath, and exhaled. And then he drew another one.

Dr. Osborn heard the sound, and so did his assistant. They looked at the body, utterly dumbfounded, and the chest moved once again.

Not yet daring to believe, Dr. Osborn gently pulled the sheet from Mark's face, bathing him in the light of the new day. He breathed deeply, and then he opened his eyes.

He was reborn.

THE END

KEN POLICARD

REDEMPTION

HUNTING
LUCIFER BOOK II

LOOK FOR THIS AD IN YOUR LOCAL NEWSPAPER

The One Million Dollar Book Review Contest is coming soon!

For more info on our upcoming contest, please visit
www.huntingchrist.com.

COME SEE IT LIVE!

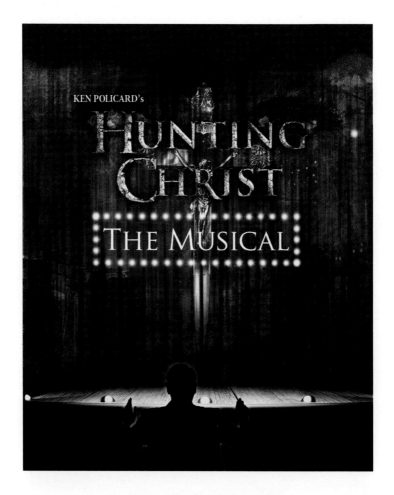

Written by: Ken Policard
Music Composed by: Cody Gillette

"Believing is seeing"

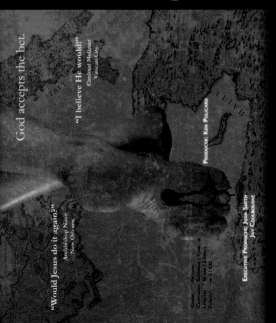

KEN POLICARD

UNABRIDGED
MP3 - CD

NARRATED BY
RICHARD KINSEY

AudioBook

M INDEPENDENT AMERICAN MOVIES

A KEN POLICARD NOVEL

HUNTING CHRIST

I AM PUBLISHING
AudioBook

The Devil bets God that Christ would be unable to achieve divinity in modern times.

God accepts the bet.

"Would Jesus do it again?"
Archbishop Nancy
New Orleans

"I believe He would!"
Cardinal Medinat
Vatican City

PRODUCER: KEN POLICARD

EXECUTIVE PRODUCER: JULIA SMITH
JAY COLBOURNE

I AM PUBLISHING presents a KEN POLICARD AUDIOBOOK
author KEN POLICARD narrator RICHARD KINSEY music CODY GILLETTE
ANNIE HOLLAND TOM WILK MELANIE SMITH
STEVE VALENZUELA RANDY MACKENZIE JAY COLBOURNE

ISBN 978-0-9846340-1-9
9 780984 634019   52450

Let he who is without sin...

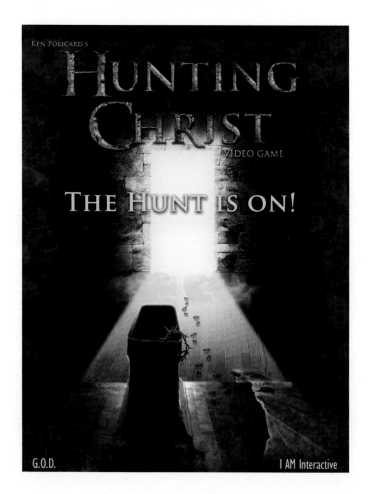

Cast the first stone!

John 8:7

www.hollywoodwalksforthemissing.org

THE PATH OF LIGHT

"The Lord is King, His Kingdom is forever. Let those who worship other gods be swept from the land!"

Psalms 10:16

*"Arise, O Lord! Punish the wicked, O God!
Do not forget the helpless."*

Psalms 10:12

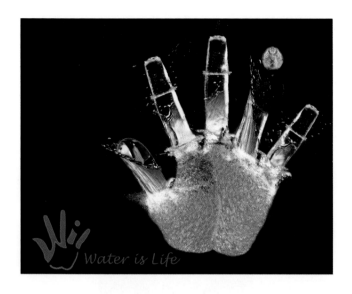

Water is Life

CHECK YOUR LOCAL SUPERMARKETS FOR
A TASTE OF W.I.L.!
"10,000-YEAR-OLD GLACIAL WATER"
www.waterislifeusa.com

To purchase the Rarest Water in the World, visit
www.seracwater.com or call (877) 745-2242

Tahoma Glacial Water – www.tahomawater.com

Akali Performance Water – www.akaliwater.com

Premium Glacial Water

Glacia Nova brings pure glacier water from Mt. Rainier directly to
you. Protected at its source within Mt. Rainier National Park, the
unique geological phenomenon of under-melting of massive glacier
provides pure melted glacial ice that froze more than 10,000 years
ago, completely free of environmental pollutants. No chemical
purification, distillation, ionization, or reverse osmosis – just
pure 10,000-year-old melted glacial ice in a bottle.

WHEN YOU WIN, YOUR FILM WINS!

MULTI-THEATER LOTTERY GROUP

Coming Soon To A Theater Near You!

www.greenlitlottery.com

"Where Your Greens Can Come True!"

 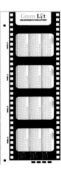 

CHECK YOUR LOCAL KIOSK & MOVIE THEATERS FOR
AVAILABILITY TO PLAY

INDEPENDENT AMERICAN MOVIES

The Hunt Trilogy

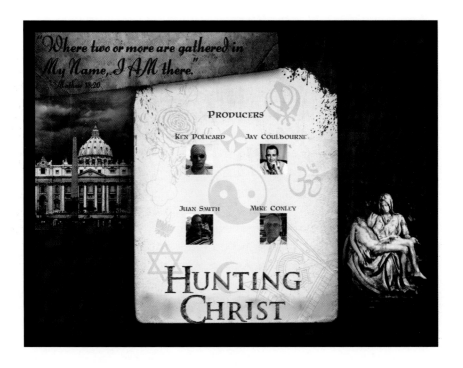

The Faces behind the HUNTING CHRIST Project!

ACKNOWLEDGMENTS

To my mom and dad thank you for your love and support. Special thank you to Pierrott Romulus, for always being there for me and my family. I've never thought of you as a stepdad, and I never will. Thank you for being a father to me.

Special thank you to Chase Hoyt, and Mrs. Karen and Mr. Robert Hoyt. Chase made sure that we had a complete package to present. The Hoyts made miracles happen so that we could get from point A to point B. Thank you for believing in us.

To my right-hand man, Producer Jay Coulbourne, our collaboration on all the artwork shows how well we work as a team! Thank you for all of your hard work and support! To Producer Mike Conley, you are our second pair of eyes. In the entertainment industry, loyalty goes a long way. Thank you for having our back! To Christopher Coppola, you are an asset to *Hunting Christ*. Thank you for hanging in there!

To Executive Producer Arnie Holland, thank you for the legal advice and, most of all, for setting up those studio meetings.

Much love and respect to Author Alan K. Dale. Words cannot express my gratitude for your support, assistance, and guidance. Looking forward to reading your second novel! Thank you for being part of "HC / BOE."

To my friend, Music Composer Cody Gillette. Loved your work on the musical "I Caligula." You are A-List! Looking forward to collaborating with you on the *Hunting Christ* Musical. Twenty-one hats off to our multi-talented friend, Narrator Mr. Richard Kinsey. Cody was right, you were the perfect choice for the voice of our Audiobook.

To my friend, Kimberly Kiplin, attorney and former Gaming Commissioner of the State of Texas, thank you for all of the advice and guidance on the GreenLit Lottery. We love you Kimberly!

To Kimberly Coleman and Rick Tebrugge, thank you for sharing your "Missing Children's Album" with us. Your tireless dedication to finding the lost is truly amazing!

Special thank you to Jeff Weis. Keep those Petitions coming, and I'll keep signing them!

. . .

Special thank you to my brothers, Patrick Policard and Christopher Aime, for their support and much love to my cousin David Joseph for showing his support at the BookExpo of America! It's always the ones that you'd least expect that will step-up and be there. Thank you David!

Special hello to my mother in-law Josette Jean Louis and to my family and friends, Marjorie Lilavois, Vani, Florence Conley, Farah Romulus, Mr. Jose Perriott, Mr. John Osbourne Smith, Titilayo Kukuyi, Adrienne Stout-Coppola, Catherin Sikorski, Emmanuelle Saget, Wikenson Alexis, Marcel Augustine, Florence Canicave, Kimberly Kiplin, Louise Ward, Nia Long, Natalie B. Becker, Ava Jamshidi, Jimmy Jean Louis, Cassandra Francois, Brianna Brown, Gabriel Watkin, Reine Roberth Jean Louise, Alan Cave, Gabriel Beristain, Dan Laustsen, David Rosenbloom, James Coulbourne, Vladimir Kurimski, Nelya Lukima, Eric "Ekaso" Brown, Jim Ross, Jonathan Cruz, Alan Pao, Matt Price, Claire Saget, Arielle Saget, Marie Yacinthe, Ted Currier, Oswold Hyppolite, Napoleon Ryan, John Bale, Jonathan Bock, Mark Horowitz, Kenyatta Hudson, Golda Aly, Naomi Saget, Guerline Trazile, Ceci Parker, Lesly Dolsant, Jennifer Policard, Gladys Benoit, Keisha Walkes, Debbie Stevens, Jason & Jordan Foster, Willy Nicolas, Patrick Nicolas, Monique Romulus, Davina Parez, Enrique Francois, Michel Benadin, Lisa Nicolas, Frank Aly, Henri J. Desrosiers, Sungwook Choe, Robert Jean Louis, Selena Dolsant, Victor Cruz, Jeff Policard, Patrick Bernard, Kengy Policard, Tahina Policard, Andre Warren, Robenson Jean Louis, William Rivera, Maria Maldonado Rivera, Danny Romulus, Herbie Bernard, Ricardo Jean Louis, Evelyn Bernard, Shanikwa Lincoln, Rodney Bernard, Yolande Degand, Davis Alexander Smith, Jean Robert Policard, and Wesner Bernard.

A VERY SPECIAL THANK YOU TO:

Tim Snider, Mark Johnson, Guerline Pierre, Jason L. DeFrancesco, Phyllis Licht, Jacob Zimer, Ambartsum Keshishyan, LD Bryant,

Karen Hodnett, Anne Marie Trouillot, Mike Alemian, Beth Roberts, Jessica Zhou, Nick Tsemberlis, Debbie Petka, Estella Nsengiyumva, Michelle Toppin, Becca Thomas, Giles Masters, Rebecca Goodrich, Michael Wilks, Bobbie Reece, Paula Scott, Brandi Carpenter, Jerry Katz, Tracy Fletcher, Michael Garrett, Paulee Zance, Sean Coulbourne, Brandon Bennett, Steve Bennett – Fortune, Steven Beer, Mark Weingartner, Jocelyne Gahimbare, Michi Nauman, Mary Fakhoury, Vernon Ryan, Wendy Pullin, Jackie Gottlieb, Phidelie Decais, Zora DeHorter, Gilde Flores, James Runcorn, Dwan Brown, John Bryant Davilla, Cathy Gesualdo, Stephen Marrero, Melanie White, Ed Koster, Roger Pugleise, Steve Rothschild, Stan Sonenshine, Andrew Knox, Joanna Adler, Mark Warren, Jeff Rice, Ryan Torres, Herby Trazile, JD. Mac, KingSun, Steve Valenzuela, Kiara Price, Rita & Jean Phillip, Pamela Bach-Hasselhoff, Aubrey Oliver, Michael McMillan, Basha, Elite, Onyx, Brooklyn Zoo, Dawn Fraser, LightYear Ent., Bad Friday Productions, Grace Hill Media, Great Minds Book Club, Amazon, Itunes, IMDB, Target, Books with Blood, Bookmasters, AtlasBooks, Ingram Book Company, BookExpo of America, and to all of those who purchased *Blood of Eden /Hunting Christ* from foreign to domestic.

Special thank you to those who "Liked" our Facebook fan page. Please visit www.huntingchrist.com to read online for free!

Special Acknowledgement to "Goodreads.com." Great site for readers who love to read, rate, and review! Your feedback matters, and makes a difference to the authors and publishers! Thank you to the first 20 readers who Rated and Reviewed the first edition of *Hunting Christ.* (*Blood of Eden / Hunting Christ* Edition) Kitty Bullard – NC, Author Nely Cab – TX, Liliana Pereira – Spain, Zulma Antepara – NY, Melanie Bennett – NY, Erica Woods-Webb – VA, Vikki Apel – TX, David Johnson – NY, Dylan Hubauer – GA, Henry Jean – Haiti, King Fryy Pacini – GA, Mary Chrapliwy – NY, Derrick Parker – NY, Erika – SD, Lauri Traverse – NY, Emii Charlotte – Venezuela, Shelby – Georgia, Diane Engel – Germany, Elizabetha – OH, and Author Becky Due.

And finally, if not for Nancy, Rebecca, Mike, Lori, Chase, Betsie, and Jay, we would STILL be editing! This project has been a team and family affair, from Genesis to Revelation. So, if this book has found its way into your hands, enjoy this fictional work with an open mind!

LETTER FROM
MR. JEFF WEIS

Ken –

I'm a Catholic and I take my kids to church every Sunday. Church is supposed to be a safe place. But Bishop Robert Finn, who is the head of my diocese (that's a regional group of churches), made our church unsafe for my children when he covered up a child sex abuse scandal.

Last month, Father Shawn Ratigan – who was a priest in a church near mine – plead guilty in U.S. Federal Court to producing and possessing child pornography. Father Ratigan used his position as a priest to take lewd images of children in his faith community.

Now a judge has found Bishop Finn guilty of covering up Ratigan's crimes – Bishop Finn is the highest level leader in the church ever to be convicted in a sex abuse scandal. *But despite his conviction, Bishop Finn still has his job as head of our diocese.*

Since Bishop Finn's conviction, groups like the National Survivor Advocates Coalition have called on him to resign, and the *Kansas City Star* published an editorial saying it's time for him to go. Our diocese needs a leader who protects children, not one who protects their abusers.

As a Catholic, I believe in forgiveness, and I think Bishop Finn should be forgiven. But as a father, I don't think he should keep a job where he could put more children in danger. Forgiveness and change can work together.

The Catholic church needs to see that it's not enough to get rid of priests who abuse children – the leaders who cover up the abuse must be held accountable as well. I know that if thousands of people sign my petition, Bishop Finn will have to resign.

Thank you,

Jeff Weis
Kansas City, Missouri

Greetings,

I just signed the following petition addressed to: Bishop Robert Finn of the Catholic Diocese of Kansas City- St. Joseph, MO., His Eminence Cardinal Timothy M. Dolan, Most Reverend Joseph E. Kurtz, and Bishop R. Daniel Conlon. Please show your support by signing Mr. Jeff Weis's Petition for the resignation of Bishop Robert Finn.

Petition Letter Drafted by Mr. Jeff Weis

I'm writing today to ask that the United States Catholic Bishops Conference support the resignation of Bishop Robert Finn, the head of the Catholic Church in the Diocese of Kansas City – St. Joseph.

In September of 2012, a judge found Bishop Finn guilty on one misdemeanor charge after he failed to report a priest who had taken or possessed hundreds of pornographic pictures of young girls. Even though Finn was found guilty in a court of law, he remains the Bishop of the Kansas City – St. Joseph Diocese. Now many members of the community feel he is unfit to lead and should resign. He is currently the highest-ranking U.S. Catholic Cleric to be convicted in a decades-long child sexual abuse scandal.

Only three years ago, Bishop Finn settled lawsuits with 47 plaintiffs in sexual abuse cases for $10 million and agreed to a long list of preventive measures, among them to immediately report anyone suspected of being a pedophile to law enforcement authorities.

Leadership within the Catholic Church must hold accountable any member who endangers children in our communities. By not supporting the resignation of Bishop Finn from Diocese of Kansas City – St. Joseph, it's almost as if the United Catholic Bishop's Conference is endorsing his actions.

Forgiveness and change can exist together. Therefore, I feel it's necessary for Bishop Finn to immediately resign. The spiritual, emotional, and moral pain that this issue has caused to Finn's fellow clergymen, diocesan employees, volunteers, parishioners and faithful must begin to come to an end.

Thank you.

Sincerely,
(Sign your name)

Dear Ken,

Thanks for signing my petition, "Bishop Robert Finn: Resign as Bishop of the Catholic Diocese of Kansas City – St. Joseph, MO."

Winning this campaign is now in your hands. We need to reach out to as many friends as we can to grow this campaign and win.

Thanks for your support,

Jeff

In Memory of our loved ones who died serving our country

In Memory of all who died serving their country world-wide

Also In Memory of all of those who died in the 2010 earthquakes in Haiti

In Memory of our family and friends

Marcelle Joseph, Edith Luisa Martin, Soraya Nicole Smith, Mary Lee Picou & Wally J. Picou, MD, Sylvia Bennett, Carmen Ville, Edith Bernard, Mr. Walt Conley, Jeanine Dolsant, Robert Jean, Alminda Ramirez, Reginald Romulus, Dezmond Bennett, Andre Ville, Barbara Labissiere, Evans Janvier, Martine St. Louis, Richelieu Jean Louis, Ketly Cangé, John Destito, Karl Dwayne White, Mildred Boone Winfield, Lenny Fichtelberg, and all of those who have died of Cancer. Your memory will live forever in our hearts!

Thank you for making a difference in our lives!

And
In Memory of my good friend
Marlon "Big DS" Fletcher.

January 12, 2010 was a devastating day in the history of Haiti. Tremors rocked Port au Prince, Leogane, and surrounding cities. Three-hundred-thousand lives were lost and an entire region inhabited by millions was leveled in a matter of seconds.

The International Humanitarian Outreach Ministries (IHOM, Inc.) was formed out of the need to organize, mobilize, and inspire stakeholder participation in addressing the Economic, Social, and Cultural needs of the people of Haiti as the whole world embarks on diverse avenues of recovery in Haiti's post-earthquake era.

"IHOM, Inc is focused on facilitating on the ground need and rebuilding in Haiti."

— Henri J. Desrosiers, President/Founder of
IHOM International

"The 10% Fund, I AM Ent., W.I.L, & IHOM are developing a program which will improve the poverty and health conditions in Haiti and in the USA."

— Ken Policard, CEO/Founder of the Ten Percent Fund

"We are providing ongoing medical care for those affected by the earthquakes."

— Christopher Coppola, Producer, *Hunting Christ*

"Our program will reduce the infant mortality rate."

— Betsie Policard, President of Global Affairs, Ten Percent Fund

"The group's main focus and mission is to provide housing for those who are still living in the tent cities."

— Juan Smith & Melanie Smith, Producers, *Hunting Christ*

"Much of our work on the ground is in liaise with non-profit organizations who have proven track records over the years."

— Jay Coulbourne, SVP of Artistic Development,
Independent American Movies

For more info, please visit us at
www.10percentfund.org
www.ihom.org
www.huntingchrist.com

"Ten Percent Fund" is a non-profit organization created for those in need, from missing children, children with cancer, and families in distress due to homes lost by turbulent economic circumstances or natural disasters. This fund is established primarily for the basis and means to contribute economically and give back to the national and international community by the donations of homes to a well-deserving family or individuals.

This is done via "Green Lit Lottery," the motion picture industry lottery. The community and churches, with the Multi-Theater Lottery Governing Group, votes for the family most deserving and in need. Overall, the homes will come from foreclosure listings typically held by the banks. This will happen through the various 50 states, as well as on a larger global level.

Furthermore, the "Ten Percent Fund" will gain strength as we personally contribute from our earnings from our companies/payrolls, alongside the generous donations of the Hollywood, star-studded community, and combined with the contributions of philanthropic individuals, groups, and corporations.

Independent American Movies is committed to donating 10% of all profits generated from the Hunting Christ franchise to the "Ten Percent Fund."

www.10percentfund.org

From my point of view, I see that there are no World Leaders standing on the frontline. America may be at war, but Americans are not! We're not at war with anybody. So, when you visit America, or if an American visits your country, remember: we're not at war. We visit because we love your culture, and you should visit us because you love America – for what we still stand for.

One Nation under God!

To the Angel of the East, West, North, and South, please watch over us as we travel to and fro.

Be blessed, and always be a blessing!

– Ken